The Women of Heachley Hall

Rachel Walkley

Spare Time Press

···●···

PART ONE

The Will

"One lives in the hope of becoming a memory."

—Antonio Porchia

..●..

ONE

I shortened the lengths of my strides, ignored the numbing embrace of a premature autumn and allowed my senses the opportunity to coax awake quiescent memories.

Years ago, as a young girl, I'd walked the same path alongside my father and knocked on the front door of Heachley Hall. The gardens boasted pungent roses and mobs of fragrant lavender, songbirds chatted exuberantly to each other and there was the crisp flavour of sea salt in the air. The house itself was a blur of grey stonework and slate with an arched porch framing an impressive door. Beyond, a dark wood. The smattering of recalled images, no different from the jumbled pieces of a jigsaw, brought with them a maelstrom of muddled emotions.

Strange how memories lingered in the form of smell, sound and occasionally taste, but visually, they easily faded into a frustrating void. Nothing else discernible remained in those memory nooks. Somewhere, waiting to be rediscovered, was a clearer picture of that day. And the reason why I'd chosen to forget it.

The garden resembled a meadow. Thistles strangled the wild grasses and verdant moss roamed wild. Once a cultivated lawn, the generous frontage had lost its beauty to the unstoppable – time and the seasons. The gravel path scrunched underfoot, leaves rustled incessantly and a crow announced our arrival with a fanfare of squawks. Approaching the weather-worn door, I smelt the decay of mulched leaves. Of the house, especially its interior, nothing came to mind; it was a vacuum waiting to be filled.

The door's diminutive size surprised me. Where was the grandiose entrance? I had been much smaller, seven, maybe eight years old, when we'd called upon Great-aunt Felicity. The visits were part of that pervasive nothingness that contained most of my early childhood.

Mr Bridge swung the key ring around his little finger. His car, an urban smart tattooed with the name of the estate agent, was squeezed next to a hawthorn hedge just outside the iron gates. He'd waited for me to arrive before crossing the threshold, as if the weed infested driveway, that cut a crescent shaped path through the lawn, was tainted in some way.

While Mr Bridge fiddled with the stiff lock of the front door, I stuffed my hands in my coat pockets and surveyed the ivy that choked the flintstone walls of the Victorian mansion. A cloak of fog swaddled the house, its tendrils swirled around the window sills, rising like a white creeper to the heights of the pointed gables where it stifled the huddled chimney pots. The poor house was smothered by nature.

He pushed the door ajar. 'So this is your late aunt's house, I gather? I'm very sorry for your loss,' he said with appropriate solemnity.

I smiled sweetly. He wasn't to know the circumstances. 'Thank you. Sadly, I only found out about Felicity's passing a few days ago.' I acknowledged his sympathetic glance before continuing. 'She died in February. Mr Porter had problems finding me.' I'd missed her cremation.

'Oh,' Mr Bridge invited me to enter first.

A flurry of yellow leaves followed us into the hallway and added to the detritus accumulating on the tiled floor.

'It's empty,' he explained after an awkward pause.

I nodded. 'She died in a nursing home. She left me the house, although...' How to explain the peculiar clauses in Felicity's will. Mr Porter had told me the details over the telephone. He'd pitched his voice perfectly for the delivery of good news: the timbre lifted almost gleefully. 'Miriam, I'm pleased to inform you that you are the sole heir to Miss Marsters's estate in Norfolk.' I'd insisted the solicitor sent me a copy of Felicity's will, along with a survey of the property. Neither document had arrived before I left Chelmsford and driven to view the old hall with its six bedrooms and hundred hectares of land.

Mr Bridge thumbed through his notes and referred to numerous – 'but repairable,' he assured – cracks in the plasterwork. The damp around the windows – 'treatable,' he encouraged. The wires hanging out of the light fittings – 'a competent electrician would fix that.' He bounced on his toes and prattled on about the 'Gothic' or 'grandiose' Victorian characteristics imbued in the architecture. The man was keen to make a swift sale.

'Such space and light. Given the size of the place, it could easily accommodate four individual flats. That's one option for a developer.' He kicked aside a dead mouse with his heel.

'Yes, I suppose,' I murmured, turning away from his clipboard to face the imposing staircase with its shallow steps. It seemed surreal to think this house could be mine.

'So, a month from now, this will be out of your hands—'

'Not necessarily.' I whipped my head over my shoulder in time to see his jaw drop a fraction. 'It would seem the sensible option, given the state of the house and grounds. However, I'm also entitled to keep the property and sell at a later date.' A later date meant a whole year of living in Heachley Hall. Felicity's will was specific – a year and a day – and then the property would be mine. Otherwise, an immediate sale would mean forfeiting the income generated and allowing a number of charities to benefit instead.

Mr Bridge's face perked up at the word *sell*. 'Naturally, we'd be happy to arrange an auction at a later time, but the house won't wait. Since Miss Marsters vacated the property some time ago, it's quite uninhabitable.'

I ignored his comment about the state of the house and I was also aware of its bleak location. I'd no clue about managing woodland either, but I was a quick learner and having nature on my doorstep, inspiring me to draw, had to be beneficial.

'According to the figures you sent me, I could be inheriting a property worth a million, potentially, of course. If I did agree to my great-aunt's stipulation, and if I happened to make it habitable during that period, I could add to the value of the property.'

He furrowed his eyebrows. 'I suppose that might depend on what you did,' he stuttered. 'I'd been given the impression, Miss Chambers, that you had no intention of living here and I, I mean Hardcastle Agents, was guaranteed the option to sell now.'

'I've not made my final decision. No guarantees have been given as far as I'm concerned.' I'd made no plans based on one telephone call with the will's executor, who clearly, given his depressing appraisal of my inheritance, expected me to sell and save myself the inconvenience of moving into a 'derelict' house. The temptation to hold off selling it lay with Heachley's potential as a marketable property, not a home. A swell of optimism nudged aside the negativity I'd carried since speaking to Mr Porter and it brought with it an unexpected enthusiasm for adventure. Making money, Dad had told me once during his last visit, was all about hard work. I, however, was a year away from a potential fortune, assuming I chose the path Felicity seemed keen for me to follow. Work, the solitary profession of an artist, I could take with me anywhere.

He began to button up his coat, sensing my views on the house were shifting. 'I hope you're right. Without renovations you'll struggle to shift this place.' He fumbled in his pocket and dug out the house keys. 'Take a look around. I've calls to make and there's no signal around here.'

I fisted the keys in my hand. 'None?' I'd considered the lack of reliable broadband unfortunate, but no mobile signal was something of a major setback.

While he returned to his car, I began my inspection of the house. The sun had escaped the cloud barrier and warmed the kitchen, highlighting the room's loftiness. Contrary to Mr Porter's doom and gloom summary, Heachley Hall wasn't falling apart at the seams. The fragile house lacked an occupation – an inhabitant. It needed a brave soul to keep it company. Was that going to be me?

Standing by the window I watched Mr Bridge dash through the iron gate, clutching his precious clipboard. The mist seemed to chase after him, shooing him off the premises. Somewhere, upstairs, something rattled. A brief sound, maybe a window fighting the invisible currents of air, which I assumed crept in through the draughty frames. Except, when I looked outside, the tree branches maintained frozen poses and the late afternoon sea mist had reappeared, draping the landscape in further stillness.

Confused by a lack of decisiveness, I picked at the loose paintwork around the window, nudging the wood beneath with my fingertip until it met a robust hardness. I wiped the paint dust off my hands and perched my bottom on the sill. It didn't creak and the lack of complaining added to my confidence that the house wasn't as ramshackle as it appeared.

Peering into the porcelain sink, I spied terracotta rust rings around the plughole. 'Pity,' I said softly. The white basin, that bore the name of the maker etched underneath the lime-scaled taps, had almost redeemed the dilapidated kitchen.

I opened a cupboard door and it hung precariously by one hinge. I traced a dark whorl ingrained in the broken door – oak. With a decent sanding down and revarnishing, it could be resurrected into a splendid veneer. The sink could also be replaced. I closed the door, carefully realigning it with the cupboard's carcass.

Around me the house whispered in the language of creaks and groans, as if to encourage me to look past its many faults. Great-aunt Felicity had lived here for decades, possibly loved the place beyond anything else. Even with my scant recollections of her, I couldn't conceive she would have deliberately let the house fall into decline. I believed she wanted me here for a purpose. The reason why was unknown, perhaps misplaced amongst her vanished things. Lost things can often be found again.

Fortune might include finding a mobile signal. I stalked the ground floor and held the device aloft, hoping for a solitary bar; just a flicker of one.

Dust billowed wherever I traipsed. From the kitchen into the old scullery, then the icy pantry, before returning to the dining room; I kicked it up around my ankles. I relied on guesswork to deduce each room's purpose; Heachley Hall was a shell and stripped of nearly everything – carpets, furniture, even light fittings.

In the drawing room hung lifeless drapes, presumably abandoned to rot in situ. I rubbed the fabric between two fingers. It possessed a friable delicacy, soft, too. The colour had faded except, buried between the exposed folds, endured a rich crimson. Above me, the wooden pole frowned, as if tired of its burden or maybe disapproving of the neglect. I sympathised.

A few shelves remained embedded in the alcove of the book-deprived library – such a travesty, I mourned with it. The lingering odour of musty paper persevered and snared itself in my nostrils. A kind of enduring smell that fitted into its surroundings. I ran my finger along a bare shelf and where the sun had faded the wood, I traced the outline of numerous book spines. Book lovers were once part of Heachley's life. I could make it so again.

Still no signal.

The bang echoed about the room and I clutched the mobile to my chest. 'What the?'

I stared up at the ceiling, expecting a rainfall of plaster dust, but the air was undisturbed. Draughts. There had to be an open window upstairs. Even with nothing to steal, the house needed to remain secure.

I glided my palm along the banister. A robust staircase that followed the walls of the hall on three sides. I turned each angular corner and wished there were welcoming portraits hanging from the walls. Or perhaps not. That would mean countless eyes tracking my every movement, spying on me. The forgotten residents of Heachley Hall, men with drooping moustaches and ruddy cheeks or elegant women with cinched waists and puppy dogs, all of them judging my decision to abandon the house to strangers. I hastily ascended.

All the doors were closed. I'd no idea which one had been responsible for the slamming. The landing, without the benefit of a window, was a gloomy corridor. The light from downstairs illuminated the apex of the stairwell, but little else beyond. I inspected each bedroom's windows for a breakage or opening, while keeping my attention on the little symbol registering the signal strength of my mobile.

Peeling wallpaper hung limply from the corners of every room. The pervasive aroma of damp wafted in tides as I open and closed doors. A cast iron fireplace remained intact in the largest bedroom. Peacocks and birds of paradise flew across the flock wallpaper. Those spies, glued to the walls, kept watch as I examined the sash windows. However, unlike the other rooms, which seemed especially neglected, this one had a residue of comfort. I stared at the overgrown grass and imagined a freshly cut lawn with croquet hoops or maybe a tennis court. The vast garden had the capacity to cater for both and much more.

The grandiose bathroom almost offered the house a reprieve from the decay. It possessed what many modern properties lack: an abundance of space. Although grubby, its potential shone through the grime. The freestanding porcelain tub was supported by brass feet, clawed like tigers and ready to scamper across the floor. Brass fish yawned beneath the taps, their open mouths tarnished by limescale. The marble sink was shallow and simple; quite usable. Above the basin and incorporated into the flaking plasterwork was a mirror, its reflective coating warped in the middle. I appeared distant and distorted; a sepia portrait of vanilla skin, umber waves of hair and copper eyes.

The toilet cistern seemed precariously placed halfway up the wall and from it dangled a hangman's noose cord. What I saw in the bowl was disgusting. The whole thing would have to be replaced.

Returning to the murky landing, I discovered another set of stairs behind a narrow doorway. The steep steps led up to the attic where two rooms matched the height of the mature cedars of Heachley Wood. Homely, relatively dust free and untainted by mould stains, which given the cold northerly aspect was remarkable. The dormer windows captured the dying dregs of sunlight. Once what I assumed was the housemaids' domain, I now fancied them as my bedroom and workroom, assuming a bed could be brought up the staircase.

The realisation dawned on me – I'd made a decision quite independently of logical processes. Although I'd been led to believe by the solicitor that there was no possibility of taking up residence here, I'd persuaded myself, purely on the basis I didn't need much, that the house had invited me to stay. The fledging idea shook off its undeveloped wings and stretched, encompassing more ideas: reclaim the fireplaces, replace a few essential things and renovate what little I could with my limited abilities and budget.

My first priority with the evening approaching was to tell Felicity's executor about my plans; I'd two days left before the deadline.

However, regardless of where I was in the house, there was nothing to indicate the presence of a signal.

I returned to the first floor and from the other end of the corridor I spied burnt mahogany or dull ebony; either way, the panel was constructed differently to the others. I'd missed a room – its door, both squat in shape and trapped inside a broad frame, emerged from the dark shadows, as if angry that I'd ignored it. From my perspective, the epicentre of the corridor's lines converged on the doorknob. It couldn't be a bedroom – there were no more bedrooms to explore. I had no clue as to the door's purpose, other than to churn up unpleasant emotions. Uprooting my feet I marched toward it; I refused to harbour any fear of an unopened door.

The brass handle reflected the hue of red in my coat. I grasped the icy metal and shivered. I turned it and the catch clicked. A tug. Then a hard yank, but the door refused to budge. I bent and examined the gap between door and frame. The catch had cleared and there was no evidence of a keyhole or locking mechanism. Determined to conquer the slight presence of dread, I gripped the knob with both hands, then rested the sole of my shoe against the doorframe and leaned backwards.

Something gave; a secret release mechanism and with the sudden loss of resistance, my heel slipped on the boards and I fell.

'Ow.' I'd landed on my tailbone. The open door swayed slightly and I nudged it further ajar with my outstretched foot. More dust clouded my vision, hiding the interior. I lay paralysed, tongued tied, half expecting a skeleton to tumble down on top of me.

Dust should settle, but when I extracted my mobile, switching on the torch app, the white particles hovered above, as if uncertain of their destination: up or down. An indoor mist had formed to create the illusion of fog or a soft veil of ash. The flurry of powdery dust triggered a sneeze. The violent exhale scattered the peculiar cloud.

I staggered to my feet, crept forward and stuck my head inside the doorway. A closet that continued behind the wall but no more than a metre deep. There were loosely fitted shelves but otherwise it was empty.

Tentatively I touched a shelf and dragged my fingertips along the edge. Redirecting the light to examine my hand, I saw a thick layer of white powder had coated the tips. Perhaps the suddenness of the door opening had chased the dust up into one billowing cloud.

I gave the door a tiny shove, and it drifted, almost loathed to respond to my gentle encouragement. Now that it was open, it was keen to stay that way. I started to lean my shoulder against it and with a few centimetres to go, it slammed shut. I knew that sound. I'd heard it before.

I laughed, a nervous titter of bemusement. There had to be an explanation, there generally was for most things, but I'd no time to investigate. The house would have to wait a little longer before I took up residence.

Giving up the fruitless search, I trotted downstairs, the echoes of my heels clattering in time to my heartbeats. I'd seek a signal in the village where I had left my car in the Rose and Crown car park. I locked the front door and dropped the house keys into my handbag. Soon it would be too dark to see the driveway. There were no outside lights, only the luminous presence of the awakening moonlight that chased the silvery cobwebs across the long grass. I hurried down the path, keen to immerse myself in the warmth of the pub.

··●··

TWO

The Rose and Crown gloriously epitomised the quaint countrified public house with blackened timber beams, an oak panelled bar, the fiery glow of a wood burner and tarnished brass horseshoes hooked on nails hammered into the wall. Alongside those rural enrichments was a flat screen TV; something for everyone, I supposed. However, the place was deserted and the absence of staff even at this early hour required me to ring the bicycle bell screwed to the bar.

A woman bustled out of the kitchen wiping her hands on her stained apron, the smell of seared meat and caramelised onions trundled after her adding to the aroma of hops. A disgruntled expression – I'd probably interrupted her in the middle of an important task – occupied her mottled face. She raised her eyebrows: bushy little things perched above her thickly lined eyes. 'Yes?'

I tried not to yawn or squeak; my dry mouth needed replenishment. 'Miriam Chambers. I booked a room for the night.'

A smile shot across her face and her chubby cheeks flushed pink, clashing with her shockingly red hair and her orange t-shirt. Nothing about her appearance seemed co-ordinated as if the notion of presentation had any place in a public establishment. My colour sensitive brain struggled to deal with her intriguing concept of harmonisation.

The cheerful demeanour froze mid-development, never truly blossoming into delight, but her displeasure at my arrival had been swept away. 'Oh, right you are.' She reached under the bar and retrieved a small ledger. 'Fill in your details here. Just the one night isn't it?'

'One. I couldn't face driving back south tonight.' I scrawled my name across the page.

'London is it?' She'd watched me write Chelmsford before commenting.

I grinned. 'Close enough.' London seemed a long way from anywhere, never mind Chelmsford.

The upstairs guest room was tucked away at the back of the inn and its décor was awash with floral motifs – the bed cover and wallpaper didn't match, one depicted red roses, the other pink carnations. I squeezed my eyes tight in the hope the garish colours might lose their potency. The addition of potpourri in the form of orange peel and juniper had failed; onions followed us everywhere.

'Bathroom down the hall. You're the only guest, so don't worry about sharing.' She handed me two keys – the bedroom and the back door. 'If you do pop out, let us know. Don't want to be worrying about you. Dinner any time after six.' She glanced at her wristwatch. 'Best get down there.' She dashed out the door.

I flopped onto the iron framed bed and dangled my feet over the sides. Tempting as it was to simply doze off – I'd been up since dawn – I had to contact the solicitor.

Graeme Porter of Porter and Flint gasped when I told him.

'You do understand that you only inherit the house after living there for a year?' he asked; the refined voice of Middle England took on a fatherly tone. 'And that at any time you leave the house for more than two weeks, barring medical problems, you forfeit the right to inherit it.'

I stared at the crack in the low ceiling, then across at the botched attempt to hide the mould above the crooked window. Earlier, I'd not noticed the flaws, now they seemed reassuring in their unimportance.

'Yes. I know it seems…preposterous.'

'Quite,' he enunciated. 'I've seen some strange things in my time as an executor, but truly, these clauses in the will are peculiar. She was most particular.'

'And she drew it up when exactly?'

There was a pause before he answered. 'Eight years ago.'

When I was nineteen and not long after Dad had died. What kind of life had Felicity envisaged for me? One of solitude, like herself, or marriage, which she'd shunned? I'd fulfilled some of her requirements, but only by my lack of success in finding a life partner and a career that didn't require me to be somewhere specific all the time. There again, taking a career break at twenty-seven years wasn't frowned upon these days, married or not. Her remarkable, and insightful view, of my unknown future made me wish I'd known her better.

Snow white hair. Braided, perhaps? Chocolate eyes. Or maybe they'd been hazel. How had I managed to forget a member of my family with little regret? The thought didn't sit comfortably with me. I soothed myself with the knowledge that losing contact with distant aunts and cousins was a common enough family trait. Sometimes, even siblings cut blood ties. I had no siblings.

Mr Porter asked again if I was sure. Answering him gave rise to the familiar bedlam of emotions: fear, excitement, exhaustion and determination.

'I'll speak to you tomorrow.' I ended the call abruptly, terribly confused by the jumble of thoughts colliding behind my sleepy eyes.

I sat up on the bed, dived into my handbag and extracted a notepad and pencil. Making myself comfortable, I sought out my salvation: a list. When faced with a demanding project, I craved the organisation of a list, just seeing it would stave off the impending panic. Once it was down on paper, I could eat, then sleep.

The list swiftly occupied two sides of paper. It had started rather simply before rambling on and on without any prioritising or timescales. When it got to financial issues, the tension in my temples sent shooting pains down my neck.

My mortgage payments would have to continue, but what about the bills?

I slumped backwards onto the lumpy pillow. The council tax on the hall would put serious pressure on my income even with guaranteed work for the year. Looking at the scrawling nightmare of needs, I would have to delve into my savings. I couldn't believe there was no cash left in Felicity's estate and I simply couldn't afford additional payments on top of my existing bills.

I dragged myself downstairs. An hour earlier the place had been deserted, now it bustled with people. The village possessed a few dozen houses, a postbox and a bus stop, yet the pub attracted patrons: regulars, given how they greeted the red-haired landlady by name.

'Glenda, pasty and chips, please,' shouted a young man with tattoos down one arm.

'Right you are, Jack,' she yelled back.

I stared at the blackboard and the smudged chalked menu. My stomach rumbled for food, but the dishes didn't appeal, my appetite crushed by nervous energy. I needed something to eat, though. 'Steak and ale pie, please.'

'Mash or chips?' asked Glenda.

'Mash, please.'

The food, when it arrived, tasted good. The kind of wholesome home cooking my mother might have given me, if I could remember. Mum had passed away from breast cancer when I was ten. Raised by a heartbroken father, I'd learnt to be independent at an early age: laundry, sewing the name labels on my school uniform and so on. My father's response to losing Mum had been long hours sequestered at his office or distant travel. My life had revolved around a fragile self-sufficiency and the occasional overnight stay with a child minder. Dad had been a microwave aficionado. He spent ages in the supermarket aisles, debating out loud whether to have Italian or Indian, peering at the cardboard covers. Politely declining his chosen package, I grabbed my fresh vegetables and fashioned a recipe off the top of my head.

Dad had never attempted to cook from scratch and if he had seen me beavering over the hob, he'd reminisced about Mum's cooking. However, I couldn't tempt him into trying my efforts, as if his taste buds needed no reminders of Mum – she'd gone and taken her culinary delights with her. Dad and I ate at different times with me at the dining table with a book and Dad in front of the television with a lap tray. Mum's food sloped off into the past, along with her stylish dresses, frizzed hairstyle and the soft edge of her soothing voice when she'd sung me to sleep.

He'd met another woman, somebody abroad, and by the time I'd left school he'd moved out there to be with her. A woman I never met. They both died in a boating accident off the shores of a Greek island. I mourned him every day, my part-time father, with his soft smile, dry wit and firm knees, which I'd sat upon many a time as a child while he'd recounted his travels: exaggerated fun tales. I believed those embroidered fantasies gave rise to my passion for the creative arts and many a picture I'd painted or drawn had been based on his florid imagery. With Dad's sudden departure, I had no link to Mum, nor perhaps the ability to dredge up the memories I'd banished.

Abandoned in the earliest stages of adulthood and battling the constancy of grief, his sudden exit also had left me financially deprived with only a mediocre savings account to fall back on when work dried up.

I washed down my meat pie with a gin and tonic.

Glenda came over to my table. 'Pud, luv?'

I sighed, returning my thoughts to the future, and slid the plate across into her awaiting hands with their bright red fingernails. 'No, thanks. What I need is an electrician.'

'Electrician?' She hovered, unfazed by my wish to talk.

'I'm moving into the area and the house desperately needs electrical repairs, amongst other things, like plumbing.' I swilled the dregs around the bottom of my glass.

'Which house, if you don't mind me asking?'

Did I mind the locals knowing I was less than mile down the road? Would they cast a sympathetic eye over my circumstances? It depended on what I told them.

'Heachley Hall,' I said softly.

'Well, I never,' she declared. 'That place. Felicity finally sold it.'

I entered the world of small village gossip with a heavy sense of foreboding. 'No, not sold. I'm her great-niece. I've inherited it, sort of —'

'She died?' Glenda slipped her broad bottom onto a nearby chair. 'I'd no idea. I knew she emptied the place. I remember the day the clearance men came. Broke her hip, you see, fell down stairs. Never really recovered mobility to live on her own in such a big house.'

'How long ago did she move out?' I leaned forward.

Glenda fiddled with her fingers, counting back, mouthing the years. 'Five years or so. Bert, my husband, he had more to do with the house. He delivered the groceries. They never liked to drive up that road, them lazy gits, so he'd drive up and drop off the bread and milk, and the like.'

'Five years,' I repeated, aghast. It explained the forlorn interior. 'She really lived there alone?'

'Maggie, her cleaner, she used to go up there every day and help her out. It was only towards the end Felicity struggled. Very independent woman, Felicity Marsters. Stubborn, too. You're her family, then?'

I traced my family tree using the wood grain, skipping over my parent's generation. 'Felicity had an older brother who died in the 1960s, my grandfather, John. She had no children. I'm her sole beneficiary.'

'So you need an electrician. Well, Jack over there, stuffing his face with pasty, his dad is an electrician. Plumber, now Bert usually does our leaks.'

'I need a new toilet and kitchen sink.'

'Bert will know somebody. Bert!' She screeched in an indiscriminate direction.

A small bearded man appeared from behind the bar. He rocked on his feet as he walked over. Perhaps, given his age, which I suspected was close to sixty, he was marred by rheumatism.

'Yes, my darling.' He tugged on his wispy beard and blinked at Glenda in an ingratiating fashion. I reckoned behind closed doors they bickered away without fear of onlookers.

'This young lady is Felicity's niece.'

'Great-niece,' I corrected.

'She's moving into the house. Needs a plumber.'

Bert's eyes widened. 'Heachley Hall? Well, I never. It needs more than a lick of paint.'

'I know,' I rolled my tired eyes up to the ceiling. Perhaps it had been a mistake to raise my issues so publicly.

'An exorcism, too.' He smirked, and Glenda thumped his arm.

'Pay no heed to him.' She laughed, rather too obviously.

'Exorcism?' I watched as Glenda's smile turned to a scowl as her husband continued to chuckle; a low rumble that bubbled up from his beer belly.

'Stuff and nonsense. All squit,' she said. 'It's Maggie's fault. She put about the idea the place is haunted. Felicity never said a word about it. All on her own every night, quite happy, no screaming for help or look of fear about her. Nonsense and rumours.'

'So why did Maggie talk of ghosts?' I remembered the closet and the slamming doors, wondering if the weird flow of air through the house was responsible for conjuring up apparitions, too.

'Ghosts? She never mentioned ghosts. Just strange happenings. It's an old house, so it creaks and groans. This pub is four hundred years old and built without foundations. It makes a racket sometimes.' Glenda halted, clucking her tongue. 'Don't fret. You'll sleep fine, everyone does here.'

'Okay,' I said slowly, not keen on the idea of dwelling on improbable supernatural happenings and accompanying village gossip. My immediate problems were based on a pressing matter – making the hall habitable for me, a living person. 'Plumber and electrician are all I need.'

'I'll get you their numbers,' Bert said and hastily retreated.

'Sorry, dearie,' said Glenda, 'he's always after a bit of excitement. We've lived here for twenty years, things rarely get exciting.'

'Sounds nice,' I said, shaking out my napkin. 'Quiet.'

'If that suits you.' She stood.

'I'm not sure what suits me. This is an experiment, a yearlong experiment. It could all go horribly wrong.'

··●··

THREE

A line of blood red ink outlined the sketch of a little girl in her pyjamas waiting for her fairy godmother. My abandoned illustration – *Milly's Marvellous Godmother* – was parked on the easel; I'd failed to settle back into the routine of work since returning from Norfolk.

Rolling across the floor on the casters of the stool, I perched on it and surveyed my little world.

I'd transformed part of my bijou apartment into an atelier: an artist's desk under the illumination of natural light – one small window – and, over the period years, I'd nourished the space with useful clutter. The bulky computer, which converted my scanned drawings into digital images, was ostracised on another table; I preferred the fluidity of a pen nib over paper or the delicate caress of a brush stroke.

My finished artworks – all collaborations with authors, specifically children's books – either decorated the walls in frames or were carefully mounted in albums. I earned a reasonable income from my hard work. Dad would have been proud.

One irksome question kept bouncing back and forth: why the palaver of living at Heachley for a whole year? Why bait me with enigmatic legal devices in order to fish me out of my sea of comfortable living? Each time doubt nipped, I pictured a vast studio with skylights and heaps of space.

In lieu of parental guidance, I needed to talk to somebody sensible. The cry for help was made by text. I invited myself to Southend-on-Sea that evening. With a steady hand, I focused on finishing my illustration. Each skate of the brush on paper recaptured my undulating attention, creating a placating distance between Felicity's house and myself.

Ruth lived in a small village to the north of the town and she greeted me on her front doorstep with a brief hug, then hurried to put on the kettle.

'Tell me,' she yelled from the kitchen, while I kicked off my shoes. 'You've kept me in suspense for two days.' Prior to my visit, I'd told Ruth I'd been bequeathed a property but detoured around the exact details of the will.

Whilst she busied herself with a teapot and mugs, I regaled her with the basics of my dilemma, the strange conversation with Great-aunt Felicity's solicitor and my impromptu visit to Norfolk. I shied away from describing the memories I'd triggered.

Ruth wore her ten years of extra age well. I'd repeatedly repressed the notion she was my secretly adopted sister or surrogate mother. Since our first encounter, I'd admired her sensible wisdom and her kindly approach to handling any problems I occasionally deposited in her genial kitchen. Our friendship stemmed from a chance encounter at a book fair where I'd dashed around the stalls, handing out newly printed business cards to publishers and agents, imploring them to look at my portfolio. I'd been fresh out of college and armed with a diploma in graphic design, however regrettably, whenever they asked about my existing published illustrations my smiley face expression had lost its impact.

Ruth – a determined and boundlessly creative teacher with a plan to write a children's book – found me hunched over a tepid coffee, mourning my failure and with space tight in the little coffee area, she joined me. Jaded by years of classroom teaching she'd written her book, the kind that appealed to young kids: rhyming couplets, a fantasyland and a faintly moralistic tale. As it happened she needed an illustrator. The outcome of our meeting had a dramatic effect on my fortunes.

The book was a commercial bestseller, lauded by reviewers and awarded prizes. My successful working relationship with Ruth had provided the kick-start I needed in the form of well-received artwork. She'd found me Guy, my agent, and instigated the illustration contract that had kept me busy ever since.

I tried hard not to use her as an agony aunt, but her generosity brought me to door, laden with the baggage of bitterness or fatigue, typically down to ex-boyfriends and work-related stresses. Freelancing was a lonely affair and as a writer Ruth appreciated the solitude. A divorcee, she sympathised with the issues caused by failed relationships, and as a primary school teacher she was an excellent sounding board for ideas. She often diverted me from my woes with witty tales about her 'kids', pupils she taught part-time. She couldn't bring herself to give up her teaching post to write full-time.

She swept aside a strand of dappled hair with a flick of one hand while dropping a herbal teabag into the pot with the other. The kettle ceased singing and the brew stewed as Ruth listened without interrupting my account, although her eyes popped wider when I mentioned the value of similar houses.

'I've done a little research on the Internet during the week,' I explained.

'So, you're going to be a millionaire after all,' she jibed, dragging up memories of a drunken night when we'd fantasied about winning the Carnegie book prize for children's books, or in my case the illustrator's equivalent, and the glory of basking in unending royalty payments at the end of our imaginary rainbow – I actually drew her a picture illustrating the evening and gave it to her as a birthday present.

I fished a document out of my oversized handbag and tossed the solicitor's report on the breakfast bar. I'd leafed through the contents and my brisk digest had confirmed everything Mr Porter had told me.

'This,' I tapped the document, 'is a preliminary report on the state of the house and land.'

'Surveyor's report?'

'A basic survey and it makes for grim reading.' I flicked through a few pages. 'Plumbing: pipes need replacing. Electricity: rewiring. Walls: replastering. Heating needed, unless I plan to rely on open fires, and a new boiler is essential. One good point, the roof doesn't leak, so buckets unnecessary. However, in my opinion, it's not as dire as he made out to me.'

Ruth poured the tea into my mug. 'But, you're not keen on living there.'

'Living there is far from ideal.' I heaved out a sigh and leaned over my steaming mug. 'I have to prove I'm living there. Just me. Utility bills, council tax, etcetera. And I'm only allowed two weeks continuous absence in every quarter of the year. At least she'd thought of vacations or her solicitor added the proviso out of sympathy.'

'What?' She spluttered mid-gulp and mopped her dripping chin with the back of her hand. 'Sounds like one of those ridiculous fairytale quests – sleep for a hundred years surrounded by thorns.' Ruth drew a sword from an imaginary scabbard and hacked at a brier wall.

I chuckled and conjured up a fragmented image of my aunt with gaps about the eyes and lips. The ivory hair remained a strong memory.

'I don't remember her much, if at all.'

'She picked you though.'

I shrugged my shoulders then blew across the scalding tea and contemplated Ruth's comment. 'Nearest and dearest, I suppose. She'd no kids, a dead brother with one child – Mum – who is also dead.'

'So your mum must have had some connection to her?'

'If she did, she kept it to herself. We stopped visiting Felicity after Mum died and Dad never mentioned her.' Dad had barely stayed in contact with his sisters never mind a distant in-law.

'Who does the house belong to during probate?'

'The solicitor is the sole executor. There were no guarantees I could be traced. Mr Porter assumed I was still in Colchester, where Dad and I lived. It was on the cusp of going up for auction—'

'And the solicitor gets his fee as a percentage of the sale?' She rolled her eyes to her arched eyebrows. 'Quite an incentive to have you sell quickly, otherwise it means he only gets what, an hourly rate until the will is executed fully?'

'Done some conveyancing before?' I quipped.

She smiled. 'Granddad left a bit of a mess for my parents to sort out.' She tore open a packet of rich tea biscuits and I nabbed one to dunk. She nibbled on the corner of hers. 'Let me bring things up to date. You're thrilled by the idea of inheriting this house, but not the living in it part, especially as you're going to be alone. A caravan in the garden?'

'Not acceptable, according to the terms. Crafty aunty. No camping out or temporary accommodation. It's the house or nothing.'

'It's all very weird, if you ask me.'

I guffawed. 'Frankly I'm confused. Joyous at the legacy, less enthusiastic about the time frame of a year. At least I'm freelance and can relocate swiftly. I can't think how it would have worked out if I'd not been an artist or I'd not dumped my last boyfriend. It's like she predicted things about me, which is impossible.'

She swallowed her tea with a few impressive mouthfuls: an asbestos tongue or more likely limited time between lessons. 'You can't do it up and then move in?'

I sipped a teaspoon's worth. 'I don't have the time. The clock started ticking the moment I agreed; I have to be in by the end of September.'

'Blimey,' she exclaimed. 'That's cruel of her. How much is it worth – the house?'

'The reality is, God knows,' I groaned. 'Mr Porter prattled on about poor location, preservation order on the woodland and nobody, whether developer or private landlord, whoever, can build on the grounds beyond the scope of the original house.'

She picked up the report and scanned over the page. 'Original house?'

I frowned. 'Not sure what that means either. It's a short walk from the village on a single-track road with passing places.' I pointed at the description on the opposing page. 'The outside is listed. I can't alter the exterior, which makes it unappealing for property developers.'

Ruth ran a finger down a few more pages, skimming the lengthy paragraphs and her face transformed into a grimace. 'Okay,' she murmured. 'Didn't your aunt leave you money, some cash to help?'

'As far as I'm aware – and to be frank, Mr Porter has been evasive on the matter – any money leftover is there to pay off outstanding debts, including the solicitor's fees for the duration of my living there, since he will need to be retained. I don't get it – why a year and a day? What is it about the place that requires that kind of stipulation? Does she want it kept in the family? If so, why not say as much in the will.'

'It's a beautiful nightmare,' said Ruth, 'a conundrum. Your aunt has cursed you: dammed if you do sell, damned if you don't.' She handed me the report back. 'My advice, Miriam, and that is what you came here to know, isn't it? Trust your feelings. You felt something in the house. Saw yourself working there. Go with it. But, be careful. You could find yourself up to your neck in debt trying to sell the place. Oh, and as for Mr Porter. Hassle him about the money. She was in a nursing home – how were the costs covered?' She slid the biscuit tin towards me.

'Good question.' And where exactly had all of Felicity's possessions gone?

Having seen the condition of the house, discovered the duration of its vacancy, and understood the significance of Ruth's hint that there had to be money somewhere, I armed myself with a list of essential repairs. Fired up by Ruth's warnings, I intended to ring the solicitor first thing in the morning and pick apart his elusive clauses.

FOUR

Any hope of forming a genial relationship with Mr Porter was about to be fractured. It didn't matter. He wasn't my solicitor, a fact that dawned on me as I dialled his number.

'I can't afford two lots of council taxes, utility bills, my mortgage – I'm not giving up my flat especially as I planned on spending Christmas there – plus the ridiculous amount of things needed to be done before I can move in.'

I paced up and down the narrow space, recalling the grand salons of Heachley Hall, superimposing them over my shrunken apartment. I'd been fooled by Mr Porter's smooth accent and forgotten to fight for my corner. Usually, my phone calls were with clients, people I knew and respected, and words came easily. I had to put aside my reticence at dealing with the solicitor over the phone, especially the lack of body language, and harden my tone.

Mr Porter's voice ruffled with limp sympathy. 'I'm sure it is a very, um difficult position your aunt has put you in—'

'Difficult, too right. I can't believe Felicity, with whom I had little contact, would expect me to live in a derelict building. She had a fall while she was living in the house, but I don't think she anticipated her absence would extend to it being left dormant for five years. I'm curious to know why she didn't make further provisions, extra little stipulations in her will, to ensure my well being?'

A vacuous pause ensued. I opened my mouth to harry him further, but he spoke. 'She'd had a stroke, shortly after she broke her hip.'

Why hadn't he told me? I expelled my frustration into the speaker. 'Severe?'

'She'd lost her speech and mobility.'

'She had no ability to change her will, did she? And I suspect there was plenty of money in the estate at the time of her stroke and it got frittered away in expensive nursing fees.'

'Probably,' he mumbled, a distancing voice, one that fed my ire.

'The money, Mr Porter,' I seethed. 'Don't tell me she didn't provide for extenuating circumstances. Nothing I've learnt about my great-aunt implied she was callous. I remember her giving me cake and dolls to dress up.'

The recollection popped into my head, along with a clearer picture of her wrinkled face, a spiral of long hair and the pearly teeth glinting by the firelight. She'd put a cushion before the open fire and I'd sat on it. Mum had warned me to stay clear of the hearth, but when I'd ignored her advice and poked at the blackened wood, her reprimand had been swiftly countered by her aunt, 'She's a sensible girl.' The words I remembered, but not the character of her voice.

The memory spike ended abruptly; Mr Porter was rallying. 'The estate has provisions. However, I assure you, these instructions are to be enacted after the house is sold or you complete the agreed time span for habitation.'

'I think it is time to have my solicitor review this will.' I called his bluff. I retained no solicitor on my behalf and couldn't afford one anyway. An eerie silence greeted my abrasive tone, then a sharp intake of breath.

'There's no need for that, Miriam.' Mr Porter had lost his haughty accent and something else surfaced, a less sophisticated tone.

'Let me make this clear,' I ceased my pacing. The threat of another legal professional had caught Mr Porter by surprise. I crowded out any chance of rebuttal by speaking quickly, determined to win the argument. My plans depended on financial security. 'I accept that when Felicity drew up this will the house was in a reasonable shape, it might have lacked modern fittings, but it was functional. It isn't now. I don't believe my aunt intended me to spend buckets of my money living there – why would I? She wanted me in Heachley Hall for a reason. I don't know what it is, but I think she saw the house as part of my future. So, the finances, Mr Porter, what are they? Tell me, how much money is left in the estate. Cash, not intangible assets.'

'I have to make contingencies—' the pause lasted longer than I anticipated and was punctuated by the shifting of papers. 'A little over twenty thousand,' he almost whispered it.

A considerable amount, but not a fortune, nothing like what the house would be worth, but it was money, more than what was in my savings account. I scrunched my trembling fingers into a fist and etched my nails into my palm. 'Twenty thousand. Enough for your fees, basic repairs and living expenses for a year.'

'Possibly, with frugal—'

'Am I not the sole beneficiary?' I hoped he flinched on the other end. He didn't answer my rhetorical question. I'd caught him: the money was mine. 'When will the money left in the estate revert to me?'

'A year and a day,' he stated clearly.

He expected me to sell and not accept the year and a day stipulation. He'd paid no attention to the living conditions of the house because I wasn't supposed to move in.

'This is what is going to happen.' I laid out my expectations, the basic necessities of living. Once habitable, I'd move in and then the year and a day clock would start ticking. He argued when I insisted on a monthly allowance to pay for essentials and I held the high ground. 'Call it a loan, whatever.'

I had the list I'd made at the pub and I told him my intention to email its contents. 'Any other improvements I elect to make beyond the scope of this list, I will cover out of my pocket on the grounds these will be recuperated when I sell the property.'

'My fee—'

'Twenty thousand, more than sufficient to cover all eventualities.' Was it? I'd no idea, but no way was he going to dictate the terms.

'When will you move in?'

'When I'm ready. Oh, the cost of hiring a van will come out of the estate, too.'

'I'm not sure I can release the funds—'

'Then I shall ring my solicitor. Oh, and I want a copy of the whole will, not parts of it.'

Porter spoke with icy precision. 'I will send it.'

The moment the call ended I punched the air and breathed a sigh of relief. I was on course to inherit a remarkable house, land, an allowance to cover the costs and when I sold the hall, it would pay off my mortgage and give me the chance to buy a decent house somewhere. Something with a downstairs toilet, no open fires, and a studio.

··●··

FIVE

The wrought iron gates with their perpendicular struts of flaking black paintwork towered over the hedgerows on each side of the entrance to Heachley Hall. Left wide open because they wouldn't budge from their sunken tracks, the gates framed the ample length of the driveway.

Ruth clapped her hands and exclaimed, 'Dickens, here we come.'

Her limp attempt at humour wasn't far from reality. Heachley Hall, the abandoned mansion, was the perfect setting for Great Expectations' Miss Havisham and her Satis House. The house portrayed a different time, before the arrival of regimental bricks and smooth mortar work. Several pointed gables crowned the upper storey, their lofty apexes topped off by small tottering obelisks. The jumbled rows of flintstone blocks transformed the walls into a patchwork of greyness. The perpendicular windows with their lead-lined miniature panes created a network of fake prison bars, while the variegated creepers that freely spawned over half the house had smothered the diminished porch. The house represented an era when romance dictated architecture not practical things like insulation and double-glazing.

The welcoming mist had slithered away, the breeze assisting in its dispersion, but the gloom lingered forming a canopy. The sun, for all its power, failed to produce an autumnal halo in the sky. Parking the rental van, I recalled the reason why I felt called to live there: Heachley might have lost its beauty, but not to the detriment of losing its character or appeal. Whatever it had in store for me, I alone would befriend it. I switched off the engine and rubbed my hands together, eager to see the interior again.

I had a mission to complete.

Where would I be without Ruth or the kindness of friends and a few strangers? I appealed for help from my Pilates classmates, next-door neighbours and a few artisans who lived around Essex. I even resorted to Facebook and Twitter to ask for some things. I usually kept my social media accounts for professional contacts and marketing my services, not begging letters for second-hand beds and electric heaters.

The response was overwhelming and deeply touching. I supplemented the hand-outs with cheap purchases from eBay and charity shops, including a slim-line fridge, a basic washing machine and a new mattress to go on a donated pinewood double bed.

When I sent him the expenses Mr Porter quibbled a little, but relented as he had done on most of my requests with the exception of the issues relating to the Internet. Once the telephone line had been reconnected, it quickly became apparent the copper wire, in conjunction with the distance from the house to the nearest junction box with broadband cable connection, was infuriatingly insufficient; a carrier pigeon would have been quicker.

'Unessential,' Mr Porter had persisted. 'The cost of upgrading the line is beyond the scope of the funds available. I would suggest you reconsider your priorities.'

'I need it for work.' However, my plea had fallen on deaf ears and I realised I'd lost that fight. Also, he was right because it would cost thousands. I would have to rely on hijacking Wi-Fi hotspots in the local area.

I'd been exceptionally busy for the last few days and accumulated everything I needed to equip a kitchen including an urn.

'Why an urn?' Ruth asked as we inspected the contents of the van. I hoped nothing had broken during the journey.

We'd departed in the dark of a blustery Saturday morning with the intention of stretching the daylight hours. I ground the gears several times before the sun rose; the hire van was a nightmare to drive as I'd little experience of such vehicles.

We'd driven past Knottisham's neat village green, which Ruth sighed longingly over, before I cautiously navigated the van's girth down the claustrophobic lane leading towards the estate.

The urn was an unfortunate necessity. 'No hot water.'

'None?' Ruth's exclamation didn't surprise me. I hadn't told her about all the plumbing issues. Kevin, the appointed plumber and friend of Bert, had managed to salvage the cold water tank and due to the presence of an insulating cover, there had been no dead rats or birds floating inside it. However, the rusted hot water tank and boiler needed replacing.

'There is no gas to the house, instead, there's an oil-fired boiler, which is a pity as it's not working. I'm currently negotiating with Porter the ramifications of fitting a new heating system. Hence the urn to make sufficient quantities of hot water until the issue is resolved.'

'Solar panels,' she suggested.

'Good idea but ludicrously expensive and it's not my house, yet. In any case, I don't care about the long-term issues. As for sunshine, during my previous visit, the sea mist seemed to blanket the house throughout the day.' Above our heads, greyness reigned.

'The coast is that close?' She glanced around as if expecting to see waves crashing over the lawn.

'Not really. There's a nature reserve between the house and sea. I suppose, a mile or so distance.'

I entered the house with filtering eyes that overlooked the grime and the fractures in the walls, but the echoing emptiness was harder to ignore. There was so much to do and I'd no experience in renovating or even the basics of remedial repairs. I'd given myself an enormous undertaking and what courage I had could easily crumble if it wasn't for the strange sense of intrigue that Heachley offered.

'Where are the brushes?' Ruth yelled, from outside, interrupting my train of thoughts with her get-up-and-go attitude.

'Dustpan and brush or long pole sweeping brush?' I shouted back from the hallway where I inspected the cobweb jungle dangling from the corners.

'Both.'

I stuck my head outside and a brutal blast of cold wind smacked my face. Ruth was rummaging in the boxes and bin liners in the back of the hire van. 'To the left, by the wheel hub.' I gestured. 'I slotted them down there.'

'Yeah, got 'em.' She dragged out two long pole brushes and thrust a brush into my hand.

'Right,' she announced, slamming the van door shut. 'Hallway first, then the kitchen, yes?'

'Those are the priorities. Plus the attic rooms and bathroom. The rest can wait.'

She started to sweep up the dust and leaves that had encroached through the open door into the hallway. The floor tiles were laid out in geometric patterns and had received a battering over time – a considerable number were cracked or broken loose. The elaborate mosaic design incorporated the geometry of triangles, squares and octagons; tiles of predominately black interspersed with grey tinged milk and lines of coffee about the edges. If I could replace the damaged ones, the floor would look amazing and impress a potential buyer when they entered the house. Inspired by the vision of a glittering hallway, complete with a chandelier, I brushed the debris into a dustpan.

Ruth crouched and poked the fringe of the dust pile. 'Odd.'

'What is?'

'Plaster dust?' She pointed up at one of the numerous cracks in the ceiling.

I followed her reasoning. 'Constant damp has probably caused the plasterwork to come away from the walls and crack. No heating for five years.' I had no plans to replaster the house. The next owner could deal with that problem.

'I don't think it is, though.' She rubbed her fingers together and held them up. The particles had a floury appearance, almost too white. 'More like, I don't know, ash. Really fine ash.' She blew on her fingers and the powder floated away.

It reminded me of the strange dust cloud that had blown out of the upstairs closet three weeks earlier. 'No idea.' I shrugged. 'Let's get rid of it.'

So much had transpired in those three weeks: utility companies contacted, accounts reactivated, services restored. I'd come up to Heachley Hall the previous weekend for a flying visit to check on progress. Bill, the electrician, installed light fittings throughout the house, and new sockets and switches in the attic rooms, then Kevin replaced the kitchen sink and toilet. When it became apparent I had a snail-paced Internet connection, Glenda had taken pity on me.

I'd lamented about the situation over a strong cup of coffee at the pub before returning home. The brief excursion had reassured me that the workmen had delivered the necessary improvements, but little else.

Glenda fleetingly patted the back of my hand. 'You're doing fine, and don't forget, we're here to help. We might be a small village but we're a big hearted one.'

I'd smiled. 'You've been very kind.'

She was polishing a brass pump handle with the end of her apron and shook off my gratitude with a brisk rub. 'If it helps, use our Wi-Fi. Bert won't mind giving you access.'

Once I settled in, I would need to send digital images to my clients and Glenda's offer warranted a bigger thank you than a smile.

Guy had not liked the idea of my moving one bit. I'd explained about the Internet problem and he reacted as if I'd been exiled to Outer Mongolia.

'No mobile signal either,' I'd confessed when I broken the news to him over the phone.

'You've got to be kidding,' he bleated. 'How am I going to chat with my favourite illustrator?'

He typically buttered his flattery with measured doses of worries and it worked.

'There's a landline. Although it isn't great. The line crackles.'

'What about the clients?'

'I'm meant to be drawing, not chatting,' I'd countered. 'I might finish the work quicker.'

Ruth hadn't minded in the slightest when I pointed out she'd not have regular updates on the drafts for her latest book.

'I'll survive,' she said, attempting a mock pout, but the frown was weakened by a humorous twitch of the lips. Smiling transformed Ruth; it stripped a few years off her face and recaptured the energy she exuded whenever children were mentioned. She needed to smile more often.

'You've promised to come back for the odd weekend, check on things and I'll be visiting, too,' she said.

'I've arranged for my mail to be forwarded. There's no need for me to make regular visits home.'

'Loneliness, sweetie, you'll pine for me.'

I'd said nothing. She was right. I'd miss my friends and my cubbyhole flat.

We planned to stay at the Rose and Crown for Saturday evening. On Sunday I hoped to have the bed installed upstairs. Bert and his teenage son, Jake, had offered to shift things around and unload the heavier items out of the van.

By the end of the weekend I expected to have established a reasonable level of accommodation. Ruth and I would then drive back to Chelmsford, return the van and on Monday, I'd load up my Fiesta with my computer, art materials and other critical necessities for the journey back north. Ruth and my downstairs neighbour had offered to keep an eye on my vacated apartment during my absence.

Ruth followed me into the kitchen and I showed her the new sink and taps. 'Not quite an exact match, but it fits the gap.' I turned on the cold tap and a jet of water spurted across the basin and bounced up the pristine white sides. The pipes knocked and banged as an air pocket raced along the tubes seeking an escape before another splash of icy water shot out. She stepped back to avoid the spluttering fountain.

'Air,' I explained. 'Kev said it would take a while to clear. He had to run the taps for ages to clear the pipes of crud. He suggests we boil the water before drinking it.'

'Lovely,' Ruth remarked with unbridled sarcasm.

I sighed in agreement.

She stroked her forefinger along the worktop. 'Granite?'

'Yes. Felicity didn't skimp on things, odd as it may seem. Everything was once good quality, just left due to her sudden departure.' On top of the worktop I'd lined up bottles of bleach and other things to clean out the cupboards.

Ruth peered into a cupboard. 'Underneath all the grime, it's quite usable. Would you want to rip out these old cupboards and put modern ones in? They're solid chunks of wood rather than veneer.'

'The doors could be sanded, revarnished and rehinged.' I gingerly touched the dangling door. 'But, I've no plans to rip out what's here. That's for—'

'The next owner,' she finished with a grin. 'Still determined to move out after the year?'

'What would I do with a big house like this? I can't afford to heat it. The garden is overgrown. The wiring is frankly archaic. The electrician was amazed how well it has lasted. He had to replace a few sockets and light fittings, and add extra ones in the attic. He thinks I'm lucky. He was quite nice about my situation.'

'Nice?'

'Insisted on fitting a decent fuse box. Said it would probably trip all the time, but better safe than sorry.'

'I'll get the rubber gloves out of the van.' She hurried off. I counted my blessings; Ruth had given up her weekend to help me and repaying her gratitude would take more than a pint at the pub. I would need to find some way to pay back the kindness shown by friends, new and old.

'Are you sure you're alright being here alone?' Ruth asked for the umpteenth time, as I stood at the kitchen window: my favourite viewing spot. 'We're doing really well on the cleaning. There's no need to unload anything in the dark, just leave it in the van until tomorrow. And don't forget, I'll be back in a couple of weeks to visit. Half-term.' She put her arms around my shoulders and squeezed them.

'Sure.' There was no point lamenting the solitary nature of my occupation. It wouldn't do me any good to paint myself as a failure before I'd spent one night in the house.

'I can't believe your aunt left it to you without explanation. Something has to be out there to explain it all. A missing letter?' Ruth picked up a dishcloth and scrubbed a mark on the worktop. Her boundless energy was infectious and I returned to wiping down the windowpanes.

'I've been over it all countless times in my head, read the will over and over, and there isn't a clue to her reasons why anywhere.' I chased a smudge of something around the glass, never quite removing it.

'Nothing in her personal effects in the nursing home?'

I shrugged. 'Possibly, but according to Mr Porter it's all gone.'

'Do you trust him?'

My hand paused mid-swirl. I'd not met the solicitor yet and consequently, my focal point remained his voice. Perhaps I'd judged him too harshly in my haste.

The window lost my attention and I turned away from the scenes of dusk. 'He's lazy more than anything else. The will had been drawn up eight years ago when the estate had more money. She hadn't intended for me to have anything until I've lived in the house.'

'Why not before?' Ruth leaned against the worktop and scrunched the dishcloth into a ball.

'I suppose if Felicity had died at home, rather in a nursing home, there'd be a larger cash inheritance. Perhaps she thought I would have pocketed the money and walked away. She wanted me to live here then give me with both the house and money, except now there isn't much cash. Porter wasn't lying about putting aside contingency money for clearing her debts, etcetera.'

'Maybe she planned to tell you, then she fell ill,' Ruth suggested.

'After she drew up the will, she made no attempt to contact me. It has to be some romantic idea I'd fall in love with Heachley, keep it, then with her remaining legacy – the cash that's gone – I would happily live here forever with a husband and kids.'

'Romantic,' she guffawed. 'Blinkered more likely.' Ruth wasn't the best choice for a marriage counsellor.

'Mad,' I half-heartedly joked. 'The will is clear, though. A year and a day. There's no escape from the clause.'

She abandoned the cloth and draped her arm around my back for another one of her encouraging squeezes. 'Come spring it will be beautiful here. You know that.'

'I know.' The house beneath the grime was full of potential; I could see the remembrance of finer days hidden away.

She picked up a brush and stomped the bristles on the hard floor. 'Another hour, then the pub?'

'Yeah, I'm starving.'

Aware of every aching morsel in my body, I was battling a screaming headache and the weight of my eyelids hung heavily. I couldn't wait to collapse into bed at the Rose and Crown.

Ruth stirred her spoon in the bowl of porridge and the steam wafted over the rim. Her enthusiasm for my family's past re-emerged over breakfast in the pub's empty bar. Now we were alone and rested, she focused on something other than books and illustrations, as we'd done over dinner.

'It's an amazing house, really. Such history to unlock.' She nudged the comment into the open.

I swallowed a mouthful of toast and took the bait. 'Amazing and scary. It's a hundred and seventy years old. I imagine at the time it was built it was quite unusual. Georgian houses were typically square with three storeys and symmetrical. This is a hotch-potch, with the front door off centre and the kitchen to the side and not at the back. Heachley Hall sought to be something.'

Ruth raised an eyebrow.

'I did some research during the week.' I'd conducted brief forays into Google while relaxing with my laptop in my comfy little lounge with its piping hot radiator. Alas, not something I'd be able to do in Heachley. I'd didn't have a settee or heating.

'Who built it?'

I shrugged. Genealogy wasn't my strong point in Internet usage; I preferred to download music and stream videos. Although, I hadn't done badly, considering my limitations. 'Not found out.

Before Great-aunt Felicity, it was owned by her father, then somebody else in the family, but beyond that, I think another family owned it.'

'You checked the census?' She scraped the bottom of her bowl.

I nodded. 'I got back as far as 1881. Before then the occupants had a different name.'

'What name?'

'Isaacks.' That's as far as I'd gone. My investigation had fizzled out – I wasn't a historian and there wasn't a website entitled "everything you need to know about Heachley Hall".

Appearing over my shoulder with a surprising amount of stealth, Glenda deposited a rack of fresh toast on the table. 'Couldn't help overhearing you ladies. Tony probably knows more about the 'ole hall than anyone in the village.'

'Tony?' I queried, smearing a thick slab of butter over a slice.

She eyed the empty teapot. 'The farm at the end of your lane. I'm sure he'd like to meet his new neighbour. Call in this morning, he won't mind.' She disappeared back into the kitchen.

Ruth leaned over the table. 'We should go. You're desperate to find out more.' She settled back in her seat as Glenda reappeared with a fresh pot.

'How well did he know Felicity?' I asked.

Glenda's fingers pinched her robust hips. 'The family have owned the farm for generations. Neighbours generally know each other, don't they?' she said brusquely, and hurried away, the kitchen door flapping on its hinges in her wake. Small village politics might prove more complex than I anticipated.

I finished breakfast in silence, my mind buzzing with questions I wanted to ask Tony. Ruth was right, I had a chasm of ignorance to fill in. Once the van was empty, we'd pay him a friendly visit.

SIX

Bert was small in stature, however, his adolescent son possessed a different build – a gangling boniness, the result of uneven growth spurts epitomised by sharp elbows and large feet. Their disconnected heights didn't hinder the pair as they heaved the mattress up the steps muttering complaints as they staggered under the weight. Bert's face turned beetroot red and sweat trickled down his blotchy forehead. He'd brought with him his own warmth. The house exuded a persistent coldness, reminding me of the impending winter without functioning radiators.

My offer to help was dismissed by Bert and instead I concentrated on bringing in the smaller boxes. Ruth remained behind at the pub having a lengthy phone call with somebody and would join me when I visited Tony. I itched to make the brief walk up the lane to see the farmer and find out more about Felicity. Glenda had kindly rung him to warn of our impending visit.

Having finished emptying the van, Bert accepted the offer of a mug of coffee and eyed the loose cupboard doors in the kitchen. 'The last time I was in this house… was at Christmas,' he said between mouthfuls of biscuit. 'I delivered the turkey and helped put up the decorations. Shame to see the place run down and empty.'

'Not entirely empty.' I pointed at the refrigerator and washing machine under the worktop: lonesome modern appliances in a vast shell of a Victorian kitchen. I envisaged the kitchen turning into a family room where a mother and children would bake apple crumbles and sticky cakes. I snapped a few mental pictures and filed them away for the marketing brochure.

He shook his head, frowning and muttering under his breath about my meagre possessions. He would remember those Christmases when the house was splendid while I lacked the memory of anything concrete. I shrugged off my inadequacies – what child remembered every house they visited, the numerous schoolrooms they cycled through on any given day or the holiday camps frequented during rain cast summers.

'Well, we'll leave you ladies to unpack.' He placed his and Jake's mugs in the sink, then he brushed his hands across his shirt, dislodging a few crumbs off his belly ledge. The crumbs weren't alone: a small layer of dust floated away in slow motion, forming speckles on the tiled floor.

As Bert and Jake climbed into the car I thanked the pair profusely. Bert swung his legs into the foot well and turned to look up at the roof. 'There's a few tiles out of place. I don't do heights,' he said apologetically. 'She had that man to help.'

'Man?' I hung onto the open car door for a moment.

'Aye. He'd come by and do odd jobs for her.' He shut the door and wound down the window. 'Can't remember his name.'

'Would Glenda or Maggie know?' Perhaps the odd-job man could tell me more about Felicity than the locals.

Bert laughed and switched on the ignition. 'Maggie moved away. Husband got a job near to Norwich.' The engine roared as he tapped his foot on the pedal. 'Posh name,' he said abruptly. 'Well-mannered.'

'Who?'

'Felicity's man. That's what Maggie said. Never saw him.'

From the porch, I watched Bert's car grind its wheels on the drive, sending the gravel stones flying. Ruth turned the corner, just missing the car.

'Ready?' she asked, joining me as I locked the front door.

'I'll fill you in as we walk up the lane. Perhaps Tony will have more to say than Bert.'

'Come in, come in.' Tony Pyke had bandy legs and stooped shoulders, as if he'd spent his life shovelling shit, which was probably quite accurate given our filth encrusted shoes. As Ruth and I had hurried across the farmyard, it had been a challenge avoiding the congealed mud and our detour around the worst of the slurry caused a scattering of squawking chickens.

We kicked off our soiled footwear on the doormat. The stench of manure followed us into his farmhouse where we were confronted by the equally strong aroma of roses – the flowers bundled into a vase on the hall table. After I'd introduced my friend and myself, the farmer's drawn face broke into a welcoming smile and he led us into the kitchen. An Aga occupied the old fireplace and copper saucepans hung from the low beams, their polished surface reflecting the light.

With its crooked walls and exposed timber, I suspected the farmhouse to be older than Heachley Hall by a couple of centuries. A few weeks ago I would have shown little interest in the vagaries of old properties, but that indifference had gone. I surveyed properties with a keen eye, trying to gauge what made them appealing and marketable. I was fascinated why a cottage with low ceilings and bowing walls, assaulted by the harshness of nature and constant occupation, still presented itself as cosy and habitable.

My hardy Victorian house even with its straight walls and spacious salons depended on human intervention to transform it into a dwelling – abandoned rooms would need an inspiring imagination to make them attractive. Tony's home probably would look welcoming regardless of its furnishing, although the copper pans and antique decorations delivered the finishing touches in style. I'd happily live in a well-maintained cottage if I could afford one, although, the small windows were a disadvantage for a light oriented worker. It led me to wonder if I should present Heachley as old or new to a possible buyer, which would they expect as they crossed its threshold?

'So you've moved into the Hall?' Tony pointed at the coffee machine. 'Cuppa?'

Coffee with fresh milk or perhaps even cream – luxury. 'Yes, please,' Ruth and I said in unison.

Taking our seats around a pine table we wallowed in the aroma of ground coffee beans. Compared to the pub, the farmhouse was seamlessly decorated. Nothing clashed or looked out of place, including the little china dogs on the windowsill, and gilt framed landscapes hung from the walls.

He asked about my plans. I didn't reveal the details of the will, only that I was experimenting with the idea of living in the house. 'Although, I don't have the income to do much to improve it.'

'Pity,' he murmured. His tone maintained a mournful edge. 'We'd heard on the village grapevine about your aunt. Sorry for your loss. Bootiful house in its time.'

The round lyrical vowels were a prominent feature of his accent. I'd steered away from my native Essex, preferring to sound neutral and unattached to a province. Norfolk speech was one I could happily listen to all day, although I doubt I had the analytical ear to adopt it myself.

'You remember Heachley Hall back then?' I asked.

Tony was probably a little older than my late father at the time of death. The signs of middle age were acutely identifiable: speckled grey hair thinning close to his pate with short wisps falling thicker behind his ears. Soft wrinkles had formed in an abundance around his eyes, tiny trenches that rippled up and down in duet to the rhythm of his smiles and frowns. Tony's weather worn face was not like Dad's, who favoured the indoor life.

'Aye, as a kid,' he replied. 'I'd play in the gardens with my brother. Felicity didn't mind as long as we called in advance to let her know, although she didn't like us wandering into the woods in case we got lost – no paths, you see.'

'She never married or anything, not even a companion?' For weeks, I'd formed a picture of a lonely grey haired spinster in a crumbling house, forlornly living out her life and shockingly neglected. But frankly nobody had given me that impression, only myself, and it was based on lost memories that I'd cobbled together with little care.

'I doubt any man could handle her,' Tony chuckled. 'Formidable lady. Kind, too. Don't get me wrong, she wasn't an easy person to like, but she had a soft soul tucked away. I think her upbringing was tough.'

The rim of my mug rested against my lower lip, poised ready to taste, but the coffee remained untouched; I didn't want to miss a word. 'Her childhood?'

'India. She grew up in India. Came over to England when her brother—'

'John, my grandfather,' I interjected, then apologetically nodded for him to continue.

'That's him. She lost her father during the war. She never spoke much about it. He died in Burma when she was young – late teens. It was obvious from what she'd told me that she'd always loved it out there and tried to stay on afterwards with her mother, but when her mum passed, well, they didn't take kindly to Felicity's presence, not in those days.'

Finally a trigger. A little clue that nudged away the pretence of knowing Felicity. Grey haired and stooped, but her face had been richly tanned and glowed with a subtle kiss of mocha warmth. Nobody in my family had spoken of her mixed race, but now in my adult recollections, her ethnicity was obvious. Her illegitimacy might explain why my grandfather lived in England and had no contact with his father and half-sister. My mother – how I wished I could remember Mum – her views regarding her side of the family had scarcely registered in my youth; Dad's relatives always took precedence.

Great-aunt Felicity had a multitude of skeletons in her closet and they were tumbling out in rapid succession. Was that why she lived in seclusion in a Victorian house, out of sight and away from awkward questions? I glued my lips shut. I had to process this revelation later, when I had the space to think.

I moved the conversation on. 'I'm trying to find out why the house was abandoned and emptied. Didn't she want to keep her belongings?'

Tony fingered his mug. 'I don't rightly know, to be honest, Miss Chambers.'

'Please call me Miriam. I gather she fell and broke her hip.'

'Tumbled downstairs. I called the ambulance.'

'You found her?'

'No, Maggie did, her domestic help. She rang all upset and not making much sense. Never one for a crisis, Maggie. I dashed up the lane and found Felicity in a lot of pain. The paramedics carted her off. Sad moment as she never came back. My wife, Liz – she's at church this morning – collected a few personal items, clothes and the like, took 'em to the hospital in Kings Lynn.' He frowned. 'Very sad.'

'She went to a nursing home, I understand.'

'A local one in Hunstanton. Liz and I visited a few times. She seemed happy and expected to come home. Very keen to get back. Social services was arranging assistance.'

'How old was she back then?'

'Eight-five.'

I sucked in air sharply through my teeth. Ruth reached over and squeezed my hand.

'I'd no idea she was that old,' I admitted, somewhat ashamed at my ignorance.

'It made no matter – those arrangements. I went to visit one day and they told me she'd had a stroke and they'd taken her to Norwich hospital. Later, they moved her to another nursing home near the city.'

'For five years she lived there.' If she'd been lonely in Heachley, she'd coped. However, a nursing home surrounded by strangers – poor Felicity, an independent, forthright woman – so like me – stuck in a nursing home and unable to communicate. Life could be cruel.

'Liz and I went to see her. She was bedridden and couldn't speak. It's quite a drive to make at harvest time. We were very busy. I'm sorry, we just couldn't keep...' He ducked his head, avoiding eye contact.

'Please don't apologise. You've been a good neighbour. Who cleared the house five years ago?' I wanted to address the critical matter of the house's decline.

Tony scowled. 'The van came charging down the lane and almost collided with my tractor. When it pulled into Heachley Hall, I was curious and went to see what they were up to, because there are scoundrels about who steal and pretend to be legit.'

'You checked?'

He crossed his arms and leant back in his seat. 'I demanded to see their instructions. Who'd authorised the clearance.'

'Do you remember a name?'

'Parker. Barker?'

'Porter?'

He nodded. 'Aye, probably. Sometime ago this happened.'

Ruth and I shot a glance at each other. 'Her solicitor. He authorised the disposal of everything, including her personal effects: photos, letters, everything?'

'I don't know. They took the furniture. Tore up the carpets. They were thorough. Liz thought they'd set fire to the trees with their bonfire. Just like before.'

'They burnt her things?' I gasped, horrified.

'They didn't care, and nobody was there to represent her,' he stumbled over his words. 'Sorry. I didn't have any way to stop them.'

He felt guilty; five years on, it still upset him. I was her only living relative and nobody, especially Porter, had bothered to contact me and check whether I'd wanted anything. Tony's unjustifiable shame fed my more legitimate version – I'd not tried to stay in contact.

'No,' I said softly, 'This wasn't how it should have been, but it wasn't your fault.'

Ruth pushed her mug aside, leaning forward. 'What did you mean about the trees catching fire?'

Tony flicked his hand, as if to dismiss his own remark. 'Oh, it was something Felicity had told me years ago. Not long after the house had been built, it caught fire and the wind whipped up the flames and blew the sparks across into the trees. The story is that the cloud of ash blew right over into the fields into the village, like snow.'

'Crikey, was anyone hurt?' Ruth's eyes had lit up. She loved a good mystery.

He shrugged. 'I don't know. The house still stands. Perhaps it was a rumour, an exaggeration. Felicity told me because I was curious about the growth of the trees. They'd come out of the stumps; new growth from old.'

I felt inundated with new information. It was time to leave. 'We'd best get back. Loads to do before we drive back to Chelmsford this evening.'

We shook hands.

'Do you remember the name of the nursing home?' I asked abruptly on the doorstep, slipping on my mud-caked shoes. I could ask Mr Porter, but this was an opportunity to stoke the locals into providing me with more information. The solicitor was useless, and obviously uninterested, in helping me with personal stuff. The less I dealt with him, the better.

He scratched his fuzzy crown as he considered my question before shrugging. 'Forgotten. Liz might know. I'll ask her.'

'I'm wondering if they kept anything of hers.' It was a long shot. However, I might get a chance to talk to his wife. What did she know about my aunt?

'Maybe.' He trekked across the yard with us; his boots better equipped to deal with farmyard detritus.

Coming to the farm gate, Ruth held back for a moment. 'Did Miriam's aunt mention a man who helped out at the house?'

For the first time Tony lost his soft features. Something moved across his face, like a shadow and it darkened the rings under his eyes. 'There was a, a gardener,' he stuttered, before bolstering his voice. 'My wife had the most contact with Felicity. We were neighbours, but your aunt was a private person. If she had other friends or acquaintances, she kept things tight to her chest.' He dragged the gate open.

'Yes,' I passed through the small gap. 'She did.'

We waved goodbye to Tony as he leaned on the gate, his shoulders slumping, relieved – it appeared – at our departure. Ruth's question had stirred up some other issue.

SEVEN

Waking early on Monday morning and extracting myself from my sleeping bag – my duvet had been left at Heachley Hall – I yawned several times, massaged my aching thighs and examined my hands; the callouses showed the signs of prolonged and unaccustomed physical labour. However, the hard work had only just started. Dad's mantra ticked over in my head, reminding me it was worth it, and I carried that philosophy with me as I returned the hire van.

My Fiesta groaned after I'd laden it to the roof with stuff: computers, art materials and more clothes. I raced to complete the packing, determined to be back on the road straight after lunch.

The note I shoved through my neighbour's letterbox was the final act, one last moment to get to grips with doubts before leaving. There was nothing else left to do but switch off the lights, turn down the heating to the lowest setting on the thermostat and secure my front door. It felt strange. I was turning my back on my cramped flat that for several years I'd been proud to call mine in order to take up residence in a neglected, unfurnished mansion with acres of uncultivated, unproductive land. The paradox caused me to both pine for my humble flat and yearn for the spacious living quarters promised by Heachley Hall.

I thought about my impending first night alone at Heachley Hall with its cavernous empty rooms and convinced myself I was on an adventure akin to a Girl Guide camping trip. I had conveyed my excitement to Ruth when I'd dropped her off.

'Don't fret about me, I'm more than capable of looking after myself,' I'd reassured as we hugged.

'You're strong, Miriam,' she said, patting my back. 'Don't let the house put you off enjoying yourself. Make some friends up there.'

I owed her so much and needed to find some way to say thank you properly. A fancy restaurant or something.

Arriving at the house in tandem with the descent of late afternoon darkness, I unloaded the car, dumping most of my things in the dining room alongside the bulk of my other possessions. With little energy left after three hectic days and many car journeys, I supped on soup, bread rolls and an apple before retiring to my attic room.

Overwhelmed by exhaustion, I crawled upstairs, changed into my pyjamas and burrowed under the damp duvet. Unfortunately, I'd not anticipated two things: the frigid temperature and the opaque darkness; the latter was stunning, if daunting. I'd only known omnipresent streetlights.

The duvet was a winter tog variety, but it afforded little warmth. I wrestled with it in the vain hope it might trap my body heat. Admitting defeat, I added extra layers of clothing and a pair of socks. Tomorrow, along with the essential shop for food, I'd buy blankets – fleece ones to snuggle into when the wind howled and the icicles formed.

During the night, neither a gale nor a cold frost kept me awake, rather, I struggled to cope with the noises outside. My familiarity with the sounds of night extended to traffic, sirens, the raised voices of pedestrians, and the aeroplanes flying out of Stansted airport. Here, with no major roads nearby, I had to adapt to other intrusions: owls hooting, foxes barking and the constant, never-ending rustle of dying leaves. I shuffled down the bed, amazed at how such innocuous, supposedly comforting, sounds of nature could disturb my slumber.

The thunderous pounding of rain on the roof woke me early. The window had misted up with condensation through which weak splinters of light penetrated. I stuck out my toes and grazed the cold floorboards and recoiled, tucking my feet back under the covers with a shiver. Summing up courage, I threw off the duvet, dashed down the staircase to the floor below and into the bathroom.

I added a rug and bath mat to my growing shopping list.

It was only October, how would I cope with a bitter winter? I would have to toughen up. Felicity had managed, somehow, so could I. My opinion of those fireplaces, which I had considered as largely decorative, changed. There was one in the dining room, the library, drawing room and upstairs bedroom, which I suspected, given the relics of decent wallpaper, had been hers.

Each fireplace had its own style, reflecting differing levels of requirement and embellishment. The one in the bedroom was basic and functional, taking up little space and a minimal hearth to trip over. The drawing room's mantel had stone carved surroundings depicting a simple scene from some Greek myth. It exemplified the Victorian love affair with the overly decorative. It had survived because it had been too large to rip out, but I noted the cracks in the figures and the poor workmanship in the detail. Whoever built the house aspired to a grandeur they couldn't afford to replicate.

The library had a wooden mantel and a degree of carved stonework, whereas the dining room had bluish Delft tiles laid around the fireplace and a marble plinth buttressing the iron grate. I suspected each of the other bedrooms once had their own simple hearth, but had been boarded over to prevent draughts; unsuccessfully, I believed, given the constant rattling of doors and creaking window frames.

I was coming around to the idea of using at least one of the downstairs fireplaces. What I needed was fuel, but I'd no experience at gathering suitable wood and I wanted to avoid buying coal.

I hurriedly dressed, grateful for the thermal underwear I'd packed. I'd two electric heaters: one I'd keep up in the attic to heat my workroom, the other in the kitchen. I switched both on, uncaring of electricity bills. Until I adapted, I had to make do with what I had and I'd no intention of suffering.

With breakfast swiftly dealt with I demisted the Fiesta's windscreen and went to explore the local amenities. I located a supermarket at Hunstanton and made a note of smaller general stores closer to Little Knottisham.

Having filled the Fiesta with food, a blanket and household wares, I returned to the Hall – my new home. Should I think of it as home? I'd not really come to terms with my relocation. Although the post office was forwarding my mail, I'd not formally changed my address. During the drive back, I'd convinced myself I was on assignment. Something temporary and necessary, rather like a secondment. However, regardless of my mental exercises in denial, Heachley Hall was now where I slept and worked.

I hadn't installed a cooker or hob, but had brought my microwave oven up from Chelmsford. The omission of the cooker left me with no ability to fry or grill. I doubted takeaways would deliver to an off the beaten track address and I already craved a bacon butty. Instead of managing with a full-sized cooker that was too expensive, I was resigned to the idea of a camping stove and putting up with their fiddly gas canisters.

Unloading my shopping into the rickety cupboards – breaking an additional hinge in the process – I anticipated a bland diet of sandwiches and microwave meals. I couldn't face arguing with the uncompromising solicitor.

Mid-afternoon and I fought to set up my computer. I crawled under the small table to reach the back panel and tried to access a USB port. The tower was a bulky and powerful enough to run the greedy graphic programs that converted scanned pictures into high-resolution images. It had nearly broken my back carrying it upstairs.

When I heard the distant trill of the telephone, I cursed, attempted to reverse out and banged my head on the underside of the table. Without a phone socket, I had to scamper down two flights of stairs to the hallway where I'd plugged the corded handset into the only socket available.

'Yes,' I panted.

Guy bellowed a greeting. The line crackled, distorting his voice. He explained about my latest project that I was supposed to be kicking off that week. 'Did you get it?'

'Last week. Is there a problem?' There were minor issues, nothing insurmountable. We chatted and hearing a familiar voice in the echoing hall was a little surreal blanket of normality, comforting me in the midst of the unknown. My restless eyes roved, seeing things I'd rather not: uneven varnish on the stairs, a multitude of broken floor titles and the sprawling highways of cracks in the plasterwork.

With the call ended, I stomped back upstairs. Charging up and downstairs was one way to keep warm.

I'd gotten halfway up the main stairwell when the doorbell rang. The bell was a mechanic ringer attached by wire to the pull handle outside the door. I retraced my steps back downstairs and through the small frosted windows I spied the outline of a person. Tall in stature – a man? I crept forward, wondering who would bother to come out here in the drizzle. Little Knottisham's welcoming committee?

The door lacked a security chain, so I drew back the bolt and created a vertical crack to peep through. The faceless man presented a slightly hunched back. His cocoa hair was slightly frizzy with damp. The knitted jumper with its baggy polo neck belonged on a fisherman out at sea. The maroon wool glistened with pearls of raindrops. His hands were buried in the pockets of his faded jeans that were torn just below the knees. Pieces of garden twine laced his boots and the excess cord was hooked around his ankles. The creak of the door sounded as I opened it wider and he turned. He lifted his face and straightened his back.

There should be dark eyes to go with the hair rather than translucent ones. The longer than typical sideburns framed his triangular jawline while thin lips and raised cheekbones offset the length of his nose that formed the centre fold of his narrow face. Young, like me, possibly. I couldn't gauge his age from his complex portfolio of features. He removed his hands from his pockets and took a small step forward.

'Good day. I mean, hello.' I craned my neck to hear his soft voice then opened the door a little more.

'Yes? Can I help you?'

'I'm sorry, forgive me, I didn't mean to startle you. Rather, I hoped I could help you.' He smiled, his lips nervously twitching in the corners.

'Help me?' I needed to be sorting out my computer issues and not speaking to strangers on the doorstep.

'Allow me to introduce myself. My name is Charles Donaldson.' A drop of rain slid down the end of his nose.

I shivered as the wind caught the door and almost tore the handle out of my hands. Simultaneously, the corner of the door whacked the side of my foot. Nearly unbalanced by my stumbling hop, I exclaimed. My caller rushed forward and grabbed my hand, preventing me from falling backwards. His cool fingered grip didn't let go until I'd righted myself. Close up, his bluish eyes appeared hollow and quite disconcerting. I jerked, snatched back my hand, and muttered a thank you. With the door wide open, he stepped into the shelter of the porch and wiped the tiny droplets of rain off his face using a sleeve.

'How can you help me?' I repeated.

'The garden – I can clear the dead wood.' He waved towards the trees. 'I'm good with my hands, making things, repairing. Chopping wood.'

'Chopping wood?' I repeated, rather more keenly.

My plan to use the fireplace in the dining room depended on finding decent firewood and using an axe with proficiency. I didn't fancy wielding a sharp weapon. Did I want a strange man on my land with an axe? Another blast of cold air raced past me, as if to remind me not to dally. Don't look a gift horse in the eye; beggars can't be choosers – Nana Chambers favoured battery of idioms that she threw about like confetti, reminding me to grab at whatever opportunities came my way.

'Come in.'

He stepped lightly through the entrance, out of the wind tunnel, and I closed the door behind him.

'Good gracious,' he declared loudly. He ignored me and strode across the tiled floor. 'It's really all gone. I'd thought something would be left, but it's everything.' His voice boomed about the hall and up the stairwell before bouncing back.

'You know the house?' I followed him, as he made straight for the library door.

He stood in the middle of the library amongst the dust, a few rusty nails and flaked paintwork, and ran his fingers through his short locks of hair. His expression was one of alarm. 'There were so many books. Hundreds. Beautiful books. All along this wall.' He pointed to the remaining bookshelves. 'She loves books.'

'Who, Felicity? You knew my great-aunt?' Any anxiety I had at having a stranger in my house was replaced by blatant inquisitiveness and excitement.

'Miss Marsters and I were acquainted, yes.' He touched a bare shelf, wiping the dust off with his fingertips. 'Friends, I should like to think. She did not mention me?'

'It was twenty years since I'd last seen her. I visited as a child with my parents. You do know she's dead? It happened about six months ago.'

He ceased sweeping the shelf and pressed his hand flat on the surface. 'No,' he whispered. 'I hadn't heard. Little reaches my ears.'

'You live in the village?'

'Nearby.'

A posh name, Bert had said. If Charles was considered posh, then I suspected I was in the presence of Felicity's odd-job man. Why had he appeared now, after all these years?

'Charles you said? You were the handyman who helped my aunt,' I confirmed. 'And you want to help me?'

He turned to face me, and I saw an intense sadness portrayed on his features, almost tearful. His wan complexion appeared sallower and under his soulful eyes, dark shades had materialised. It would seem nobody had told him and given his connection to the house, I wondered why he hadn't been told.

'I would be happy to be of service.' He didn't look happy.

I thought of my long list of outstanding jobs, many of them beyond my basic abilities at do-it-yourself. 'I have little money. I'm afraid I could only give you the minimum wage. An hourly rate, cash in hand.'

'That will be quite acceptable.' He straightened his shoulders, his eyes brightening. 'The house needs much doing to it. I had not been aware of its state. She's been gone longer than I... How strange to see Heachley empty. It's not right and you must have some decent comforts restored. A young lady such as yourself cannot be without succour.' He bounded towards the door and once again I strode after him as he headed back to the front of the house. 'She baked: cakes, bread, pies.' He flung open the kitchen door. 'The oven.' He halted before the hole in the wall. 'Was here.' His voice deflated.

'Was it?'

I peered into the large letterbox shaped chamber. The iron frame and door must have been ripped off, maybe by the clearance men. The miniature chasm was a blackened shell crumbling inside, about a metre deep and surrounded by exposed brickwork. Below the oven was an iron door welded in place. I assumed behind the shutter was where the location of the coal fire was. Previously, I'd ignored the strange nook, unsure of its purpose, but it made sense — a large flat surface for baking. I stuck my nose into the darkness and inhaled: hot metal and yeast. Another memory of visiting Felicity? Or was the house harbouring more forgotten things on my behalf, slowly leaking them into my subconscious? I stepped back and looked at him.

He stared at the gap with his moonlight eyes. 'Yes. She spent much time in this room.'

'It would have made great pizzas.' I grinned, trying to cheer him up, but he didn't respond in kind. 'Would you like a tea or coffee, Charles?'

He walked around the perimeter of the square room — a slow ponderous walk — as if to reacquaint himself with the layout. He studied each side, from the wall of oak cupboards regimented into two rows, each a uniform size and tarnished by overuse to the stretch of granite worktop under which I'd installed my fridge and washer. The exposed brick wall housed the carcass of the absent oven and opposite it, the sash window, which reached to the ceiling, letting in sufficient light that even on a dim day I needed no electric bulbs.

'No, thank you.' Charles halted by the sink. 'This is new, but the cupboards.' He looked over his shoulder at the broken doors hanging from their hinges, 'those need repairing.'

'I've only had the time to sort out a few essential things. I moved in at the weekend.' I switched the urn on. I needed a coffee to warm my chilled bones.

He examined one of the damaged hinges, poking the metalwork with a long finger. He didn't wear a ring, but that meant nothing these days. 'She's been gone a while.'

I couldn't tell if it was a question or a statement. His words hung unanswered, as if he was finding his own way to the answer.

'Five years. She took ill and had to leave suddenly. You didn't know?'

He paused with his fiddling and sighed a heavy one heralded by a sharp inhale through his nose. 'I wasn't needed, so I stopped coming.'

'She'd ring you, I suppose, if she needed you. Do you have a number I can contact you on?' I wondered where I'd left a notepad and pen.

'Number?'

'Telephone number to reach you.'

'If you don't mind, I'd prefer to simply call by now and again.' He pointed at the cupboards, ignoring my open mouth as I tried to fathom how that might work out. Charles, on my doorstep – how often? He gave up on the hinge. 'Would you like me to repair these?'

'The cupboards? Wow, that would be great. I was going to sand them down and revarnish, but it would mean taking them all down—'

'I can do that for you. There are tools in the outbuilding. Well, there were…' He'd left the room before finishing his sentence.

I'd not explored the gardens or the small collection of buildings behind the back of the house, one of which looked like an old garage, the others possibly stables. He marched up to one and pulled on the door. It resisted, briefly, before the bottom scraped along the cobbles of the courtyard. 'Here,' he declared inviting me in.

There was the taste of wood; its bitterness was there at the back of my tongue, reminding me of a cooper's workshop in a distillery. Except there were no barrels. Instead, more cobwebs strung together into a hammock that reached from one side of the makeshift workshop to the other. The converted stable had survived the blitz of the clearance with remarkable fortune. A table, manufactured out of planks, took centre stage under the rotten frame of the window. Laid out on its surface was a collection of carpentry tools, each one covered in crumbs of curled shavings caught in a mat of webbing. Shark tooth saws, old chisels with crinkled handles and a claw hammer. Propped against a wall, an axe. The sharpened edge glinted, catching a shard of light that chased us through the door.

'It's all still here. Just as…' He brushed some of the sawdust off the table with a sweep of his hand. 'Nobody wanted these?'

The tools were in reasonable condition. 'I've no idea why they were missed. The house was cleared when she fell ill.'

'A blessing for us, then? I can make good those cupboards and if you like, chop wood for the fire. Would that be of assistance to you Miss… I'm sorry, I don't know your name?'

'Miriam Chambers.'

'Miss Chambers.'

I nearly giggled at his sincerity. 'Miriam, please.'

I expected a blush or something transparent, because his eyes dropped awkwardly to examine the flagstones. However, his skin remained pale. 'Miriam,' he said softly. 'Pretty name.'

He picked up the axe. 'Best start before the rain comes down heavy again.'

Charles, the reinstated handyman, went out of the shed towards the wood. I observed him as he paused for a moment to swing the axe and survey the trees. Ahead of him lay fallen branches and a tangle of undergrowth; an unexplored wilderness on my doorstep. The rain had brought with it a sea mist that swirled between the trunks of the oaks and beeches, catching the floating leaves in its wake. With long strides and undaunted by the bleak weather, Charles navigated an unseen path. The cold instigated a rampage of goose bumps across my shoulders and I darted into the scullery or utility; another empty room I'd chosen to ignore.

By the time I'd reached the kitchen window Charles had vanished. I hovered there for a few minutes, listening to the urn whistling. I brewed a coffee and headed back up to the attic. I still had to hook a printer up to the computer. I would miss the Internet and the connection to the outside world, but not the spaghetti cables.

I lost track of time while tinkering and cursing at the error messages; the printer refused to feed paper. The deluge of rain on the roof snapped me out of my frustrating battle. How could I have forgotten Charles so easily?

Reaching the ground floor, I paused to listen and other than the pattering on the windowpanes; I heard nothing. It had been over two hours since he'd gone to chop wood. With the light fading fast, I hurried outside, sprinting across the courtyard to the shed. There, lined up against the wall, was a mountain of chopped logs stacked neatly and with the bark side up. The shiny axe was propped against the wall.

'Charles,' I shouted out of the door, but it was obvious he'd gone home. I felt somewhat guilty that he'd done all this backbreaking work and left without me paying him. I'd no way of contacting him, which seemed a peculiar arrangement and one that made little sense.

··●··

EIGHT

The dining room, the smallest of the reception rooms, was the easiest to heat since it faced east and caught the morning sun. Scattered about in boxes and crates, my worldly possessions — those things I considered useful and important enough to bring with me. They would need unpacking, sorting, but without cupboards or durable shelves, I had no storage. Perhaps if I asked Charles sweetly, he might build me some cupboards.

I rifled in one box and dug out my iPod and docking station. The soulless house needed some kind of sound. I'd made a decision not to bring a television. My existing flat screen was bolted to the wall and given the hassle of mounting it in the first place, I'd no plans to dislodge it. I'd not seen an aerial on the roof of Heachley Hall and I suspected Great-aunt Felicity had no interest in televisions. However, I couldn't stand the silence. While I worked, I'd often listened to music and I concluded the radio would suffice for the duration of my stay. The television would distract, keep me from work and since my spare time was better spent renovating the hall's interior, my evenings shouldn't be wasted watching reality TV or soap operas, not that I cared much for them.

Armed with my entertainment system, I headed upstairs to continue my fraught attempts at starting some real work. As I passed the landing I noticed the closet door was ajar, which was odd given the effort required to open it. I reached out to shut it and it rocked, waving slightly, and as my fingers touched the freezing doorknob. The door slammed shut; the noise reverberated about the house and the vibrations reached my feet.

What was it about that door? I wiped my clammy palm on my trousers. I refused to be freaked out by stupid draughts.

Later, after I'd eaten another round of soup and bread and treated myself to a cupcake, Ruth called. I lacked a chair in the hallway – another oversight. While I brought my friend up to speed with my news, I leaned on the dusty wall.

'Do you trust this Charles?' The line hissed rhythmically, and I adapted to the interference by filling in the odd constant or missing syllable.

I pursed my lips and traced a thin crack in the wall with the tip of my finger. 'Yes, I suppose.' He'd done what I asked – chopped wood – and far more than I'd anticipated. 'It's just, he turns up the day after I arrive, but didn't know Felicity is dead.'

'You didn't find out for months. She'd been gone for five years, living on the other side of the county, debilitated and unable to communicate.'

'You would have thought Maggie or somebody would have told him.'

'Rural communities aren't like The Archers, they don't live in each other's pockets. He came by, saw your car and chanced it.' Ruth had grown up in a tiny village and understood country life, whereas I'd lived all mine in towns or cities. However, I couldn't imagine a reason why Charles happened to be down my lane without an explanation.

'He didn't give me a mobile number.' I slid my back down the wall and crouched.

'No reception in the area, remember?'

The line went silent – almost silent. It was as if somebody was listening: splintered sounds stuttering down the line.

'Is he good looking?' Ruth fizzed with unsubtle questioning; she had to be smiling.

I pictured the man in his scruffy clothes, which were at odds with his educated tone of voice and gentlemanly phrases. 'Yes, kind of, but slightly gaunt, as if he's been ill.'

'Perhaps he has been unwell and he's just getting back into things. There aren't many opportunities for young men in rural places; he's doing what he can. He probably makes a fine living helping lonely young women.'

I sensed her smirk on the other end of the phone. I laughed, forcing it out. 'Well, he found me quick and he offered to sort out the kitchen cupboards.'

'So, see it as good fortune. He knows the house – given he was friends with Felicity – and you might find out more about her.'

'Possibly.' Then I spied it, above my head: the doorbell cable was detached. A flurry of butterflies escaped my belly. What had forced it loose? I stared at the thin wire linking the pull to the bell, which hung close to the ceiling. I would need a stepladder to fix it.

'Ruth?' I began, tentatively.

'Mmm?' Her voice crackled.

'When I first met Bert, he implied the house was haunted, or I should say Maggie had told him that.' I held my breath waiting for her reaction.

Why was I contemplating such a ludicrous idea? I rested my chin on my knees and used my spare arm to hug my legs. The hallway was polar and my thick jumper had lost the battle.

Ruth snorted, an almost derisory response. 'Surely Felicity would have been alive when Maggie told Bert. Felicity didn't die in the house.'

'I guess ghosts are supposed to die in the place they haunt. She was cremated; perhaps her ashes blew over to here.' I traced my foot along the edge of a floor tile and swept aside the accumulated dust with my toes.

'Do you believe in them, ghosts?'

'No,' I exclaimed sharply. 'Nonsense. I don't believe in them. If I saw one I might, but I haven't.'

'So it's gossip, Miriam. The bored inhabitants of Little Knottisham filling the airways with chatter about the supernatural. Do you think if Felicity had lived in a modern house, rather than an old hall, there'd been this rumour? Ignore it.'

'Perhaps Charles can give me more details, assuming he's party to it all.'

'There, good idea. I'm glad you're making friends. I won't have to worry about you much.'

I smiled. Ruth, the motherly type with no children of her own, taking care of me. 'Don't worry. I'm fine.'

'I'll be up soon.'

'I'm looking forward to it. I've so much to do. I'm sure the time will fly by.'

'It will, just keep busy.'

I eyed the wire. Bert might have a stepladder. I would fix it myself; make sure it didn't come loose again. There were no invisible ghosts in this house. What haunted it was shabbiness and malfunctioning things.

'Sleep well,' she said, except the 'well' sounded more like 'ell'. I had come to some frozen kind of hell, a money pit of a mansion. I needed to sell it so I could payback for a year of living in a freezer populated by weird dust.

NINE

I needed a sat nav in the car. I've just driven down the same street in King's Lynn for the third time. Eventually, I parked outside the hardware store, grabbed my shopping list and proceeded to dash around the shop in a crazed, haphazard fashion.

I should be drawing pictures of guinea pigs – little furry animals chased across the farm by an angry goat. I'd envisaged a sequence of comic strip illustrations created in watercolours and finished in ink; the author had already approved the draft. The hard graft was producing the finished thirty-two pages by Christmas.

To help relieve the stress of standing in the checkout queue, which crept along at a ponderous pace, I tried the breathing exercise I'd learnt at Pilates. Inhale through the nose – wait, count and hold – release slowly through the mouth. I whistled through pursed lips, then repeated, allowing my lungs to expand. The woman standing behind me took a step back, as if I was contagious. Perhaps I should find a Pilate's class nearby, something to do on the cold winter evenings.

The glacial house ate into my bones. Waiting my turn in the queue, I took refuge in daydreams, imagining a fragrant bath or better still, a blistering hot shower with billowing steam and the prickling spray massaging the tortured muscles of my back. Unfortunately, I had to manage with a bowl, a sponge, and a quick wash in front of the heater. I fought the temptation to sneak away and pay for a hotel room for the night so I could bask in the luxury of warmth. I doubted my expenses extended to those tactics on a regular basis, but even if I did break the rules, would Mr Porter know? How would he ensure I was keeping up my side of the bargain? No doubt he would spring a visit on me, something unexpected.

I'd not anticipated a few binding clauses in a will could successfully hold me hostage to a ridiculous situation. 'Stubborn to the core' – my father's frequent reference to my less endearing trait. I couldn't contemplate reversing my decision – the money from the sale remained an enticing lure.

The queue shuffled forward. Somebody at the front had picked up the wrong item and a helpful assistant had gone to fetch the correct one. Clutching the wire shopping basket in my hands, I surveyed the lighting department, which was small in scale and dominated by uplighters and halogen bulbs. I fixated on the few traditional lampshades hanging from the display racks. The bulbs in my house remained bare and unadorned. Seeing the shades, which I'd walked past with determination, I craved the decorative cones with their frilly edges and bright colours and with it came hankerings for other trivia: the coasters on coffee tables and gilt-framed photographs. For my kitchen, I needlessly desired a spice rack, silicone oven gloves and a tea cosy in the shape of a cat. Never one for green thumbs, even the droopy houseplants on display called out to be placed on the windowsills of Heachley Hall. I closed my eyes and drifted back into the realm of imaginary delights. There, on sunny mornings, I'd draw back the insulated curtains and wriggle my toes in the soft carpet pile.

No, it wasn't to be. What was the point of filling the house with transient comforts when I was unswerving in my wish to sell the place? I ceased my unfocused attempt at meditation, opened my eyes and stepped forward, dropping my basket on the counter with an unapologetic clatter. I would stick to improving the fabric of the house and its permanent features. More importantly, I needed to return home. I'd guinea pigs to draw.

Back at Heachley Hall in Charles's shed, I laid out the sanding tools: a block and sheets of emery paper, a small paintbrush and a large tin of oak stain varnish on the workbench. Next time I went to King's Lynn, I would ask Charles to join me and he could pick the best hinges. However, he wasn't around to ask. Would he turn up? I hoped he would.

I headed upstairs carrying a mug of coffee and sat in front of my desktop easel. I picked up a pencil and sketched a dumpy guinea pig with extraordinary long whiskers. Calmness descended. The pencil glided, guided by my steadying hand and my pulse no longer thrummed in my temples. It seemed only in the moment of quietness with the tools of my trade arranged about me did I find peace of mind, the tranquillity of knowing I was doing something I loved. The rustle of leaves outside slipped away into nothingness, as did the rain drumming on the window. I had no awareness of either, only the soft whir of the heater in the background, pumping out some warmth. My knuckles ached with the cold.

I took a break. Repetitively humming a tune, I washed-up the mug in the kitchen sink. When I turned to face the cupboards, one of the broken doors was missing. Charles had removed the door. I must have left the back door open.

Did he like coffee? With milk? I gambled Charles was a coffee drinker and made him one. The rain had stopped, and I crossed the yard. Around the perimeter of the small yard a forest of nettles and hollyhocks grew, and between the cobbles, tufts of grass and moss softened the edges of the worn stones. I stumbled on the slippery surface and spilt a few drops of coffee.

The damaged cupboard door lay on the bench. Charles was bent over and sanding off a residual layer of lacquer using the emery paper. He'd fashioned a square block of wood and wrapped the paper about it. I'd forgotten to purchase a sanding block.

'I brought you a coffee.' I placed it on the edge of the bench away from where he was working.

'Thank you. You didn't have to.' He blew at the veneer of sawdust and the tiny shavings scattered, revealing a richer, natural colour. 'See, the wood beneath is in good condition.' With little effort, he held the bulky door up to the light.

'I didn't buy any new hinges,' I explained, 'I didn't know which ones were best. Next time I go to King's Lynn you should come with me and choose the right ones.'

He picked up one of the hinges he'd removed and held it out. 'Just like this one. I'm sure you will find a good match. Take it with you. My time is best spent here.'

'Oh. Okay.' I hid my disappointment. I'd hoped he'd come with me but it seemed Charles had little intention of spending his spare time with me. On the table there were several carpentry tools that I hadn't provided him, including a plane and metal file.

'Were these left over from Felicity's time or did you bring them?' I pointed at the small collection.

'Your great-aunt kindly provided me with these implements.' He touched the handle of the file with a gentle caress of his fingertips, almost lovingly. 'She was always most generous.'

'I wonder why the clearance men didn't take them?'

'I don't know. Let us be grateful for their lack of persistence with regard to the outbuildings and their surroundings.' He dusted down his jeans and the sawdust flew off in all directions. 'I'll come and fetch the next door. You don't mind if I remove them all? I'd rather varnish them at once.'

'Sure.' I shrugged. 'Whatever you like. I didn't pay you for chopping the wood.'

'No matter. Why not pay me when I've finished the doors.' He followed me out of the shed.

'If you're okay with waiting.' I crossed the yard.

'Quite okay,' he spoke hesitantly.

I stood in the kitchen and hugged my cold hands under my armpits. The shed had been freezing – how did he work in those conditions? He wore similar clothes to the first time I'd seen him, except the jumper was a different colour: dark blue instead of crimson.

He'd brought a screwdriver with him and immediately attacked a lower cupboard that hung at an angle from one hinge. The door looked like it had been kicked. I blamed the clearance men – thugs.

Charles removed the hinge. 'I'll need new screws, too. These are rusty. Same size as this.' He passed me one and I slipped it into the pocket of my fleece jacket. My teeth chattered.

'You're cold,' he remarked.

'I'm used to central heating.' I cocked my head to the defunct radiator under the windowsill.

'Felicity liked open fires. She said they were magical and enchanting to watch.' He wrestled the door onto the floor then propped it up. 'She'd sit by them, staring.'

'Didn't she want a television?'

'No. She had one once, but her eyes were not good. She preferred to read. She had this little magnifying glass to help.' He scrunched up his eyes, squinting at some imaginary page.

'I've a radio. I'm going to try to manage without a telly.'

'Radio is wonderful. Voices travelling across the air, speaking into your ear.' He waved his hand in front of him. 'Like a private conversation.'

'I need the company,' I grumbled. 'Big house and just me.'

'No gentleman callers?' He raised his eyebrows.

I dropped my gaze. 'Once upon a time there was a charmless prince but no happily ever after. In fact, I've entertained a few. However, for the time being, I'm single and unattached.' I could list them – a string of names etched into my catalogue of failed relationships – but what was the point of raking over has-beens. Perhaps two had captured my heart sufficiently that I mourned their unprovoked departure. The rest I'd happily ditched with trifling aftershocks on my part, although one had attempted to cling on like a limpet.

Charles smiled at my lacklustre description of my love life. 'So, now you're the princess in the tower. Yes? Awaiting your glorious Norfolk prince?'

I laughed. 'Too, right. Trapped I am, unable to escape. Ensnared by the curse of a dead aunt—'

'Curse?' His delicate eyes had widened, and an additional paleness draped over his already colourless pallor. 'What madness comes again to Heachley?' he muttered.

I shrugged, sympathetic to his comment, but I found him a tad melodramatic in temperament. 'A year and a day. My confinement here is bound by her last will and testament. Only if I live here for the specified time do I own the place properly.' I tapped the granite surface of the worktop. 'Hence my minimalist approach to moving in. I'm not committed to living here.'

I'd yet to fathom out Charles's facial expressions. We'd spent relatively little time in each other's company, mostly polite and business-like in nature. What he showed me seemed to be shock, almost an admission of horror on his part. 'I cannot believe she would be so cruel as to bind you to this place,' he hissed.

'Oh, it's my choice,' I hastened to explain. 'If I don't stay, it will be sold and I'll forfeit the value of the property. I confess—' I placed my hand over my heart, '—I'm after the gold pot at the end of the rainbow, assuming Heachley sells. The money.' I swayed, as if to swoon with delight.

His worried expression diminished. 'Not truly trapped,' he concurred. 'I do hope you stay, even if it means you are less than comfortable. I shall endeavour to assist you in whatever way I can. I owe your aunt that much. I'm relieved she didn't seek your misfortune in this arrangement.'

'Don't you find it odd that she'd seek to put such a lengthy proviso on my stay?'

'She had her reasons, I suppose.' He backed away from me and bent to pick up the door.

He'd not really tackled my question, but why would he? It was a family matter. When I was better acquainted with Charles, I might ask him what he meant by owing Felicity. In the meantime, I wished the house wasn't so cold.

'I've got so much to do to make Heachley Hall fetch a decent price. Actually, you could do me a favour.'

He straightened up without picking up the door. 'How may I help?'

'I want to light a fire in the dining room, but I've never lit a fire indoors before now.'

'Ah, I'll show you.' He bounded past me. 'Come, Miriam. It is an art, lighting a fire, and you'll do well to learn, then those teeth of yours will stop chattering.'

I slipped my tongue between my teeth, halting the tremors. What else had he noticed about me? My limp hair, the ink stains on my fingers? Little things that shouldn't be out of place, but were?

I tucked my hair behind my ears. 'Thanks.'

On his knees, Charles inspected the fireplace. He pulled out the grate and peered up the chimney before reaching up with the full length of his arm. 'I can't feel any blockages, but it probably does need to be swept.'

He described it as an art and watching him construct a pyre, I agreed. A couple blocks of wood at the base, then a layer of kindling. He stuffed a few scraps of paper into the crannies to act as an ignition point.

Charles lit the corner of a piece of paper and sheltered the tiny spark with his hand. The flame flickered uncertain, and for a second I thought it would die. The paper caught and the fire travelled along its length meeting another piece, and like dominoes falling, the scraps burnt in succession until the kindling was ablaze.

'You need a fireguard.'

'I don't expect I'll need a fire down here every day.'

'The house will get colder over winter.'

I didn't doubt him. The flames licked their tongues around the blackening bark, crisping the edges. Grey smoke puffed out in response and the wood hissed and spat out its liquefied sap. I held out my hands, rubbing them before the embryonic heat.

'The wood is damp,' Charles remarked, tapping the nearest unlit block lying on the stone hearth. 'It will smoke for a while.' He sat back on his haunches and crossed his arms.

'No matter, this will make a huge difference.' I hunkered down on my heels next to him.

He tossed another chunk of wood on the burning pile. 'You like this room?'

'It's smaller compared to the others. I just find big rooms intimidating. I live in a small apartment. I remember something about this room from Felicity's time here. Perhaps a table, I don't know.'

'It had oak panelling, so high.' He pointed to a ribbed line running around the walls.

I stepped away from the hearth; the fire generated an inferno of heat. 'That explains the marks on the walls.'

'She asked me to remove the panels.'

'Felicity?' A stupid question because who else did he mean.

Charles rose and ran his hand over the surface of the wall. 'Too dark for her tastes. She liked light shades or patterns. She put up hangings, like tapestries, she'd brought them back from her native India.'

'Native? You make her sound like a foreigner.'

'Do I? She made Heachley Hall her home, but everything in it spoke of a different place. It was very exotic and colourful. I can't believe it's all gone. A great pity.'

I agreed with the sentiment. 'I suspect the clearance company pilfered much of her things. The will's executor hasn't been…thorough.'

He turned to fire and poked the disintegrating wood with a stick. 'The smoke is rising. Let's go outside and check it's emerging from the chimney.'

Outside in the cold I stamped my feet while we waited for the smoke to poke out of the chimney pot. I spied a damaged roof tile.

'Can you fix them?' I pointed to the loose tiles.

'Yes,' he said, with a nod of his head. 'There's a ladder behind the shed.'

'There is? I don't want you to do anything dangerous.'

'Have no fear for my safety, Miriam, I will come to no harm.' He grinned, a remarkable charming expression that enveloped his face, and, for a moment, his pale irises darkened as his pupils dilated.

I snatched a breath and lost the ability to speak. I was blushing. Even in the cold air, I felt the heat of a blush bloom over my chilled face. I wanted to deny the existence of the prickling sensation at the back of my neck, the warning buzz that came when I was in the close proximity of a man. It was no good. His masculine energy had awoken something forgotten, something banished to the back of my mind: my neglected love life.

While watching the wisps of smoke, my last so-called beau superimposed itself over the grey skies. Jordan Buller bounced onto the memory stage, grinning and wrapping an appreciative arm around my shoulders. A thickset bloke with chubby cheeks and a nervous giggle when we… I opened my eyelids to find Charles raising an eyebrow in my direction, his head cocked to one side. I said nothing to explain my abrupt daydreams. Instead, I stuffed my hands in my trouser pockets. I'd been harsh in my recollection, more likely it had been Jordan's bottomless generosity when it came to nights out or gifts that had kept him attractive and good company. However, it had taken me a few months to see that he had little else to offer, and neither had I.

Satisfied the chimney was functioning correctly, we returned indoors. Charles collected his next cupboard door and headed to the outbuilding. I started to climb the stairs, reforming the image of a comical guinea pig in my head.

I reached no farther than the mid-flight of steps when a knock at the front door halted my ascent.

·· ● ··

TEN

B ert dragged the stepladder out of the boot of his estate car.
'Thank you.' I opted to stay out of the rain and shouted from
the doorstep. 'You didn't have to bring it up straightaway.' I'd
called the pub earlier in the day to beg for the favour.

'No problem. Glenda says you might need it for a while.'

'Are you sure? I don't want to be a bother.'

Bert carried the metal stepladder into the house and propped it
against the wall. 'Really, you can have it. I'm sure you'll find plenty
of use for it.' He glanced up at the ceiling and I followed his gaze.

The cobwebs hung from the corners, tangled and dusty – had
they been spun recently or years ago? For how long could a spider's
web last?

'I'll be able to clear those.' Then I gestured towards the door.
'And fix the bell.'

Bert swivelled and flicked the loose wire with his finger. 'Did I
make you jump with my knock?'

I managed a feeble chuckle. 'Just a little.'

The house had captured Bert's attention. He crossed to the
bottom of the staircase where the individual steps had lost their
sheen and acquired the dull imprint of countless footprints. Ruth
and I had swept the whole set, hoping to re-establish the stairs'
former glory. However, the wood needed a proper polish to
retrieve the gnarled grain in the oak and deepen the colouration.

Bert remained fixated on the blank wall at the bottom of the
staircase. 'That must have been the location of the doorway.' He
pointed at the cracks in the painted plasterwork.

'Door?' The fractures had formed in their meandering a

particular perpendicular arrangement. I stepped back and mapped the outline of a hidden doorframe.

'Here.' He gestured with an arm, sweeping it from one side to the other in an arc. 'The other end of the house stood here. Must have been grand in its time.'

'What other end?' I skated my palm along the wall and felt a small indentation – a perceivable difference in the thickness of the plasterwork.

'I thought you knew.' Pink freckles appeared on his cheeks, as if my ignorance embarrassed him as much as it did me. He ruffled his ginger beard, twirling the ends through his fingertips and twitched his nose. The man had a plethora of little eye-catching habits that overlaid an endearing boyishness on his wrinkled face.

'The house – t'were much bigger until part of it burnt down.' Bert had confirmed what Tony had said about fire, but the farmer hadn't mentioned the shrinkage in size as a consequence of the damage. The revelation explained the clause in the mysterious will regarding building an extension out to where the original house once stood.

I moved farther away from the wall and tried to picture the layout of the building. As well as the blocked door next to the bottom of the stairs, upstairs the landing came to an abrupt end – passed the bedroom where Felicity had slept, to where the strange little closet occupied a stretch of wall. If that opening had been the continuation of the original house, then the symmetry made more sense: a stairway sweeping up the three sides of the central atrium, climbing to the gallery where the bedrooms led off around the landing.

'How much bigger?'

Bert pulled a face. 'Don't rightly know. This fire happened long ago, a hundred years or so, at least. Although, it's still the talk of the village. Probably because it's common knowledge that Heachley Hall could once have rivalled some of the grander stately homes in these parts.'

If he referred to Sandringham, I doubted Heachley Hall had been that spectacular in comparison. Outside, where the missing wing once stood, was a neglected and overgrown garden area with a formal layout of rose beds, low hedges and dwarf walls. The rooms possessed no viewpoint of this garden because of the absence of windows. The extent of the garden appeared to represent the scale of the original building.

Bert cleared his throat. 'I reckon you could see the original size by going in the cellar. The burnt-out rooms were demolished but the foundations remain underground.' He tapped one of his boots on the tiles and the metal toecap echoed across the hall.

The cellar.

Mr Bridge's appraisal had listed the presence of the basement—'Nothing of value down there.' In retrospect, I suspected he hadn't explored it and had probably stuck his nose in and dashed out. Bert, who licked his lips and bounced on his heels like an expectant dog awaiting his daily walk, had aroused my inquisitive nature. I also owed him a favour.

'Let's take a look,' he suggested. 'I can spare a few minutes.' Bert's watch remained covered by his shirtsleeve – Glenda maintained Bert's schedule. 'We'll need a torch.'

He waited in the kitchen while I fetched the LED torch from my bedroom. Since he took it out of my hand, I let him take the lead. The entrance to the cellar was in the scullery. A rickety door with a loose doorknob and a small sliding bolt. Bert aimed the torch light down the stone steps and its beam lit up another door at the bottom. The paint had peeled off the surface leaving the darkened wood bare and splintered in places.

On my own, I'd never have dreamed of going into the cellar. It seemed a pointless exercise to know what lay beneath my feet. My reticence wasn't born out of a fear of dark places, merely the thought of a dank smelly cellar with rats and probably an accumulation of junk.

Bert gave the lower door a nudge and it creaked – a high pitch groan, as if we'd awakened the portal from a slumber. Protesting doors seemed to be a common feature of Heachley Hall.

I peeped over Bert's shoulder, which wasn't difficult given his short stature. A pungent smell emerged out of the gloom and it wafted up my nostrils. I wrinkled my nose at the unpleasant concoction of aromas: damp, mildew, wet stone and stale air. Thankfully, I didn't smell anything putrid.

Bert banked the light from left to right, gradually uncovering white-washed walls, which had flaked off in places to reveal red bricks. Alcoves were scattered about the outer perimeter wall, forming sunken tombstones with their arched recesses. Alien to the original fabric were the steel support columns – a later modern addition to re-enforce the house. Rubble lay strewn across the uneven flagstones: splintered wooden planks, shattered bricks, broken glass and all manner of fragmented man-made materials.

'Careful with your feet,' Bert warned, stepping farther into the cellar.

He kicked aside a piece of glass with the steel-capped toe of his cowboy boot. With his back to me, Bert's rocking gait and bowed legs gave the impression he'd just dismounted a fat horse. Swaying side to side, he continued to explore with the torch as we crept forward, tiptoeing past the worst of the rubbish. He hovered his light towards a far wall. Neat rows of small round holes had been chiselled out of one section.

'What are those for?' I asked.

'For storing wine bottles,' concluded Bert and since he was a pub landlord, he was probably correct. 'Kept them cool and safe. This area must have been a small wine cellar. Given its proximity to the kitchen, they might have had a cold storage area for meat and cheese. Any cupboards have long gone.' He shone the torch on the smashed wooden shelves then shifted the beam. 'Coal bunkers.' The metal boxes lined the opposite wall and beneath their shuttered doors, the coal dust had turned flagstones the black.

'I wonder if there's some left.' I meant it as a joke, but Bert was curious, which meant I had to follow him. We moved out of the light cast by the open door and with only the torchlight for guidance we examined the coal bunkers.

Bert lifted one lid cautiously and peered inside. 'Empty,' he said.

The box contained nothing, not a scrap of coal. He moved the torchlight up the grubby walls until he exposed the wooden slats of the low ceiling. A small trapdoor lay directly above the bunker. 'Coal chute for deliveries.'

He circled the light about and uncovered more nooks. In one corner was a pile of wheels: big bicycle ones with snapped spokes and shredded tyres. There were also small tyres joined by an axel.

'Pram wheels?' I guessed.

'Maybe. Right size.' He kicked one and the axle sheared away with a clatter. 'Come on, let's see what it's like on the far side.' He aimed the light at the gap in the wall between the partitioned sections of the cellar.

I followed his footsteps as we scrunched our way through the debris of a forgotten basement. I hugged myself protectively and focused on the narrow beam of the torch. That proved hard, the darkness drew my attention away like a magnet.

Thick blackness, almost solid and touchable. What lurked in it was a mystery since without the torchlight it was impossible to see even a glint or outline of what lay hidden in the murky depths of Heachley's cavernous cellar. Pitch black some might say. Pitch, like tar, is glutinous and oily, and I seemed to swim across it, suffocated by what felt like a lack of breathable air. With each footfall, the icy moisture increased the turbidity and only the blue glow of the LED bulbs offered salvation from the oppressive weight of darkness.

I blinked several times before focussing hard. Were rats scurrying through the scattered trash? The more I imagined what could be hidden in the invisible spaces of the cellar, the more I heard accompanying sounds: fluttering, scuttling, squeaking and then a dismal creak.

I halted while Bert continued to creep forward. My ears were alive to the subtlest of noise, especially our breathing, which filled the fetid air with exaggerated rasps – quite unnatural, as if forced. I held my breath and listened.

It sounded like a sigh or a small rush of air. Had something brushed past me? I froze, waiting for it to happen again. Nothing.

I muttered a curse.

'What?' asked Bert, glancing over his shoulder.

'Just my imagination getting carried away. I felt something.'

'I think there're bats.' He waved his torch up into the rafters. Cobwebs and an abandoned wasp nest hung in the crevices, but no sign of bats. 'Do you want to go back up?'

I shook my head, then realised he couldn't see my gesture. 'No, I'm not scared, just the darkness plays havoc with my imagination.'

Bert chuckled and held out his hand. 'Here, hold my hand if you like.'

My heart had already kicked up a thrumming racket in my ears before he'd even offered his comforting hand. What alarmed me? Was it the nothingness inhabited by vermin? The detritus of bygone inhabitants and the vacuum left by neglect? No, what troubled me was how a once splendid house sat upon such a bleak place and that amongst the aged foundations lurked rubbish and crumbling brickwork. Even the addition of later structural supports worried me.

Modern houses had deep foundations and damp courses. Building regulations dictated the beginnings of a house. Heachley Hall had been built in a time when custom determined the structure. I didn't like what I saw down here because it reminded me of the fragility of things we assumed to be strong and reliable.

I took Bert's hand, not out of fear, but because I detested the cellar; a useless space without a function and destined to be forgotten or misused. If I intended to keep the house, I would fill it in.

'There.' He reached out with his torch. 'There's the current outer wall. See beyond, the cellar continues.'

It did; the flagstones vanished as we stepped onto dirt. The natural ground beneath the house, soil and ground down stones, congealed into a platform. It squelched slightly and sucked my shoes in. I gasped and gripped Bert's hand tighter. The temperature dropped, and my breath hazed in front of me forming a white cloud. He flashed the light about the cellar. The whitewash had disappeared and in its place the walls were charcoal black and barely perceivable in the darkness. Entrenched beneath and about Bert's feet, dust: the familiar white particles I'd seen floating about upstairs. Somehow the plague of dust managed to seep up through the floorboards, and then beyond.

I sniffed. The air smelt different, too. Even after decades, I detected burnt wood: an acrid lingering odour, like a bonfire in a neighbour's garden or a firework popping off at a display – invisible, but there.

Bert stretched out his arm into the void. 'Looks like it was several yards longer, perhaps two extra rooms down this side of the house?'

'Yes,' I murmured, uninterested in the dimensions. 'So, all this burnt down?' The scale of the fire, the heat generated to blacken the cellar walls and obliterate the missing salons, must have been substantial. With no fire service to battle a blaze, the fact the rest of the house survived was amazing.

'Don't rightly know,' Bert answered. 'T'were pulled down, I should think. Fire must have caused a lot of damage.'

A door slammed shut and the noise reverberated along the cellar in waves, shifting the air into a breeze. An icy blast of air caught the back of my neck. Dust swirled up from the floor billowing into a white mass, while at the same time, projecting out of the walls, a veil of soot formed a blackened cloud. The two seemed loathed to touch one another and shrank away to be conquered by gravity. Awoken by the abrupt disturbance, squealing and scuttling sounds emanated near my feet. Bert spun around and blinded me with the torchlight. He let go of my hand. With my heart pounding against my breastbone, I emitted an unintentional cry of alarm.

'Draught catching the door,' he declared.

I'd enough of weird air currents. 'Let's get out of here.' I snatched the torch out of his hand and hurried to retrace our steps.

Back in the scullery I switched off the torch. Bert secured the door, heaving it to with a yank of his arm. My near asthmatic throat squeezed tight and I rasped breathlessly – I'd dashed across the cellar to reach the stairs, scattering unknown objects with my feet, hoping they weren't furry and alive.

'That was fascinating.' He grinned, turning to face me, then his expression altered: his moustache drooped, and the smirk disintegrated.

I blinked, adjusting to the bright light, and bit back a less than polite retort. 'You said this house was haunted,' I reminded him of the conversation at the weekend. 'Did you fancy a little ghost hunt, is that it?' I blurted.

He started, surprised by my acidity. 'I said Maggie thought that,' he corrected. 'I'm sorry, I should never have mentioned it. She liked to watch those paranormal telly programs. You know the type, hidden cameras in old houses. Drove her husband nuts with her spooky stories. She thinks anything more than twenty years old is haunted, including our pub. Saw things everywhere. Forget it.'

'I bloody can't, can I.' I walked into the kitchen and he followed on my heel. 'I don't believe in ghosts,' I added over my shoulder.

'Nor do I,' he said, 'I do like old houses and this place has mysteries to solve; it makes it fun. You should see your time here as an adventure.'

'An adventure,' I snorted weakly, making short shrift of his lightly directed humour. I didn't mean to be hostile. It was time to lose the strange sense of misconstrued antagonism towards Bert.

The fear of financial ruin, of drifting without purpose, was crowding my thoughts. Lighten up, Dad would have said, after one of his increasingly frequent trips to Greece. At the time, he'd bombarded me with seemingly frivolous advice, which I'd treated as insulting. She, the invisible Aegean beauty who had tempted him out of his austere office and into her olive skin arms, had edged Dad into a flamboyant lifestyle, so unlike the penny counting one he'd practised when Mum had been alive. Would he have been so flippant if my mother had survived and she had inherited Heachley? I couldn't blame Dad for seeking succour in the company of another – she had relieved him of the constant burden of grief. Such a pity his renewed exuberance for fast living hadn't extended to learning how to steer a speedboat.

I turned away from the empty oven hole and dismissed the memories. 'I'm sorry, I shouldn't have snapped. I'm a little stressed. This place is a millstone around my neck,' I said.

Bert replenished his sanguine cheeks. 'You don't have to go down there again.'

'I don't plan to.' I lay the torch on the worktop and sighed. Amongst the angst about my impending austerity, the image of a once splendid hall had recaptured my curiosity about my aunt. 'But you're right, I am intrigued by the cellar's secret. Didn't Felicity have anything to say about the fire?'

He shook his head. 'No. Ghosts, the fire, she showed no interest in discussing them. Considered it all a storm in a teacup. To be frank, she didn't say much to anyone. In recent years, before her accident, she rarely visited the village and relied on Maggie. Although—' he tugged on his beard, '— she did say Maggie should know better than to speak about things she didn't understand. Yes, that was what she said, now that I think about it.'

I stared at the bank of cupboards. 'Charles might know about the fire. He and Felicity had a friendly relationship, perhaps she told him about it.'

'Charles?' Bert straightened up.

'Her handyman. He's back and is fixing the cupboard doors for me.' I pointed at units and the two with the missing doors. 'He's in the shed right now. Let's go ask him.'

It was my turn to lead and Bert followed me outside across the rain sodden yard and into the shed.

It was deserted. No sign of Charles. The doors lay on the bench, sanded and smooth and next to them, his tools neatly arranged. I picked up the discarded mug; the coffee dregs had thickened into a black gloop at the bottom.

'Oh,' I shrugged, apologetically. 'He's gone.' I checked my watch. It was past four o'clock and the dim room, like the other outbuildings, didn't have electricity. 'Probably went home. It's too dark to work in here.'

Bert picked up the sanding block. 'He didn't come to say goodbye?'

'We were in the cellar. He must have thought we'd vanished into thin air.' I laughed at the irony. Shy Charles was content to come and go as he pleased.

Bert nodded. 'I best get off, too. Glenda will be kicking up a fuss.'

I showed Bert out, thanking him once again for delivering the stepladder.

'Come to the pub this evening for a meal. On the house.'

'Bert, I couldn't. You've been so generous with—'

He wagged his finger at me. 'I insist. I dragged you into the cellar—'

'No, you didn't, I was happy to go down there.'

'You wouldn't have considered it if I hadn't mentioned the fire.'

An awkward pause descended, because he was right. The fire intrigued me not the cellar. He'd graciously offered me recompense, I should accept. 'I'd love to come to the pub.'

'Jolly good.' He fished his car keys out of his jacket pocket and I let him out the front door. I waved goodbye as he drove away, but I didn't think he saw me standing in the porch.

Alone again, I eyed the doorbell and its dangling wire. I couldn't be bothered to fix it. Those restless guinea pigs needed longer whiskers.

ELEVEN

I wolfed down my food reminiscent of Oliver Twist – shovelling forkfuls into my mouth in rapid succession. I fought the temptation to creep over to the bar and ask for seconds. Ensconced in a cold house, I burnt calories, which in turn created a bottomless appetite. There was no danger of gaining weight while I lived at Heachley Hall.

As I stabbed at the last morsels of flaked fish and chips, Glenda joined me, wiping her fingers on her apron as she wriggled into a seat.

'Thank you.' I dabbed the napkin around my chin. 'It's very kind of you to feed me.'

'You look starved. You'll turn into a waif.' She rested her hands on her rotund belly and chortled.

'Not likely.' I twirled a loose strand of my hair, catching my fingers on the knotted ends. Upstairs was a lovely bathroom with a shower and tub. I craved for a hot bath above anything, even food. 'I don't suppose you could do me another favour? Would you feel put upon if I asked if I could have a bath or a shower? I didn't anticipate how much I'd miss hot water.'

Her eyes widened. 'You don't have hot water?' she shrieked. 'How can you live like that?' She scraped back her chair. 'I'll get you some towels. Take as long as you like. Good grief. I shall be having words with Kevin. How could he leave you with no hot water.'

I rushed to follow her back to the bar. 'It's not his fault. I only asked him to fix the cold water supply.'

'Now listen here, dearie.' She leant across the bar and ground her thumb into the wood, twisting it back and forth. 'Don't let these men walk all over you. I'll give him a ring and insist he sorts this out.'

'Glenda,' I called after as she disappeared into a back room. 'Drat,' I muttered to the swinging door.

Lying among the fragrant bubbles I nearly nodded off. The bath water lapped over my body, warming my bones and redeeming my frozen core. I took my time to dry, redressed and return to the bustling bar downstairs. My damp hair hung around my face and I relished its smooth feel.

Glenda was busy serving customers and I hung back, waiting for the opportune moment to say thank you for her hospitality.

She spotted me and waved me over. 'I've spoken to Kevin. The earliest he can come out is Friday. Let's see what he can sort out for you.'

Friday was the day after tomorrow, I hadn't expected anyone that quickly. 'I'm really grateful—'

'Say no more. Us girls must stick together.' She gave me a swift wink and returned to serving the next customer.

The short drive up the lane took no more than five minutes and throughout the journey I yawned. By the time I'd located the porch light switch and illuminated the keyhole with sufficient light, I'd made up my mind to go straight to bed. Turning on the heater, I peeled off my clothes for a second time that evening, put on my thermal pyjamas and burrowed under the damp duvet. The promise of hot water gave me something positive to focus on, otherwise, I struggled to find anything encouraging about my circumstances.

In the morning, I slipped on my slippers and heavy dressing gown, and scurried downstairs in search of an essential cup of coffee.

Sunshine blazed through the frosted glass of the front door, dancing across the tiles of the hall, and the brightness cheered me up.

Entering the kitchen, I let out a shriek and jumped back a step. 'Charles! How did you get in?'

The dazzling light reflected off the screwdriver in his hand. He lowered his arm to his side unperturbed by my outburst and he greeted me with a surprisingly sincere smile. 'Good morning, Miriam.'

'The door,' I jabbed a finger towards the back of the house. 'It was locked. I locked it.'

'Ah, I found the key. Felicity used to leave a key under a stone by the back door. I found it.' He seemed pleased with himself and his pale eyes sparkled for a second. Usually they possessed an empty dullness to them.

'Oh,' I walked past him to switch on the urn.

'You don't mind? I didn't mean to scare you. I like early mornings.'

'It's fine, but I'd rather you didn't just walk into the house without me knowing. At least call out or something, so I know you're here.'

'Of course. I'm sorry, I took advantage of the key. I forgot that was Felicity's arrangement, not yours.'

'I don't mind the key.' My swift declaration came without much thought. I'd just granted him permission to come and go as he pleased. The freedom I'd gifted him should unnerve me, but it didn't. Given my isolation, having somebody was a comforting afterthought. 'I came to see you yesterday, but you'd gone already.'

'I had?' He furrowed his eyebrows, then gave an indeterminate shrug. 'I had something urgent to deal with. I apologise.'

'Please, don't. You must have others.'

'Others?'

'Clients. People you help out?'

He smiled, as if amused by my question. 'Probably, but at the moment, you have my time. I'm sure when needs must, I shall be busy elsewhere.'

His response contained the usual vagaries, a recognisable feature of Charles's style of communication. I'd dealt with monosyllabic men before, something of a speciality of mine, but at least he didn't grunt and ask for another bottle of beer, which was Ruth's sad experience. The urn started to hiss and I spooned out the coffee granules into a mug. 'Fancy one?'

'No, thank you.'

I hovered waiting for the urn to reach temperature and wondered how to interrogate him without appearing inquisitorial or unpleasant. 'It was a pity you'd gone. Bert was here, and I wanted to introduce you to him.'

Charles hesitated, clearing his throat before speaking; another peculiar, and somewhat endearing mannerism of his. He refused to make eye contact with me. 'It is of no importance. I'm not a man for idle chit-chat.' He turned away and fiddled with one of the doors.

'Not idle. He and I had visited the cellar.'

Charles's hand froze, poised halfway between hinges. 'Why? I mean, it's just a cellar.' He reclaimed use of his arm and jabbed the screwdriver at the lower hinge.

'To see the original foundations. He says part of the house burnt down years ago.'

'It did,' Charles said softly. His shoulders had gone rigid and the grip on the screwdriver tighter.

I shrank back a little. Had I angered him? 'Do you know much about it? Did Felicity tell you anything?'

'Not that I remember.' He rotated his wrist, attempting to release the screw holding the hinge in place.

I persisted. 'You talked about this place. You know it so well.' I pulled on the urn's tap and a gush of steaming water landed in my mug, splattering liquid over the rim.

'Perhaps not as well as you might think.'

He'd lied, I felt sure of it. He kept his back towards me, but the tension in his body remained. There was no point pushing him; we were barely friends and I couldn't afford to alienate my rather useful handyman, not while I had a monopoly on his time.

I hunted around for a slice of bread to toast. As well as soup, I would be living on a diet of jam and toast for the foreseeable future. 'Okay, my mistake. I guess Felicity really didn't speak much about this place.' I'd intended to sound dismissive, but it came across as grumpy and frustrated.

Charles released a harsh expiration of defeat. He turned and directed his gaze straight into mine with an unswerving focus. It startled me how his eyes lacked vibrancy, because the rest of his body reflected confidence, a fluidity of movement rather similar to an athlete and a superlative comfort of being in his own skin, except the pallor on his face remained pasty and untainted by an expected flush of annoyance at my sulky remark.

'She was very fond of this house, more so than many would know. A lonely woman on her own, pining for another time, she'd come to rely on Heachley as a sanctuary. We understood each other well enough. If there are stories to tell, then they remain with her, not me.'

At last, something of an explanation. He'd maintained a distance with Felicity, just as he seemed determined to do with me. 'I understand. I'll leave you to it.' I nodded towards the upper hinge.

'Thank you.'

I slotted the bread into the toaster and waited, praying a fuse didn't blow. He reached up for the upper hinge, stretching his tall frame higher until he stood on tiptoes. As he did, the sleeves of his jumper slipped down to his elbows. I suppressed a cry. From his elbows to wrists, his skin had puckered into blotchy red scars – an intermittent patchwork of discolouration.

The toast shot up and I released my paused exclamation, using the toaster to mask my reaction to seeing his arms. He lowered the door and the sleeves dropped back down, covering up the red blotches. He seemed unperturbed by the exposure.

'I'll take this to the shed.' He left me to scrape rock hard butter over my toast in a haphazard fashion. Felicity's life held my curiosity, but Charles's should be none of my business.

TWELVE

Before I started work I fixed the doorbell, ensuring the wire was secured and unlikely to loosen. Pleased with my efforts, I retreated to my den in the attic. On a blank piece of paper I sketched a farmer. Needing inspiration, I stole Tony and next to his bandy legs, I drew the naughty billy goat with giant horns about to launch his attack on the unsuspecting guinea pig. It was a bad habit – stealing real-life people for my illustrations.

I heard a distant metallic clunk and paused, cocking my head to listen. There it was again – a dull chink – the doorbell. By the time I'd raced downstairs, I expected my visitor to have given up and left. However, the woman outside had patiently waited and when I opened the door, she smiled in greeting.

She was neither young nor old, and she'd bundled her chestnut dyed hair into a neat bun. A pair of letterbox shaped spectacles were perched on her long nose, and the lenses enlarged her eyes into dark moons. Bright red lipstick smothered her plump lips and her cheeks were as rosy as her mouth. Behind her, parked up next to my Fiesta, a black Toyota Rav-4 and a thick coating of dried mud encrusted the bonnet and wheels, forming splatter marks that Jackson Pollock might have admired.

'Miriam isn't it?' she asked, her voice deep and husky and quite at odds with her feminine appearance. 'Sorry to disturb, but my husband said yew were after some information, and I thought rather than drop a note or ring, I'd pop by and say hello.' She spoke with a thick dialect: a slow drawl of vowels, stretched and songlike.

I couldn't place her. 'I'm sorry—'

'Liz. Liz Pyke.'

'Of course. Sorry, I've been lost in work and… Do come in.' I waved her into house and led her into the only room downstairs with a sense of normality – the kitchen. I switched on the small fan heater and offered her a drink, which she declined. She stared at the disassembled kitchen units and I explained about the absence of some of the doors.

'Felicity would have appreciated your efforts to sort this place out,' Liz said sweetly. Too saccharine; it reached my ears as patronising.

I salvaged a faint smile. 'Did Felicity talk about her family? I know so little about her.' I leant against the worktop and tried to appear nonchalant as if there was nothing exciting to know.

Liz tucked a loose strand of hair into her bun. Unhurried in her action, she tested my patience. 'It's been a few years and she was a reclusive woman. I tried to encourage her to attend church or join the Women's Institute, but she declined, politely of course. She liked to bake, and she donated the odd cakes for stalls, if I asked. I usually stuck a note through the door and Maggie would turn up at our house with a fresh cake.'

'Maggie seemed to be more than her cleaner. Why didn't she have a full-time carer?' Where had Maggie gone? The questions stacked up in my head.

'She treated Maggie like a gopher. Bert and Glenda, too.' Liz hesitated, as if to suddenly recall who I was to Felicity. The moment of embarrassment was fleeting. 'Sorry, that's sounds cruel. Let's just say she knew how to get the most out of people. She'd sit in her library, blanket on her lap and book in her hand with the house gradually falling apart around her. She seemed content as long as somebody was there to run her errands. Never one for the village, if she went anywhere it would be Old Hunstanton and the seaside. She'd take a taxi. When she put her mind to it, she was reasonably capable of looking after herself. Until she fell.' Liz placed her handbag on the worktop and rummaged inside it. 'Here this is what I came to give you.' Liz handed me a piece of paper: *Beechwood Care Home. 01603900201.* 'The nursing home where she ended up.'

'Thank you,' I tucked the note into the back pocket of my jeans. 'There's a small chance they still have some of her things.'

'Possibly. When she left here she asked me to collect a silly box from her bedroom to bring to the hospital. She said it contained photographs and letters, and other things. I guess, even though she was optimistic about her return, she removed them as a precaution. As I said, she kept things to herself. Something she'd been used to doing.' Liz shrugged, and her glasses slipped down her nose a fraction.

I wished I could remember what Felicity looked like, how she behaved in the company of my parents. I thought hard and pictured a woman with bronze skin, wrinkled and weather worn. It reminded me she hadn't gained that swarthy appearance living in Norfolk.

'Because she was different?' I suggested

'Different?' Liz pulled a face.

'Mixed raced.'

Liz lowered her voice. 'It didn't bother me nor Tony. I expect she'd got the odd look with her dark skin and pale eyes. Some of the locals didn't think it appropriate for her to live in this house.' Liz's cheeks blushed as bright as her lips. 'Not many, just a few,' she swiftly added.

I frowned, disheartened by the notion I might be living amongst the narrow-minded. 'I'd thought such things didn't matter so much these days.'

'Oh, maybe not now, but back in the sixties and seventies people were a little more prejudiced.'

'Because her mother was Indian? I know she was born in India.'

She puckered her plump lips, creating a ring of wrinkles about her mouth. 'To be honest, I don't think it was her colour. She wasn't that dark, not like some. No, it was because her mother and father never married, even after his first wife died.' The pause tested my patience. I urged her on with nod. 'She was the outcome of an adulterous affair. Her brother, John, had refused to speak to her or her mother. According to Felicity, after their father died, John returned to England leaving her behind and washed his hands of them. It was only when both her mother and brother passed away that she left India.'

Her brother – my grandfather – a man who'd died long before I'd been born, when my mother had been a small child. 'So he lived in the house up until then?'

'What? Oh no. Hated the place, I gather. His father had rented it out during his time in India and John carried on the duty of landlord. Several families lived in this house for three or more decades. My late father remembered John visiting occasionally; he'd stay in the pub. Dad knew quite a bit about our neighbours – the tenants; he liked to call by and chat.'

'My grandfather made an impression, if your father remembered him.'

'John created quite a scandal,' Liz chortled and the folds in her neck wobbled in time to her feeble laughter. 'My, my, what a family, the Marsters. The last tenants of this place had a daughter, Mary Branston—'

'Mary, that's my grandmother's name.' I leapt off my resting perch, eager to hear more. Finally, more skeletons were tumbling out of the closet.

'Because she is your grandmother. He took one look at her and swept her off her feet, or so I'm told. Except, she was twenty years his junior and her family didn't agree with the match.'

Mary had raised my mother a single parent, rather like my own father. She'd spoken little of her husband or any other members of either family, the Marsters or the Branstons. I'd not even known her maiden name. Liz and I, between us, had painted a portrait of fragmented families with little cohesion. I wished I taken to my grandmother, but what I remembered was a constant string of ailments and senility.

'Poor Gran. I think she worked hard to provide for Mum. After Mum died, she was broken, never really recovered.'

'How sad.' There was little comfort in Liz's expression. She swivelled on her feet and ambled around the kitchen, peering into the bare cupboards and the cavity left by the absent oven. 'It's not the same place. Such a fine house it must have been. Felicity couldn't keep on top of it. She cocooned herself in the library and couldn't be bothered with modern conveniences or technology. I think she tried the television, but she had no fascination with it. Whenever I called by, which wasn't often as she seemed uncomfortable having visitors, I noted the decline, the chipped furniture, holes in the carpets and the flaked paintwork. If it wasn't for the wall-hangings.' Liz clucked her tongue, glancing around. 'Such a shame,' she muttered.

'Yes. It's hard work keeping a large house in good order,' I admitted. 'I'm failing. I haven't even cleaned out the drawing room.'

'I gather it once had a painted ceiling.' She raised an eyebrow.

'It did? Wow.' My enthusiasm failed to muster in the tone of my voice. 'Well, not now,' I added.

She couldn't hide her curiosity, so I showed her the room and the plain ceiling. She muttered some more words of pity, as if unsure whether the state of the house distressed me.

'I vaguely remember visiting here,' I explained. 'But not this room. I think I ate cake at the dining table. Was there a long table in there?'

Liz touched the old drapes, poking them with her fingertips until they swayed. A plume of dust billowed out towards her, enveloping her in a sheen of white powder. She jumped, emitting a mild exclamation and waved her hand about her face. Backing away from window, and between excessive splutters of coughing, she spoke almost harshly. 'I don't know. I never went into the dining room.' As she crossed to the middle of the room, she brushed her clothes down with a flick of her wrist.

'I'm going to turn it into a living room for the duration of my stay.' I needed an ordinary room with furniture and warmth.

She asked me what I did for a living and I told her about my current project. Her face transformed from chiselled sharpness into something softer. 'I've a grandchild. He loves books. He's nearly a year old.'

'This book is set on a farm.' I regretted telling her that the moment the words left my mouth. She insisted on seeing the progress, which meant ascending to my workroom. She dawdled, taking her time to reach the attic and grabbing the opportunity to stick her head around each of the bedroom doors. She muttered indiscriminately as she snooped, admitting she hadn't been upstairs before. When she peered into the bathroom, her scowl turned into an aghast expression. I heard her mutter, 'How could she let this place get so run down.'

I ignored her grumbling. In my workroom, I'd laid out the drawings on the table.

She pointed at the half-finished illustration of the farmer. 'My, he looks just like Tony.'

I scrambled to collect up the sheets, embarrassed that my caricature had been more accurate than I intended. 'Is it?' I said, with feinted surprise.

She glanced at her watch. 'I have to go; time to feed the chickens.'

Walking back into the kitchen to collect her handbag, I bumped into her back as she froze on the threshold. I squeezed past her and found Charles crouched on the floor with a screwdriver. He rose and brushed down his jeans. There was an uncomfortable pause while I waited to see if Liz recognised him. Her lips pouted into a funnel, as if she was weighing up her thoughts.

The seconds dragged by. 'Charles, this is Liz.'

Charles offered his hand, extending his arm like a rigid pole, and Liz shook the tips of his fingers.

'Pleasure to meet you.' The genteel words were at odds with his icy tone.

'She lives on the farm at the top of the road, Tony's wife,' I explained.

'Charles, yes, I know,' she said softly, and he flinched, snatching back his hand. Grabbing her handbag off the worktop she stepped backwards. 'I really must go. Good luck, Miriam, with the nursing home.'

I followed her out, but she stopped in the doorway and turned. 'Charles.'

He'd returned to his crouched position, the screwdriver poised in his hand. 'Yes?'

'You were the gardener,' she said, continuing to stare at him, clutching her handbag to her chest. She seemed rooted to the spot.

With his back to her, he slowly continued to rotate the tool, working hard to loosen the screw. 'It's a big garden. Lots to do.'

'Ye-s,' Liz stuttered, then lifted her voice. 'I saw you in the grounds once. So you're back.' She shrugged, as if the spark of memory lost its relevance. 'I'm sure Miriam appreciates your help as much as Felicity did.'

He glanced up at her and fixed his pale eyes on hers. They had gone cold, an almost menacing expression. I'd not seen Charles show any animosity and it unsettled me. He shifted his gaze back to the hinge and squeezed the handle of the screwdriver.

'I do my best,' he said, and we left the room.

Liz opened her car door. 'Anytime you want more eggs, just pop by.'

I repeated my gratitude regarding the nursing home's number. She revved the engine and sped down the drive. Unlike the affable Tony, Liz had shown an unusual level of interest in my family, but not in a forthcoming way. As for Charles's cool reaction to Liz, it left me feeling uneasy, as it did her too.

When I returned to the kitchen, Charles had gone. I'd questions to ask, a multitude of them buzzing around my head. I massaged my temples, wishing that those puzzles would fly away and leave me alone. But my priority had to be the will and the need to dig into the past and find out why Felicity had chosen me. Why she'd elected to use such an unusual way of bequeathing her home. However, it was as if somebody or something was protecting her, preventing me from seeing the truth. But what?

The wind howled outside. Coming from the direction of the coast, it rushed across the grounds and attacked the trees, forcing them to bend and twist, before throwing its invisible weight against the walls. An endless whistle emanated from on high where the chimney pots perched on top of the roof. Heachley Hall responded to the gale with creaks and groans, muttering to itself in the language of crumbling mortar and loose tiles. An odd duet – wind and house – and the two did battle, relentlessly and without taking a pause. The wind had somehow penetrated the house, creating a draught about my ankles and my spine goose bumped with the frigidity of that ceaseless current.

I went back upstairs, picked up my drawing of the farmer with his bandy legs and tore it up. I sketched out another and this time my farmer had straight long legs, as if on stilts. No more distractions: I'd a job to keep and money to earn. The cold house was providing me with nothing but bills and Felicity's past could wait – what difference would ringing a nursing home make when it was warmth that I needed. I removed the paper with the telephone number from my back pocket and put it to one side.

When darkness descended, I lit the fire in the dining room, copying Charles's technique. My first attempt failed. The yellowing newspaper – discovered bundled in the scullery – curled up, turned brown and the tiny flame died. Scuppered by the paper's fragility, it disintegrated into slivers. For my next attempt, I used printer paper and a few discarded envelopes. I twisted the sheets into substantial twigs. The flame flickered, teasing its prey. Then, as I gently puffed, it caught and spread.

For a while, I gazed unblinking at the awakening fire and the smoke. I'd nowhere to sit, so no ability to enjoy the rising heat. I circled about the room, my reflection captured by the window each time I completed a circuit. Reaching out, I touched the glass and the cold pane stung my palm. All the warmth of the room was rapidly vanishing through the window. I'd have to buy curtains and a pole.

The idea sparked another and rather like the thriving fire I envisaged a rug before the marble hearth, a small sofa and a lamp stand. I would sit in the evenings with my iPod and a book in my hand, and the time would pass. I so desperately needed this year in my life to fly past.

My sublime mental picture vaporised the moment the doorbell rang. The clank echoed through the house. I checked my watch: seven o'clock. On the other side of the frosted window, the outline of a man. Not Charles, too small; not Bert either, too slender.

I opened the door sufficiently to cast light into the porch. 'Kev.' I stepped back to let the plumber in. 'Glenda said you'd come tomorrow.'

'Aye. I finished earlier than I planned.' He yanked on his belt buckle. The fidgeting continued – he scratched his scalp as he patrolled the kitchen – before ducking under the worktop to check the layout of the pipes that fed the sink and washing machine.

The vacant hole, which once housed the oven, drew his attention. 'You've got no cooker,' he exclaimed. 'Yea gods woman, you can't live without a cooker.' He shook his head and put his hands on his hips. 'How you going to cook a decent breakfast.' He ended his reprimand with a grin.

I replied with an agreeable smile – I missed sizzling sausages. 'I know. I'm thinking of getting one of those camper stoves.'

With another shake of his head he inspected the radiator, then plodded upstairs to examine the bathroom. I passed the time waiting for the urn to heat up so I could make him a coffee.

'Right,' he said, accepting the mug from me. 'I know you have little money to spend, but frankly, whatever you have would be worth spending. This is what I propose. Get a cooker—'

'A cooker?'

'Aye, a cooker. A Rayburn. It's like an Aga, you've heard of them?'

I nodded.

'They're oil burning heaters. It will heat your hot water, and if you can afford it, a few radiators, too. Oh, and it will cook you breakfast.'

'Where would it go?'

'Here, in this hole.' He pointed at the brickwork. 'Plenty of space and re-enforced floor. I can pipe the hot water to your taps upstairs in the bathroom which is directly above us.' He gulped down his coffee, quite unperturbed by the scalding temperature. 'You can't survive with that.' He jabbed a finger at the urn. 'Oh, and get yourself some convection heaters, oil ones, not these daft fan ones.'

'How much? The Rayburn?' I held my breath and his answer was what I suspected. Dismayed by the cost, I deflated. I would have to break into my precious savings. Mr Porter's contingency money wouldn't stretch to that amount plus the forthcoming bills.

'I don't know, Kev, it's a lot—'

'It's a selling point for the house. Think of it; old style cooker right here. Then you can rip out that useless boiler.' He referred to the mammoth beast that stood dormant in the corner of the scullery.

Kevin proceeded to talk about valves and feeder tanks, I cut across his incomprehensible words. 'When could you fit it?'

He pulled at a pocket size diary from his jacket. 'Well, now,' he mumbled, thumbing through the pages and squinting at his notes. 'Early November. Can you manage 'til then? Glenda was convinced you'd freeze to death or something.'

Glenda's influence stretched way beyond the confines of a village pub. I had an idea how I might thank her.

I jerked a thumb at the urn. 'I can manage.' Ruth and I would find some way to cope.

After Kevin had gone, I heated up a ready-made meal in the microwave and sat on an old milk crate by the fire – I'd found the makeshift stool under the sink in the scullery. I nibbled on the bland food, opting to eat the portion straight from the container to avoid washing up. Numbers floated around my head. The cost of fitting the cooker and a hot water tank would take a chunk out of my savings. Nevertheless, that was what it was there for, wasn't it? An emergency pot, which I had imagined would see me through spells when contracts dried up. Fortunately, my popularity with authors kept me employed; I could risk spending a little of my savings.

The flames wavered, losing their potency as they desperately tried to extract the last combustible element out of the diminishing piece of wood. Sod it. I would contact the bank and arrange for a release of cash. Then, once Kevin had sorted out the estimate, I'd order a Rayburn and two convection heaters for the attic rooms. I scraped the plastic container clean with my fork. Pity the carton wasn't combustible. I couldn't afford to waste anything. My finances were about to be squeezed tighter.

Having dismissed money matters, my mind wandered back to my mysterious aunt, Liz had revealed a little more about Felicity and I wasn't sure I liked what I heard. She painted Felicity as cut-off from the world around her and alone. The idea of a manipulative old woman fitted with the quirkiness of the will but not with my scant recollections of Felicity herself – she'd embodied a warm, colourful spirit. The thought of contacting the nursing home unnerved me. Was I going to find out more things about my aunt that I would rather wish were best left unknown?

THIRTEEN

The Rayburn wasn't the only thing I ordered online in my endeavour to keep busy and distracted from dwelling on Felicity. Opting to have lunch in the pub on the Saturday, I hijacked the Wi-Fi and bought some furnishings for the dining room, including bright orange drapes and a purple rug. I'd gone psychedelic with my colour scheme and not through choice; they'd been the cheapest options for each item I needed. Whether on eBay or some discount online store, I shopped sparingly. By the time I'd finished my stodgy pudding, I'd amassed a sofa, rug, uplighter with a spotlight and enormous curtains to cover up the draughty window. The pole I'd have to buy from the hardware store.

After lunch I drove to King's Lynn. The traffic was horrendous, a nightmare of barging cars hounding each other for a tiny space on the road. After only a week of country lanes, I'd adapted to the rural life far quicker than I'd anticipated.

I purchased the curtain pole and hooks then armed with my sample hinge, I identified a reasonable match. In the kitchen section, a range of door handles tempted me and unable to resist, I bought a dozen brass knobs that possessed sufficient antique styling to fit in with the cupboard doors and with the simplicity I preferred.

I left the hinges and doorknobs in the shed for Charles. He'd removed all the doors by the end of Friday and stacked them against the wall ready for the varnishing stage. I admired his meticulously workmanship: he'd sanded them into smooth surfaces, removing the tarnished lacquer and accompanying stains.

He didn't appear on Saturday. Even handymen had the weekend off. Somewhere, he was having a life, relaxing with his mates or going by his introverted nature, maybe he preferred to remain at home, the location of which remained a mystery. He'd no car nor bicycle, and obviously came and went by foot. Nearby, he'd said, which meant sufficiently close to walk. Yet I'd not seen many houses between the village and the farm, only a few smallholdings that once might have been part of Heachley Hall's tenancy.

After my Saturday shopping trip, I spent Sunday morning cleaning the library. I should have been working on my illustrations – time was tight – but the house beckoned, and I frittered away a couple of hours chasing the white dust about the floorboards and wiping down the remaining shelves. Pleased with my efforts, I unpacked a box of books I'd brought from Chelmsford and created a dinky library on one shelf. Apart from those few books, there was nothing else in the room.

The library, along with the drawing room, looked out onto the formal garden to the rear of the property. Once a sweeping lawn with terraces, unwanted growth had overburdened the neglected landscaping – brambles and bindweed swamped the remnants of flowerbeds. The garden resembled a meadow. The rain stayed away, and after lunch, I heaved on my Wellington boots and ventured out to explore. I'd been at Heachley Hall a week and was on the cusp of my first outdoor adventure.

I began my trek in the smaller garden that had once borne the weight of the southern aspect of the house. Below my feet, underneath the soil, lay the cellar. Tracking along the dwarf walls, which formed the boundary of the garden, I wondered if they represented the original perimeter of the house. If so, they outlined reasonable sized rooms. Beyond the low walls, there was a small forest of spiky monkey puzzles, camellia, tangled honeysuckle and dense rhododendrons, that in the spring would burst into a flower and display a multitude of colours. The evergreens formed an impassable barrier and buttressed the outer wall of the estate.

Amongst the rhododendrons, rogue trees had sprouted out of old stumps: immature and thin about the trunk, they'd grown in isolation. Tony had referred to the damage the fire had done to the woodlands. I guessed I'd found the evidence.

Turning my back on the evergreens, I wandered towards the back of the house to admire the bay window of the drawing room and the smaller library one. I skirted the edge of the larger overgrown lawn and my boots protected my shanks from the long, wet grass and other pervasive weeds. I'd need an industrial sized lawn mower to undo the years of neglect.

As I continued to walk around the house, I stumbled upon the trap door for the coal chute under the window of the scullery. The bolted doors were too small for a man to squeeze through. I gave them a kick and was pleased to note my foot hadn't smashed through them.

Next to the back door were the outbuildings that were collected around the small cobbled yard. Behind the garage was the wooden ladder that Charles had mentioned; it appeared in good condition and usable. I wasn't sure about the ramifications on my part if he fell from the roof, but he'd offered and I needed his help.

To this side of the house, especially around the sheds, the trees closed in and swayed over the part of the roof where my attic space occupied the corner. Tilting my head back, I saw additional shuttered windows next to the two rooms I used. There had to be other rooms up there. I suspected they'd been accessed using a stairwell eaten by the fire. It meant there were attic rooms with no access point and, oddly, nobody had bothered to knock a doorway through the wall. Possibly a hundred or so years with no visitors. Rather freaked out, I added it to the pile of not-my-problem and carried on my explorations.

Beyond the outbuildings, the estate stretched out for many acres and much of it woodland. Fighting for space the warped and gnarled oaks formed a disfigured arboretum of ancient trees, whilst their neighbours – pine trees and firs – stood orderly and perpendicular. I weaved between the trees, trampling through undergrowth of mulch and stumbling on the hidden roots.

The waning light cowered behind overhanging branches. The gloominess sucked the saturation out of the colours. What should have been a deluge of ambers and lemon yellows dancing in the daylight was a dull blur. Across the trunks of fallen trees a patchwork of lichen covered the bark, but even their palette of greens and saffrons lost out to the grey soup that had descended over Heachley Wood.

I looked over my shoulder to find the house had quickly vanished. If there had been a path leading through the woods, I couldn't discern the route it traversed. My breath fogged the air, steaming out of my lips and nostrils in white puffs and it wasn't the only thing obscuring my vision. The mist rolled towards me like watery waves; first, undulating about my ankles, then the wisps of white surged up to my knees. I'd not seen fog like it before. My experience of foggy days was urban based and rarely so uniformly dense. Glancing up, I'd lost the tops of the trees and the cloudy sky beyond.

As I soldiered on deeper into the ancient woods, the trees closed in tighter; their branches tangled together into a single mesh of twisted vines and dangling ivy. Icy droplets of mist wet my face and settled onto my coat, and the enveloping cold thwarted my progress. I swivelled on the spot. A haze of whiteness had formed a shifting barrier, plugging the gaps between the trunks and hiding the mass of trees as if to usurp the forest's natural authority.

By the house I'd been sure I'd felt a light breeze, but not in the midst of trees, where nothing swayed or disturbed the opaque fog. The penetrating frost had stiffened the leaves, contorting them into unnatural poses and the still air was heavy with condensation. I remained glued to the spot, unsure what direction to take next. Did I go back to the house or on towards the perimeter stonewall? It had to be somewhere nearby.

The blanket of dew continued to swirl, almost forcing me to retreat away from my intended destination – the farthest point of the estate. I heard a twig snap, then another. A crack, crack of broken branches. I'd no idea where the sound came from. One second from the left, the next the right. I spun, pursuing the sound with my ears leaning in different directions.

Snap. Crunch. The splintering of a pinecone?

My heart raced, and I began to walk backwards. My heels caught on the buried roots and I stumbled and crashed onto my backside.

I exclaimed a string of curses and pressed my palms into the soft ground. The needles slithered over my fingers like tiny worms, rapidly burying my hand, while the dewy wetness seeped through my clothing. I scrambled up.

My heart pounded, its pulse thrumming in my ears and I tore through the trees, hurrying back to the house, away from the strange noises. My Wellingtons grew heavy. Dead leaves stuck to the soles and hampered my efforts. The oppressive mist continued to battle with me, and I batted it aside with my hands. I'd not realised I'd come this far into the woods; the return journey seemed longer, more arduous.

Having lost sight of the house I halted and listened, but the only sounds I heard were my wheezes and chattering teeth. At last, the miasma parted, and I caught a glimpse of familiar stone and a slate roof; one of the outbuildings, possibly Charles's shed.

The mist thinned and disintegrated into nothing, and within a few metres of the house, it vanished. The afternoon light, which I'd convinced myself had turned to dusk, lit up the flintstones turning them silvery. Colour returned to the fallen leaves and the grass was once again a lush green. I dashed over to the back door, flung it open and slammed it shut behind me. Leaning against the door, I turned the key in the lock and closed my eyes.

It took a few minutes to catch my breath. I kicked off my boots, and with shaking fingers, I removed my coat and switched on the lights. For a while I stood before the fire I'd lit in the dining room and warmed my hands, until a burning sensation penetrated my cold fingertips and my thundering heart calmed.

Unsettled by my experience, I struggled to keep my thoughts focused on work. Images of swirling fog and the possibility of a strange presence lurking within it supplanted the comical farm characters I should be drawing. Defeated, I trudged downstairs and tried Ruth's number. No answer. With the phone still in my hand, I impulsively rang the Rose and Crown. Unsure as to my motives, when Bert answered, I stumbled over my words. In the background there was chatter and a football commentator blaring out from the TV.

'Sorry,' I stammered. 'I went into Heachley Wood and, just. It's silly but I heard weird noises, like something was in there with me.'

'Rabbits,' he suggested.

'Except, do they crunch on pinecones? It sounded heavier. Solitary.'

'Ah. Muntjac then.'

'Muntjac?' I'd no idea what he meant.

'Deer. They're common in these parts. Probably came through a hole somewhere. They like forests.'

'Deer?' It made sense, I supposed, the sound of footfalls. How big were muntjac?

'Aye. Some of the farmers take a pop shot at them from time to time. Tony has a gun licence, he's been known to shoot a few.'

'Shoot them? Why? Deer are beautiful animals.'

'They make a fine venison stew. We sometimes offer it on our menu, except,' he paused and snorted, 'I blame Bambi. Nobody likes to eat deer, not the hoity-toity types.'

I didn't take offence, because I was quite unprepared for what lurked in the woods. I apologised for disturbing him with my impulsive call.

'If you want advice, just ring. It's no bother.' His kindly comment dismissed my embarrassment. I said goodnight sweetly and hung up.

Muntjac in the woods seemed a good enough explanation. But, for now, I'd trust the woods to take care of themselves and I'd stay in the house.

The next morning, working hard on my drawing, I rethought my decision to ignore the nursing home and questions about Felicity. My adventure in the garden had once again poked my natural curiosity. I refused to be daunted by fog and the noises of furtive creatures. The reticence, which had kept me from exploring Felicity's past, now seemed excessive and over-thought. I had every right to know the reason why I was inhabiting an abandoned house, bound by the stipulation of a year and a day.

I shuffled through my papers and found the note with the

nursing home's number. It rang and rang, then switched to a recorded message, informing the caller to ring a different number. I noted the number down. It had a different dialling code that I didn't recognise as local.

This time my call was answered after two rings.

'Twilight Care Homes.' The woman's voice sang. 'How can I help?'

'I was after Beechwood Care Home.'

'Beechwood.' She paused. 'The facility closed in April. All the residents were transferred. Can I send you details of our other homes? They all provide service to an excellent standard.'

'Actually, no, that's not what I'm after. I wanted to trace the details of a resident who stayed at Beechwood.'

'I'm afraid we can't release confidential information about any of the residents.'

'She was my great-aunt and she died in February at Beechwood.'

'I'm sorry for your loss,' she said swiftly.

'Thank you. What it is, I didn't have a chance to see her before she died and I'm trying to trace any belongings she might have had left. I only found out recently that she'd died and I'm her sole beneficiary.'

'One moment.'

I waited for a response while listening to muffled voices.

'When Beechwood closed, all their records were transferred to the head office here in Peterborough. As for unclaimed personal possessions, I'm sorry we don't know what might have happened to them. Usually a home will store items for six months, but you said she died back in February, and then the closure,' she hesitated. 'Is it possible somebody else collected her things?'

'I don't think so. The will's executor didn't mention anything.'

'Look,' I heard a pen tapping in the background. 'I could give you the email address of the former manager of Beechwood. She works at another home, not one of ours. She might remember your aunt.'

I was gracious with my thank yous, even if I was disappointed with the lack of information. I wrote down the email address and the name *Mrs Eva Kendal.*

After a brief outing to buy bread and milk, I dropped into the Rose and Crown to compose the email on my mobile, pleading the case of a sad niece in desperate need of information about her long lost aunt, requesting she contacted me by telephone if it was possible. Probably exaggerating the sentiment of the message, a touch of guilt caused me to pause before hitting the send button.

By the end of the day I'd heard nothing back and as Thursday drew to a close, I concluded my attempt to find Felicity's missing box was doomed to failure. Mrs Kendal, for whatever reason, hadn't responded to my email.

FOURTEEN

During the week, I'd tried to put aside my unnerving trip outdoors. Regardless of what had caused the noises in the wood, it hadn't followed me back to the house. However, while I contemplated my farmyard illustrations, my concentration wandered and I battled with the depictions conjured up by my vivid imagination – the exotic mists with tentacles and claws. The scary images reminded me of my vulnerability – living alone in an empty house – however, for an illustrator, they were fantastic fodder for inspiration.

Downstairs, Charles came and went in his haphazard style and I would occasionally bump into him in the kitchen. If our paths didn't collide by the cupboards or in the hallway, I felt a touch bereft as if only he alone could conquer any twinges of loneliness. On Wednesday, with the sun shining through the windows and the sky a marine blue, he announced his plan to fix the roof tiles. While he clambered over the roofs, I anchored the bottom of the ladder with the sturdy weight of my foot. He moved with agility and navigated the apexes of the gables by swinging his body around the chimneystacks. His dark hair glinted in the bright light as he precariously balanced on a slope and stepped across the space like a tightrope walker. I alternated between holding my breath and gasping at his apparent lack of fear. If he fell – the thought was not bearable. Such a disaster meant I would have lost a newfound friend, somebody who provided me with much needed company and a connection to Felicity and my family.

I shouted up on one occasion to warn him of his hazardous location. He cheerfully told me not to worry. 'I've been up here before.'

He slotted the dislodged tiles back into place and even volunteered to clear out the muck in the blocked guttering; a deluge of water overflowed every time there was a torrential shower.

On Friday morning, he put the final touches to the cupboard doors. Each unit – half a metre wide by a metre high – had been neatly hung, aligned and evenly distributed, forming two rows of six cupboards. A layer of varnish glazed the doors and the grain in the oak stood out in a breath-taking array of patterns. I ran my hand over the smooth finish, examined the brass hinges and knobs, which although old fashioned in design, were perfect for the antiquated surroundings of Heachley Hall.

I complimented the handyman on his efforts and quality of workmanship.

He ducked his head and shrugged off my compliment. 'Thank you, Miriam. I appreciate your kind words.'

The awkward moment continued when I had to pay him. Cooped upstairs in the attic, I'd little idea of his schedule or hours of work. Charles shuffled on his feet, stuffed his hands into the pockets of his jeans and tried his best to look most uncomfortable while I tapped away on my mobile's calculator. The previous day, during the grocery shopping in Hunstanton, I'd drawn a fair size wad of cash out of the bank's machine.

'Maybe four, perhaps five hours a day?' I suggested. 'As an average.'

He scratched his head. 'Probably. I don't keep track of time, not while I'm busy.'

'A bad habit of mine, too.' I concurred. 'My friends don't think I have a watch.' I calculated the amount – a hundred and fifty pounds – and he accepted the payment with little fuss, rolling the notes into a bundle and jamming them into his pocket.

We discussed what needed doing next and I remarked his sanding and staining skills would be handy for sorting out the battered wooden stairs.

'A mighty amount of wood,' he declared, from his position at the bottom of the staircase. He counted the steps with an outstretched finger, calculating the effort involved.

I remembered his makeshift sanding block. 'I will have to get you an electric sander. You can't do it by hand.'

His eyebrows furrowed, and he pulled a grimace. 'Electric?'

'I'm sure I could buy a cheap one. I'm also sourcing some replacement tiles for the floor.' I pointed at the cracked tile by my foot. 'Also, I wanted to paint the dining room, which I can do myself, and once the plumber has finished, I was thinking about painting the kitchen and bathroom, but I might not have the time.'

'Plumber?' Another quizzical expression spread over his face.

'Kevin is coming the week after next to install a hot water system based around a cooker range.'

I showed him where the Rayburn would go. 'I can have fresh hot meals, instead of re-heated junk. Unfortunately, I can't offer Ruth anything special when she comes for the week. She arrives tomorrow.'

'The week?'

'Yes.'

He pursed his lips. 'I don't think it would be a good idea for me to do the stairs for a couple of weeks. I'd get in the way.'

It made sense and I couldn't persuade him otherwise. As much as I looked forward to seeing Ruth, I would miss Charles's interludes, the way he smiled when I said hello or the little pucker of his lips when he concentrated on a task.

'I'll come back in two weeks.' He paused by the back door. 'You'll need more wood to burn. I'll go chop some now before the light fades.'

I watched him from the scullery door as he ambled into Heachley Wood, swinging the axe, quite unperturbed by the gloomy destination. In the distance, I could see the white haze, waiting to greet him and it sent a shiver down my spine.

'Charles.' I called out, but he kept going. I slipped on my Wellingtons and bolted after him. 'Charles, wait.'

He spun, snapped his back straight and tightened his grip on the axe at the same time. 'Miriam. What's wrong?'

I caught my breath; alarmed by his rigid stance. 'Have you ever seen muntjac in the woods?' I asked breathlessly.

He shifted his grip on the axe into a looser one. 'No, I can't say that I have, but they are shy creatures and unlikely to stray near to the house.'

'I came out here, on Sunday, and heard noises, like footfalls. Bert thought they were caused by deer.' I expected him to laugh and I was, in retrospect, embarrassed by the need to ring the pub for reassurance. 'I was just, chatting with him,' I added, lamely.

Charles merely cocked his head to one side and his eyes smiled, creasing at the corners. 'All sorts inhabit the woods – badgers, foxes, rabbits – they are not quiet.' He stared up at the branches, then back at me. 'In the spring, a chorus of birds will sing from dawn to dusk. You're quite safe, have no fear. Just watch the roots, they can send you flying.' He kicked the exposed root by his boot.

'The mist.' I'd seen the way it had behaved, coiling its antennas about my legs, then chasing me out of the woods. How to explain that to him?

'Yes?'

'It felt alive.'

'Feeling alive and being alive are different things.' He reached out to a nearby tree and spread his fingers over the bark. 'Does a tree feel this, my touch?'

I snorted. 'Of course not. It doesn't have a nervous system or brain.'

'Yet, it is alive.' He let his hand drop to his side.

'Until you chop it down.'

'Would it know – the sap, the bark, and the leaves – would they know they'd been cut off from the roots that sustain them? They have no feelings.' There was an expression in his face that I couldn't quite pin down. He'd lost the smile lines and gained something else – sadness?

I hugged my arms. The branches above us groaned and bent low as if to listen. His explanation re-enforced my apparent weakness: yet again, I had dipped into the art of personification and perhaps it was an artist's natural trait, to give life to objects in the same way I would to a human being. 'I imagined the mist is alive, nothing else. But there are no unnatural happenings here in this wood. Is that what you're saying?'

'I'm saying you have the ability to imagine it is alive. The mist never knows if it is or isn't.' He gave me a crooked smile and took a couple of steps, before pointing up at the sky. 'The light,' he reminded.

'Yes, sorry. I shouldn't detain you.'

I didn't see him again that day and consequently, I'd forgotten to pay him for chopping the wood.

FIFTEEN

'He's done a brilliant job,' Ruth said, as she admired the glimmering cupboards. 'Pity I've missed meeting him.'

'He finished yesterday. He'll be back in a couple of weeks to do the staircase.' I poured coffee into two mugs.

She clapped her hands together. 'So, what next?'

I had a list and I ran my eye over the piece of paper. 'How about we take down those dreadful drapes in the drawing room and burn them?'

'Sounds fantastic. I love building bonfires and it's nearly Guy Fawkes Night!'

'Remember, remember, the fifth of November,' we chanted, giggling, as I tossed a lighted match onto the heap of disintegrated curtains. The fire in the middle of the front lawn blazed with autumnal shades and the smoke billowed across the grass, fanning the trees.

'I hope the sparks don't catch,' I fretted, remembering the previous fire.

'Too damp,' said Ruth. 'In any case, that mist will put them out.'

The plume of grey collided with the fog and the two waltzed, forming a smog, until the mist smothered the heavy smoke particles. As the fire crackled, snacking on the dregs of shredded curtain fabric, the smoke lost its battle and floated to the ground. Gradually, there was nothing left for the bonfire to consume and we kicked the fallen leaves on to the glowing embers until they smouldered.

I shivered, and peering up at the clearing skies, I spied the brightest stars punctuating the darkening backdrop. 'Might have frost tonight. I'll light the fire in the dining room.'

We trudged into the house leaving behind a heap of ash and charred remains.

'You'll have to change the names of the rooms,' Ruth said, hanging her coat on the end of the bannister rail.

'Why?' I slammed the front door shut and the bell above jingled.

'Dining room with no table?' She grinned. 'Drawing room. Sounds terribly posh.' She pinched her nose in and puckered her lips, trying to pull a snooty face.

I giggled. 'All right. How about large completely useless room.'

'It's big enough to play badminton in—'

'No it isn't,' I huffed, although I'd wondered about a table-tennis table.

'Just think you could turn this place into a sports club. Tennis courts outside—'

I gave a gentle shove and chivvied her into the kitchen. 'At least the sofa arrived or else we'd nowhere to sit in the evening.'

'You spoil me,' she mocked, then changed her tone to a pleading one. 'Let me spoil you. Pub for food?'

Later, with both of us more than tipsy, we staggered back from the pub, walking the mile or so up the dark lane with a torch shining a path in front of us. We dragged our weary limbs up the two staircases to the attic room. Approaching the top of the second flight, we both froze. Somewhere below something was rattling furiously and with energy.

'What's that?' Ruth whispered, peering down the narrow stairwell.

I tried to ignore the familiar sound, although it seemed worse than usual. 'The draught. None of the windows fit snuggly and without curtains there seems to be a natural ventilation system.' I nudged her, and she resumed her climb.

'I could never live here,' she muttered.

The noise grew louder, almost frantic, and it seemed to chase after our feet. We hurried and stumbled over the remaining steps. Once inside the bedroom, I kicked the door shut. 'There, quiet now.'

Standing breathless and still, we listened. Silence.

'Oh God,' moaned Ruth, collapsing on the airbed on the floor. 'I must be pissed.'

'Me, too.' I flopped backwards onto the bed. 'I need to get away from here. It's going to stay dry tomorrow, so how about a trip to the sea?'

'What about your list?' Ruth rolled onto her side.

'Sod it. Fresh sea air is what I need.'

Ruth yawned and hiccoughed at the same time. 'Sounds, good,' she slurred, her eyelids drooping.

The fresh air idea had merits up until the point we began walking along the beach. We braced ourselves before each gust of icy wind, the approaching whoosh of each squall heralded its buffeting arrival. With a scarf wrapped about my neck, my ears swathed by a woollen hat and fleecy gloves protecting my hands, the wind still managed to chafe and penetrate all the futile layers until it assaulted my body.

'Fuck,' I muttered, as I bowed my head and fought against the next blast of cold air.

Ruth, who had borrowed another of my scarves, flapped her arms up and down. 'Do you know you can see the sunset across the sea, even though technically we're on the east coast?'

I pictured the map of East Anglia in my head and sure enough, she was right, Old Hunstanton faced west, not north or east. 'Pity the sun is hiding.'

'Let's keep walking,' she suggested, stuffing her hands in her coat pockets.

The beach was too long for us to explore thoroughly on a bitter autumnal day. Rain had compressed the sand and our shoes sank into the grains, leaving behind a trail of soft footprints. On our right, the waves crashed effortlessly onto the shores. To our left, the cliff face offered little protection. Weary of battling wet sand and the wind, I halted. Facing the wall of chalk and limestone stripes, the layers triggered a wave of butterflies in my belly.

'I've been here before.' I rotated, taking in the view, and the landscape. 'Yes, I have.'

My nose dripped and the cold bit into my toes. The salt air had whipped my cheeks until they felt raw. I didn't remember the cold, instead, I had a recollection of blue skies and blazing sunshine. 'I was holding somebody's hand. I must have been small; I had to look up.'

'Your parents, your dad?'

I started pacing circles in the sand and tucked my chin under the edge of my scarf.

'No, no. It was Felicity.' The picture I was constructing in my mind took more shape and the details crystallised as I weaved colour into the image. The smell of seaweed cinched my nostrils – that had been there, too.

'Felicity,' Ruth exclaimed.

'Yes, yes,' I said excitedly, and I hurried to describe my memories. 'She was trying to explain to me about the sun setting, just like you did now, except, I didn't understand the compass points back then, too young. Her hand pointed across the shimmering water and I shaded my eyes.'

'You're sure it was Felicity and not your mum?'

'She wore a sari. How could I forget her clothes. She dressed unashamedly – a bright yellow sari. She loved the sun.' I smiled. 'Funny thing memories, what triggers their return.'

'I'm glad you're remembering her, but I can't take this ridiculous cold a moment longer. Let's find somewhere to eat.' She turned on her heel and retraced her footprints in the sand.

We argued, politely, about who should pay for the food in the lighthouse café. She won, as Ruth generally did.

I sliced up my sausages and stabbed a piece with the fork prongs. The cold gave me a good appetite. Ruth rolled the sausage across her plate and toyed with it.

'There's something I need to tell you,' she said.

I glanced up and she had a pensive expression on her face. 'What's up?'

'I've met somebody.'

The fork made it halfway to my mouth and it remained there, hovering expectantly. 'Who?' She hadn't mentioned anyone before now.

'He's divorced, two sons aged ten and eleven. He's a teacher and called Mick.' She rattled off the details, then pressed her teacup to her lips and sipped.

I didn't want to appear surprised, but I struggled to hide my stunned expression. I blinked several times. 'When?'

'I didn't want to say anything until I was sure – a few weeks. We met at a union meeting. We're both reps.'

'So it's serious?' I chewed on my food, ruminating on her revelation.

'That's why I'm telling you. I feel awful—'

'Why?' Her last word jarred. She'd given up her time to help me.

'Because I'd told you I would come up for weekends, but things are progressing and now I don't think I'll be able to commit to as many. It's the only time I get to see him.'

I put down my knife and fork and leaned forward. 'I'm so pleased for you. Go for it. I can cope up here, plenty to keep me busy work wise. I'll pop down to Chelmsford now and again, we can meet up.'

'Sure?' She held the teacup tight in her hands; avoiding eye contact.

'Yes. Good grief, why wouldn't I be?' I picked up my cutlery and continued to eat. Ruth's shoulders relaxed, and she blew out a long breath through her lips.

'Thanks. I've been dreading telling you.'

'Well, you shouldn't have done.'

She tucked into her food as if her appetite had been switched back on. Mine disintegrated. I'd lied. I would miss her weekend visits. I'd been banking on them for my sanity's sake. But I couldn't blame her decision. Older than me, she couldn't afford to waste time, not if she wanted the children she longed to have. We ate in silence. Ruth scraped her plate clean and I left my second sausage chopped up and uneaten.

We abandoned the idea of beach combing and drove into nearby Hunstanton to explore the small town. We found the library – I noted down the opening times – and a sports facility Ruth reckoned I should join, if only because it gave me somewhere warm to go and a chance for a swim.

'Too expensive,' I declared, after scanning their membership fees.

When the light started to fade, we returned to Heachley Hall, sat on my recently acquired second hand sofa and embraced the fire's warmth whilst chatting about Mick. With encouraging smiles, I showed nothing but enthusiasm for her new boyfriend.

The weather proved more suitable for outdoor activities on the Monday; the wind had dropped, and the sun peeped out from behind the clouds. Ruth and I spent the morning raking up the crisp leaves then burning them on yet another bonfire.

My clothes and hair reeked of smoke, Ruth's too, but she didn't complain. She poked the fire with a long branch, before making trips into the overgrown rhododendrons to break off dead twigs and smaller branches to add to the pyre. She had her back to the house, but I didn't.

A shadow moved. I blinked, uncertain whether it was a creature or a person. However, even with the swirling white plume of smoke, I was sure I'd seen something next to the outbuilding closest to the garden – another disused stable. One of its walls helped form a narrow passageway running down the side of the house.

'I think I might have seen someone.' I circled around the bonfire. 'I'll go check.'

'Charles?' Ruth called out as I hurried across the overgrown meadow that constituted the back garden.

Wellington boots afford little protection above the knee. My trousers were sodden, and due to the length of the grass, the wetness had soaked through my jeans, cladding my thighs in a cold jacket. The chafing effects of the icy denim burnt and hindered my pace. I dashed into Charles's shed, but there was no sign of him there. Doubling back, I crossed the courtyard and opened the back door.

'Charles!' I shouted, then held my breath to listen for a reply. I walked through the scullery, the kitchen and out into the hallway. At the bottom of the stairs, I yelled his name again.

Nothing. I must have imagined something in the smoke, an illusion created by the heat haze. I frowned – last night my ears had been playing tricks. Today it was my eyes. I re-entered the scullery and walked past the cellar door. It was ajar, and the faulty bolt was missing. I searched the floor at my feet, but there was no sign of it, only the familiar white dust that crept up the steps from the cellar.

I cautiously stuck my head around and peered into the gloomy stairwell. The darkness proved impenetrable, I couldn't even see the door at the bottom. I puffed out my cheeks, contemplating whether to go down to investigate. I ought to check the lower door was shut as leaving it open would only add to the existing draught.

I stomped down the steps, making my presence felt in order to scare away any mice. The temperature dropped, and my breath mushroomed in front of my face: my own personal mist. I touched the wall with my fingertips, using it to guide my descent. I hadn't brought the torch; I couldn't remember where I'd put it after last night.

Putting my foot down, I misjudged the distance. My knee and hip jarred on the stone floor. I'd reached the bottom before I'd expected. I yelped as the pain jolted up my leg. Limping forward, I reached out and poked the air with my forefinger, searching for the door. The cellar breathed on me. An expulsion of air whistled past my ears, and with it I heard the scurrying of the dreaded mice and the gentle flapping of the bats' wings. Still no door. I edged half a foot closer and jabbed forwards with my finger until I hit the door. Fumbling, I hunted around the wooden panel for the doorknob and the moment I found it, I yanked on it. As I slammed the door shut, the cellar expelled a final puff of frigid air.

I ran up the stairs, shut the upper door and leant on it.

'Was it Charles?' Ruth asked when I went back outside.

'No.' Standing over the fire I rubbed my trembling hands together. 'Ruth, have you been in the cellar?'

'No, well, not the actual cellar. While you were in the bathroom, I went down the steps, but it was so bleeding dark and you said there are mice down there, and I'm not great with mice, so I bottled and came back up.'

'You didn't open the second door at the base of the stairs?'

'Another door? Didn't see one.' She shovelled a load of dead foliage onto the fire. 'Why?'

'Nothing.' I shrugged. 'Just, the door was ajar.'

'Oh, I might not have shut it.' She grimaced, mouthing 'sorry'. 'You should mend the bolt.'

'It's gone, fallen off.'

'Wasn't when I opened it. I noticed the missing screw.'

'This morning?'

'Yep.'

'Oh. Strange. I've only just noticed it's gone. Perhaps, the other screws got worked loose,' I peered over my shoulder at the house with its grim walls that were especially dire when framed against the backdrop of greying skies.

I jerked and snatched a quick intake of air. Another shadow – this time the upstairs window: Felicity's bedroom. I wasn't going to stoop to the superstitious claptrap about ghosts. The house was unoccupied, devoid of human company. I'd probably seen a reflection of the trees in the glass.

'I'm going crazy. Forget it. The bolt's got kicked under something in the scullery. I'll look later.'

I mimicked my restless thoughts by kicking the plastic bags by my feet and remembered why I'd brought them outside in the first place. 'Let's go pick apples.' I scooped up the bags.

'Sound's good.' Ruth dropped her makeshift poker and I handed her a couple of bags. I followed her and just to make sure, I glanced over my shoulder at the window. Of course there wasn't anything to see but silvery glass.

We collected enough edible apples to fill several carrier bags.

'I'll store them in one of the sheds. They might last through the winter.'

We dragged the bags through the overgrown lawn and deposited them in an abandoned outbuilding, opting to hang the handles from convenient hooks in the hope the fruit would remain out of reach of the mice and other vermin.

For lunch I heated up ready-made soup in the microwave. Afterwards, we returned outside to clear the paths and cut back the ivy from the windows and porch. The fire burnt for most of the day, filling the air with a constant acrid smell until the smoke irritated my throat. The ash floated on the invisible currents as if reluctant to land. Its passage – the swirl of white particles – resembled like a flurry of snowflakes.

After dusk, using hot water from the urn and a large washing up bowl, we took turns bathing before the fireplace. I ached in numerous unseen places and my palms had again developed callouses. I'd not drawn for days, consequently, I'd slipped behind my schedule. However, time spent with Ruth was important. I needed companionship and together we'd ticked off a substantial part of my immediate to-do list. The other, longer list, the one buried in my head, I ignored.

On Tuesday, we concentrated on the bedrooms that I'd repeatedly neglected to attend to. Silvery cobwebs hung from the ceilings and across the windows, creating lacy curtains of tiny spindles. A shame to destroy them. Layers of dust covered the wooden boards. Good quality floorboards, that if cleaned and polished wouldn't necessarily require carpets to hide them. The walls were a different matter. I picked at the peeling wallpaper and the flaked paintwork peeked out from behind the tears.

Ruth swept the floor with the big brush while I attacked the cobwebs with a tea towel hooked onto the end of a long stick. She left the room to empty the dustpan.

'What's this for?' she shouted.

In the hallway I found her examining the closet door. 'Cubbyhole, storeroom.'

She gripped the doorknob and pulled it.

'Sticks a bit, I said.

The door sprung open and Ruth stuck her head in the pokey little room. 'Odd place for a storage room.'

'I thought that, then, after I went into the cellar, I realised this once wouldn't have been here. Where the door and closet are now, it would have been an extension of the hallway leading to the missing wing and the extra bedrooms. For some reason, when they blocked this wall, they created a closet.'

She held the doorknob and gave it a twist. 'Odd.'

'What?'

'There's a doorknob on the inside.' She opened the door wider.

I stared at the knob – a round brass one – just like the one on the outside, but not a perfect match. Whereas the outer one had tarnished, the inner one was shiny. 'That's weird. I don't remember it being there before.'

Ruth rattled the handle. 'You probably wouldn't be looking for it. I mean you'd have to be on the inside to notice.'

Regardless, it seemed odd that I hadn't noticed, and I'd been sure I'd taken a good look inside. I sniffed. The air in the closet was heavy, as if weighted down by time. On the outside, the dust had collected, but inside more lay on the boards and shelves. Ruth stepped back and gave the door a shove. It lingered, as if harbouring an indecisive soul, then slammed shut.

We both jumped back. 'It's just a stupid closet,' I said quickly, refusing to engage her in the haunted house theory. 'Best get back to it,' I murmured.

Ruth went back to sweeping while I chased the spiders away.

Having worked hard for two days I drove Ruth to Norwich for a day out. We visited the cathedral and castle before touring the shops for some retail therapy. My shopping list was unfortunately long, and I couldn't afford much of it. I treated myself to warm clothes, a pair of leather boots that were on sale, and a few kitchen items in preparation for the arrival of the cooker the next day: pans, a casserole dish and other essential implements. As I watched the amounts stretch my credit card closer to its limit, I bit my tongue and halted the despairing gasp.

Ruth had the good grace to keep quiet about my money stresses. She deflected the topic during the journey back by talking about her forthcoming book. My head buzzed with ideas for illustrations. However, first I had to finish my farmyard tale.

The cooker arrived late Thursday morning. The deliverymen had taken several wrong turns before finding Heachley Hall. 'Your place isn't on the satnav,' the driver grumbled. 'Lane is too narrow.'

They'd reversed the truck up the drive and wheeled the huge

cooker in on casters. I showed them the space under the old oven slot where it was to go. One of the men installed the Rayburn, but didn't do the plumbing for the hot water; Kevin would do that. The engineer ensured the hotplates heated up and demonstrated how to control the thermostat. The smell of burning oil and hot metal quickly filled the kitchen.

'It will settle, the smell,' the engineer reassured, packing up his tools.

He left a manual, cookbook and half-drunk mug of coffee. By late afternoon, seated on two old crates and pouring over the cookery book, Ruth and I basked in a pleasant swathe of heat.

'We should go shopping for ingredients and make a casserole,' I suggested, tossing the book onto the worktop. The lovely cooker seemed an extravagance in my empty house.

'This was a good decision, Miriam. I know you're worried about money, but down the road, you'll get it all back and more.'

'God, I hope you're right.' I rolled up my sleeves. 'I'm hot!'

Ruth burst out laughing and I, relieved at last to have some semblance of a normal kitchen, joined in.

Our last day together and we spent it washing down walls. Eventually, I would paper over the cracks and redecorate my newly established sitting room. By late afternoon, Ruth announced it was time for her inevitable departure. I buried my disappointment behind a facade of bravado. I didn't think for a minute she believed it.

We hugged, and I heaped gratitude in her ear. 'You gave up your holiday for me!'

She patted my back before releasing me. 'Come down for Christmas.'

'I'll be at Aunt Valerie's'

'After that. Come for New Year.'

Thank goodness, it meant I wouldn't be with my aunt's family for the whole duration of the festive season. I squeezed her hands in mine, demonstrating my appreciation with tear pricked eyes. My throat had seized up and words failed me.

The gravel crunched under the wheels of her car and the

headlights lit up the imposing gates leading to the lane. Once the sound of the engine faded, I went indoors and bolted the front door. I leant against it and listened. Nothing. Not a peep. For once, the house didn't creak, rattle or groan. There was no doubt in my mind; I was quite alone.

SIXTEEN

Since Ruth's departure I'd been catching up on work. With the exception of trips downstairs for food, I spent my weekend cloistered in the attic. My only outing had been to the Rose and Crown to hook up to their Wi-Fi and download my latest emails. Scanning the list, I'd hoped for news from the nursing home, but still nothing, which deflated my mood.

Guy had asked for extra commissions to my existing project: illustrations on the inside covers. Guy saw money; I saw pressure. I'd lied to him by pretending I had no issues with time and accepted the extra work without quibbling. Back at my desk, I'd proceeded to gnaw the end of my pencil.

Due to my persuasive agent, I paid little attention to Kevin and his friend Ryan while they ripped out pipes, drilled holes through walls and ceilings, and lifted floorboards to expose rusting pipes. Sequestered in my den, I beavered away rather oblivious to their activities, unless I allowed thoughts of steaming hot bathwater to infiltrate – my patience was hanging by a thread. I left them to help themselves to drinks and the only time our paths crossed was when I shooed them out of the bathroom for a pee.

The metallic burning smell of the Rayburn had gradually receded. I was determined to master the art of slow cooking. I stewed casseroles of root vegetables and lamb for hours, then savoured the results in the evenings by the warmth of the fire.

The rest of my meagre order of furniture arrived during the week. The orange curtains that clashed magnificently with the purple sofa, when hung didn't quite make the distance to the floor, creating an unfortunate draught that shot across the room at ankle height. However, the synthetic fibres of the rug cushioned my soles and the lopsided uplighter cast a reasonable glow. It almost felt homely.

However, my tolerance of background noises slipped away and by Friday, I'd grown tired of the constant banging, the radio blaring out thrumming pop songs or the latest football banter. The two men chatted incessantly, both shouting over the radio and the drilling until eventually their voices reached my sanctuary in the attic – my workroom was situated right above the bathroom. I stuffed cotton wool in my ears.

Sometime around midday, the house fell silent. Downstairs I found them packing their tools into the van.

'Come.' Kevin gestured towards the kitchen. 'Let me show you.'

There'd been issues, unexpected extra expenses caused by previously invisible problems. He rambled through matters, bemoaning the ancient pipework and lack of conduits between the two storeys.

'Right mess.' He thumped the kitchen wall. 'Had to run the pipes up this way, rather than along under here.'

I half listened, not caring about the details, only that it was costing more than the original estimate.

'However,' he announced with a snort, 'you've got your hot water.' He turned on the kitchen tap and after a few spurts, water streamed out. I stuck my hand underneath the flow. Scalding! I whipped my hand away.

Kevin escorted me to the bathroom and demonstrated the hot water supply extended to both the sink and bathtub. Within seconds of the tap being turned on, the steam rose out of the old tub, misting up the brass taps.

'You've enough hot water to have a bath every day. That Rayburn is cooking all the time. There's your tank.' He pointed to the corner of the room.

There was no danger of missing the enormous cylinder, which stood on a raised plinth and held upright by struts extending from the walls. Pipes and valves stuck out of the insulated tank like rigid tentacles on a steel body.

'If you box this in with some wood panels, it'll make a nice airing cupboard for yewself.'

Another job for the versatile Charles. 'Great,' I said. 'Thanks.'

'And this,' he grinned, obviously pleased with himself, 'is me surprise.' He rapped his knuckles against the old radiator.

I reached out to touch it: roasting.

'It weren't bad, this radiator. I flushed the grot out and replaced the valves. It's gravity fed, so you'll need to turn it off in the summer or else you'll cook.'

I pressed my palms against the metal casing and the warmed my chilled fingers. He'd kept it secret and it was a lovely surprise. I'd heating downstairs in my kitchen and now in the bathroom, too. 'That's brilliant. Thank you.' I rubbed my heated palms together.

'Doesn't cost much extra, running the pipes alongside the others. Once you've made a hole.' He jerked his head towards the gap in the floor where the pipes vanished.

With a shaky hand, which was borne more out of shock at the amount than nerves, I wrote out the cheque, and Kevin stuffed it into his jacket pocket. With a nod at Ryan, they climbed into their white van and drove off.

That evening I sank into the bathtub, wine glass in one hand and a rather damp book in the other. I'd tuned the radio into Smooth FM and dotted a few candles about the room. The combination of mellow lights cast a mural of shadowy patterns on the walls.

Behind me, the ugly, but well insulated hot tank gurgled as it refilled. I wriggled my toes and burst the foaming bubbles. This would do. Now, I would cope with the winter. Given my crushing workload, the six weeks to Christmas should zip by.

I closed my eyes. The radio crackled and briefly lost its reception. The room descended into near silence – the tank had replenished, but the water continued to drip: soft pips echoed inside the cylinder. In amongst the varied gentle sounds I heard something else. Humming?

Perhaps. It sounded similar to the soft buzz of a distant bee, except it tracked the melody on the radio – an old Sixties classic.

I shot up. The water sloshed around my waist and the bubbles disintegrated.

'Who's there?' I called out. I swallowed what seemed like a massive lump in my throat and listened, trying to siphon out my thumping heartbeats.

The strange accompaniment ceased. The water around me stilled and I stared at each of the flickering candles in turn. What had I heard? The radio regained its signal strength and abruptly returned to life. A different song, less melodious and more rhythmic.

I settled back in the bath. My ears were playing tricks on me. A week of plumbing racket had desensitised my hearing and I'd forgotten the quirky sounds of Heachley Hall. I picked up my book, wetting a few pages as I located my marker. I sighed. Another weekend alone. I couldn't wait for Monday and with luck Charles would be back to help with the varnishing of the staircase and the construction of the airing cupboard. Those two tasks should keep him occupied and provide me with companionship.

The book flopped to one side in my hand – I couldn't concentrate. I stared at my toenails poking out of the water and I tapped them against the edge of the tub.

I was excited about seeing Charles again. Why was that? He came and went with a peculiar confidence and we'd spent little time in each other's company. The man was an introvert and uncommunicative for the most part; he'd revealed nothing of consequence about his life beyond Heachley Hall. Had he been in prison? Was he embarrassed about his background? He seemed educated and he spoke with a degree of elegance – posh, as Bert called it. However, Charles wore string for laces and there were patches sewn on the elbows of his jumpers.

Elegance wasn't something that sprung to mind when I thought of Charles, rather he maintained a love of humbleness – an endearing trait. Something about him drew me in and I grappled with the need to know more about him. If I chipped away, perhaps he'd eventually open up and tell me. But I had to tread carefully. If I scared him off with my prying, he might not come back and that would be a pity.

SEVENTEEN

'Miriam Chambers?'

I twirled the telephone cord between a finger and thumb. 'Yes? Who's speaking?' I said somewhat breathless from my rapid descend of the stairs.

'My name is Eva Kendal. You sent me an email a few weeks ago. I've been on holiday and I've only just caught up with my inbox.'

I flipped through my contacts list, trying to place her. A local accent and not one of my clients. It took a couple of seconds for her name to register. Ten o'clock on a Monday morning and my brain needed another injection of caffeine. 'Beechwood Care home, you were the manager.'

'Yes, that's right. I don't work for the company any longer.' She had a soft voice, the kind you could imagine soothing a troubled person. 'Your email said you were trying to trace the personal effects of Felicity Marsters.'

'Yes, my great-aunt. Do you remember her?' I perched on the milk crate, which I'd left by the phone socket.

'Oh most certainly, although poor woman, she had limited mobility and her speech was badly effected by the strokes. I do remember the sparkle in her eyes and she had some degree of understanding of her situation, unlike some of our residents. She clung on longer than we'd anticipated.'

'I had no idea she'd been ill until after her death. I'm particularly interested in her personal things, especially a box which contained documents and other mementos.' I held my breath while Eva clucked her tongue.

'I don't recall anything. It was some time ago.'

'Nobody came to claim her things when she died?' I gripped the cord tighter.

'She had no visitors, beyond those who took it upon themselves to visit for charitable purposes, but they were rare.' Eva sucked in a quick breath. 'That isn't unusual, I should say, her not having kin visit. Her account was settled by her solicitor; he had power of attorney.'

'Mr Porter?'

'Yes, his name rings a bell.'

'Did he visit?'

'I don't think so. We spoke on the phone. I don't recall him mentioning a box of documents.'

Her answer didn't surprise. I pursed my lips, muffling a growl of annoyance. Mr Porter had shown little if any curiosity in the past life of an invalid ninety-year-old. No wonder it took six months to find me. His preferred choice had been a swift auction. 'So what would have happened to her things?'

'Well, we had a storage room and things were generally kept for a period, until it became apparent nobody wanted them. Of course, Felicity died shortly before Beechwood closed.'

'The room was cleared, you don't remember if—'

'I'm sorry. I left before the actual closure.' Another sharp intake of breath from Eva. 'I wasn't happy with how they handled it. So uncaring – dumping the residents here and there in other homes, splitting up friends. I voiced my concerns, but felt powerless. I resigned.'

'I see.' I tipped my head back and lent it against the wall. 'You don't—', the doorbell clanged above my head. 'One moment, please.'

I put down the handset and unlocked the front door – Charles. I greeted him with a broad smile and he responded in kind, tugging slightly at a lock of hair. I waved him in. 'I'm on the phone.'

Charles stepped across the threshold and closed the door as I reclaimed the handset. 'I'm sorry, Eva, just the front door. Do you have any ideas about what might have happened to Felicity's things once the home had closed? They wouldn't have thrown the box away, surely? Not while her will was in probate?'

Eva released a puff, an almost sigh. I imagined her on the other end of the phone, uncomfortable and fidgety at my line of questioning. Opposite me Charles stood straight backed, his eyebrows unusually quizzical and knotted together.

'I'd assume,' Eva continued, 'they were sent to Peterborough, to the head office.'

'I spoke to them. They said they didn't have anything and gave me your details.' I sensed an impasse, as if I'd become stuck on a merry-go-round and was rapidly going nowhere.

'Oh. That's not promising. Who did you speak to?'

They'd been no names; I should have asked. 'Some woman in admin.'

'If I were you, I'd go back to them and try again. Ask for the manager. Really, they shut that place in such a hurry.' The soft edge of her voice disintegrated, and a residue of anger surfaced.

'I will. Were there any staff at Beechwood who would remember Felicity, perhaps they might be able to help?' I pursued.

'I suppose. I didn't deal with the residents on a daily basis – too much paperwork.' She laughed half-heartedly. 'Let me see. Staff turnover in the last year or so was high; the writing on the wall must have been obvious.'

I glanced at Charles. Rather than going to his shed, he remained rooted to the spot, attentively listening, almost craning to hear the other end of the conversation. It was a level of intrusive behaviour I'd not witnessed from him before now. I turned to one side and blocked him out of my view.

Eva clucked her tongue repeatedly. 'I'll try to come up with a couple of names. Everyone was scattered to other nursing homes and some to new jobs. Such a shame.'

'Why was the place closed?'

'Money. The building needed renovating. It wasn't especially suited to the needs of the residents – people living longer, but often more infirm. I suggested they downgraded the place to a residential home, rather than nursing care, but they opted to close it.'

'So if they'd gone with your plan, and my aunt had survived, she would have been moved anyway?' Eva was right, the situation hadn't been fair.

'Yes, more than likely. She needed round the clock attention and would have been placed in a nursing facility. But the decision was taken out of my hands.'

I tried not to judge her for abandoning her clients; Eva Kendal might smack of insincerity, but she probably had her own career to consider.

'Sorry,' she rushed to say, 'I've got to go. I'm ringing from work.'

'Yes, of course. Thank you for calling.'

'I wish I could be more helpful.'

We said goodbye and I hung up. 'Drat,' I muttered.

'Problem?' Charles's piped up and I turned to face him.

'I've been trying to track down Felicity's possessions, the ones she took to the nursing home where she died. They seemed to have vanished. I was speaking to the last manager of the home, Eva Kendal.'

'Possessions?' He followed me into the kitchen.

'I'm not sure what they were. She kept them in a box. Liz – Tony's wife – thought it contained papers. I was hoping to find out more about my family and why she left this house to me.'

Charles displayed an unusually deep frown. 'I assume she left it to you as you are her nearest living relative. I don't believe she would want this place left to a stranger.'

'But why this year thing. Why?' I slammed a mug down on the worktop. 'Sorry,' I grimaced. 'Not your problem.' It was time to move on. I pointed at the Rayburn. 'Look at my new cooker.'

Charles stepped over to the mammoth appliance. 'Impressive.'

I showed him hot water gushing out of the tap and then, beckoning him upstairs, the tank in the corner of the bathroom and explained the airing cupboard idea.

He peered around the cylinder. 'I'm sure I can put something together.'

We agreed he should stick to the original plan of restoring the staircase to its former glory before dealing with the cupboard. When I mentioned the electric sander I'd bought, he furrowed his eyebrows.

'It's cordless,' I explained. 'I checked it out and it's easy to use. I've bought loads of emery papers, including different grades. I wasn't sure which would be best. It will work brilliantly on the steps and bannister, but you'll have to sand down the spindles by hand.'

Returning upstairs to work, I left him to practise. Around lunchtime I emerged from the attic and halted on the landing above the hall because below people were talking. Two male voices passing back and forth in rapid conversation. Neither of them was Charles. My stomach churned with shock – had he opened the door to somebody and why hadn't I heard the doorbell?

I tiptoed down the stairs and as I turned the corner, I encountered Charles on his knees sanding a bannister spindle with a sheet of emery paper. There was no sign of the sander. Resonating around him were voices discussing the political issue in Russia: a news bulletin on the radio. I was relieved. The house hadn't been invaded by strangers.

He stopped the circular motion of his sanding hand and glanced up. 'You don't mind Radio Four, do you?' He pointed a finger between the balusters to the floor below.

I leant over the bannister. He'd placed the radio on a crate and plugged it into the only socket in the hallway. Chunky in size and with the antenna extended to its full length, the radio's reception compared to my battery driven one, wasn't bad. The model with its wooden casing and dial buttons reminded me of one Dad possessed, which in turned had belonged to Nana.

Nana Chambers was another one of my relatives who had come and gone leaving little trace or impact on my life. Along with my grandfather, she had spent most holidays abroad enjoying sunny beaches or pool sides, letting her skin crisp into a leathery jacket. Eventually, tiring of dull England – as she'd frequently claimed – they'd both uprooted themselves and gone to live in the Costa del something. My father shrugged off their emigration and shown no interest in visiting. His sisters had raced off at every opportunity to spend time with their parents, basking in the sunshine and drinking tequilas. 'Why can't we go?' I'd asked Dad countless times. His replies had varied from lack of time to unnecessary expense. The reality had been he'd been busy courting another woman and visiting Greece on a regular basis.

Nana had a great deal of tolerance for the sun, but not the healthy diet of the local Spanish. According to my aunts, she'd stuck religiously to eating chips with everything and consequently her heart clogged up. My forgotten grandfather, who'd spent most of his last years fishing, followed her to the grave not long after having never bothered to interfere with her cooking choices. Dad had gone to their funerals, but he'd not taken me. I guessed he adopted her radio and brought it home.

Dad had enjoyed Radio Four. 'Sure, why would I mind? I can't hear it up there. I like the radio, but I can't work and listen to speech.'

'I find it passes the time.' He slid his hand along the bannister. 'I thought I'd start with the bannister, then do the steps.'

'Whatever you like.' I continued downstairs. 'Do you want a sandwich?'

'No, thank you. I had a big breakfast and I can last till later.'

Before I returned upstairs with a plate of sandwiches and an apple from my orchard, I left him a coffee on the crate next to the radio.

Later, spying through the window the first stars in the darkening sky, I stretched, rose and carried the empty plate downstairs. The radio was silent and unplugged. The untouched electric sander and the emery paper lay next to the crate. I switched on the kitchen light and discovered the coffee mug I'd left with Charles laying on the drainer, rinsed out and dry. I'd failed to hear his departure, again.

An odd guy – his habits shaped by his solitary nature and unpretentious attitude – evasive, too. While I sketched and coloured in pictures of cartoon animals, he'd sanded a handful of spindles and perhaps, two metres of bannister rail. Charles wasn't in a hurry. But I didn't mind. If it kept him busy and here, under my roof, then technically I had company, and if all we managed to say to each other over the coming days, perhaps weeks, amounted to little of substance, then it was more than I'd expected when I'd arrived a month earlier.

EIGHTEEN

Before I left to spend Christmas with Aunt Valerie in Wiltshire, I paid Glenda and Bert a visit. Any spare hour or so I'd had in the last few weeks had been nabbed for one small project – a drawing of the Rose and Crown in ink and water colours. The gift brought an almost teary smile to Glenda's robust features. An appreciative Bert hammered a nail in the wall by the bar and hung the picture there.

I visited my flat in Chelmsford. The first night, I laid on my bed wrapped in my sleeping bag and cried. There seemed little explanation for my breakdown, other than fatigue and probably frustration at how little time I'd had to discover more about Felicity. On a positive note, my illustration project had been completed, although I'd had to fight with Wi-Fi connections at the Rose and Crown and the slow transfer rates before Guy declared he'd received everything. The author had sent me a complimentary email in reply.

My time in Chelmsford should have felt like a glorious homecoming, however, my two nights in the flat served to remind me that for the next few months it wasn't my home. Putting aside the sombre reality of my situation, I revelled in the luxury of a shower by letting the hot spray pummel my aching back.

The television became my constant companion for the duration of my stay. While gorging on crisps and biscuits, watching the kind of tripe I'd normally considered a waste of my precious time. I didn't shift from my armchair and with my laptop glued to my kneecaps, I hogged my social media accounts. My neglected Facebook account burst back into life as I caught up with friends.

I tweeted inconsequential soundbites every few minutes and retweeted strangers. My fingers tapped away on the keyboard.

Eventually I ventured out, once, with my friend, Frankie, who worked at the local college as an assistant in the art department. I'd met her there during my studies. The day before Christmas Eve I painted my lips with gloss and she dragged me out to one of Chelmsford's less salubrious pubs. We spent the evening hollering over the headache inducing grind of music.

Naturally, she'd been curious about my circumstances in Norfolk, but the constant battle with the background noise shrank our conversation down to one or two words flung across a small table. We gave up communicating, got drunk and staggered back to my flat. I rocked her in a bear hug before she clambered into the back of a taxi. Frankie hadn't exactly taxed my intellect, but she'd given me a decent forgetful night out. After two months of self-inflicted exclusion at Heachley Hall, one night of frivolous fun was a luxury.

The long drive along the M4 on Christmas Eve gave me time to think. Guy had more work lined up for me in the New Year; good opportunities that would keep me busy, and I also had Ruth's new book to work on, too. I carried a drawing pad with me wherever I went and I sketched out ideas in the services car park during one break. If the author liked my rough drafts I hoped to win the commission.

I hit the road again and conjured up half-baked illustrations as I drove. Between mental pictures, I fretted about Heachley Hall. Cars zoomed past my Fiesta while I thrummed my fingers on the steering wheel and reviewed my situation. Charles had finished the stairs and constructed a fair sized airing cupboard with three useful shelves. My next plan had been to redecorate the living room, but when the replacement tiles I'd ordered for the hall arrived early, I'd reprioritised my task list.

Before I'd left, Charles, crawling about on the mosaic floor, had examined the old tiles. 'They've lasted well,' he'd muttered. He poked his finger in a crack, then bounced up onto his feet. 'I'll start in January, when you're back.'

I'd promised to buy adhesive once I returned in the New Year. 'I'll see you then?' I'd ventured to ask, hopefully, as he'd crossed the threshold of the front door.

'Of course.' He'd turned to face me, his head cocked to one side and a crooked smile shaped his lips. 'I look forward to it.'

A wary pause ensued as I lowered my eyes, unable to maintain his fetching gaze and ran my finger along the edge of the doorframe, 'Sure. Yes. Me, too.' I dropped the awkward words one at a time like Morse code.

Just one smile and the blood rushed to my cheeks. I nearly glanced away, embarrassed by my reaction. There was an air of expectancy about him. He'd hovered, locking his gaze on me, forcing me to hold him in a visual embrace. Strip away his worn-out clothes with their hand-sewn patches, the man had something classy lurking beneath. The confident pose: straight backed and square shouldered and his eloquent speech devoid of the Norfolk dialect. It always surprised me as I expected him to drawl in a similar fashion to Tony or Kevin. When I'd asked him about how he planned to spend Christmas and New Year, he chewed on his lips, and gave a small shrug. No mention of his home life.

'Don't worry about me,' he'd said, then changed the subject back to floor tiles.

When goodbyes became awkward, it meant something else was going on; a thought which continued to unnerve me.

I thumped the steering wheel and swore loudly at a Passat that under cut me. The sooner I reached Valerie's the better. A wandering mind had dangerous properties.

'My darling,' Valerie screeched, dashing across the driveway, as I unfolded my legs and slammed the car door shut. 'Well done.' She wrapped her arms around me, hugging me to her skimpy bosom. Valerie considered driving to Devizes a challenging endeavour only to be undertaken by the bravest. The week before she'd implored me to come by train. 'We'll pick you up from Swindon.' I'd won that battle swiftly when I told her the price of a ticket compared to the expense of driving. My aunt lived in a bubble when it came to the cost of anything.

'They're all here,' she announced, propelling me towards the front door.

The all aspect meant a crowded house. As well as Valerie and Uncle Dave, I had my cousins, Yvonne and Lucy, plus Lucy's husband Justin and their pint-sized son, Toby. I paused by the door. 'Yvonne hasn't brought Legolas, has she?' I cringed, remembering how the over excited Labrador had chewed my sandals during my last visit.

'Kennels. Simply not enough space.' Valerie dropped her voice. 'I'd never say this to Yvonne, but he's a beast to look after. Such a relief when she'd realised it was either the dog in the car or the presents. She couldn't fit in both.' We both giggled.

I braced myself for a gaggle of enthusiastic relatives and held out my arms for the inevitable crushing embraces of each one in turn.

Between watching films, washing up dirty dishes and playing snakes and ladders with Toby – again – I snatched moments alone. My business website, which I haphazardly updated, needed an overhaul to bring it up-to-date with my latest projects. I jotted down notes and immersed myself in the world of Internet connectivity, something I pined for at Heachley.

By the time I returned to Chelmsford, I had a list of things to do and for the duration between Christmas and New Year, I kept myself busy. Feeling pleased with myself, I repacked my suitcase with fresh clothes and drove to Southend to Ruth's house.

Mick was a beefy guy with black rimmed glasses, which he pushed back up his nose every few seconds. When he shook my hands he squeezed my knuckles, then as an afterthought he edged forward to peck my cheek.

'Miriam, lovely to meet you.'

I was intruding on their special time together. It felt obvious in the awkwardness of the moment. I asked about their respective Christmases.

'Mother,' Ruth groaned. 'She's a talking machine and Dad watched everything on telly: all the usual repeats and whined the whole time about the lack of originality, and then contradicted himself by claiming he missed the old shows. Blah blah. I read loads.' She grinned with the last comment.

Mick lined up the mugs. He appeared quite at home in Ruth's domestic haven.

'I had the kids on Boxing Day along with my parents.' He opened his mouth to say something else, then shut it again. His thick eyebrows twitched, knotting together across the bridge of his nose. He shrugged off the pause. 'It was different. But I suppose there were no slanging matches to upset the boys.'

I shuffled on my feet, not knowing what to say. 'So, is it just us for the evening?'

Ruth confessed they'd invited someone called Matt. I suppressed the eye rolling, because her cheeks went pink when she mentioned he was single. Ruth liked to play matchmaker for me and her attempts so far had not given rise to any new boyfriends.

'Matt who?' I asked folding my arms across my chest.

'You don't know him.'

'Teacher?'

'No,' she tut-tutted, an exasperated expression. 'A nurse practitioner. He works at the hospital.'

'And how did you meet him?'

Ruth traced a finger along the edge of the worktop, flitting her eyes over to Mick.

'My brother.' He poured hot water into one of the mugs. 'Matt's my brother.'

'Oh,' I kept my mouth in a round shape. Didn't Matt have friends of his own to spend the New Year with? I said nothing, and Ruth changed the subject to ask about Heachley Hall. As we settled onto the comfy chairs in her lounge, I brought her up-to-date on my endeavours to renovate the place.

She rubbed her shoulder up to Mick's side and curled her legs to one side, stuffing her feet under a cushion. He wrapped an arm about her neck and caressed her with the tips of his fingers. I examined my coffee and described the staircase and airing cupboards.

'Guy lining up more work for you?' she asked.

'Not as much. I think he's busy taming another illustrator to his ways.'

'Perhaps he's realised he needs to hang back,' Ruth suggested, raising her mug to her lips. 'Give you some breathing space to sort your place out.'

'Probably,' I said weakly.

A silence ensued. I couldn't stop staring at Mick's roving hand. It ran down Ruth's arm, tucked itself around her waist and gave her a little squeeze. She giggled and snuggled even closer to him. I backed myself deeper into my armchair and slurped on my hot drink.

'And Charles?' Ruth's interrogation continued unabated as she cuddled Mick.

My scalp tingled when she mentioned Charles, so much so I raked my fingers through my hair to combat the fuzzy sensation and pursed my lips. 'Coming back to replace the broken tiles. Then, he might do some decorating. He says he could have a go at plastering, too.'

'A jack of all trades.'

'Beats me hands down, then,' Mick guffawed and took a swig from his coffee before continuing. 'I can do IKEA, but anything that doesn't involve a screwdriver or hammer, I'm stuffed.' A broad smile filled the lower half of his face. He had appealing features with a light dusting of bristles around his lips and chin. Along with a twitchy nose, the seemingly unconscious adjusting of his glasses, he scratched the back of his neck, too. I unnerved him, and it re-established the idea that my presence was inconvenient.

I retraced the conversation. 'He's been a handyman for a while I think. Gardener, too.'

'That garden needs so much work,' Ruth agreed. 'We'll come up and help in the spring, won't we, Mick?'

For a split second his lips drooped, then he nodded, rather too briskly. 'Sure. We'll help. In the spring.'

Spring seemed a lifetime away. One month of winter and I couldn't wait for the longer days and the warmer nights.

'Thank you,' I murmured. 'I can't promise many home comforts and—'

'I thought,' Ruth interrupted, 'We could stay at the Rose and Crown, then you don't have to worry about beds and things.'

Things. I imagined them canoodling around my house or squashed on my dinky two-seater keeping each other warm. Did I want that kind of company? Ruth, yes, she was useful on her own and easy to accommodate, but a couple? I fidgeted, swallowed the last mouthfuls of my scalding coffee and ignored the burning sensation in the back of my throat.

'Makes sense. I mean, you're my guests and I'm not expecting you to spend the weekend gardening,' I said.

Ruth blinked hard at me, opened her mouth, then snapped it shut. I instantly regretted the sarcasm. I leapt to my feet. 'How about a walk? I've eaten far too much at Valerie's and need to exercise.'

Unsurprisingly, Mick's brother turned out to be not my type and my opinion wasn't helped by a fourth glass of wine.

Mick cooked a delicious evening meal of pasta and ragu, Ruth provided the cheesecake and Matt brought the wine. I gnawed on my lower lip when I realised I'd brought nothing for the evening. Ruth patted my hand as I apologised for my lack of foresight.

'You've got enough on your plate, sweetie,' she said.

'Gosh, yes.' Matt leaned across the table. He possessed the same bushy eyebrows as his brother. 'Ruth says you live in a stately home.'

My cheeks went hot, and my fork clattered on my plate. 'No I don't. It maybe bigger than average—'

'Average,' Ruth shrieked. 'Each room is the size of my ground floor.'

'No they're not,' I squirmed on my seat. 'The drawing room is large—'

'Drawing room,' Matt settled back in his seat. 'Wow, sounds grand, ostentatious.'

I stabbed at my penne. 'It's empty, devoid of any furniture. The house has nothing to make it grand or—' I snorted, '—ostentatious. The wallpaper hangs off the wall in places, the glass rattles in the window panes, the ceilings are cracked, the pipes—'

'Miriam,' Ruth cut across me, 'You're doing a fantastic job. The house isn't derelict. Shabby, yes, but it will sell.'

I focused on Ruth's soft smile. My racing heart calmed, and I briefly closed my watery eyes. The stress abated, and I nodded. 'Yes, you're right. Sorry. It's a grand house, not a stately, but not average and it will sell.' I opened my eyes and smiled back at her. The optimism returned; I had to cling on to it somehow.

She wiped a dribble of tomato sauce off her chin. 'Good.' She turned to Mick. 'This ragu is lovely, darling.'

For the rest of the meal Mick and Matt argued over who was the better cook. Both seemed to have been raised to look after themselves, which would appeal to Ruth and should to me, but Matt lacked something. There was no sense of common ground between us, nothing to draw us even into a decent conversation.

When Ruth switched on the TV for the Big Ben chimes at midnight, I held back while Ruth and Mick conducted a protractive kiss. Matt's eyes widened watching his brother's embrace and he stepped towards me. Before he could touch me, I held out my hand.

He hesitated, staring at my palm before taking it in a limp shake. 'Happy New Year, Miriam. Good luck with the house.'

'Thank you. Hope you get that promotion,' I offered in return. He stepped back and we both waited for Ruth and Mick to disengage.

I hugged Ruth close and she whispered in my ear, 'I'm here for you, sweetie. I haven't forgotten you and I mean it about the garden. Matt was Mick's idea, sorry.'

She squeezed my sides and released me. I wiped my watery eyes with back of my hand. 'Thanks for the invite. I don't know what I'd do—'

'I couldn't possibly let you spend your two week break with both of your aunts.'

I laughed, hiccoughing and the room spun around me. 'I should sit down, I'm drunk.'

Matt left after breakfast and New Year's Day proved to be leisurely and relaxed. We watched a film, ate a late lunch and went for a walk along the sea front and pier. Mick and Ruth held hands, but otherwise, they'd stopped short of groping each other.

I crushed my fledging jealousy. Ruth deserved happiness and my enthusiasm for their relationship grew over that cold first January day. I laughed at Mick's poor jokes, which Ruth seemed content to tolerate. Or perhaps they were good jokes and my sense of humour had hit rock bottom. Who was I to criticise – the queen of unsuccessful affairs had shunned yet another male opportunity. The next day, I left for a brief stopover at Chelmsford before returning to Heachley Hall.

If there was one man I keenly awaited seeing, it was Charles.

NINETEEN

Weeks had passed since I'd spoken to Eva Kendal and the impression I'd been left with – that she'd forgotten about Felicity's box – was probably true. There hadn't been a peep from her about following up, so I decided to take action into my own hands and chase up the head office of Twilight Care Homes in Peterborough.

The hallway at Heachley Hall was beyond chilly, and the ambient temperature transported me to what felt like the arctic tundra. My exhales mushroomed out of my lips and formed a smoky mist. Perched on a camping stool I'd acquired at a car boot sale in Hunstanton, I dialled the number and asked to speak to the manager. It took several minutes of persuasion to make it past the receptionist and be allowed to speak to a Mr Craven. I explained my situation, the missing personal effects of my great-aunt. When he asked me to describe the box, I floundered, unable to provide any details other than it contained documents and photographs. I'd only Liz Pyke's description to go on. He promised to investigate and ring back. Somehow, as I lowered the handset, I suspected it would be another false promise.

I'd only been back a day and the freezing temperatures indoors, never mind outside, had drilled into the core of my bones. The pipes hadn't frozen in my absence and Kevin had assured me that the vulnerable pipes had been sufficiently lagged with insulation, but his reassurance didn't convince me. Luck wouldn't always be on my side, something would give eventually: a wall would collapse, the roof tiles would slip off on mass in a storm or the cellar would flood. I'd mapped out all the possible disasters and believed them to be imminent.

A spate of negativity was how I generally started the New Year. Annually, I predicted doom and gloom, and each year, those scenarios failed to arrive. However, my mood swings didn't stop me from projecting my worst fears into my daydreams. The arrival of Charles later that morning perked me up, until I noted his old clothing and no new boot laces either.

'So what did you do for Christmas?' I asked, unable to resist poking my nose into his affairs. There had to be something exciting in his life beyond me and Heachley.

He knelt on the cold floor and picked at the edge of a cracked tile. 'The usual,' he muttered.

'Are you Jewish?'

He laughed as he shook his head.

'Atheist? Do you hide away at Christmas, like Scrooge and bah humbug callers?'

Resting back on his heels, he looked up at me. 'Scrooge?' He furrowed his eyebrows.

'You know. Charles Dickens. *A Christmas Carol*. The three ghosts, past, present—'

'And future. Yes. I remember, now.' He rose, a sad smile on his lips. 'It's been a while since I read that one, not since I was a boy. Maybe I am Scrooge, waiting for my salvation.' The corners of his eyes turned down. I'd made him sad and I hated the expression he showed, it made me upset how quickly he became morose.

'No, not Scrooge,' I hastened to add. 'He was miserly and uncaring. That's not you.'

'Isn't it?' The frown on his face deepened and he moved away, heading towards the scullery door. 'I need tools.'

'I bought adhesive.'

I hurried after him and his long strides made quick work of crossing the hallway. In the shed Charles collected together what he needed: brush, paint scraper and a hammer. I slid the tub of PVA glue across the table towards his hand.

'This is what they recommended. And also, the guy in the shop said to use beeswax on the floor when you've finished. The tiles are in the corner.' I pointed at the boxes that had been delivered weeks ago.

I carried the tub of glue into the house for him, then stood around, wondering what else to do. I'd given up on asking him if he wanted to a drink, he always turned me down.

Charles reappeared, sniffing the air. 'You've lit a fire.'

How he missed the smell when he walked in, I didn't know. The stench of damp wood smouldering in the fireplace reeked throughout the house.

'Earlier, in the living room. I'm sketching down here. A new project, I don't need the computer or easel.' I'd left the pad on the sofa. There was another reason – the opportunity for him to pop his head around the door and say hello. A small and heartening antidote to loneliness.

I told him all about my assignment as he smashed the first tile with a hammer, disintegrating it into bits. Using the dustpan brush he swept away the debris of the tile and laid a new one in its place, checking the fit.

'Monsters from outer space,' he repeated the premise of the book. 'And this is for children?'

'Friendly aliens, but they have to look like monsters. They're lost and they come to Earth for directions. I can design the monsters myself, the author has given me a few ideas, but it's down to me.' I loved it when I could be entirely creative with my drawings. I bounced on my heels and imagined a hairy monster with two heads, one for talking, the other for eating. I should be drawing by the fire, but chatting with Charles proved both productive and gratifying.

'This doesn't scare children?' He painted the glue on the back of the replacement tile.

'Younger ones maybe. It's meant to breakdown preconceived ideas. The monsters are an allegory for foreigners in general and the book is to teach kids not to pre-judge those who don't look or talk like us. I mean, you know, human and aliens. British and immigrants. That kind of idea.' I fumbled.

'An admirable fable.' Charles gently laid the tile in the empty space.

'Didn't reading *A Christmas Carol* scare you? Especially the last ghost, the one who didn't talk?'

143

He paused, and his body stiffened. 'I don't remember,' he murmured. 'Should ghosts frighten or terrorise?' He glanced up at me.

'Bad ones, surely. Those who mean harm.'

'Is that what ghosts do, hurt people?' He pressed down on the tile with a grunt of exertion.

I shrugged. 'I don't know. I don't believe in them. It's all nonsense and probably meant to scare children. Don't be bad or the bogey man will get you.' I waved my hands in the air and made whooping noises.

A faint smile trickled over his face. 'But not your monsters, because they're nice and friendly.'

It was time to knuckle down to work. 'Very friendly,' I agreed. There were hundreds of tiles in the floor mosaic and probably a few dozen were damaged or loose. It had taken him fifteen minutes to repair one, then he'd have to wax the floor. It amounted to several hours work. I smiled, knowing I'd have company nearby. 'Put your radio on if you like. I don't mind it in the background.'

I left him to work, leaving the door ajar, so I could listen to the gentle music.

The fire blazed in the hearth, generating copious heat for my wriggling toes. Outside of the living room window, the grass remained crisp with white frost. I blew on my cold hands and picked up my pencil. Replaying our conversation, it dawned on me he hadn't answered my original question – what the hell had he done over the Christmas?

I hurtled down the stairs, out onto the landing, then down the next lot of steps. The telephone trilled louder and with an urgency that had even penetrated my den in the attic. Charles hovered by the telephone, his hand outstretched.

'I'll get it.' I skidded across the tiled floor and snatched at the handset. 'Yes? Miriam here.' I wanted it to be Mr Craven, to have him announce he'd found Felicity's things safely stowed in a storage box somewhere and in it would lie the answer to my question – why was I here?

'Miriam, are you ready for this?' Guy's abrupt style greeted me.

I rested my shoulders against the wall and rubbed my fingers across the creases in my forehead. 'For what?' I waved the lurking Charles away and he tiptoed to the other end of the hall where he'd been working.

Half an hour later I hung up. He'd sweet-talked me into more work. Another project to sit alongside my existing one, plus the drawings I was doing for Ruth, which we handled directly between us, rather than through Guy. Now I would have plenty of work to keep the winter month's flying by and a long list of things still to do in the house that hounded me whenever I wandered into any room. Three days after I'd returned to Heachley and the rhythm of my life had returned to drawing, eating and sleeping.

I sank my bottom onto the lowest step of the stairs and buried my face in my hands.

'What's wrong?'

I peeked between my fingers. Charles came over and crouched before me, his hands clasped between his knees.

'Just, too much going on,' I sniffed.

He touched my chin with his forefinger using it to lift my head – the gentlest of nudges. Those voluminous eyes of his with tiny pinpoint pupils stared right at me. 'Tell me.'

'I need money, so I'm working my socks off and I don't usually take on this much work. My agent's given me another book to work on and it's a good contract and the author is well-known. But, this damn house.' I thumped the step next to me. 'The rooms need painting, some of the floorboards need replacing and there's the rotten window frames. Oh, and the jungle garden needs a chainsaw. Argh!'

'Miriam, I'm here to help.' He settled on the step next to me. 'What else is bothering you?'

Charles's radar of perception often surprised me. He refused to stop at the obvious and rightly suspected that other things heaped stress on my shoulders.

I sighed. 'Felicity. I was hoping to find out more about her and why she left this place to me. She wanted me to live here and went out of her way to make it the better option, even with the lack of money up front, but I'm not convinced she simply saw this place as the pot at the end of the rainbow.'

Propping his elbows on his knees, he leant forward, entwining his fingers together. 'Can't help you with that. She kept secrets for a reason and they died with her. However, I liked Felicity and she always had time to talk to me.'

'What about?'

'Books, primarily and her time in India.'

'You said she'd quite a library.'

'Yes. A mixture of novels, art books, pamphlets about travelling abroad, others about different religions. Lots on India, its culture and people. I borrowed a few. I love history books and maps. She had a big atlas.'

My ears had pricked up when he mentioned the one thing I hoped I had in common with my great-aunt.

'Art books?' I queried.

'Illustrated tales from India. Great epics with exquisite plates. Postcards, too.' Charles waved his hands at the walls. 'Tapestries. She draped these walls in colourful pictures and didn't care much for the cracks forming behind them. The rugs were from Persia or Nepal. The pottery in the kitchen – bright and nothing like what I use.' He coughed and waved a dismissive hand. 'You know, china and porcelain, old stuff.'

I tried to imagine what the house might have looked like: exotic sculptures, symbols of religion, perhaps Hindu elephant gods or a chubby Buddha sitting cross-legged. 'Was she religious?'

He chuckled softly. 'No, not really. She didn't care for a particular religion and was very broad in her tastes. She had a crucifix on the mantelpiece in the drawing room alongside a statue of some Hindu god.'

I smiled. Felicity embraced life with an openness I admired. But then I remembered the bonfire Tony described, when Felicity's things had been unceremoniously burnt. 'Why didn't he sell her things?'

Charles straightened. 'Who?'

'Effing Mr Porter. Didn't he want to make money out of this place? So why not sell her things rather than burn them.'

'Probably because much of her things were foreign in style.'

'Around here, maybe, but in other parts of the UK it would be common to have Indian art decorating houses. Birmingham, Leicester, Manchester all have Asian communities, so why did he get rid of it all.'

'Did he?'

I opened my mouth then changed my mind. I'd assumed Porter told the clearance guys to burn her things, but perhaps he hadn't. Perhaps, he had no idea what the contents were and had relied on local people to deal with the clearance, that led me to wonder if they'd burnt what had no value and sold the rest without telling him.

'I supposed it could have been sold. So where's the money?' I pondered.

'Seems to me you have some questions to ask.' Charles stood, and a puff of dust fell from his trousers.

'Do you think you could remember what was in the house? Help make a list?'

He didn't answer straightaway. He wandered back to where he'd left his tools. 'I only know about a few rooms, the downstairs ones. I couldn't tell you the value of anything.'

'All I need is a rough idea of what was here. If only I could find Maggie and ask her. She would have cleaned all the rooms.' I rose, turning to climb the stairs. 'I doubt this will come to anything. Knowing Mr Porter, he'll have some excuse for what happened to the contents of the house.'

'She wasn't proud, Felicity,' Charles said, his attention on the broken tiles at his feet. 'It's quite possible the contents had little commercial value. She spoke of a love of markets and bazaars, buying things for her mother. I think she wanted to recreate her life in India between these walls, and it had nothing to do with intrinsic value.' He paused, then spoke softly, 'She missed the warmth of the sun, the colours, the monsoon storms.' He lifted his head and the whites of his eyes shone under the light.

'Why didn't she go back?'

He shrugged. 'Because she'd no family there. Her mother gone, no sisters or brothers. If she had other relatives out there she never spoke about them. Ever.'

How I regretted not knowing her better. If only my parents had visited more often. 'Family. Me and Dad, we were it. Except, we never bothered to visit her once Mum died.' I ran my hand along the smooth banister; Charles had polished the surface into a sheen. 'When Ruth was here we went to Old Hunstanton. While we were on the beach, I remembered being there with Felicity. I must have been a young child.' The same image over and over: the sand sifting between her painted toenails.

'She loved the sea. The waves.' He blinked and turned away, bending over to pick up the hammer.

'Do you go swimming in the sea?'

His back stiffened, half bent. 'As a boy. I swam, yes.' He straightened. 'Felicity lived by the sea in India.'

It explained the happy expression on her face. Those memories re-emerged with clarity, unlike the house, which I barely recalled. 'She wore a yellow sari, that day on the beach.'

He nodded and raised the hammer, before pausing, ready to strike. 'Colourful, aren't they, those kind of dresses. She wore them in the summer when the weather was good. In the winter, she preferred the clothes of the local women, trousers and woolly tops.'

Another tile was obliterated and the sound of the harsh demolition ricocheted throughout the hall.

'I'll email Mr Porter. Ask him for an inventory of the contents prior to clearance. See what he has to say.' I started to trudge upstairs.

If only I had thought to question the solicitor in detail before now. I'd been naive and made mistakes. Trudging into my workroom, I flicked open my laptop and composed a sharply worded email to the infuriating Mr Porter. Later, I would head out and hook up to the Rose and Crown Wi-Fi to send it. If there was one person who seemed bent on keeping me from finding out about Felicity, it was her solicitor.

TWENTY

'I'm sorry, Miss Chambers, we've no record of Miss Marsters's possessions.'

A week after my original call, Mr Craven called me back. Seven days of frantic project planning. Lunchtimes spent at the pub, scoffing Glenda's mayonnaise drenched sandwiches while sending emails back and forth to confirm deadlines, then back to Heachley to print off contracts or King's Lynn to pick up more art supplies.

'They have to be somewhere, unless they were destroyed. Who would authorise their destruction and wouldn't there be written agreement? There might have been important documents in that box: letters, even a new will.' I huffed. He'd listened in silence to my mini tirade.

'If there was paperwork, I'm afraid it was left at Beechwood with the owners.'

'Owners? Sorry, I don't understand. I thought Twilight owned it?'

'Yes, it did. Twilight acquired Beechwood Care Homes about a year before its closure. The business was sold to us, but not the building. The property passed back into landlord's hands after we closed the facility.'

My fingers curled into a fist. 'So they could still be sat at Beechwood in an empty building?'

'I've no idea if it's still empty.'

A red mist descended in reply to his limp remark. I spat out my next question, not caring how rude I sounded. 'Who exactly owns the place then?'

'Dominion Estates. A property agent, which is in turn owned by an investment company. A decade ago they bought up lots of large houses for the purpose of turning them into nursing homes. They maintain the properties and the facilities, and rent them to specialist care providers. However, our standards of care made Beechwood unsuitable for long-term use. After we acquired Beechwood, we moved the residents to other facilities in our group and closed it down.'

So why acquire a nursing home if it was substandard? My question bore no relevance to my original request, but I felt sorry for those staff and residents who'd been shuffled off to other places. Felicity might have been one if she'd lived. How would she have coped? The little I'd learnt about her gave me the impression she'd been proud of her independent spirit, and her Indian heritage, too. However, none of those things would have been demonstrated: a frail, mute geriatric was invisible.

'We always have the best interests of our clients at heart. It is necessary to maintain their care to high standards.'

No, it was necessary for the balance sheet. Take the income of the residents, discourage expensive staff from transferring and close it down. I tapped my pencil on the desk, annoyed, but there was little reason to continue the conversation.

'Do you have a contact number for Dominion Estates?'

I wrote down the email address and telephone number. It would mean more ringing around and explaining my situation. Why was I so intent on pursuing this lost box of papers and photographs? I'd started and I damn well was going to finish the investigation. Dad had been wrong; I wasn't stubborn, I was determined. Felicity would have admired my tenacity.

I scribed another email to a faceless company, pleading for my dear aunt's precious legacy, all that was left of her long life, which wasn't a lie, there wasn't anything at Heachley of hers, nothing. The email sat in my outbox ready to be sent later that evening. I punched up my latest picture and began to tweak the saturation and hue, softening my pencil strokes into a continuous blur. My two-headed monster-cum-alien morphed into a gentler child-friendly beast.

A few minutes later, I was answering the telephone yet again. The number on the display was one I recognised, but rarely heard from: Mr Porter.

The silky voice I'd heard months ago hadn't rematerialised since then. Instead Mr Porter filled the airways with a snappy business tone. 'I can assure you, Miriam, nothing of value was burnt. The men disposed of non-recyclables, damaged furniture, old mattresses, curtains. Much of it was in terrible condition. They informed me nothing was destroyed—'

'Her books? The tapestries? The Persian rugs?' I persisted, cutting through his rambling excuses with a razor acerbity.

'The books were sold to a second-hand vendor. As for the tapestries, I've no idea where your inventory comes from, but those items weren't listed on mine.'

My heart hit my breastbone in rapid succession of thumping beats. The list Charles had given me wasn't complete, he couldn't remember everything, but he'd taken me around the house, pointing out where furniture and other objects had been situated. Considering the time lapse, he'd a remarkable memory for detail.

'There were various sculptures of deities. Indian artefacts? For God's sake, they ripped out an antique oven.'

'The proceeds of the clearance was given to me as a lump sum, I've no indication of what sold individually.'

'Seriously? You didn't think to find out?'

'It had taken some time to acquire power of attorney and the nursing home bills were mounting. The clearance provided for nearly five years of fees. I can assure you, the income generated from the sale of Felicity's stuff was quite generous.'

Stuff. The word riled, as did his unsympathetic attitude. Somewhere, in amongst her things, her private letters and documents, was the address of my father. How hard had anyone tried to contact her living relatives – me, primarily? Would I have halted the clearance or happily let Mr Porter and his power of attorney take charge of the situation? With a sad realisation, I anticipated I would have shown little curiosity. More regrets. More angst at my lack of interest. The only reason I was sitting on a camper chair in a frigid, empty mansion on a cold winter's day was because Great-aunt Felicity had insisted I live here for a year and day.

'I want a list of what was sold. I don't care if you don't have one and I don't care this was five years ago. I want to know what happened to her books, her pictures, her tapestries. Just in case when I sell this place and make my fortune, I decide to buy them back.'

It was a futile reason. Whatever survived would have long ago exchanged hands, perhaps several times. The trail was dead.

'Miriam—'

I slammed the phone down.

'Miriam—'

'What?' I snarled, then leapt to my feet. 'Oh, God, sorry, Charles, I didn't mean to shout at you.'

'I've made you a coffee. Sounds like you need it.' He stood close to the kitchen door, waggling his thumb over his shoulder and I followed him in. 'I've made a start on the dining room walls. I filled the holes left behind from where the panelling had been fixed.'

With my palms flat on the granite surface and my shoulders hunched over the worktop, I cried. My tears dropped into the coffee mug, splashing into the dark liquid. I didn't know why those conversations – both with the care home manager and the solicitor – had upset me. Behind me, Charles hovered, his shoes shuffling on the floor.

He placed his hands on my arms and turned me around. I unceremoniously sobbed into his sturdy chest. I bunched my arms between us, hugging myself and burrowed my nose into his woollen jumper, expecting a waft of unsavoury body odour, instead, the pullover smelt of soap and lavender. Another surprise to digest: Charles's clothes might appear worn to death, but they were fresh and patched up. The sweet aroma tickled my nostrils and I sniffed, trying not to sneeze. Propped against him, leaning into his steady frame, I perceived underneath his ruffled exterior a sinewy brawn packed into a slender build. He'd the physique of man who neither worked out nor sat around watching TV.

Gently, and with little more than his fingertips, he patted my back. 'She wouldn't have wanted you to be upset. It would never have been her intention to see you sad. I'm sure,' he soothed.

I put aside my frustrations with the solicitor, because there was nothing I could do – water under the bridge. If Mr Porter wanted to redeem his poor form, he might instigate his own investigation into the integrity of the clearance company he'd employed, but I doubted it. After all, if he was in on a scam, why expose himself? And if he wasn't, he'd not want to admit to his apparent incompetence. I was starting to hate the man.

Finished with my ridiculous outpouring and somewhat embarrassed by my need to cry on Charles's shoulder, I eased backwards and wiped the tears from my hot cheeks. 'Stupid. I mean, it's not as if she's here.'

He plucked a rogue strand of hair out of the corner of my eye then whipped his hand away as if I'd stung him.

'No, she's not here.' He gestured about him as he spoke. 'Wouldn't it be lovely if she was? Imagine how proud she'd be of you and your achievements. She'd stand here, in this kitchen, baking her cakes or making a chicken pie, asking about your day.'

'Chicken pie? Yummy.' I rubbed my belly in a mock display of hunger at the image he created of a busy Felicity enjoying her kitchen – my kitchen.

'She kept hens in the garden.'

I raised my eyebrows. 'She did?' I took a sip from my mug of coffee – not bad given the tears it contained.

'Lots of eggs and she'd no compunction about eating the hens either. Wrung their necks when needed.' He strangled an imaginary chicken with his hands.

I flinched at his dramatic re-enactment. 'Gosh. You didn't volunteer to do it for her?'

'Me?' He laughed, tucking his hands behind his back. 'I'm a coward. She once asked me to lay snares in the woods to trap rabbits and I called her cruel.'

'Did she do it herself?'

He shook his head. 'No. She wasn't that adventurous. We planted carrots and potatoes instead.'

'Where?'

He took me out into the frosty garden after I'd drunk my coffee and along by a garden wall towards the back of the overgrown lawn was a long patch of soil covered in dead foliage; the relics of nettles and brambles. Charles kicked about and found a bamboo stick. 'For the sweet peas.'

He drove the stick into the hard ground and leaped over the weeds in an animated display of gardening expertise, gesturing here and there, as he suggested rows of onions and lettuces. I laughed at his energetic dance and he grinned back. I couldn't wait for spring and the rebirth of a vegetable patch.

TWENTY-ONE

The last week in January I woke up to a white world. During the night, the sky lowered a blanket of snow and it covered the landscape in brilliant whiteness. I first noticed the extra lightness in my bedroom as I lay waiting for my alarm clock to beep. The alarm was necessary, because without it I could happily waste the morning lying under the warm duvet. Drawing back the curtains and wiping away the veneer of condensation, I pressed my nose to the icy glass. The treetops level with the roof were swathed with a couple of inches of snow; it balanced on the branches and the smallest of twigs.

I grabbed clean clothes out of my wardrobe. The canvas armoire, which I'd bought off eBay, housed most of my day-to-day wear. Having dressed, I slipped on my pumps – bare feet in Heachley Hall was not advisable due to both the cold and the odd exposed nail jutting out of the floorboards – and I hurried downstairs to the next storey.

The master bedroom provided the best view of the back garden and I flung open the door and raced to the window. The snow lay two or three inches thick. Sufficient to hide the low-lying grasses, but not the long blades of the untended meadow that continued to smother the main terraces. However, even with the tallest fronds sticking up, the whiteout was complete. The rhododendrons had cowered under the weight – their branches bowed – and the snow had been shifted onto the ground. The trees boldly took the burden and without a nudging wind to loosen the flakes, the snow had coated every horizontal level, highlighting each branch like a marker pen. Where the snow hadn't reached, the frost had managed to paint its own silvery effect.

I stamped my cold feet on the floorboards. Behind me, the fireplace lay dormant. With the house turning into a perpetual fridge, I decided today I would light all the fires, leave the doors open and heat up the place. The Rayburn did an excellent job of keeping much of the downstairs sufficiently warm. But the first floor remained icy.

On the opposite side of the house I had a view of the front garden. To my surprise, the lane had been cleared of snow and what remained lay banked against the verges and under the hedges. Tony must have a plough attachment for his tractor and gone out early to clear the lanes around the village. Over the previous weeks, he'd often stopped by to check I wasn't freezing to death. He'd brought eggs and cheese, sometimes a gammon. Some poor pig had been sacrificed on his farm and I tried to avoid thinking about the real-life world of farming. My meat typically came from the supermarket shelves.

The snowstorm had long gone by the time I rose, and the blue skies had turned the shimmer of whiteness into a tinkling glassiness. Outlined neatly in the frozen bitten snow was the sparkling outline of footprints. They tracked up to the front door, then back to the gate. The postman had made it through to deliver the morning mail.

I bounded downstairs and scooped up the envelopes on the doormat. Two bills and a postcard from Ruth. She had spent the weekend in York with Mick. Lucky girl. Her life was on the up and I'd not seen her since Christmas, but our regular phone calls kept us close as if she was there, right next to me. I could even imagine her soothing face as she batted away my frustrations at my failure to unearth that infernal box.

Flicking the card over, I read her delight in finding her book on sale in a bookshop. She'd done an impromptu book signing for the few children present. I tucked the card behind the other letters and pursed my lips at the credit card company names embossed over the envelope windows. More money oozing out of my account. Mr Porter had seen to the utility bills, which didn't amount to much, with the exception of the heating oil for the Rayburn. He'd not answered my request for more information on the clearance. My patience wouldn't last forever.

'Hello.' Charles came out of the living room, shaking dust off his jeans. 'I've lit the fire.'

Every weekday I came downstairs to a warm room and whether Charles was there or not to greet me, it always felt as if he was somewhere in the house. If there was an opposite of cold comfort, Charles epitomised it.

'Thanks.' I followed him into the kitchen. He'd finished painting the dining room, including the ceiling and completed the laborious task of gouging out the rotten wood from the window frame and applying wood filler. He planned to paint the frames. He'd also sanded down and revarnished the mantelpiece. As usual he came and went in his unregulated fashion and my constant need for firewood kept him busy chopping wood.

I laid the letters on the worktop and pointed out the window. 'Beautiful, isn't it?'

'Yes,' he murmured, shoving his hands in his pockets. His pale complexion seemed whiter than I'd previously seen. He must have walked to Heachley in the thick snow wearing his silly boots. Poor man. I blinked and gazed out the window at the footprints formed in the snow; the postman had left those marks. Where were Charles's?

I pivoted on the balls of my toes and faced him, folding my arms across my chest.

'What?' He slipped his hands out of his pockets and he rocked back on his heels.

'What time did you get here?'

He shrugged. 'Not long.'

'So why can't I see your footprints in the snow?'

His shoulders snapped backwards as if I'd struck him and he swallowed hard; his Adam's apple bulged in his neck. 'I didn't come that way,' he stuttered.

'Oh, what other way is there?' I tapped my foot on the floor. 'Charles?'

He gestured with his head. 'I'll show you.'

I followed him to the back door and he opened it. Down the side of the house, leading back and forth to the outbuildings, were footprints. Layered over each other, they'd trampled down the snow into a mushy mess of mud and powdery flakes. Some of the prints led off into the wood. 'I've been chopping wood and lighting the fire.'

'Yes. I know. So you let yourself in by the back door, but where is the path from the front?'

'There isn't one.' He shut the door and leaned his back against it. 'I come through the woods.'

'Every time you come here or just when the weather is bad?'

'Always. It's the easiest route and most direct.'

'I don't understand.'

He puffed out his lips. 'I'm sorry. I should have said. I live over there' – he gestured with a thumb over his shoulder—'the other side of the wall. It's crumbled in places and I climb over. It saves me coming around the long way.'

'I see. You don't have a bicycle? Wouldn't that help?'

'I prefer to walk.'

'In the rain? The howling wind?'

He guffawed, 'I don't think it makes much difference on a bicycle and anyway, the woods give me shelter. It's a nice walk and I enjoy it.'

'You live towards Docking?' Could he not say for once?

'Kind of.'

I walked back into the kitchen and filled the kettle. The urn had been demoted to under the counter and no longer needed. Charles sloped in behind me, a deep frown on his face. 'I'll get back to—'

'Have you been a prisoner, locked up for something? Is that the reason why you don't like to say anything about your life outside of Heachley?'

He'd stuff his hands back in his pockets and returned to examining the floor. 'No, Miriam, I have not been in gaol.'

'I could understand, wanting to keep that part of your life secret, then making a fresh start.'

He repeated his declaration, the second time, he looked straight at me and I flinched as those pale eyes drilled me.

'Right. No prison. So, you're ashamed of your upbringing, something like that?' I persisted, leaning on the counter.

He shook his head. 'My parents are gone, like yours. My brother emigrated and he's estranged. It's just me.'

'You, on your own, in a house somewhere nearby, and you walk across the fields, climb over my wall and traipse through my woods to paint walls for me?'

A smile slipped over his tense expression and his eyebrows lifted. 'In a nutshell.'

'Why? You're a bright man. Why haven't you got a decent job?' He shrivelled again, the shoulders drooping under my interrogation. He edged backwards, as if he wanted to charge out of the door. I held up my hand, signalling him to halt. 'Please, Charles, I don't want to make you uncomfortable. I'm trying to understand.'

'There really isn't anything to understand. I don't need much. My ambitions don't lie far away. I don't want to line my pockets with money. Is that hard to accept?'

Yes, dammit, because I coveted owning mansion and the million or so quid it represented. The secrets of his life placed him at a constant emotional distance from me and I hated the implication I might never know him better. Something about him forced me to keep up my questions. 'And you don't want me to know where you live?'

'It's not necessary, is it?'

'I could give you a lift home.'

'I like walking,' he reiterated, his voice hardening.

'In the snow?'

'In the snow. Do you like driving in the snow?' He parried, crossing his arms and mirroring my own stance.

It terrified me. My little car had no ability to hold the road in icy conditions, never mind the snow. I'd already told him I'd nearly slid off the road on the way into Little Knottisham. My reticence to answer his question showed: I gnawed my lips.

'Why do you come here, Charles?' I pleaded.

He reached up and ran his hands through his dark locks of hair, flicking them away from his pale face. 'I came for work, originally, yes. It's what I do: gardening, carpentry. Now, I don't know. If I'm being honest, I keep coming back because I can't help it, and...' he ducked his head and I lost sight of his translucent eyes. 'I have to be with you.'

'Be with me,' I whispered, my pulse raced, a syncopated thrumming in my ears. 'Are you coming on to me?'

He raised his head. His eyebrows knitted together. 'Coming on to you?' he queried.

'Is this some long drawn out chat up?'

He stepped backwards again. My harrying of his personal life seemed to strip away his confidence. I'd not seen him stumble so much over his words before now.

'I want to help you. Felicity would have approved.'

'Have to be with me?' I reminded him.

'Poor choice of words. I meant to imply, I'm obligated to help you because of my friendship with Felicity.'

His tune changed once again. Now, he'd dragged in my aunt as an excuse. My belly knotted itself with butterflies: it bothered me. I preferred the implication it was entirely down to me.

'She's gone. You didn't even visit her in the home, so why care now?'

'I tried. I would have. I don't have a car and...'

'Tony would have taken you. They visited.'

Charles's lips thinned into a line. 'I'm not friends with them, especially her.'

'Liz? Why not?' I harried.

He screwed his face into a barrel of frustration, then released a muffled exhale as he unscrewed it, dropping his arms at the same with an audible snap to his sides. 'For heaven's sake, Miriam, it's personal. That's the whole point of this conversation. I have a private life and it has nothing to do with you. Now, do you want me to paint the window frame or not?'

I huffed, 'I'm not sure what I want you to do.' I'd forgotten my coffee. I yanked open the fridge door and poured a generous helping of milk into the mug. The liquid overflowed and slopped over the side onto the granite. I closed my eyes. I couldn't believe I was on the verge of dismissing him. The realisation frightened me. Most weekdays he kept me company for a few hours. Having him around was a comfort and I'd grown accustomed to his inconstant visits in the house and I relished them, bundling up each and every instance, no matter how brief or inconsequential, into some kind of goodwill package to keep and hold on to in the stillness of the empty house. No, he couldn't leave.

'I'm sorry. You're right. It's none of my business. I'm so wrapped up with work and the mystery of Felicity. I've not heard from Eva Kendal, the owners of Beechwood or effing Porter in ages, and I feel isolated.'

'Perhaps you need a break. Some time in Chelmsford.'

I laughed. 'In a warm house, yes and a hot steaming shower.'

'A shower, yes, very nice,' he murmured. 'So, the window frames?'

The tensioned between us had swiftly thawed, unlike the snow outside. 'If they're not covered in dew.' The windows dripped condensation most mornings and recently, the watery film had frozen into sheets of ice through which light danced, projecting shadowy fractals around the room.

'If they are, then I'll replace the dodgy floorboard in the bedroom upstairs, instead.' The creakiest rotten boards had been targeted and those that could be reused he hammered back down, others had to be replaced and he'd shaped the boards from planks of oak he harvested from the woods. It had saved me the cost of the timber.

'Thank you,' I held the mug in my hands, its warmth unnecessary – the heated conversation had driven up my body temperature.

He edged towards the door. 'I'll find the paint—'

'I left it in the dining room. Too cold in your shed, it would spoil. You must be impervious to the cold.' I'd more than once offered him the opportunity to use a downstairs room to do his carpentry, but he'd politely declined each time. The man was beyond infuriating with his evasiveness and steadfast determination not to breach the interior beyond the necessary.

'Hardened. Another reason to keep busy. Keeps me warm.' He grinned, a half-hearted attempt at humour. I listened to his footsteps on the hallway tiles. That job he'd meticulously finished earlier in the month and to a high standard. When I'd paid him, he'd rolled the notes into a ball, before stuffing them in his back pocket. Why did it seem like I paid for him to be at my beck and call?

That wasn't fair. Charles was a craftsman, not a Casanova. He didn't care for me that much. It had to be guilt, something to do with Felicity and he was covering it up.

I had to chase up Eva and Dominion Estates. I needed that elusive box to have the answers.

The wind picked up during the night and the snow slid down the roof, flying off with a whoosh. Having been woken by the noise, any attempt at going back to sleep was interrupted by flashes of Charles' face.

What bound him to Heachley wasn't an employment contract or an obligation based on guaranteed employment; I made it up as I went along. It dawned on me that what troubled me was that he might simply not turn up one day. He deserved a better paid job and working conditions, and I wouldn't be able to stop him if he walked away. What if he did? Without his help, how would I tackle the list of things that needed doing? I tossed around, curled into a foetal position, and buried my head under the covers.

Again, the snow moved and landed with a thud below. The unhappy house groaned with the burden of winter on its tiles and chimney pots. The chance for sleep faded further.

Charles Donaldson – the handsome introvert who plagued my wakefulness – seemed reticent to tell me anything substantial about my great-aunt. I'd teased a few facts out of him – her eccentricity and love of India – but he hadn't actually provided me with much depth or understanding of her psyche. Perhaps I'd gifted him with too much knowledge. He was just the handyman-cum-gardener, and why would he understand her motives for bequeathing this place to me? Charles's thirst for information remained focused on distant countries and cultures, and it had been those subjects he'd prised out of Felicity's library.

We had our own particular conversations. When I needed a break, I'd often sought him out in one of the rooms where he laboured to fill cracks or replaced rotten floor or skirting boards. Slowly and methodically he worked, and in the background his radio blared. If he wasn't listening to Radio 4 or the classical music stations, he chose Jazz FM.

'Who's that playing?' I'd asked on more than one occasion and he answered without hesitation.

'You like jazz, why?'

'It doesn't clutter my mind with emotions, rather it keeps me company without impeding.'

I'd taken that to mean I was unwelcome. 'Sorry.' I'd backed towards the door.

He held up his hand and the signal halted me. 'No, not you. My own thoughts impede. Things I care to forget.'

'Oh.' What things? I'd murmured to myself, but I never asked him.

His mental stimulation came in other forms – quiz shows or debates: I yawned at that kind of endless droning. Once I'd marched in on him listening to Woman's Hour. He'd shown no embarrassment when I queried his tastes.

'Felicity liked it,' he'd shrugged.

So much of what Charles spoke about was confined to the world according to Felicity.

I started in bed and the covers fell off my shoulders. He was her love child, was that it? It proved to be momentarily idea that failed to blossom when I pictured his face – the supreme pale skin, brown hair and translucent eyes – all of which were at odds with Felicity's mixed ethnicity. Why if he'd been her son had she not left Heachley to him? I slumped back down and yanked the duvet back under my chin. A stupid idea.

A spine tingling creak. The eerie low squeal was followed by a long drawn out scraping sound. Was something being dragged along the wooden boards?

I inhaled sharply, held my breath and slowly opened my eyes wide.

The faint trace of moonlight offered little assistance. Another solitary creak – shorter and shriller – even more like a squeak.

I sat again, but slowly, drawing myself up on my elbows. I concentrated hard on listening. Again, the isolated creak. Not in my room, but close by and unlike the wind outside that buffeted and whistled in a random fashion. The sound indoors possessed rhythm – footsteps?

The wind paused, heralding the onset of silence – the creaking had ceased. Regardless of my anxieties, I had to investigate.

Sticking my legs out, my heels then toes touched the rug. I rose, reached out with my hands, and hunted for the door handle. I stubbed my toe on something, and hopping about, I cursed under my breath. I needed light. Back tracking, I crashed into the bedside table before fumbling for the lamp switch.

The spotlight blinded me. I waited for my pupils to shrink. Gradually, I refocused on the attic bedroom. The source of my stubbing was evident – I'd tripped on a boot. I kicked the offending item under my bed. Facing the door once again, I listened. Nothing – not a peep.

I squeezed the door handle with my trembling hand, nudged the door open and poked my head out. Peering around the small landing that separated the two rooms, I jumped. A dark figure greeted me.

I groaned, 'Idiot.' Clutching my hand to my chest, I inhaled slowly: the light behind me had cast my shadow against the wall opposite.

I lowered my eyes and my attention was drawn to the floor just outside the bedroom door. I crouched and ran my finger along the wooden board. White dust coated the tip of my forefinger. The same ash like substance that came and went all about the house. It formed a trail from my door towards the staircase. Switching on the landing light, I tracked the dust downstairs, then into Felicity's bedroom. Flicking on the light switch, I entered. There the trail stopped, the powdery particles had spread themselves around until they disappeared into the cracks between the boards.

Squatting on my haunches, I searched for footprints, something to identify the source of the residue. Lightning flashed about the room, the air crackled with electricity and my scalp fizzed with static.

I leapt to my feet and the onslaught of cold air triggered a bout of shivers. Outside, a gust of wind rushed towards the house and from above, a bank of snow cascaded off the roof, blanketing the window with a shower of whiteness. Simultaneously, the force of the squall smashed the snow against the pane and high in the sky, thunder cracked. I tottered backwards. The draught swirled around my ankles, picking up the dust and billowing it upwards into a cloud. Behind me, the door slammed shut.

I screeched, then I held my breath. From out of the silence came a solitary pop and the light went out. The power had failed.

The darkness swathed, impenetrable, rather similar to the glutinous cellar air. I froze and only my heartbeats drummed in my ears. Snatching a trembling breath, I softly panted and slowly stretched out my arms, daring to explore the pitch-black space.

For those seconds of darkness, I believed in ghosts. They surrounded me, those invisible phantoms who haunted and put fear into the minds of sane people. They were there with me. How many? Who were they? Whoever I'd imagined, they had to be the cause of the sudden onset of my unexpected terror. What else could make my body shake and my brain freeze, but the spirits of the dead? I snatched back my hands, fearful something would grab at them, pull me into, what? An abyss? A void?

'Felicity?' I murmured. 'Is that you?' Wretched silence greeted my strange question. Not even the wind or the house uttered a noise; nothing bothered to reply.

Seconds of paralysing inactivity, which felt a lot longer, the light flickered back on. I blinked, desperately seeking focus. I spun around and checked I was alone. The room was empty. Combing my fingers through my tangled hair, I groaned my relief, hoping it might displace the ridiculous pummelling of my heartbeats and shallow pants of breaths

'What the hell is the matter with me? I don't believe in ghosts.' Felicity was gone and why would she haunt here anyway? I waited for some semblance of calmness to embolden me. 'I don't believe in ghosts,' I repeated through gritted teeth.

With a firm grasp I snatched at the door handle and threw the door open. I stomped upstairs, back to my little room and burrowed under the duvet.

'I'm going nuts.' Charles was right; I had to spend the weekend at Chelmsford. The sooner the better.

TWENTY-TWO

Ruth poured over the drawings laid out on her dining room table. While she perused, tapping her finger on her lips and nodding repetitively, I nervously waited for her appraisal. She might be my friend, but during those moments, she was my client, too.

'Well?' I broke the silence. 'I've not gone overboard on the colours, have I?'

She shook her head. 'They're perfect.'

I slumped into a nearby chair and puffed out my lips. 'Thank God. I'm up to here—' I levelled my hand with my nose '—with work. What with my monsters, the new project with robots, now clowns. I'm spinning around.'

Ruth offered a smile of encouragement. 'Don't fret. I'll show these to my editor. We'll discuss how to layout the text, then update you with any changes needed.'

My mobile bleeped. I'd connected to Ruth's Wi-Fi to download my emails. Most had been sent in the last couple of days. I scanned down the list. One in particular caught my eye and I bolted upright in my seat.

'What is it?' Ruth asked, collecting up the pieces of paper scattered across the table.

'This Dominion Estates who own Beechwood, they've replied to my email.'

She paused in her gathering. 'And?'

I squinted at the small text. 'We apologise for the delay in reply—'

'Nice of them.'

'We can confirm we have no property belonging to Twilight Care Homes, nor any of Beechwood's former residents. Any assets were stripped out by Twilight Care Homes upon termination of their lease.' I scrolled down the screen.

'Did you really think Dominion had anything?'

'No. Why would the landlord keep things left behind by a bunch of geriatrics? Oh okay, listen to this, they confirm the contractors refitting the building should have contacted Twilight before disposing of any unidentified items found.'

Ruth perched on the edge of the table and folded her arms. 'Contractors?'

'Yeah, seems the place has been taken over by another care provider. Dominion Estates has no involvement with refitting as long as it falls within the scope of the lease, blah-dee-blah. Regards, mister so and so.'

'So, you're back to blasted Twilight again.'

I pocketed my mobile and my head lolled forward. It was a road to nowhere. I had to face the fact Felicity's last possessions on this Earth were gone. What a sad state to live to ninety and have nothing to show for all those wonderful years of life.

Ruth snorted, 'Mr Porter—'

I wanted to ring the solicitor's neck, instead I held up my hand. 'Don't go there. He's gone into hiding and not replying to any of my emails.'

'Eva?'

Another fruitless avenue of enquiry. 'Nothing either and I don't want to hassle the woman. What's the point? I don't think she gives a damn.'

Ruth slid into the dining chair next to me. 'Try a different tactic.'

'Meaning?'

'Heachley has a history, one that's probably recorded in newspapers and letters. If Felicity had any secrets to tell, then perhaps, so did somebody else.'

'I suppose.' I wasn't convinced. Everybody told me Felicity had lived a life of a recluse.

'Try the local library.'

The idea warmed over the rest of the weekend. The combination of a hot shower, a delicious lunch with Ruth and watching a movie with a bottle of wine had a magical effect on my motivation. Driving back to Heachley Hall on Sunday, the traffic was unusually heavy, and the long journey provided me with the opportunity to plan my investigation and the robots, too.

There were no hushed tones in Hunstanton library.

Shaking the droplets of rain off my coat, the first sound to greet me was the shriek of a small child. In the middle of the children's corner was a toddler dismembering the contents of a large box. Each picture book he extracted with his grasping hands landed on a tottering heap. The little boy's mother sat on her bottom by the box, staring blankly at her mobile phone. Her eyelids drooped while her fingers fluttered over the screen. She jerked her head up and popped her eyes open wider. She dropped the phone into her lap and raked her fingers through her hair; the shiny nails glinted under the lights. Pressing her palms into her shadowy eyes, she shook her head.

'No, Flynn.' She scooped up the books and attempted to rearrange them in the box. Snotty nose Flynn screeched and proceeded to snatch books out of the box as fast as his mother could put them back. The tears added to the streams of mucus puddling on his chin and upper lip, and the viscous threads dripped into the box. I cringed, my sympathy stretching out to those books, which an author had spent hours lovingly constructing into a literary adventure, only to have them turned into a breeding ground for contagious bugs.

In the opposite corner sprawled on a beanbag armchair was an elderly man clutching a walking stick with marble knuckles. His head lolled to one side, slack jawed in his dream world. A spot of drool on the corner of his lip waited for release. His stuttering snores collided with the whoops of Flynn and the futile admonishments of his exasperated mother and blended into a peculiar orchestration. How quickly I'd become accustomed to a different kind of silence.

The librarian ignored the noise. Her nose was inches away from her computer monitor and the forefinger of her right hand occasionally stabbed at the keyboard.

I cleared my throat. 'Excuse me—'

'Oh, yes, hello.' She rolled her chair back, her smile broadening. 'How can I help?'

'I'm not sure.' What the hell was I looking for anyway? 'I'm researching the history of a house and its occupants. It's called Heachley Hall and I'm wondering if you have anything about the local history.'

She pursed her lips and clucked her tongue on her roof of her mouth. 'Not heard of Heachley. There's a small collection of publications covering Hunstanton and the local area.'

She directed me to a lower shelf in the Reference section. I crouched to inspect the contents of a box: a few thin books on King's Lynn and the history of Norfolk, other pamphlets on county life, farming and a couple on Norwich. What did I expect, a treasure trove of information waiting to be unearthed?

I thumbed the corners of the booklets.

'Sorry,' the librarian said, 'not much, I know. If you want more things, like family history, you'll need to visit the county archives in Norwich. They'd have newspapers on microfilm, birth and death certificates, local businesses, so on.'

'I naively hoped there would be something about Heachley. There was a big fire there once, a hundred or so years ago.'

'I suggest you look for newspaper reports then. Sorry, I've only lived in the area for a couple of years. I don't know much about local history.' She backed away. 'You can check what's available on the computer, over there.'

The small bank of computers lined one wall. 'Thanks.'

Left to my own devices, I placed the box on a table, and flicked through the small selection of publications, most of which had not made into a hardback format, or even a decent binding.

I nearly missed it: an A5 sized booklet made from thin paper, almost like tissues except glossy. With a simple cover and title – *Hunstanton's War* – and a picture of an observation post, it came to no more than fifty pages or so. There were several short articles written about the various experiences of people living in and around Hunstanton during the Second World War. The first was told by a farmer near Docking, who had a German fighter plane crash into one of his fields. Another described the impact of labour shortage on farming and the role of the Land Girls.

Towards the back of the booklet I spotted the photograph. In black and white, as with all the pictures in the publication, the house was easily recognisable with its small turrets on top of the gables. The caption beneath read, *Heachley Hall, Royal Observers Corp Station.*

I grabbed a nearby chair, perched on it and poured over it. The brief article had been written by somebody who'd been stationed at the house. However, as I read, it was apparent much of his recollections were not about Heachley, although those who worked there had admired the tranquillity, rather the author described the camaraderie and role of the Corp.

Two names stood out in the text: Hubert Marsters – the landlord, who'd leased the house for the duration of the war and had lived in India before dying fighting the Japanese in 1943 in Burma – and his son John, who continued the leasing arrangement.

I stroked my finger across the two names: my grandfather and great-grandfather. There was nothing else revealed or hinted at in the article. The house had served a purpose and done its duty. Scanning through the start of the pamphlet I checked for the name of an editor and publication date. Apart from individual names in the articles, the overarching author was the *Historical Society of Hunstanton and Docking.* The publication date: 1957. Examining the photograph, I wondered if it had been taken in the 1950s at the time of the article or during the war. The branches of the trees were bare, the chimneys were devoid of puffing smoke and the gardens in a decent state.

I scanned the picture and article using the library's computer and copied the file to a flash memory stick that I carried in my handbag.

'Found anything?' the librarian asked, coming to stand alongside my chair.

'Yes, a photograph and an article.' I showed her the booklet. 'That's my house.'

'Yours?' she exclaimed.

Explanations were too complicated and I brushed over them. 'Yes, kind of,' I stammered. I turned back to the monitor. 'I'm trying to find out if this historical society still exists or if there are other publications by it.'

The librarian, her curiosity roused, which didn't surprise me given her usual clientele were either asleep or dismantling her displays, helped me search, but we found nothing.

Glancing at my watch, I sighed. 'I have to go soon. Perhaps I should go to Norwich.'

The librarian agreed and went to fetch me a leaflet about the library services there. While she hunted through her desk drawer, I perused the shelves, picking up novels – when did I have time to read? I selected a couple of lightweight romances, then spied a macabre cover: a raven on a clawed hand – a ghost story, according to the blurb on the back.

'Here, you go.' The librarian handed me the leaflet. 'Taking those?'

'These two, but I'm not sure about this one.' I held up the ghost book.

'It's a good read, I gather. Full of suspense.'

I chuckled, 'Probably not a wise choice for me. Some say the house I'm living in is haunted.'

Her eyes sprung wider and she leaned forward on the desk. 'How exciting. Have you seen anything? People walking through walls, objects moving?'

I almost mentioned the missing cellar bolt, then I decided it was trivial. Nothing else had disappeared or moved, but there again, my house was somewhat devoid of objects. 'No. I don't believe in haunted houses. The previous occupant, my great-aunt, died elsewhere and before that, lots of people lived in the house.'

'Is that why you're interested in the house?'

'More because I want to know why my aunt stayed there and who lived there in the past.'

'Perhaps she is bound to it,' the librarian's spoke softly, which was unnecessary; there was nobody within earshot. The mother and child had vacated the premises while I'd been busy scanning and the elderly man hadn't moved from his seat. 'Powers that keep her there, even after death.' The librarian's voice wobbled. She was twice my age, at least, with dark hair and a collection of rings on her fingers, which clattered on the keyboard. Mascara laden eyelashes ringed her blue eyes, and she blinked sharply, as if surprised by her own hissing pronouncement. Her words came across as melodramatic, somewhat over the top. I clutched the books tight to my belly and hid my shaking fingers. Did my trembling signify fear or annoyance?

'What do you mean?' I glanced over my shoulder at the sleeping gent and he snorted, jolting himself awake. For a few seconds, he scratched his head, disturbing the few wisps of grey hair sprouting from his balding scalp.

'Well,' she whispered, 'your aunt might have died elsewhere, but her spirit could have been called back to haunt the house.'

I loosened my grip on the books, slid them across the desk towards her, while wishing I hadn't mentioned anything about the house. 'Except, the house is quite innocuous.' Another lie. Heachley Hall spoke to me every day, chatting away with its creaks and groans, the odd door slamming, the layer of dust that drifted from room to room. I went into denial whenever anyone implied I lived in a haunted house.

She held the bar scanner to the back of the ghost book.

'Not that one, please.' I snatched it back, putting it to one side. 'Don't have time to read three,' I added lamely.

After I'd gathered up my things, my handbag and books, I stepped out into the rain. I could eat lunch in town or head back to Heachley Hall. The choice was easy – a small cafe would suffice. One thing Charles never bothered with was lunchtime and if he wasn't there to share his lunch with me, then I'd enjoy a meal out.

'So, the house was let to the Observer Corps during the war,' I informed Charles when I returned home later in the day. He was applying putty to the edges of a drawing room windowpane. The air reeked of linseed oil. My assaulted nose spontaneously wrinkled and I stifled a sneeze with the back of my hand. He carried out the task with remarkable ease and skill; pushing his thumb into the putty, while leaving even amounts spread along the edge of the wooden frame. Until I came to Heachley, I'd never lived in a house that didn't have sealed metal units.

'And you read this in a booklet in the library?' Charles asked. He rolled a small amount of putty between his fingertips to warm it. In the background the radio played softly, floating a voiceless melody across the room. He'd plugged it in on the far wall.

'Yes.' His lack of interest in my discovery surprised me, but there again, perhaps Felicity had told him about how the hall was used during the war. Maybe, she'd had a copy of the pamphlet on her bookshelves and he'd read it himself.

Before I could ask, he shot a glance over his shoulder. 'What else did you find out?'

I sighed, heavily with puffed cheeks. 'Not a lot. I should go to Norwich and visit the library there, they might have more information.'

'What are you hoping to find?'

His reflection in the windowpane showed his eyes narrowing to form letterbox slits. I moved closer to the window and inhaled the potent aroma of linseed. Opening up to Charles had become easier over time; he seemed genuinely interested in my situation and often encouraged me with ideas for improving the house, especially when my mood darkened and I lost sight of the end-point: selling the place.

'Since I can't find Felicity's secrets here, I thought I might find out more about the house and its previous occupants. The librarian recommended the archives in Norwich, but when do I have the time? I've deadlines to meet.' I couldn't afford the charges either and would have to do the research myself.

Bending over the windowsill, he hunched his shoulders and bowed his head, hiding his face away from the reflective properties of the window. 'Secrets?'

'The contents of her box. Frankly, I think it was chucked away and nobody has it in them to admit to it. By nobody, I mean Eva Kendal.'

'It's becoming an obsession, that box.'

'You reckon.' I scoffed. It had, but then so had Heachley and the need to earn my fortune. 'It fills my time between drawing pictures of tin can robots.'

'No more two-headed monsters?' He picked up the knife and began to smooth the putty, focusing in on his task.

'I'm taking a break—'

The rapping of a distant knock interrupted.

'Hell-oo,' the woman's voice sang through the hallway. Charles' shoulders stiffened again and the knife skidded across the putty, scoring a line into it.

Liz Pyke appeared in the doorway. 'I'm sorry, the back door was open. I tried to ring but you couldn't have heard the bell.'

The Wellington boots were spotless. Green with an adjustable strap, they probably were the most expensive boots available. The tweed coat, the silk scarf draped around her neck and fedora hat, which had a fur velour finish – unlike my woollen knitted style – added to the country woman profile. The attire shouted money, which I didn't associate with agricultural living. What little news I read about rural life showed farmers struggling to make money, but here was Liz looking the part of the squire's wife.

Detecting the pervasive smell of putty, she scrunched her nose up and halted by the door. 'I'm intruding. Clearly you two are busy talking, so sorry.' Her apology grated, because her voice had an insincere flavour to it.

Charles, his nostrils twitching, remained by my side with rigid limbs. Gripping the putty knife, his knuckles turned white. He detested Liz Pyke – his body language shouted it. I stood between them and almost expected him to shout abuse at her. He'd refused to explain the reason for the acrimony and if I were to insist and demand an answer, would he stay or quit?

'Would you like a tea or a coffee?' I asked Liz.

'Oh, neither. I stopped by to see if you needed anything. We've plenty of eggs. Always eggs.' She rolled her eyes up into the brim of her hat.

'A dozen would be fine.' I didn't need that many, but it felt rude to decline her gift.

'I'll go get them out of the car.'

Before leaving the room, I dispatched a swift smile to Charles, but he'd already turned away to face the window. Eggs clearly didn't interest him. I followed her to the front and she opened the boot of her RAV-4. On the back shelf were rows of egg boxes.

'Don't you sell them?' I asked, accepting the egg box.

'These are too small. All they want is large ones.'

Who 'they' were, she didn't reveal. She slammed the car door shut and hovered, glancing about the grounds. 'Grass has grown very long,' she remarked.

'Around the back is horrendous. I've no idea how I'm going to cut it.' The back lawn was officially a wilderness and a breeding ground for mice and rats. The problem was escalating up my to-do list and would only deteriorate further once the spring arrived.

'Cut it?' She set off at a pace, around the side of the house and into the back garden. She knew where she was going, and I traipsed behind, clutching the egg box to my chest. With her hands on her hips and legs astride, she stood by the dwarf wall that marked the boundary of the top terrace. She reminded me of a general surveying an army. I smothered a grin; she'd make a great caricature and I mentally painted those exaggerated expressions, then filed away the image for future projects.

'I wondered about a scythe—'

'Good grief, Miriam, you'll be here for years using that. I'll speak to Tony.'

'Tony?'

'He has a contract with the local authority for trimming hedgerows and verges. He's got all the equipment. He could get the tractor around the back if he went around this side.' She pointed towards the spacious area where the demolished wing had stood.

'The woods impede on other side.' She spun around and grimaced at the encroaching trees. 'These ought to be chopped down.'

'There's a preservation order on the woods.'

'Not this close to the house,' she declared. 'The boundary for the preservation order covers the acreage of Heachley Woods, but not the gardens. Felicity let the new saplings grow and did nothing to curtail the existing trees. They practically overhang the house. She never wanted anything done to this place. So much potential wasted.'

I wanted to put the eggs down. My hands were shaking, both from the cold and the raw energy that burst along my nerves. 'Potential?' How did Liz know all this stuff about Heachley?

'Oh yes. Can't you picture it?' Her face lit up and she stretched out her arms, as if to embrace the gardens. 'The soil is excellent quality for farming. The far end is hardly visible from the house and to the side, where the wood has overgrown, it could be cleared and made into decent fields. Then you would be left with a copse for game. Specialist butchers would buy up wood pigeon and pheasant, not forgetting muntjac.'

I gawped, unable to stop her enthusiastic description.

'Then, the house. Turn it into a lucrative bed and breakfast. Think of all those tourists in the summer who visit the beaches, they'd love this place.' Her arms dropped to her sides and she stuck her chin out from under her hat. Her eyes remained hidden from view under the brim. 'When exactly will this place go up for sale?'

I snapped my jaw shut. Such a mercenary attitude and it jarred badly. My lips trembled, and I couldn't speak. For those few seconds, she reminded me of Mr Bridge, who'd eyed up the abandoned mansion with pounds signs imprinted on his eyeballs – at least that would have been the way I'd drawn him in a cartoon. Liz showed the same eagerness to see Heachley transformed into something intolerable: a boutique hotel or a grotesque shooting range for the local wildlife, or an extension of a farm – what else?

My stance thawed. 'Later in the year,' I squeezed out the words through gritted teeth. The effrontery of the woman, breezing in, warming me up with eggs and Tony's good nature, then alluding to her designs. How could she afford to buy Heachley?

'She should have sold it years ago.' The bitterness in Liz's voice hung in the air between us. She had an agenda which I hadn't anticipated and I'd wrongly assumed she was Felicity's friend. What she wanted was Heachley Hall and its land.

I came close to telling her to get lost, to leave my property. But the swaying grasses caught my eye. She'd offered to cut it for nothing and I needed it done. I inhaled, plastered a fake smile on my face. 'Probably. She couldn't look after it on her own.'

She paced along the flagstones. 'We tried, Tony and I, to make her see sense, but she was a stubborn old battleaxe. Glenda and Bert didn't help. Always giving her what she wanted – help with the shopping, deliveries and Maggie, too. She worked for nothing most of the time.'

'Felicity was fortunate.' My lips twitched with the pressure of maintaining that smile.

'Then there was Charles,' she spat his name out and glared at the house. I looked at the drawing room window, expecting Charles to be stood there with the putty knife observing our little chat, but he wasn't.

'Charles?' I queried, my lips drooping slightly.

Liz's prim face with its powdered cheeks twisted into a scowl. 'I'd forgotten about him. I bet he whispered in her ear, I'm sure of it.'

'He's just the handyman. The gardener, you said.'

'Just – there's a lot of misunderstanding in that simple word. He'd a hold on her, I'm convinced of it, now that he's here again. It's reminded me things are not what they appear around Heachley. Watch your back, Miriam. Felicity fell, remember?' Liz spoke with a crazed conviction, as if a cascade of thoughts tumbled into her mind one after the other without much reasoning.

I folded my arms, determined not to be bowled away by her ramblings. 'Tony said it was an accident.'

'That's what Maggie said, but she never saw it happen and Tony, who's not one for stirring up muddy waters, didn't have the courage to ask how she came to fall.'

'This is ridiculous. If Felicity had been hurt by somebody, why wouldn't she say?'

'Because,' Liz hissed, placing her back to the house, 'she was afraid.'

'Of what?' I wasn't exactly sure what Liz was trying to imply.

'This house,' she gestured over her shoulder, 'It wouldn't let her go. A colourful woman who lived an exciting life in India turned into a recluse. Doesn't it seem odd to you? There's rumours about this house.'

Finally, she touched on something that intrigued me. 'And Charles, what about him?'

Liz shrugged, throwing up her arms. 'A malingering type. One who latches on to old folk and milks them for money.'

I laughed, unable to agree to the idea of Charles showing interest in money. I had to thrust the notes into his hands when I paid him. 'I doubt he's interested. He comes and goes and doesn't stay too long.'

Liz snorted, stuffed her hands in her coat pockets and cocked her head towards the garden. 'So, the grass. Would you like Tony to come by?'

'Oh yes, please,' I forced the muscles in my face to respond and the smile returned.

The moment her car left the drive I raced back into the warmth of the house. Liz had entered the house on her own, creeping quietly enough for us not hear her approach. What had she heard Charles and I talk about – Felicity, her secrets, the box that Liz herself had retrieved and took to the nursing home five years ago? Had she looked inside it? Who wouldn't resist peeking inside a mysterious box? She mentioned documents and photographs; she must have sneaked a peep.

The light flashed on the telephone, a red spotlight frantically blinking: I'd a missed call. I'd left the unit on a pile of directories abandoned on the floor. The last number I'd dialled remained my failed attempted to reach Eva Kendal earlier in the morning. I scrolled up to retrieve a list of incoming numbers from the caller display: the most recent caller I didn't recognise. It had occurred during my trip to the library.

Slowly, I set the phone down and chewed on my lip.

'Miriam? Is there a problem?' Charles stood over by the kitchen door, wiping his hands on a tea towel. 'What did Liz want?'

I passed him and entered the kitchen, depositing the egg box on worktop. The smell of linseed followed behind with Charles. 'Were she and Felicity friends?'

He guffawed. 'Felicity hated her.'

I slumped against the windowsill. All this new information confused me and seeing the peculiar spark of animosity in Charles's eyes came as a surprise. 'Hated. That's a strong word. I thought given she and Tony visited Felicity when she fell ill that they were friends.'

'Liz represents everything Felicity hated about Little Knottisham.' With a sudden snap of his wrist, he tossed the tea towel onto the Rayburn and it flew across the hot plates and came to rest in a heap.

I straightened up. Drip-feeding me information was becoming an irritating practice of Charles. 'Rumour-mongering and the like?'

'No, not so much that, although what community doesn't suffer from gossip.' He waved his hand dismissively through the air. 'No. What Felicity saw in Liz Pyke is somebody who believes she is above everyone else. The pillar of society.'

'The squire's wife,' I mumbled.

'Yes, exactly.' Charles had excellent hearing. 'Liz wants this place.'

'I know. She told me outside she couldn't wait for the auction. How can she afford to buy Heachley?'

'Liz has the money. The Watkins, her family, have owned the farm and surrounding land for generations. Tony married Liz because her father had no sons to run the farm. She is dripping in money. He, from what Felicity told me, lacks the ambition of Liz. She will stop at nothing to get this place. And, unfortunately, I don't know if you can stop her, unless… well, it doesn't matter what I think.' From anger to despair, and now with his luminous eyes, he almost seemed desperate to convince me that Felicity never wanted this outcome.

I slumped against the worktop. 'Felicity told you this?'

'Yes. This isn't the first time Liz has tried to buy Heachley. She pestered your aunt. Kept turning up on the pretext of asking for cakes and badgered her, promising Felicity a fair price and a chance to retire somewhere smaller.'

'And Felicity said no.'

'Each and every time.'

I shook my head, disgusted at Liz's tactics. 'Felicity was eighty odd and Liz visits the nursing home until… That's why she stopped going to see Felicity.'

'Why?' Charles's eyebrows shot higher.

'After the stroke, Porter obtained power of attorney because Felicity couldn't communicate her wishes. Liz probably gave up visiting because she'd no way of persuading Felicity to change her mind.'

'And Mr Porter?'

'Now, that would be interesting if Liz tried to influence him, encourage him to put it up for auction and not find me? Surely he had Felicity's interests at heart – the will is clear. I have the choice when it comes to the future of this place, nobody else.'

'A year and a day. She wants you to live here so you are discouraged from putting the house up for sale and Liz can't acquire it?'

'But that isn't what the will states. After the year the choice is still mine: to stay or sell.' I reiterated. Did I want Liz to have Heachley, to turn it into a bed and breakfast and hunt muntjac in the woods? Oh God no.

The expression on Charles's face showed pain, an etching of fine lines appeared on his forehead. 'Why did she do it?'

'Liz?'

'No,' he whispered, 'Felicity. The will, trapping you here.'

I shook my head. 'I'm certainly not trapped. But I can't live here, not without more income. This place will be sold and consequently, it might go to somebody who doesn't deserve it.' I remembered what Liz had said about the house, holding Felicity bound to its walls. 'Charles, do you think Felicity's fall down the stairs was accidental?'

'You think Liz … harmed her?' He stuttered, his brows knotted into a quizzical frown.

She'd been accounted for elsewhere, hadn't she? 'No, not Liz. I meant, somebody else.' It remained a ludicrous notion to mention haunted houses. 'Forget it.' I slapped my hands on my thighs. 'I've wasted a day on all this crap. I'm going upstairs to work.' I needed to clear my mind of all of this.

Charles called after me as I climbed the stairs. 'I'll be off, then. See you tomorrow.'

I heard the anxiety in his voice. 'Sure. Tomorrow.' I reassured him because what would happen to me if I lost faith in Charles?

Dragging my heels upstairs, I couldn't stop thinking about what Liz had told me – the implication that my aunt was a victim of some kind of deceitful enterprise to take Heachley from her. But nor could I fathom Charles betraying Felicity or acting on Liz's behalf; he clearly shirked her company and fervently told me how much Felicity hated the woman. Liz coveted the house to such an extent she spied on me, waiting in the wings for me to sell it. So would I? Would I give her the opportunity to buy when I still had no clue as to why Felicity had me living here? Nothing about Heachley Hall made any sense.

TWENTY-THREE

A picture of a blazing fire sprang into my dream. The wood spitting sparks across the hearth and up into the air before coming down onto the rug. The tiny flames munched on the fabric with sharp amber teeth.

I leapt upright, my eyes blinking in the blackness and my heart racing. I couldn't ignore my strange nightmare – had I failed to extinguish the fire in the sitting room prior to going to bed? I couldn't remember. Somewhere on my bedside table lay the little torch. I hunted about, grasping it tight before switching on the beam. A halo of light bounced off the far wall and dazzled my unprepared pupils.

With my feet encased in cold slippers, I scurried down the first flight of stairs, sniffing the air, testing it for the smell of burning embers or worse, a roasting fire. Nothing of the sort accosted my nose. Reaching the main flight, I steadied my pace, not wishing to follow the fate of Felicity and end up head over heels. I held the bannister, grateful for the guidance. Beyond the splayed beam of the torch hovered the familiar darkness, and it refused to show anything of what awaited me downstairs.

I pressed my hand to the door of the sitting room, feeling for unwanted heat, but the wood was cold. It creaked as I pushed against the handle, edging the door ajar, then wider until the torch lit up my make-shift living space.

Unlike my dream there was no sign of flames or leaping sparkles. I crept closer to the fireplace. The torchlight focused on the grating and hearth. Its appearance puzzled me. Although I couldn't recall putting the fire out, neither had I a memory of arranging it so: the dregs of a burnt log buried under a pile of ash. When I moved my hand closer to the small pyre, I felt a plume of warm air; there was heat left in the fire. I poked at it gently with the poker and a wisp of smoke rose for a fraction, then collapsed.

Someone had arranged the fire to keep it alive, but not fully burning. I stepped backward, my heartbeats pounding harder.

They came rushing back; all those annoying references to haunted houses. Especially Maggie's belief in the macabre, which Bert had based on her obsession with television programmes. What if the preoccupation began after working at Heachley Hall, after spending more and more of her time with the ageing Felicity? She'd seen the dust, heard the bangs and creaks and watched the mist hang around the windows. She must have done, just as I had. Had it led to a fascination with the supernatural?

I shut the door behind me and hurried back upstairs to my bed. For a long time, I lay with the torch on my chest, the beam rising and falling in time to my rapid breathing. Sleep refused to return. I kept it at bay with my churning thoughts.

Nothing made sense and I so desperately wanted my experiences, my discoveries about Heachley to make sense. When sleep arrived, it did so in a creeping fashion, sliding in beneath my drooping eyelids.

After breakfast, I cleaned the kitchen while in the background the radio droned something musical. My brain, forced awake by caffeine, wasn't in the mood for drawing.

As I squeezed the mop into the bucket of water, Charles turned up and he heralded his arrival with a rap of his knuckles on the kitchen door.

'Good morning,' he greeted my back. 'Not as cold today.'

Since he'd walked, I wasn't going to argue with him. The Rayburn – Kevin's amazing idea – removed my fear of cold mornings, and it was probably why I hung about in the kitchen for longer instead of working.

'Watch the wet floor,' I warned.

'I was going to tackle painting the window frames today, if you can tolerate the smell.'

I leaned on the mop, puffing out a sigh. 'Sure.'

He furrowed his eyebrows. 'Not still upset about Liz? You look flustered.'

'Slept badly. Weird dream.' I drained the water out of the bucket into the sink. 'Actually, more than a dream.'

'Dreams aren't always meant to be understood.'

'This one was like a warning. Except, it turned out to be something else.'

He chuckled. 'Now you've lost me.'

'The fire in the sitting room.'

The laughter died on his lips. 'What about it?'

'I'd forgot to put it out before I went to bed and in the night, I woke, panicked and came down to check on it.'

'And?'

'Somebody else must have tampered with it.'

Charles followed me into the sitting room.

'See,' I pointed at the heap of ash.

He scratched his head. 'It's been banked down.'

'Banked?'

'The ashes are layered over the remaining embers to trap in the heat. It keeps the warmth in and makes it quicker to light in the morning. I should have shown you how to do it.'

'But you didn't. So who did this?'

He crouched, pushed aside the smouldering ashes and started to reconstruct the fire with fresh kindling and wood. 'What are you saying, Miriam?'

'It doesn't make sense. I'm sure I didn't do this.' Perhaps I had, but unintentionally with my last prods of the poker. 'Is it safe, like that?'

'Banking it down is safe, but you ought to have a fireguard, too.'

I slumped onto the nearby sofa while Charles stirred the fire back to life. I took a deep breath and made my stupid confession. 'I don't think I'm alone here. I've got it into my head that Felicity's ghost is keeping me company.' I cringed, waiting to hear chuckling or some other humorous riposte at my silly idea.

With the poker in one hand, and the other clutching the mantel Charles rose.

'Felicity haunting here?' He shrugged his shoulders. 'I suppose it's possible.'

I jumped to the edge of the sofa, my back rigid. 'You think so? I mean it's ludicrous isn't it? I said I don't believe in any of it and in any case, she died miles away and—'

'She'd never harm you. I'm sure of it.' He propped the poker against the hearth. 'I know you don't want to believe in ghosts, that's understandable, but if she was, all I'm saying is she'd not put you in danger. Why would she harm you?' He looked at me expectantly.

'You think she'd protect me?' I waved at the fire, which had burst into life, cackling in the background with its own kind of laughter. 'Like making the fire safe at night?'

Charles swivelled and stepped away from the heat of the fire. His pale eyes had narrowed to pinpoints and he brushed a lock of hair away from his brow. 'I can't explain what you saw last night. Do you feel threatened?'

I clutched my hands between my thighs, rubbing them up and down, drawing life into the cold fingertips.

'No. Except, Felicity fell downstairs.'

Always I came back to that sudden accident and the lack of witnesses. The resulting train of events meant my great-aunt never came home again. Perhaps she yearned to return so much, she made her way here in another form.

A soft smile transformed Charles's tense expression. 'That doesn't make sense does it – her ghost causing that accident? Felicity's ghost couldn't have been here while she was alive.'

His correction snapped me into line. Something else, something that went beyond one person – the house. Leaping to my feet, I paced around the sofa.

'I know. But what if the house itself has a strange effect on its occupants? Making them do odd things? Perhaps I did bank the fire down then couldn't remember. Or I did it in my sleep. Maybe it's not a conscious state, some kind of spirit. A poltergeist?'

He rolled his eyes to the ceiling, his lips twitching. Was he laughing at me?

I stomped my foot. 'Stop it,' I snapped.

He jerked, his eyes widening. 'I'm sorry. This must be unpleasant for you. You're here on your own; it's bound to make you feel uncomfortable. It's a big house. An old house.'

I flapped my arms; the rush of nervous energy agitated me like a double dose of caffeine had been shot into my veins.

'Yes, it's hard. Bloody hard. I lay in bed last night, running through it all. Felicity breaking her hip. Liz visiting her in the nursing home, not as a friendly neighbour, but badgering her to sell. Then Felicity had a stroke. Was it through stress? Had Liz driven her to it?'

Charles grabbed my flailing hands. 'I can hear music.'

'What?' I exclaimed. I didn't hear anything, I only felt the touch of his hands on mine – I froze and, in the stillness, he was right, there was music.

'In the kitchen. I think you slept badly. You're tired. Your thoughts are all jumbled up. I can tell you're not making sense. Trust me, sleep will make it better.' He squeezed my hands between his cool palms.

I wanted to argue, pick holes in his explanation, but my fatigue gnawed. 'Suppose,' I grizzled.

He led me back into the kitchen, one of my hands still captured in his. 'Come, let's dance. It's excellent at chasing away worries.'

'Dancing?'

'Naturally.' He grasped my hand higher and rested the other on the ledge of my waist. 'Waltzing.'

I laughed. 'Waltz? I don't know how. I'm more of a bopping, hip-hop girl.'

'Hip-hop?' he frowned. 'Very un-ladylike. You're mistress of Heachley Hall. You should dance with eloquence.' He snaked his arm further around my back, drawing me closer to his chest. My chin nudged his shoulder, and I tilted my head. Rather like his clothes, he smelt natural, although this time I detected the scent of pine needles. With a gentle squeeze, he guided me, walking me backwards while maintaining a faint smile.

'Footwork needs practice. Lightly on your toes,' he sang.

I snatched a breath between giggles. 'Charles, I'm wearing slippers.'

'We'll cope. Follow my feet.' He swirled me around and I trod on his right foot.

'I'm hopeless.'

'Don't look down. Look at my face.'

My cheeks burnt with heat. Look at him? I blinked under my fringe and peeked up. He held his head to one side, the small side-burn showing on one cheek. For a second, his eyes twinkled, quite different from their usual hollow appearance.

'Why, sir,' I murmured, 'you're making me blush.'

'Indeed,' he smiled, twirling me around again. 'Left foot, not right,' he corrected, as I made a guess at where to move.

The music, which I barely noticed, had the right kind of rhythmic beat, but otherwise had nothing waltz like about it. Yet somehow, Charles fitted our little dance to the rhythm. I concentrated on mirroring his feet. My slippers slithered on the damp tiles and he snatched me closer, preventing me from sliding. I responded by pinching his sweater between my fingers and thumb, anchoring my balance.

Something else. I blanked it out. Forcing it deeper, but for a fleeting second, it was there, toying with me, making its presence felt. That tingle, that zap of energy that comes when a man touches me. I glanced up, past the smooth outline of his chin and stared over his shoulder out the window avoiding eye contact as if he might draw me in deeper with his gaze.

The song ended, and he released his grip on my waist and hand. 'There. You're smiling now. Much better.' A soft smile of satisfaction broke across his face.

My silly night-time excursion had been briefly forgotten. 'Yes, thank you.'

'This house won't hurt you and I don't believe it would have harmed Felicity either,' he said softly. 'What happens beyond its walls and the gates, that's a different matter.'

I agreed. The mystery lay farther afield. I just needed to figure out where.

Charles's musical interlude had deflected and calmed me. It was time to refocus on other matters. Work, my obligations to my clients, they lay beyond the boundaries of Heachley. Charles and I parted company each to our own chores, but part of me knew it was too late and denying the organic response was futile. It had happened during that brief swirl in his arms. I no longer coveted just the house for myself. I wanted him, too.

····●····

TWENTY-FOUR

As I chipped away at February, pining for the first snowdrops and daffodils to fight their way through the undergrowth, I mastered the art of focusing on work and ignoring anything that might persuade me into thinking I lived amongst the spirits of the dead or some other spooky world. I slept better, too. Charles had been right, sleep was a great cure-all.

While Charles painted the hallway – he'd convinced me he could manage the height of the stairwell on his own – I completed my alien storybook and moved Ruth's project up the priority list.

Clowns became my focus. I whittled away half a day at the library, poking around the book box the defiant toddler Flynn had dismantled a few weeks before, checking out the current offerings. Not much on circus life, it appeared.

If the librarian remembered me, she said nothing. She merely nodded in my direction when I arrived and left.

My little bubble of tranquillity was burst by a text message, which arrived as I unlocked the car in the library car park. Sent by Aunt Valerie, it declared – without any negotiation – of her intention to visit Heachley along with Aunt Grace, her younger sister.

I groaned, head-butting the steering wheel. One aunt was hard work, the pair of them would induce a migraine.

My aunts, who'd always claimed they were there for me since Dad's death, remained unreliable when it came to offering useful advice. Practical day-to-day stuff, fine, but with big life changing decisions they quickly lost any common sense. To add to the illusion of usefulness, they had a habit of deliberately disagreeing with each other. They detested the idea that one of them might be better informed than the other, and in the absence of an arbiter, they batted me back and forth, wearing me down in the process until I gave in to the loudest opinion.

Ping-ponging text messages back and forth, it became apparent they planned to stay the weekend on the outskirts of Cambridge in an exclusive hotel, along with my uncles. And while the two men meandered about the golf course, they – my not-so adventurous aunts – would endeavour to track me down and come for lunch.

I anticipated they would get lost driving on the country roads, which they did.

Late on the following Saturday morning, the telephone rang.

'The satnav can't find you, darling,' Valerie crackled, her stress levels easily discernible. 'We've been up and down these silly little lanes.'

I provided them directions over the phone until their mobile signal cut out and several minutes later, they edged along the driveway, the car wheels grinding on the gravel and announcing their arrival.

They gaped in duet as they stepped out of the Mercedes, while underfoot their high heels sunk between the weeds and chippings. Foolishly, when I'd first informed them I was moving into Heachley Hall, I'd downgraded the scale of the property to something probably no bigger than a country manor house, rather than an imposing mansion. My intention had been to keep in check their curiosity about Felicity's will and stem their general tendency to interfere with anything that smacked of status or wealth in the hope they might stay away from me. With their visit, my attempt at curtailing their busy-body natures came to a dramatic conclusion.

Opening the front door I welcomed my aunts with an awkward smile. 'Hello.'

'Miriam,' Grace shrieked across the drive. 'This, this house. You never said your mother's side of the family had this kind of money.'

Valerie shot her sister a stabbing glance. 'Now, Gracie, we said we wouldn't mention poor Anna.'

'I remember Malcolm saying this place was a disaster in the making.' Grace marched up to the porch, sweeping her gaze back and forth across the frontage.

'Nor Malcolm, either,' Valerie reminded her sister. She threw open her arms, entombing me in a perfume laden embrace. 'Darling, this is wonderful. How lucky for you to inherit such an amazing property.'

I cleared my throat and accepted a peck on my cheek. 'It's not quite a disaster, but it isn't exactly…' I hunted for an appropriate word similar to road worthy and gave up. 'You'll see.'

Charles's touching up of the hall with a lick of paint had worked a treat for improving the first impression of the house. Along with the polished tiles and varnished staircase, the vestibule had recaptured much of its original grandness. What it lacked were pictures, mirrors and decorative lighting: the light bulb swinging in the draught wasn't the most inviting picture.

I closed the door behind me.

'My, my. So spacious,' Valerie admired, re-buttoning her half-opened jacket. 'Cold, too.'

I'd lit the downstairs fires at dawn, but due to a frosty morning, they'd had little impact on the ambient temperature of the house. Upstairs was even worse.

Any attempt at keeping the facade of grandiose fell down the moment they entered the sitting room. My hotch-potch of furniture and lack of carpeting quickly dispelled any ideas I secretly lived the life of luxury.

'It's like Yvonne's student days all over again,' Valerie muttered, raising her eyebrows higher until she rested her attention on the cracked ceiling.

I smirked. 'It's all I need.'

'But you don't have a telly.' Grace swept about the perimeter of the room. 'Not one in the house?'

'A radio is fine. I'm busy working.'

They lauded the Rayburn, rubbing their hands over the heat. 'This is more like it.' Valerie tapped a cupboard door. 'Original?'

'Yes.' I wanted to praise Charles's work, but I zipped my mouth shut – too complicated.

Then, their frowns reappeared when I showed them the scullery with the rusting hulk of the disused boiler still waiting to be ripped out, the stained sink and the rotten slats of the wooden drainer.

'Obviously I will get around to this room. Probably remove everything, leave it bare for the buyer to do as they wish.'

Grace's mouth, which had sprung open when we entered the scullery, failed to shut as we toured the rest of the downstairs, if anything, her jaw seemed to loll lower when I showed her the empty bedrooms.

'Where do you sleep, darling?' Valerie asked.

'Upstairs in the attic.'

'The attic?' she wailed, melodramatically.

'The rooms are smaller and easier to heat,' I explained.

Behind the veneer of lipstick, Grace's lips had turned bluish. I'd grown accustomed to the cold and forgotten its impact on the uninitiated.

When I opened the bathroom door, Grace visibly braced herself, as if she was about to be shown a frozen version of hell. Knowing how my aunts rate hygiene, I'd spent much of the previous day scrubbing the kitchen and bathroom to a standard way beyond my own needs. I could do little about the sparseness of furniture, but at least they couldn't fault me on cleanliness. First thing Saturday morning I'd lit scented candles in the bathroom, polished the brass taps and turned the radiator up to maximum. Heat billowed out of the room the moment they stepped into it.

'Oh,' Grace almost sounded disappointed. 'It's not bad, really. Nice big tub.'

I sighed, relieved I'd passed this test. The slightly more comfortable attic rooms ended the tour and when I offered to take them outside to show them the overgrown garden, they declined, preferring to view it from an upstairs window.

Valerie wiped away the condensation from the windowpane. 'It's vast. All this land and woods.'

I hedged a guess at the thoughts running through her scheming mind. 'Unfortunately, Auntie, the gardens can't be built on, nor Heachley Woods. Whoever buys this place has to be committed. It will take some looking after.'

My aunt pouted. 'Shame,' she mumbled.

We returned to the kitchen where I laid out a buffet of salad, cold beef and warm bread, which I'd baked in the oven. I suggested we ate before the fire in the sitting room. My aunts occupied the sofa, their plates perched on their knees, while I used the folding chair from the hall. The fire sizzled in the background as we munched. I awaited their verdict. It didn't take long to arrive.

'Such potential,' Valerie declared.

'But you'll have to make sure you get the house properly valued,' Grace sipped orange juice from her glass.

'I won't have much say in setting the guide price.'

'It has to go at auction?' Valerie enquired.

'Yes. The will stipulates auction only. I guess Felicity thought it might go for a better price if parties bid against each other.' Liz certainly might fight for Heachley. The thought didn't comfort me.

'And you have to live here until October. Oh, my poor thing,' Grace leaned over and patted my knee, consoling me like her pet dog. 'There has to be some way of having you move out. You can't live like this.' She waved her hand in a vague direction and enunciated the last word with distaste while her nose wrinkled.

There was no point arguing what exactly she meant by 'this'; it would be beyond Grace's cloistered upbringing to appreciate how far up the scale this house was compared to the lowliest accommodation frequented by the less fortunate. I might lack furniture and decorations, but for what I needed, the place functioned adequately.

While they tried to outwit each other with solutions to my supposed problem, I sat on the sidelines, my plate resting on my lap and my chin tucked down. I'd expected their competitive streak to raise its ugly head. Neither of them wanted to do me out of my inheritance, so they plotted how to cheat the stipulations in

Felicity's will. The sisters bickered and suggested increasingly preposterous schemes.

'Rent somewhere, nearby—'

'But, Valerie, I have my place down in Chelmsford—'

'Sh, dear. It's too far, you need to be close by in case this solicitor calls by to check on you.'

'He hasn't so far,' I admitted, then bit on my tongue with regret.

Grace's eyes popped open, latching onto my last few remarks. 'If he hasn't, then move out and keep your name on the electoral register and for council tax, you can send him the bills as proof.'

'But he might visit,' I added, because I'd no doubt he would at some point, just to spite me. 'He never said he wouldn't.'

Valerie frowned. 'Too, risky, Gracie, she has to stay nearby, then she can pop up the road.'

'Val, she can't live in a cheap B&B—'

'Mo-ney,' I sang over the top of them.

'You'll catch pneumonia staying here.' Grace tugged on the lapels of her tweed jacket. She'd not removed her scarf.

'I've been here since October and managed to survive,' I smiled, then nibbled on my buttered bread. I'd excelled myself at bread-baking, perhaps there was more of Felicity in me tucked out of sight.

Things started to get farfetched when Grace wondered if they could bribe somebody at the solicitor's office to warn of an impending visit. Then I could rush back – from where – to meet him on the doorstep.

'She'd have to leave a few things about to make it looked lived in,' pointed out Valerie. 'A bed.'

I glanced at my watch. It was time to end the pointless debate. 'I appreciate your concerns, but I'm happy here. I've got all I need.'

'Don't be daft,' Valerie snapped. 'It's not healthy being here on your own for weeks on end. You're young, you should be out there,' she jabbed a finger at the window, 'finding yourself a man.'

She'd hit on the crux of her annoyance. Here I was, their niece, whose mother had left not a clue about Heachley Hall, destined to inherit a mansion without recourse to marriage or career. Envy had finally arrived, and neither of my aunts had successfully hid the sentiment.

I placed my empty plate on the hearth. 'It's only temporary. There is plenty of time for me to get hitched. Anyway, I'm not alone. I have neighbours and friends.' Thank goodness Charles didn't work weekends.

'And what if you decide to stay on?' Valerie's grilling continued unabated.

'I'm not staying here. I don't want to.'

'And if it doesn't sell?'

'It will. At least, there's somebody who wants to buy it.'

'Who?' Valerie's voice shot higher.

'The neighbouring farmers.'

'Farmers?' Grace's eyebrows rose.

'Wealthy farmers. They have plans for this place and that's that.'

Money dismissed their concerns for me. The reminder of the potential worth of the estate put paid to their scheming ideas. I had to stay to the end, and they knew it, because they wanted to say there was money in the family even if it wasn't theirs to fritter away. I rolled my eyes at the introduction they might foist upon me – have you met our niece, she's a millionaire – I closed my eyes and buried the smarmy voice.

After lunch I showed them my latest illustrations. They deluged me with niceties: cute, sweet and charming being the most common. I thanked them, increasingly aware of the sycophantic tones. I was to stay in touch and keep them up-to-date with the renovations and in return they would send me articles from home and interior design magazines. Anything to help me with my enormous project. I kept my lips tightly shut, not mentioning I intended to do the bare minimum and most of my focus in the coming months would be on the garden.

By mid-afternoon, my headache had blossomed into a pounding pain across my temples. I guided them towards the porch door, thanking them for their time and reminding them my uncles were probably in the club house waiting for their return.

Ultimately their visit buoyed my optimism. Whether they'd thought I would have cried on their shoulders in despair or have gone crazy with solitude, I'd presented myself as robust and on top of things. I grinned, unashamed at my success in keeping my interfering aunts at bay. They had no need to be involved and I would maintain the status quo for as long as possible.

It wasn't just about the money any longer. I actually felt at home. The sensation had crept up unnoticed and as I twirled around and congratulated myself, and Charles, on the replenished hallway. I had to truly acknowledge Felicity's unexplained hunch that I would take to this place.

TWENTY-FIVE

Mr Porter paid his visit at the end of February and I was given my opportunity to ask him about Felicity's possessions. My hope in tracing the box remained despite the setbacks.

He arrived with two days warning and if he anticipated finding the house in a terrible state, he kept quiet. Instead, he muttered a smattering of appreciative words about my efforts, especially with regard to the kitchen. As for evidence of habitation, there was no doubt that I lived in the house. He examined each room: the desk littered with sheets of drawing paper, the laundry drying on a clothes horse before a fire and the smell of bread baking in the kitchen. The small habits of life on display and they confirmed the truth – I'd no reason to practise the deceitful schemes of my aunts. The house was fit for purpose, almost comfortable and with winter slipping away, the interior arctic conditions had improved.

'What exactly did she have with her at Beechwood when she died?' I began my interrogation with a straight back. I was determined not to bend.

'Naturally, she left some clothes behind at Beechwood,' he admitted, while ponderously stirring his coffee. 'Not much really. She had no way to occupy herself in her last years. The radio seemed to be her companion.'

'No papers in a box?'

A split second of a blank expression, then he shook his head and drew his lips into a dismissive pout. Did he know nothing about the box?

I pressed on. 'When she was taken to hospital, after her fall, a neighbour brought a box of things – she'd asked specifically for it.

Nobody seems to know what happened to it.' I studied him, ready to pounce on any hint of deceit that might inch its way on to his sour features.

'Probably of little importance, then. Old dears are not always in their right minds; they like to keep things – knitting patterns, recipes – things of no significance. The home would have disposed of such things.'

I scowled and crossed my arms – his indifferent attitude only confirmed his ignorance. 'She didn't knit and she was stuck in hospital, not cooking school. Whatever was in that box, she wanted it close by.'

Mr Porter slurped on his coffee and shrugged. Meeting him in person, I'd gained little insight into the man. He'd ruined my preconceived ideas of his appearance: portly, middle-aged with wispy hair and ruddy cheeks. I'd been wrong. Tall, angular about the shoulders and jaw, and topped off with a mop of black hair, he was far younger than I'd imagined. Perhaps in his thirties and married – I spied the gold band on his finger.

'Your aunt remains a mysterious woman,' he declared. 'I should be going. Thank you for showing me around. Good luck with everything. I hope this leads to you fetching a decent price.'

I smirked. Unlike the original auction, which Mr Bridge had come close to obtaining, this sale would line my pockets and nobody else's.

Less than an hour after he'd left, the telephone called me back into the hallway.

'Yes,' I answered, pressing the handset to my ear.

'Miriam Chambers?' The timid voice was nearly drowned out by crackles and hisses.

'Yes. That's me. Can I help you?'

'Actually. It's probably me who can help you.'

I waited, bracing myself for a cold caller trying to sell me something unwanted. 'My name is Pauline Myers. I work at St Mary's hospice—'

'Hospice?' She had my attention.

'I'm sorry for not contacting you, I've been super busy and I forgot. Eva, that's my old boss, contacted me, and suggested I should get in touch.'

'Eva Kendal?'

'That's right. I worked at Beechwood for nearly a year, until it closed. I looked after your aunt.'

I clenched the handset tighter, taming my breathing and praying finally I'd have some news. 'Felicity. You knew Felicity?'

'I was her primary carer before she passed away. Very sad condition. Felicity was locked in, that's what we say, after her stroke. Unable to communicate other than blinking. We tried all sorts of things to help her, but she was never one for technology. She loved picture books, especially of India and places like that.'

'I'd been hoping to speak to somebody who was with her at Beechwood. I'm so glad you decided to ring back.' The excitement unleashed a flurry of nervous expectation.

'Eva persuaded me. She'd contacted me earlier in the year, said you were after information. When they closed the nursing home, I changed jobs and it's not easy to keep up with my former colleagues.' The soft voice grew louder, her confidence growing.

'I wanted to know if you remember a box. I don't know what it looked like or how big it was, but it contained papers, possibly photographs.' I crossed the fingers of my free hand.

'Oh yes. It was kept in her wardrobe. A rectangular box: colourful, shoebox sized and sort of woven.'

Distinctive in style and difficult to miss. I swallowed hard. 'Do you know what became of it after she died?'

'It was bagged up with the rest of her things and put in the storage room until somebody collected it. Next of kin, usually.'

'And did anyone?'

'I'm not sure. You see, it's funny you're interested in that box, because it's bothered me for ages.'

'What has?'

'It got a little chaotic after April, last year, when all the residents moved out. I went with some to settle them into their new homes and when I came back, I happened to be in the storeroom and Felicity's possessions had gone.'

'Gone?'

'Yes. I asked, because I was a little curious, but nobody I spoke to could remember who took them. She had no visitors, you see, at least not while I cared for her.'

I pressed my fingers to my temple, trying not to blame myself for Felicity's lonely existence. 'Did somebody throw them out?'

'Possibly. But it would have been logged and there was nothing in the logbook.'

'Logbook?'

'Yes, it was kept in the storeroom.'

'What happened to the logbook?'

'I'm sorry. I took up a job offer at the hospice and didn't stay to the end.'

'I see,' I deflated. I'd risen to the height of excitement, expecting some form of definitive news, but what I'd been left with was nothing more than a continuation of my existing problem. The box hadn't been found.

'Thank you, Pauline, for contacting me. I'm very grateful.'

'Oh, I wish I could have done more for your aunt. I went to her funeral.'

'That's kind of you. Unfortunately, nobody had traced me and I didn't know she'd died.'

'A few of us staff went to say goodbye and there was one other person there, who I didn't recognise. It wasn't you?'

'No.' My absence now pained me. 'What did she look like?' I asked.

'Red-haired, shortish. Middle-aged, maybe a bit younger.'

'Did she give her name?'

'No, she hurried off at the end of the cremation; tearful I thought.'

I groaned. 'If you do remember anything else, you will call me?'

'Of course, but I'm afraid, there's little else to tell. She, your aunt, never spoke a word.'

I thanked her again and hung up. The idea of a mute old lady, clinging onto life for no great purpose brought the prickle of tears to my eyes. I wiped them away and sighed.

A pang of guilt gnawed at my guts. Pauline's recollections had exonerated Eva: she had been asking around. However, what little I'd unearthed about Felicity's box painted a picture of neglect but not deceit or deliberate acts of malicious behaviour. If it had gone, it probably had been thrown away. The logbook? Lost too or buried in Twilight's head office. Did I really want to badger that place again and listen to Mr Craven deny all knowledge of its existence?

All I'd truly uncovered was there was a solitary mourner at the funeral. Who was she?

Perhaps it was a result of seeing me in the flesh or the evidence of my efforts in turning Heachley Hall around that led Mr Porter to undergo some kind of transformation. That was my positive take on his latest news. My cynical view was that he didn't want to be held accountable for screwing up and picking a dodgy clearance firm.

He wrote to me and explained he had followed up my concerns regarding the actions of the company and had identified some issues.

Standing in the kitchen, I tore the envelope into pieces. 'Issues!'

Charles stuck his head around the door. 'Miriam?'

'Nothing,' I huffed. 'Something too late to resolve.'

He edged into the room. 'What thing?'

I glanced over the contents of Mr Porter's letter. 'The clearance company he employed to empty the house has gone bust. Their activities are under investigation by Trading Standards, amongst others.'

'Standards?' He pursed his lips.

'The company had a habit of selling things on the side. It's likely some of Felicity's nicer things, in particular her rugs and tapestries, which Mr Porter failed to record properly, were sold on and not passed back to the estate. Plus, they might have burnt numerous personal items, things that wouldn't sell.'

'Oh dear,' he murmured.

'Quite.' I held up the letter. 'He apologises, but sadly, it's unlikely the sold items will be recovered. Unless I want to fight it in the courts.' I scrunched the paper up in my fist and threw it across the room. 'It's not right.'

Charles reached out, captured my hand and gave it a squeeze. 'It's not your fault. People aren't as honest as they appear, and you weren't to know.'

I sniffed, and he let go. 'Sorry. Stupid of me. It's water under the bridge.' I stared across the kitchen. Droplets of rain cascaded down the windowpane. Beyond the glass, the omnipresent greyness had returned, aided by sea mist and low clouds. My misery existed alongside that murkiness. 'I hope the sun returns. Tony is coming next week to clear the lawns.'

'He's a decent enough chap.' Charles scratched his chin. 'There'll be plenty to do with the spring arriving. I take it you'd like me to help in the garden?' He raised his eyebrows optimistically.

It was something of a rhetorical question. How I took Charles for granted bothered me to the point of shame. I paid him haphazardly for his equally sporadic hours of work and he never complained or demanded more money. He seemed to possess boundless levels of energy. If he ever yawned, he hid his gaping mouth and if he suffered with hunger, he kept to his particular mealtimes.

Since our little waltz in the kitchen, we frequently lapsed into awkward pauses or moments when our eye contact bordered on the bashful. I left unspoken the emotions I'd kindled in my heart and since his feelings remained undisclosed or maybe non-existent, I'd no means to communicate those tiny flames of desire. When I lost my concentration during work, I'd sketched a little drawing of Charles, then scrubbed it out. Those meandering sidetracks nudged their way into my daydreams, especially when I replayed a conversation or one of Charles's odd comments about something he'd heard on the radio. He'd seemed keen to talk, then when I'd pushed for a more personal context – asking him what his friends thought on a matter – he'd dry up and excuse himself.

People were allowed to be shy and reticent. Why should he divulge his personal life? What about Felicity? Had he allowed her into his circle of trust? Which led to an irritating realisation about his relationship with my aunt: he'd trusted her, but not me. What would I need to do to prise him open and why – each and every day – was there this need in me to know him better?

He scooped low and picked-up the chewed-up letter. Unfolding it, he smoothed the crumpled paper out. 'She wouldn't have minded.'

Enigmatic Charles struck again. 'What?' I asked.

He gestured about him. 'Losing everything. She understood it would come to her in another life.'

I'd missed the obvious – her devotion to a different place – I sighed, more at myself than him. 'She believed in reincarnation?'

'She'd been raised a Hindu.' Charles's habit of leaking snippets of information about Felicity at salient moments made me wonder to what extent he had really known her. He'd left me with the impression she'd preferred distance. Charles, too, was an expert in creating an uninformative veneer of politeness. Given his age, he could only have known her for a few years, yet, somehow he'd formed a lasting connection.

The idea of reincarnation appealed; it fitted with the house. 'Perhaps that is what a haunting is. Some other life bleeding into this one, leaving an impression of itself. I'm sure I can feel her, sometimes, especially at night. I've tried to ignore it.'

He handed me the letter and I lay it on the worktop. Something to file away, but perhaps not forget.

'Is there anything else you need?' asked Charles softly.

There were the practical things that needed doing in the house, but my hesitation was due to a strange rush of adrenaline that greeted his question – was he referring to something more? Had I detected in his gentle manners something similar to what I felt towards him? However, sadly, nothing showed on his face; no hint of what else he might mean by his nonchalant enquiry.

There had been plenty of missed opportunities to recapture the intimacy that I'd come to crave from him. Those that resulted in fleeting contact – like slipping his finger over mine when he handed me something or the adjustments to the scarf around my neck before I went out – were too infrequent to build upon. I held back the intrusive personal questions, lacking the courage to dig deeper for fear he might scarper and not return. Now I failed dismally to answer his own.

'No, thank you. I mean, sure, please help with the garden.' I crushed my disappointment.

He opened his mouth, held it there for a second and then pressed his lips together. He turned on his heel and I watched him walk into the scullery and back outside – his haven from me or memories of Felicity?

TWENTY-SIX

Throughout the winter months the Rose and Crown remained something of an oasis in the desert of my social life. It acted as a hub, the focus of my limited network around Little Knottisham. I'd become something of a local celebrity and recognisable fixture. I usually visited on a Wednesday evening and again on Saturday lunchtime. Other times, I came and went according to an intermittent need to transmit important files.

Before I'd left for Christmas, I'd established a particular corner of the taproom as my domain and the locals would greet me by name with a brisk, 'How yew doing, Miriam?' It proved to be the quietest spot in the pub and afforded me both an electric socket for my laptop and the warmth of the fire. During January and February, I'd learnt the names of the regulars, especially those who lived out a second life propping up the bar, rather than supping at home. Glenda, always busy in the kitchen while Bert pulled the pints, would come and sit at my table for a few minutes each time I came by so she could check up on my progress. She offered her opinions, whether I wanted them or not. She'd reviewed all of my illustrations, nodding her approval at each picture as if she'd become the sage of children's books.

As for my call with Pauline, Glenda failed to recall the red-haired woman. 'Some kind soul I suppose,' she suggested. 'I'm sure Maggie would have gone, if she'd known. But, she's a little brunette.'

Heachley Hall gradually had lost its attraction. I'd not kept secret my intention to sell the place and there was the odd enquiry about when the sale would happen, even though the value of the property was beyond the reach of most of the inhabitants. What they did speculate about was who might buy it.

'Pykes,' The name rumbled around the pub each time the question came up for discussion. 'She'll nab it.' The gossip reiterated what I'd learnt from Charles and Glenda, who'd confirmed when I'd probed her that Liz fancied herself as Heachley's owner, but Glenda hadn't added anything further about Liz's relationship with Felicity and laughed off the idea of anything malicious on Liz's part.

'She's thinks she's the queen of Knottisham, but she's harmless,' Glenda had said with a loud chuckle. I thought Glenda wore that crown and I preferred it on her head. She patted my arm and hurried back to her domain behind the bar.

The other contenders for buying Heachley were a boutique hotel chain, a retired cabinet minister and a minor royal – this idea, I assumed, grew from the relative proximity of the Sandringham estate. However, to their collective disappointment, I'd not been approached by anyone of magnitude.

The patrons had never satisfactorily resolved my curiosity towards my neighbours. Liz Pyke generated scowling expressions, whereas Tony was generally well liked. My earlier enquiries about Charles had resulted in blank looks. After the incident with the footprints in the snow when he'd told me he walked over from Docking direction, the troop of regulars, mainly men, rolled their eyes to the timber beams.

'Probably went to a different school to us,' one proposed initiating a debate about the local population.

'Assuming he was born here. Could be a traveller, one of those.'

'Some like to travel, others never go more than a few miles.'

The banter around the bar had dried up, as it had on most occasions. I'd given up asking if anyone knew anything about Charles. By the beginning of March my place in the community had been accepted and nobody batted an eyelid when I inhabited the corner.

The next time I arrived for my usual Wednesday lunch, Glenda loomed close by as I set up my laptop.

'Thought you'd like to know Maggie has been in contact me with me and she asked about Heachley.'

I dropped the cable. 'Really? Where is she? Can I meet her?'

Glenda slipped into the seat opposite. 'Steady up,' she chuckled.

'Did she leave a contact number?'

'She was in a bit of a dither, to be frank. Her mum's been ill, she's separated from Fido—'

'Fido?'

'Her puppy dog husband, whom she should have left a long time ago.'

'So, no contact number.' I slumped in my seat.

'She was curious about you, though. Wanting to know what had happened to the old hall. She hung up pronto, so I think she had to go.' Glenda scraped back her chair and collected up a couple of empty glasses from the nearby table. 'There's one slice of steak and kidney pie left. I kept it back for you.'

I smiled, sweetly. 'Thank you.'

'Peas and mash?'

As if there was any other option with the pie. I nodded. 'Not too much gravy, please.' My appetite had slunk away; I suspected I'd caught a cold.

'You're far too skinny.' She frowned. 'If your mother were alive, she'd fatten you up.'

I kept the wan smile fused on my face a little longer. 'Probably.'

I'd no idea what my mother would have made of my life. She should have been the one to inherit Heachley Hall, along with my father. Every time I pictured that scenario, my intention to sell the place wavered. Could I create an idyllic family haven where we would live happily ever after? But reality bit quickly. I tossed the fantasy aside and replaced it with unglamorous creaking floors and clanking pipes. The fuse box continued to trip at least twice a month, casting me in darkness. The last time had only been the previous week, when I'd used the iron in a different socket to usual. Consequently, I'd covered the socket in tape to remind me it was faulty and best avoided. Half the antique electrical outlets in the house were dangerous.

Glenda returned to her place behind the bar and I concentrated on my next proposal: another farmyard story. The publisher had received my last one with admiration and they'd commissioned a second joint adventure from the author and myself. Personally, I'd rather draw aliens.

The following day I told Charles about Maggie's call. He raised his unfathomable eyebrows and said nothing.

With the onset of warmer weather, he'd spent more time in the garden. However, due to a deluge of rain the previous day, Tony's promised arrival of heavy-duty cutting equipment had been delayed. Charles, unperturbed by the wet foliage, set about lopping and digging up the brambles and generally redefining the borders. We discussed how to deal with the growing pile of garden waste that would only become bigger once Tony set to work with his hedge trimmer and industrial sized mower. 'Burn it,' Charles suggested.

I disagreed. 'Too much smoke. Also, it's environmentally unfriendly, burning waste.' A tad hypocritical on my part. Ruth and I had burnt leaves and a curtain. But Tony was about to add a mountain of cuttings.

He battered his long eyelashes for a few seconds, but didn't argue.

What else? 'I could hire a shredder and turn it into compost.'

He whistled, sucking in his breath. 'That's going to be a mighty amount of compost.'

'There'll be space to store it at the back of the garden.'

'Still, that's a lot of mulch.'

'What did you do with it when you worked for Felicity?'

'Burnt it.'

We smiled in unison. 'Okay, let's see what Tony has to say, he might know how to deal with it.'

Charles's smile dipped. 'He's coming here?'

'Soon, I expect. Not sure when. He's doing me a favour. I can hardly demand an allotted time.'

Charles nodded, pursing his lips. 'No, true. I'll concentrate on clearing the paths at the back, shall I?'

Not long after, he disappeared behind the bushes wheeling the barrow he'd resurrected from one of the sheds. How quickly he merged into the shrubs and undergrowth, allowing the garden to consume him whole: a man very much at home outside – more so than indoors.

Too many things whirled around in my head: work related issues, the house, Felicity's infernal box and Charles, my dancing partner. I flitted between tasks, unable to settle, and blew my nose with increasing frequency. No longer could I ignore the cold, both the resurgence of wintery weather and viral versions.

By Friday afternoon, having returned from a disorganised trip to the supermarket for food I didn't fancy and unable to face drawing, I relented to fatigue and opted to sit before the warmth of the sitting room fire. I heaped extra logs onto the burning embers until the sap hissed and leaked between the shards of blackened bark. The sizzling noise was melodic, a gentle tune for my tired ears, and as I gazed at the flames, my eyelids drooped. I snuggled deeper into the crook of the sofa and my head lolled.

'Miriam!'

I jerked awake, snapped my heavy head up and ricked my neck muscles in the process. I smelt a different kind of burning: acrid and chemical.

One end of the rug was on fire. On the hearth lay a burning piece of timber and shooting out of it, sparks. Charles stamped on the flames. One corner of the rug had caught. I leapt to my feet to assist, but he waved me back. I wore slippers, while he had boots.

Starting a fire in a hearth might be a challenge, but an unwanted one ignited with relative ease. Having escaped the fireplace, it sought the most inflammable material in the room and feasted on it.

'Your laces,' I pointed at his boots; the dangling string had caught fire like a candle's wick. He dabbed tentatively at the fuse with his hand. Smoke rose between his feet.

'Damnation.' He dragged off his pullover and used it to beat the flames.

I dashed into kitchen, grabbed the rim of the half full washing bowl and carried it back to the sitting room. The water sloshed around and spilt over the sides. With little thought for aim, I upended the contents onto the rug.

The flames extinguished, but the plume of smoke remained and coiled around our ankles. Charles knelt by the undamaged end and began to roll the rug up. Underneath, where he'd exposed the floorboards, the dirty dish water trickled through the crevices and disappeared into the dead space below.

'Oh my God,' I breathed heavily, pressing my palm against my clammy, hot forehead. 'I fell asleep.'

Charles grabbed his discarded pullover and rose. 'You'd put far too much wood on the fire, so it toppled over.' He didn't attempt to mask the rebuke. 'Foolish girl,' he added and kicked the rolled-up rug. Smoke wafted out of one end.

I chewed on my lip. 'Sorry.'

Now wearing only a white t-shirt, which although shabby managed to accentuate the sculpting of his biceps and pectorals, he examined his sweater for damage. I couldn't stop staring at his arms and the peculiar blemishes that meandered along them. I itched to reach out and trace one. Numerous unanswered questions bubbled away in my head.

Seeing my unguarded fascination, he flinched then scowled. He shifted backwards and stretching his arms above his head, he hurriedly covered up his body. Embarrassed by the need to stare at him, I turned away and focused on the fireplace.

'I waited too long. I mean, I should have made a fireguard,' he muttered, bending over to pick up the rug.

'It's not your fault.' My voice shook; the delayed burst of adrenaline hit hard. My legs wobbled, and nausea filled my empty belly. What if I hadn't woken up? Even worse, what if Charles hadn't been here?

He rested the rolled-up rug over his shoulder. 'I'm sure I can find a sheet of metal, perhaps use part of the old boiler and make it into a guard.' He shifted the weight of the rug and the pungent smell of charred fabric penetrated my snotty nose.

My stupidity riled not only me, but him, too. He kept shaking his head and clucking his tongue.

I shrivelled. 'Charles—'

'Sh,' he whispered. He brushed the knuckles of his spare hand over my cheekbone. 'Good fortune I came into the house to use the bathroom.' His thinly set lips, which he'd pressed into a line, softened into a gentle smile. He heaved the rug one more time, allowing it to drape over his shoulder and he walked towards the door.

Glancing back, he eyed me. 'You should go to bed. I'll bank the fire down.'

'Thank you.' I sniffed, plucked a tissue from my trouser pocket and unapologetically blew my nose. Then, with my fingertips, I touched the spot on my flushed cheekbone and held them there.

In bed, I snuggled down under the duvet. My embarrassment at setting fire to the rug had been obliterated by the realisation Charles had taken care of me. That little premise warmed my bones as much as the convection heater. Falling easily into sleep, I floated the cusp of an idea that he would always take care of me, wherever I lived.

TWENTY-SEVEN

By Monday the weather and my cold had sufficiently improved for me to hang out the washing. On the southern side of the house, Charles had speared two poles into the soggy ground and rigged a line between them. While I pegged the bedsheets onto the line, a car pulled up on the driveway.

Out of the vehicle stepped a small woman, rather neat in stature, and she wore leggings and a hugging sweatshirt. The colour of the hair caught my eye: red.

'Hello!' I called out.

She halted near to the porch. 'You must be Miriam.'

I carried the empty laundry basket and picked a path through the long grass to meet her. 'Yes. I'm Miriam.'

A tentative smile shaped her lips, which twitched nervously. 'I'm Maggie.'

Now, up close, I could see the roots of her dyed hair. Streaks of auburn and caramel almost hid the ashes of her natural colouring. Glenda had described Maggie differently. Just by visiting the hairdressers she'd easily, and unintentionally no doubt, disguised herself.

Following me into the house, Maggie gasped at the bare bones of the house, but not at the rattles and creaks as the wind tracked behind us; the whispering chorus of the house I'd grown used to over the previous months.

'What a draught,' she'd remarked. 'It's so, empty.'

She poked her nose around the library door, muttering and shaking her head at the fractured plasterwork and vacant shelves. Seeing the kitchen cupboards, her face had lit up; something familiar and while she waited for me to fill the kettle, she traced her fingers along the edge of a cupboard door.

'These have come up a treat.'

'New hinges and handles.' I almost mentioned Charles, but changed my mind. There would be no sidetracking Maggie onto other topics.

She swung one open. 'I'd no idea everything had gone.'

I switched on the kettle and cleared my throat. 'What happened – the day she fell – were you here?'

She peered inside the nearest unit and inspected the row of cereal packets. 'Oh yes, I was here in the kitchen. Gave me such a shock. She came down with a clatter – her walking stick – and I panicked seeing her lying at the bottom. She was calm, never one to get flustered or upset, but I could see she was in terrible pain.'

'Why did she fall?' The kettle started to whistle.

'Why?' Maggie closed the door and shrugged. 'Old legs. I told her to fit a stair lift.'

She described an anti-climax. I'd anticipated Maggie finding Felicity alone and unconscious at the bottom of the stairs, something more sinister than a simple slip. I'd created a dramatic scenario in my head based on what? My fertile, suspicious imagination, and little else.

'And you called Tony?' I dunked the teabag up and down in a mug; the tea stained the water in swirling patterns.

'I know. Silly me. I should have rung for an ambulance, but he dialled the emergency services from the farm then came here straightaway, and stood at the gate looking out for the paramedics. I went with Felicity in the ambulance.' She reached out, accepting the tea mug offered to her.

We relocated to the sitting room and I prodded the fire back to life with the poker. Maggie sipped on her tea, peering over her shoulder at the sparsely furnished lounge. 'This was the dining room.'

'I use it as a living space. The other rooms are too big to heat.'

'It was always a challenge keeping this house warm. The central heating barely functioned and she wouldn't pay to have it fixed. I

214

don't think she had much money left by then. She'd inherited a considerable amount from her father, but it couldn't last forever. She never had a job.'

She rambled on for a few minutes, describing how Felicity recycled everything, hoarding books and clothes, even clothing from jumble sales.

I snatched a question when she paused to breathe. 'Did she take anything with her?'

'With her?'

'In the ambulance?'

Maggie blinked a few times. 'Not that I recall.'

'Oh. It's just Liz Pyke told me—'

Maggie's frown lines deepened and she snorted. 'Liz? She wasn't here when it happened. She visited the hospital later and went back to fetch a few things for Felicity, if that's what you mean. I stayed with Felicity until she was comfortable in the ward.' She rested the mug on her lap. She had large hands with calluses between the knuckles and chipped nails. 'They moved her to a nursing home to recuperate. Frankly, she and I argued about her future. I believed she should stay in the home longer, but she was miserable there and I agreed when she came back here, I would extend my hours. But then she had the stroke. So sad, we – Bert and I – had planned this homecoming for her. She'd even agreed to have the stair lift fitted.'

I joined her on the sofa and her face remained in profile as she stared into the fire. Her nose, which was dainty and small, twitched like a rabbit's.

'They moved her after the stroke. Did you see her at Beechwood?' I tried to sound nonchalant, as if my questions were rudimentary and lacking ambition, but ultimately, my destination was the nursing home.

'We moved to Norwich, my husband and I, and I tried to stay in contact with Felicity by visiting when I could. She'd recognised me, even after I dyed my hair – new look for a new life. I saw the spark in her eyes when I entered the room. I read to her, brought her new books, her favourite foods. But then…' She tightened her grip on the mug.

'Glenda said your mother's ill.'

'I ended up living with Mum. My husband didn't want to move again. It's fine, we were on the ropes anyway.'

'I'm sorry.'

'Oh, don't apologise, not about him and me. We're good, probably better apart than together. I wound him up no end. I came up to see him. I rang the pub and Glenda told me you'd moved in, so I decided to call by on the way back.'

'I'm very grateful to have this chance to talk to you. I know so little about my great-aunt. You went to the funeral?' Pauline's description fitted Maggie: it had to be her.

'Yes. It was reported in the local paper's obituary column and my husband spotted it. That last year of Felicity's life flew by. I kept meaning to visit her. But Mum took priority—'

'Of course. It was kind of you to visit Felicity when you could. I'd no idea she'd been ill. The solicitor didn't put much effort into finding me.'

'She mentioned you a few times, recalling what a lovely child you were – sweet Miriam, she'd say, but of course, you're not little now,' Maggie added with a whimsical smile.

I hugged my knees. 'She remembered me?'

'Oh yes. Your mother, too. Always sad when her name cropped up; she'd go watery eyed. So young, she'd say.'

My eyes brimmed with tears. 'I wished I had the chance to know her; Felicity, that is. To be honest, I don't remember Mum much either.'

'When Felicity died one of the care assistants rang me – Lucy. We'd become good friends you see, she'd offer me advice about how to look after my mum and we chatted on the phone several times. I went to the cremation, just me and a few of the other staff, but I had to dash off at the end of the service.'

I swallowed a hard lump in my throat. 'Beechwood closed down not long afterwards.'

'I know. Lucy was concerned about Felicity's things.' Maggie shot a sideways glance. Her expression was taunt, paler than when she first arrived.

'Things?' My eagerness raised the tone of my voice. I slouched backwards in the chair and tried to mitigate my excitement.

'The clothes had already gone. They'd all but forgotten about it and with so much upheaval, Lucy thought it might get destroyed or mislaid. So, we arranged to meet up and she handed it over to me. I don't think she was meant to, me not being a relative, but nobody seemed to care anymore.'

'It?' I crushed my palms together in a minor act of prayer.

'A box.'

I closed my eyes, 'And you have it?' then, held my breath.

'Yes. In the car. I hope you don't think I would steal anything of Felicity's.' I opened my eyes to see her trembling lips and her nose twitched faster.

Maggie was no thief, not in my opinion, because she'd answered my prayers. I reached over and touched the back of her hand. She flinched, possibly misinterpreting my relief and I withdrew it.

'No, not at all. I've been searching for that box. I'm just grateful it's been found.'

She'd been sat bolt upright, her shoulders rigid, as if expecting me to burst into anger, but instead, I'd unleashed my enthusiasm and gratitude. She fumbled in her handbag for her car keys and smiled. 'I'll go get it.'

I paced the room waiting for her return. I needed to stay grounded and not succumb to over-excitement. I'd built this box up to be the answer to all my questions. What if it was nothing but holiday postcards and things she'd brought back from India? Maggie described Felicity as a hoarder. Nevertheless, I wanted the box my aunt had treasured to contain something of value, of significance.

I peered out of the window and watched Maggie unlock the boot of her Ford Focus. She extracted the box, propping it on her hip as she slammed the door shut.

Pauline had called it colourful and shoe boxed size, but not a shoebox. It wasn't made from cardboard and neither was it the kind of storage box sold in a typical shop.

I opened the front door for Maggie and she thrust the prized container in my direction, before I'd even had the chance to shut the door. She offered it to me in a manner that smacked of desperation, as if the box was diseased.

'One minute,' I held up my hand. Without a dining room table, I'd nowhere to put it. I dashed into the sitting room and unfolded the collapsible camping table, which I used in lieu of a permanent one. I placed the table by the sofa.

'There will do.' I pointed at it.

Maggie rested the box on the surface and stood back. 'Chindi. That's what they call it.'

She referred to the Indian technique of using colourful woven scraps of material. Long threads of cotton or other stiff fabrics, trapped in lines. The lid was held in place with a hook.

I fingered the loose threads, which had frayed and poked out in a spiky pattern. 'I take it you know what's inside.' My stomach churned, wanting to know, but also not daring to peep inside. Would it be letters, another will, or something about my mother or grandfather?

'Yes. An odd collection of things. Some photographs of India over the years. A few of Felicity's mother. The rest is to do with some woman and the fire that happened here.'

Intrigued, I unhooked the clasp. 'Nothing about the Marsters family?'

'Not obviously, more to do with—'

A rattling interrupted Maggie and the door creaked. Charles. He'd taken his boots off, leaving him standing in heavily darned socks. His damp hair clung about his cheeks, zig-zagging along the line of his jawbone.

'Maggie,' he exclaimed with wide eyes.

'Charles?' She spun on the spot, clutching a hand to her chest. 'What are you doing here?'

If I expected a warm embrace or even a shake of the hands, neither happened. An immediate, unnatural silence fell and only Maggie's heavy breathing disturbed it. I lifted my hand off the box lid. Charles was staring not at Maggie, but the box.

'I was in the garden,' he said softly, his gaze fixed. 'Pruning.'

I fidgeted with the hook, embarrassed by the awkward pauses. 'Charles has been helping me. He cleaned up the kitchen cupboards, the staircase, lots of things. He's very versatile.'

'Yes,' Maggie rocked on her toes. 'Felicity thought so, too.'

'I'll leave you to talk,' Charles backed out of the room.

'Charles,' I hurried to the door, but he'd already covered the hallway. 'Please don't go.'

Whether he heard me or chose to ignore me, I didn't know. The back door slammed.

'Odd,' I said, re-entering the sitting room. 'I'd have thought he would be pleased to see you. It's been a few years.'

Maggie picked her handbag. 'I should go, too. Let you look through this stuff in your own time. I'm sorry I didn't come by before now. I've hung on to this for far too long.'

'No, honestly. I'm glad you had it. I'm not convinced the nursing home would have bothered to keep it. Please thank Lucy, won't you.'

'Sure.' She slipped the bag over her shoulder. As she crossed the hall, she paused, examining the tiles. By her shoes, a sheen of dust covered the floor, the white particles a stark contrast on the black tiles. 'Funny how spooky this house gets. I thought I'd gone mad when I worked here.'

I clenched my hands into tight fists, unsure whether I wanted to hear about her theories. 'Why did you think it was haunted?'

She furrowed her forehead, perturbed by my directness.

'Bert told me,' I clarified.

'Oh. Bert. Gossip queen,' Maggie guffawed. 'This, for one thing. Haven't you noticed this white dust?' She scuffed the tip of her shoe on the floor. 'Bleeding everywhere. Plus, the doors banging and strange noises lurking behind closed doors. Sometimes I thought I saw movement in the shadows. That horrible cellar – I refused to go down there. Black hell, I called it.'

I laughed, half-heartedly. 'I know, I've had the same experiences. I think it's Felicity trying to warn me about something, like she's still here.'

Maggie frowned. 'Can't be her. This place gave me the creeps while Felicity lived here. She, on the other hand, didn't give a hoot. Laughed at me if I commented on anything peculiar.'

'And Charles?' I hedged.

The frown dragged her cheeks lower and before it could slip off, she hoisted the strap of her handbag higher onto her shrugging shoulder. 'Whatever Charles thought, he kept it to himself. At least with me.'

'You didn't stay here with her as she became more infirm?'

'Me?' Maggie shook her head and snorted. 'Originally, I came a couple of mornings to clean. Then, as she grew frailer, I found myself here most mornings, helping her up, getting her dressed. I'd come back in the evenings to make sure she'd eaten and put her to bed, too, if needed. I cleaned for a couple hours on the odd day, but otherwise, she was alone. Charles, I suppose, might have kept an eye on her, but he was the gardener, nothing else. It was pure luck I was here when she fell.'

'Oh. That means she was alone.' Like me, listening, contemplating. How had she survived three decades of this place? I masked a grimace with my hand.

'She liked it. Believe me, she didn't need company. Solitary creature — Felicity Marsters. If she went out, she'd use a taxi. Growing up in India she'd probably gone by rickshaw. She'd no shame about who she was.' She smiled, briefly, a transient alteration in her expression; for the first time, she elicited a modicum of warmth. Exhaling deeply, she pursed her lips. 'She should have stayed in India.'

'So, no ghosts,' I repeated, somewhat surprised by Maggie's apparent disinterest in the subject.

Her red dyed hair matched the sudden blush of her cheeks and she jabbed her finger in the direction of the dust at our feet. 'Oh, there are spirits here in my opinion. I didn't say there weren't. And, I can take a good guess at who haunts this place.'

I leaned forward focusing my eyes on her mouth. 'Who?'

'Look in the box,' Maggie said softly, her lips articulating the words, while her eyes darted around. She bowed her head, moved closer and spoke into my ear as if to avoid a spy listening in. 'The only reason she kept that box by her was because she was fascinated about this place, especially that fire. She was obsessed by it.'

I ignored the parallels with my search for the truth. 'The fire?'

'Yes,' Maggie hissed, 'and the Isaacks. She told me she'd gone, years ago, back in the sixties, to the record office in Norwich to find out more.' She rattled her car keys. The visit was over.

I opened the front door for Maggie. She glanced up to the sky and clucked her tongue. The mist had descended, almost hiding the gates.

The rain pattered on the car's roof and she pulled up the collar of her coat. 'If you want my opinion,' she said hurriedly, 'this house is haunted and has been for years, and long before Felicity arrived.' She drove off as briskly as her tongue.

I said nothing. What could I say without frightening myself.

With Maggie gone, I returned to the Chindi box and opened it. The contents bundled together at the top were a collection that bore witness to Felicity's life over many years, including faded photographs of different locations in India. The contrast in the pictures had bled out, stripping out the vividness and leaving behind a flat impression of what must have been amazing temples, paddy fields of rice, statues, vast rivers and deltas.

Lying under them, a few black and white pictures of a woman with long black hair tied back and her beautiful dark eyes dolefully staring into the camera lens. At her side stood a small girl with big teeth and paler eyes: Felicity. One sepia photograph was stuck onto a cardboard frame and the uniformed officer captured within had a remarkably handsome face; something of my mother perhaps in those faraway eyes. The portrait was labelled Major Hubert Marsters: my great-grandfather and Felicity's father.

Tucked into the back of the frame was crumpled notepaper. I smoothed them out to discover love letters written with a slanting style in ink and signed by Hubert. No dates bar one letter, but the first part of it was smudged, and only the year was legible: 1932. Hubert, simply addressing the recipient as his beloved, had expressed in brief eloquent terms of endearment his wish to join his Indian mistress. Quite poetic. However, he then went on to confess his obligation to Lily – my great-grandmother – and John had hampered his efforts. At some point after that last letter Lily had died and he had been free to bring his mistress and daughter to live with him. Unfortunately, he'd never married the nameless woman, leaving my great-aunt illegitimate and shunned as an outcast.

Rummaging through the photographs, I found no trace of my grandfather, John, Felicity's half-brother. No remembrance of her sibling or any inclination to explain his absence from her life. The feud between them had lasted a long time. So why had he left the house to her, not my grandmother, when he died in 1965?

I put the family photographs and letters to one side. Beneath them were other documents: a mixture of originals and photocopies. I placed each one on the table, side by side, trying to work out a pattern or explanation for their presence. Felicity had an eclectic interest in the social welfare of unmarried mothers in Docking. Not a subject matter that was unfamiliar to her given her own status as illegitimate. However, the names weren't of anyone I recognised as part of our family, but there again, she'd gone back over a hundred years. The photocopies of newspaper articles had streaks across them, the typeset heavy and inky, making the print hard to decipher. There was also a letter from the Board of Guardians to the editor of the *Norfolk Chronicle* – dated February 1873 – it referred to the fate of the poor in Docking workhouse.

An increasing number of unmarried, destitute women have been admitted to the workhouse in the last year, many with child or encumbered by existing offspring, whose parentage is unknown. Little can be done for these paupers other than to feed and clothe them. Unfortunately, the lack of experienced midwives at the workhouse has recently led to a number of deaths during childbirth.

These sad events include the late Nuri Sully who died within hours of her stillborn child and without any attendance by a midwife. The parish considers such deaths could be avoided if their meagre funds were augmented and more money given to specifically provide for the care of these destitute inmates, many of whom have been abandoned by greater personages in our society.

The name Nuri Sully appeared again in an undated extract from another local newspaper. The poor woman had died in childbirth. The burial notices in the *Docking Gazette* stated she'd been buried in a coffin provided by an anonymous benefactor and her body interned at Little Knottisham parish church. Felicity had shown an unusual amount of interest in one vagabond woman abandoned by her family. Turning over the paper, somebody – Felicity? – had penned on the back:

Real name of Beatrice?

Who the hell was Beatrice?

The remaining newspaper clippings came from the *Norfolk Chronicle* and referred to an event I already knew about: the fire at Heachley Hall. Two were published within two days of each other at the end of January 1873, the other a while later in 1875.

January 26th 1873

The flames could be seen for miles about and as far as the coast at Hunstanton. The inferno brought the residents of Little Knottisham running to assist the desperate family and servants in their attempt to save the property from total catastrophe. The consequences of the fire at Heachley Hall have yet to be fully assessed, however witnesses agree a third of the great house has been lost to fire damage and much of the woodland around it caught the sparks and burnt to cinders. The efforts of all those who assisted, risking their lives to enter the property to save valuables, have been lauded by the Mayor of King's Lynn, who offered his condolences to the owner, Mr Henry Isaacks. The cause of the fire is unknown, but it is considered fortunate the house did not burn down in its entirety.

January 28th 1873

With great sadness, the police have disclosed that the eldest son of Henry Isaacks, Christopher Isaacks, died in the fire at Heachley Hall. The heat of the inferno that engulfed the wing was so great that his remains have not been found. However, he was seen at the window by those who fought the fire and he was known to be in the house at the time, while the rest of the family and servants attended church. Valiant attempts were made by several local farmers to reach Mr Isaacks, but unfortunately the young man was unable to open the windows or smash them. His apparent inability to assist in his own escape has led the police to declare the poor man was swiftly overcome by the thick choking smoke and the intensity of the flames swept his body into the ashes.

Inhabitants from the surrounding villages have been coming to Little Knottisham church to sign a book of condolence left there by the family, who have not returned to the sad scene, preferring to take up residence in King's Lynn for the foreseeable future.

April 21st 1875

Heachley Hall and its surrounding lands have been sold at auction to the Marsters family. The new owner, Major Rupert Marsters, whose father played a vital diplomatic role in the Indian mutinies, was born in India. He has returned to England to assist his brother, James Marsters, in the management of a spice company, which is the family's primary business in India. The house has remained vacated by the Isaacks since the tragic fire that took the life of Henry Isaack's son, Christopher. Plans have been drawn up to repair the house in preparation for the arrival of Maj. Marsters and his family. It is understood the demolished wing will not be rebuilt.

Somebody had died at Heachley Hall and not quietly in their bed. Christopher Isaacks had burnt to death. The impact of the fire on the Isaack family was devastating; they'd never come back. My ancestors, the Marsters, had owned Heachley Hall for longer than I'd appreciated. The fire had happened in 1873, the same year as Nuri's tragic death – was there a connection? Two years later,

Heachley was sold at auction and lived in by the Marsters until when? My grandfather and great-aunt had been born in India. Why had Hubert and his family lived there and not in Norfolk, and in his absence, what had become of the house? Who had the tenants been?

I wanted answers. I'd dreamt of opening this box and finding letters, perhaps an exchange between my mother and her aunt in which Felicity had been asked to honour some agreement or duty of care towards me, her only surviving relative. Maybe even Felicity's plans for Heachley, her vision of its future. My greatest ideal would have been a letter addressed to me, explaining why she'd added the binding clause of a year and a day to her will. Why, dammit, was there nothing about her life at Heachley Hall? Felicity's box had created yet more questions. I combed my fingers though my hair and scrunched my hand into a fist. I'd discovered a trail of incompleteness, the skeleton of a story. Why had she stopped researching?

With everything spread across the table, I waited for something to leap out at me. The rain thundered on the windowpane. The minutes ticked away unproductively. Defeated, I gathered up the papers and bundled them back into the box. At least they were back at Heachley Hall, where for a few more months they belonged. After that, the box would probably take a journey alongside my other possessions, losing its significance until some day I would open the box and once again ponder the reason why I lived in a rundown mansion.

Except, I refused to let that be the end of my research into Felicity's will, or the house's past.

Maggie had inferred the man who burnt to death in the fire was the ghost of Heachley Hall. The quirky happenings, which plagued the house, had a source, an identity, supposedly. I hooked the lid in place and stroked the fibrous material and noted my trembling fingers. Was I worried about the implication of a ghost? Was I ready to believe in anything supernatural? That wasn't me; only in my imagination and at the end of a pencil did I allow things to become unreal.

Picking up the box, I carried it into the library and placed it on an empty shelf. There it would stay. No way was a ghost going to ruin my last few months in Heachley Hall. However, my curiosity had been awoken, but not about Christopher Isaacks and his domestic tragedy – fires burnt down many houses. Nuri Sully and her sad demise had captured Felicity's imagination for some reason and I still had no explanation why. If Nuri was buried in the churchyard, then maybe there were records of her birth and her parentage at the parish church. I regretted not pursuing the archives and seeing all those names was like a spur in my side – I should finish what Felicity started years ago.

My rambling thoughts were interrupted by the persistent rain: I'd left the washing out on the line.

Once I'd loaded the sopping washing back into the machine for a spin, I went in search of Charles: what had made him react so negatively to Maggie's appearance?

There was no sign of him in the outbuilding.

He'd been working on manufacturing a fireguard out of a sheet of metal, which he'd dug out from another building. It lay on the bench where he'd been hammering it flat. Some of his tools were arranged in a neat row on the bench while others hung from wall hooks. Above his bench was a small shelf with a solitary occupancy: the radio. It stayed here when he went home. Propped against the stack of freshly cut wood, the lethal axe with its sharp edge glinting. Throughout the winter, the firewood had never run out. Not once had I been left without sufficient fuel. Always, when I came with my basket to collect the hued logs there stood dry ones, separated from the damp ones. I learnt to know which pile to use and which to leave for later.

The light coming through the window seemed barely sufficient, yet he coped without complaining while beneath my feet, the uneven floor had been swept of wood shavings. The smooth cobblestones, round like beach pebbles, were shiny islands in the hardened sea of concrete. He took pride in his workplace, as if it was an extension of his own home.

How had I come to rely on this man to such an extent? This remarkable individual who appeared most days for a few hours, technically a trespasser, climbing over a wall and choosing to chop wood in a murky wood. Why had he kept himself busy here in an unheated shed with no lights and with little companionship? Selfishly, I wanted the reason to be entirely down to me and not some loyalty to my departed great-aunt.

With the garden springing back to life, and less to do inside the house, Charles often elected to wheel a barrow of tools and disappear into the farthest points of the estate. Unnerved by the box's arrival and Maggie's gloom ridden depiction of Heachley, I wished he would remain indoors, close by, humming a tune with a paintbrush or trowel in his hand. I'd become increasingly needy with my expectations of Charles and the comfort it brought.

I backed out of the shed. Yet again, his ability to come and go had thwarted my attempt at interrogation. Perhaps I unfairly wanted his attention when it suited me. I'd have to wait to reveal the contents of the box to him. Nevertheless, the momentum of my enthusiasm wouldn't be abated. I returned to the house and grabbed my handbag and car keys. The churchyard beckoned.

TWENTY-EIGHT

Little Knottisham parish church, St Cuthbert's, hid itself in a copse on the outskirts of the village. Built using flintstone, and possessing unstained windows – probably not the original ones – and a small tower, the narrow church was penned in by its cemetery and surrounding walls. I parked my car on the lane outside and strode up to the porch abutting the nave.

The door was locked. I rattled the latch several times half expecting it to spring open. According to the notices pinned to the board in the porch, the church spent much of its time locked. The congregation had shrunk and shared its vicar with a neighbouring village.

I weaved between the headstones in an arbitrary fashion. The sun edged out from behind a cloud and the recently mowed grass shimmered with slippery wetness. A few surnames etched on the headstones matched the names of the locals I'd met during my time in the village, including the Pykes, whose family occupied one corner plot. Passing one headstone, which stood lopsided, I spotted an even more familiar name: MARSTERS. Crouching on my toes, I traced the carved lettering, which had been obscured by lichen and moss. I wished I'd brought paper and chalk since rubbing over the gravestone might have made it easier to read. Picking away at the white fungus I revealed the name:

JAMES MARSTERS

Chiselled in copperplate style numbers, his birth year – 1844. He had died in 1890. A distant ancestor of mine, but whether a cousin or of direct lineage, I didn't know. My knowledge of my family ceased with Hubert. James' wife, Georgina, passed away in the early part of the twentieth century and she lay with him.

Next to James' grave, a fresher one stood, with a headstone made out of polished marble. The names on this grave were much clearer:

Lt Col. RUPERT MARSTERS
and his beloved wife
OLIVIA.

Born in 1846, he'd lived to a good age, dying in 1934, whereas she had succumbed earlier in 1913 at the age of 65. Rupert Marsters was the man who purchased Heachley Hall, according to the article in Felicity's Chindi box, and James was probably his older brother. Although these men must have had strong connections to India, they'd both been buried here in Little Knottisham.

The third grave, which had a larger more ornate headstone, revealed its occupant to be Frederick Marsters, born in 1868 and died in 1933, the year before Rupert. Potentially a son of either Rupert or James. The wording of 'beloved husband and father', implied a wife, but she hadn't shared Frederick's grave. Hubert – probably the offspring of Frederick – had inherited Heachley before the Second World War and leased it out. All of these men could have lived at the Hall at one time or another.

I touched each gravestone in turn and tried to make some connection to my family. Hubert had been buried in India, so I'd no grave to visit for him. John Marsters, my grandfather, rested in a London cemetery. Felicity, cremated in Norwich, my mother likewise in Colchester, and my father's ashes had been scattered on a Greek island with his lover. Only one other Marsters – Mary, my mentally fractured grandmother – had been buried and she lay next to John, squeezed into his grave. Her only dying wish was to be with her husband. My attempt at sensing a connection, some kind of energy conduit between me and my deceased ancestors didn't happen. I smirked. What did I expect? I'd known nothing about them, nor cared to until Felicity's will brought me here.

I streamed a thin puff of air through my lips creating a long sigh, while behind me a shadow, caused by the sun, disappearing behind a cloud, stretched across the graveyard, dimming each headstone in turn. The sun's shrinking rays lit up a final headstone before vanishing.

Tilted backwards, almost toppling over and a few feet behind James's grave, stood an isolated stone cross. Approaching the small memorial, I squinted, struggling to read the name. Only when I knelt close enough to touch it, and skate my fingers along the first few letters, did I realise who lay buried at my feet: Nuri Sully. Her birthday unknown, but her death was marked as 26 January 1873. The same day the fire ravaged Heachley Hall and killed Christopher Isaacks. Below her name, in smaller letters, a reference to a daughter – her stillborn offspring.

For several minutes I crouched, gazing at the name, trying to assimilate its significance. The blustery wind swept around me, rustling the yew trees, which lined the graveyard and hid the outer wall. The evergreens' discarded thin leaves littered the ground, killing off the grass and leaving it muddy and bare. It was into this harsh ground that Nuri Sully had been interned, unlike the Marsters family members, who were surrounded by lush grass. For a woman described as destitute, she'd been given a burial and headstone, something she'd perhaps not anticipated as she lay dying in the workhouse. However, the grave's solitary position smacked of necessity, almost an obligation on the part of the benefactor who'd paid for it, rather than love or kindness.

Perhaps, my trip to the church had not been fruitless. I'd discovered a link and not to my relatives: Christopher Isaacks and Nuri Sully had died on the same day. What this new discovery signified, I didn't know.

A handwritten note had been stuffed through the letterbox during my absence. Resting on the doormat, I nearly trampled on the folded piece of mud-splattered paper. In a chaotic scrawl, Tony informed me that tomorrow the weather would be dry and he would arrive early in the morning to mow the lawns and cut back the jungle of hawthorn hedgerows.

I checked the time – the school day had finished – and I dialled Ruth's home number. I itched to tell her about Maggie, the box and the graveyard visit.

She listened attentively, prompting me when I rambled on and skipped over some salient point. I drew breath and waited for her verdict.

'So-oo,' she drawled, 'this box mainly contained photographs of India and her parents. Basically, nostalgic stuff.'

My shoulders slowly drooped as I exhaled. 'Yes, I suppose.'

'I don't want to kill your excitement, sweetie, but the rest was buried at the bottom.'

'Meaning?' I pressed my fingers into my temple, the familiar ache immediately returned.

'Just…'

'Go on,' I urged.

'She missed India more than anything. What you found, those few newspaper articles, sounds like half-baked research. Like she started something then gave up. One trip to the churchyard and you've confirmed there's a Nuri Sully and she died the same day as the fire. Yet, Felicity, it appears, didn't do any further research.'

'Maggie said she'd gone to the archives.' The librarian in Hunstanton had recommended the same course of action to me.

'But when? It couldn't have been in recent years because she was too old and infirm. So she had an interest in this woman and the fire, but never followed it through and forgot—'

'But she took the box with her to hospital—'

Ruth cut back swiftly. 'She asked for a box which contained photographs of her mother and father. A distinctive box that Liz easily could identify and find. If Liz had peeked inside it, she saw things of no importance, and it's probably why nobody cared about it. If there were scandalous things in it, do you think Liz would have forgotten and shrugged off this box – the nursing home, too? They would have recognised documents of legal importance, like another will, and acted on them. If there was anything else Felicity had held on to, she left it behind at Heachley and never asked for it. It's all gone, and probably burnt by the clearance guys. Sorry.' She'd softened her tone at the end, aware of the significance of what she was saying. This was it: there were no more secrets.

I groaned in frustration. Ruth had easily dismissed my discovery as insignificant. 'Maggie alluded to something,' I ventured.

'She'd probably done what you've done. Focused on those few documents, which for a ghost hunter is great fodder. The fact is, and I'm sorry to burst your bubble of excitement, they were like leftovers, forgotten things. Felicity simply wanted the picture of her parents. The rest she couldn't be bothered with.'

'Why?' I snapped at the wall right by my nose.

'Because it's a coincidence,' Ruth said gently. 'A woman dying in a workhouse and a fire on the same day? It's local history and nothing sinister.'

I huffed. Ruth couldn't see my scowl, but she'd hear my grumpy tone. With relative ease, she'd deflated all my discoveries into little consequence. There was nothing to explain Felicity's plans for Heachley, nor Maggie's suspicions of a ghost, other than a man dying in a house fire, nor was there anything a solicitor would find of value.

'Drat,' I muttered.

'You've been expecting so much from this—'

'I know, I know,' I didn't want a told you so, not that Ruth would present it in such a demeaning fashion, but it sure felt like one.

'Look. It's Easter soon and I promise to visit for a few days. Without Mick.'

I cringed in shame at her suggestion. Ruth had noted my reaction to their constant displays of affection.

'Oh, you don't have to leave him behind,' I piped up.

She snorted. 'Don't be daft. We both know what you need. We'll get drunk, eat calorific cakes and burn more stuff in the garden. How about that?'

I gabbled, relieved and overwhelmed. 'Yes, thank you. That's kind of you. I'm sorry. I'm sulking.'

'Nonsense! How's my clown?'

Work – the distraction I depended upon. 'Good, but I'm scrapping the juggler. He looked like an octopus.'

'If you're not happy with it, that's fine by me.'

'I'll come up with something else, I promise. I'm low on inspiration at the moment.'

We drifted into talking about the book. Her story, which was pitched at helping children adapt to starting school, was about a circus school. Each act, from clowns to jugglers, trapeze artists to acrobats, had a tale to tell about enjoying school.

My black mood lifted. Tomorrow the garden would have its facelift and soon I would pass the halfway point – six months. The more I focused on tidying up the garden, the less the house would interfere. No more wondering about dust blowing about the rooms. If there was a ghost, he – assuming Maggie's theory was the reason for the anomalies – could haunt away. I didn't care.

·· ● ··

TWENTY-NINE

The tractor's rude engine woke me. An unfriendly rumble that ricocheted its way into my twisted dreams, displacing the image of a misty graveyard haunted by octopus jugglers with the bland walls of the attic. Squinting in the dimness I located the fluorescent glow of the alarm clock: seven o'clock! I scrambled out of bed, flung on some clothes and careered downstairs.

Tony had made a start on the front lawn. The tractor dragged behind its wheels a large spinning attachment and a vast bucket. My fears about the cuttings lying strewn across the newly mowed grass were unfounded; the cutter incorporated a collector bin.

When Tony spotted me waving by the front door he halted his sweep and cut the engine.

'Mornin', Miriam.' He grinned and pushed his flat cap back off his wrinkled forehead.

'Tony, brilliant, you're here.' I enthused. I stomped my frozen feet on the gravel and the gravel stones flew up. 'Er, coffee?'

He held up a large flask. 'I'm alright, thank you.' The grin spread wider.

'The cuttings – what did you plan to do with them?'

He scratched his ruddy nose with a grubby thumb. 'Add to our manure. If that's okay. Unless you want them for yourself?'

'No, no.' I held up my hands. 'Keep them.'

He chuckled. 'Reckon they'll be a fair amount. I'll clear the lawns, then swap over to the hedge trimmer.'

I beamed, 'You're a star.'

His rosy cheeks flushed brighter and he switched the engine back on. The tractor juddered, spluttering, then the flail began to rotate, sending loose grass flying. I backed away and headed indoors.

Working proved impossible. Both the noise and the hypnotic distraction of observing Tony plough up and down the garden terraces proved too entrancing. He swiftly carved a path into the rear garden, exposing fresh shoots and obliterating the nettles and hollyhocks without mercy.

What lay beneath was not, unfortunately, lawn tennis grade grass. I'd have to work hard to kill off the dandelions, daisies and other weeds. I'd need to hire a ride-on mower, otherwise, Tony's wilderness clearance would prove to be pointless.

After the lawns had been cut he drove away back down the lane to the farm. I assumed to switch to another trailer attachment. Standing by the library window with an empty coffee mug, I admired the transformation and bounced on my tiptoes. Then, out of the corner of my eye, a fleeting glimpse of dull redness between the trees. Was that Charles arriving?

I dashed to the back door, eager to meet him. Zipping up my fleece jacket and pulling on my Wellington boots, I slammed the back door shut. If Ruth was dismissive of Felicity's box, perhaps Charles could be persuaded to share his thoughts. The previous day, he'd certainly stared hard at the box, clearly alarmed by something.

I hung by the outbuildings waiting for him. When he failed to arrive, I skirted the outside of the sheds, then tracked along the edge of the wood to where I thought I'd seen him. While I stepped between the conifers, farther to my right, pinecones and twigs snapped – muntjac roaming? The tractor should have scared them off. I froze, listening to the undergrowth crack and rustle until the odd sounds grew quieter and distant.

I hovered, uncertain, trying not to lose courage. Since the time I trekked into Heachley Wood and the mist had chased me out, I'd done nothing more than stick to the fringes. The cold weather had paid some role in my reticence to explore, but not entirely.

Deep amongst the tree trunks, the mist lurked. The white swirl drifted close to the ground, slithering in waves, some dense patches, others not so. I continued to walk the imaginary boundary between the landscaped garden and the woods, my path punctuated by shrubs and overgrown borders. Hedges, once probably the victim of excessive topiary, had grown up above my head. They hid unknown cultivations out of sight and smothered the original landscaping.

I called for Charles, but no response came back. The last hedge to curtail my exploration was the massive hawthorn that stood alongside the perimeter wall. The stonewall rose at least two metres tall with black flints forming teeth shaped parapets and their razor sharp edges reflected the morning light.

Somewhere, Charles had breached this wall. Turning my back on the formal gardens, and keeping sight of the boundary enclosure on my left, I should come to the gap he'd used.

The woods thickened. Younger saplings that had sprung up untamed forced me to wind a convoluted trail. At no time did I lose contact with the wall, even when the voracious climbers attempted to overwhelm the man-made structure with greenery.

The mist travelled with me; an unwanted companion. Coming from the direction of the sea, its fluid tentacles crawled over the wall, bunched around the exposed roots and congregated in the hollows of the trunks. My brisk exhales snorted out of my dripping nostrils – invisible, noisy and nervous – no match for the silent sea breath and its persistent presence. I trod my path with determination, my head ducked so I could avoid eye contact with the annoying fog.

I paused. In the distance, I heard rumbling again. The tractor was back ready to hack down the tall hedges. Some ten minutes of walking had brought me deeper into Heachley Wood than I'd ever been before. The wall remained visible, intact and looming. It should turn to the right at some point and bring me closer to the house and eventually the front gates.

Where was the gap that Charles climbed through?

The trees spread themselves apart, opening up their branches and letting in more light. The ground cleared of brambles and detritus and I came across logs, splintered and split into sections.

This had to be where Charles cut the firewood. I'd not anticipated the distance from the house. The man must toil for hours lugging the chopped wood to the shed.

Alongside the wall the growth of clematis, honeysuckle and the ubiquitous ivy diminished, and in its place a stream flowed, its water crystal clear. The delicate noise of liquid tumbling between stones punctuated the other sounds of the wood: bird song and trees rustling in the breeze.

The mist that had been so apparent further back had gone. I'd come to a clearing right in the corner of the woods where the wall redirected itself and created a sheltered spot. I'd reached the farthest point of my estate. There, quite unspoilt and swathed in ivy, stood a log cabin.

The roof perhaps once slated had been covered in layers of conifer branches, pine needles and thick moss. At the front the window had been repaired using masking tape to cover the cracks in the glazing and the door, which was made from planks of wood nailed together, fitted the opening with no gaps. A brass knob kept it closed.

I was starting to understand its purpose. Tall enough for a person to stand up in and the size of one or two small rooms, it had been maintained, although not beautified nor transformed into a genteel summerhouse. I guessed it served a more necessary function: shelter.

Did I call out for him or barge through the door and demand an explanation? Neither. I peeked through the window, but my reflection and the dim interior thwarted my curiosity. With thumping heartbeats echoing in my ears, I approached the door and rapped my knuckles on it. Without an answer to invite me indoors, I turned the handle and entered.

I snatched a gasp. The clean interior had been made habitable with basic pine furniture: a table, bench, two shelves fixed to a wall and a wooden storage chest on the floor, which was covered in hessian mats. Those were the only items visible, the rest of the space had been partitioned by a long black drape. Reaching out, my fingers quivering uncontrollably, I swept the makeshift curtain aside to reveal a low trundle bed with quilted blankets. Hanging from the hooks in the walls the familiar clothes: polo neck knitted jumpers, faded jeans and darned socks.

A lantern torch was next to the bed, and alongside it was a wind-up radio with a crank handle. I bent over and switched it on. A voice blurted, crackling but distinctive. I turned the radio off.

I returned to the rudimentary living space. The lone shelf housed books: a motley collection of travel guides, small atlases and a few on plumbing and carpentry techniques. The table and bench possessed the features of the homemade: functional but lacking the refinement of varnish or mercury level straightness.

What the interior lacked seemed stranger for its absence: no cooking facilities, pots or pans, in fact hunting around, not even food or flasks of water. There was a copper bowl, tarnished and dinted with an ancient crusty bar of soap nestled in its bottom; it smelt of lavender. Another familiar characteristic of the cabin's occupant.

I rummaged in the wooden chest and found a few more books, pencils and paper, upon which were scribbled designs for my airing cupboard and including a recent one: the fireguard.

The paper slipped out of my hand and fluttered onto the floor.

He'd lied to me. I'd tried countless times to give him the chance to open up and explain his circumstances. It had never crossed my mind he'd be homeless – a vagrant living on my estate.

I groaned, cursing him, both annoyed by his deceit and pitying his situation. He'd lived in a freezing hut throughout winter – why? How?

He could afford to buy new clothes, bootlaces and soap with what I paid him. Perhaps it wasn't that bad. Maybe this primitive accommodation was a temporary abode, somewhere he dossed in the week when I needed him, then at weekends, he travelled farther to his real home. There, he'd have warmth and hot food. Except, he'd never stopped using string for his laces. What a blind idiot I was! I slumped onto the bench, burying my head in my hands in disbelief. Nobody chose to live like this. He came here to hide, but from what and whom, and for how long?

The lid of the chest remained propped up. I dug down and pulled out a square tin. The decoration on the outside was vintage and chipped in places, but the brand was legible: Carr and Co Biscuits.

I clawed at the rusty lid, fighting with the tight fit, and it flew off with a clatter. Inside were papers and unlike Felicity's, these were originals. The fine paper felt friable, like tissue, the curling corners tinged with damp and each required me to handle it gingerly. I lay the various documents out on the table. They represented a passage of time and glancing at the visible dates, a considerable amount of time had passed since the first had been written.

A day ago, the names written would have been unknown to me, but now having seen the contents of Felicity's box, Charles's collection of secret papers mirrored some of her research.

Love letters, not many, but addressed to Bea and signed by Kit. The brief handwritten missives divulged a love for what must have been a forbidden sweetheart. They referred to secret assignations and trysts in remote places.

Glancing through them, I arranged them in what seemed like an appropriate order. Then went back and read them carefully.

My darling Bea,

There is a barn east of Watkin's farm where we can meet on Sunday afternoon. It has fresh hay and an easy path from the house. Make haste at three o'clock. I will bring ale, bread and cheese, and we shall picnic. Do not speak of this to any of the other servants. I trust you appreciate this matter is of great personal risk to us both. I cannot wait to have you sit upon my knee again. Look for my next letter in my coal scuttle.

Yours affectionately,

Kit

Watkin's farm – Liz's family name and the farm was still occupied by them decades later. I smoothed the creased letter flat with a trembling hand and cocked my ear to listen, holding my breath.

Charles could be here any minute. But, for now I was alone. I picked up the next wafer of paper.

My darling Bea,

The weather is fine again this Sunday and I wait with much impatience to look upon your pretty face. I will take the trap to the beach and meet you there. I cannot risk us being seen travelling together. I will bring you back to Knottisham in the trap when it is dark and drop you close by the lane. The next letter I shall leave behind the basin in my chamber.

With sweet kisses,

Kit

Why were these love letters in Charles's possession? He knew I was interested in the history of Heachley and yet he'd kept them from me – I trusted him! With a pounding heart and churning stomach I read on.

My darling Bea,

How close we came to discovery. You must not loiter in the hallway with the expectation of finding me. I have included notepaper so that you may practise your letter forming and write to me instead. It is best if we do not meet for a while until my mother ceases her questioning.

Affectionately,

Kit

An admonishment, but at the same time, Kit had sought to educate his lover. The pair were not matched in station and I was pretty sure who Kit was by now. I lay the letter to one side and eagerly picked up the next one.

Dearest Bea,

Since word has reached Father of our affair and your subsequent dismissal, he has confined me to the house and grounds. I hope this letter reaches you as I have entrusted it to the groom and his daily excursion to Docking to collect parcels. I await news of your condition. I pray you are mistaken as to its nature.

Yours,

Kit

Dearest,

I have heard no news from you and fear Father is intercepting your notes. I'm accompanied wherever I travel by Father or my brother, my account is withdrawn and I have no allowance. My mother has taken to the morning room and her sewing, refusing to discuss my heartfelt wish to be reconciled to you. It has given me much time for thinking upon our sad situation. I hope these words are not too difficult for you to read, but I fear our future is doomed to failure. With great regret, I seek release from the promises I gave you in haste and hope you understand my family honour depends on your good behaviour and continuing secrecy. Do not come to Heachley, I beg you, as the scandal it would create would be too much for my family to bear. It is over and there is little more I can do for you given my confinement. My father intends to send me abroad until the gossip has died down. Those to whom you have entrusted yourself will take good care of your health.

I've given this note to our faithful groom. Please do not plead with him, as the poor man has little influence.

With affection,

Kit

In just a few sheets the little saga had unfolded into something nightmarish. Charles had kept a tragic love story buried in a tin for what purpose? Had Felicity seen these letters? They fitted perfectly with the newspaper articles in the box. More importantly, they were personal and probably belonged to somebody other than Charles or Felicity.

I snatched up the next scrap of paper.

Kit.
My darling.
    I am at the workhouse. Please come fetch me and take me
away. I am desperate. My head hurts. Please, I beg. Do not forget
me and the child I carry.
    Love and kisses. Bea.

This last forlorn letter, written in a cruder hand on a scrap of crumpled paper, was unlike the elegant copperplate workmanship of the others, and its contents revealed the saddest episode. I had my connection made solid. The poor Bea, dismissed by her lover, was Felicity's enigmatic Beatrice, who in turn had been given the name Nuri at birth. The man, whose signature throughout had been Kit, must be Christopher Isaacks.

Why Kit had rejected his pregnant lover was encapsulated in a harshly toned note, signed by Henry Isaacks, and penned in the autumn of 1872. Beatrice, a servant in the household at Heachley Hall, had been dismissed – their affair exposed.

October 12th 1872
Miss Sully,
    Due to your gross misconduct, your services as housemaid are
no longer required and with immediate effect, you are requested
not to return to Heachley Hall or make contact with my son.
Your belongings have been left at the public house in Little
Knottisham under the care of the Landlord.
    Your dismissal is a matter of disgrace to not only yourself
but this family and our loyal servants.
    Henry Isaacks

The final letter written on thicker notepaper was addressed in an elaborate hand to Mr H Isaacks and signed, the Master of Docking Workhouse. It had been dated some days after the death of Nuri Sully.

The following letters were found in the personal possessions of the late Nuri Sully. Please dispose of them as you see fit and do not ponder upon their nature. It is not for a decent gentleman to dwell upon the misfortune of the destitute, nor those who are migrant to our shores. I return them to you as they should not fall into the wrong hands. Her remains, with those of her stillborn daughter, have been brought to the undertakers and as you requested, she will be buried as swiftly as possible at St Cuthbert's. We have been unable to trace her relatives, but as they are gypsies, it is unlikely they will be found without considerable expense.

I express my condolences for the loss of your son.

A Gypsy. Now things began to make more sense. To fall in love with a servant, especially in prudish Victorian times, had been a tragic mistake for Christopher, but to make pregnant a Gypsy girl, a Romany, would bring dishonour to both families. They'd abandoned her as harshly as the Isaacks.

How had Charles come by the documents?

The expression on his face when he'd seen the Chindi box had been one of alarm. He'd ignored Maggie, not out of rudeness, but because he'd panicked. Had he ever rifled through the contents in Felicity's absence, before Liz brought the box to the hospital, and removed those letters, the true substance of her research? If he had, he'd wilfully interceded in Felicity affairs. But why?

I thumped the table and the fragile letters jumped. Carefully, I gathered them up and put them back in the biscuit tin.

I had to decide whether to wait for him or return to the house.

The door creaked, and a slither of bright sunlight struck the table. I had my answer.

Colour, the relic of a faint blush, drained from Charles's face in the briefest of seconds. He gripped the doorknob tight and froze on the threshold. The light behind him shone past; his eyes were unfathomable hollows, darker than I had ever seen before.

Unable to rise, my feeble legs seemed extraordinarily heavy. We stared at each other, unblinking, waiting.

I licked my parched lips. 'Why didn't you tell me?' My voice shook, unhinged by both his presence and my inability to rage at him. I felt disappointment, yes, but not anger.

He opened his mouth a fraction, but said nothing. He'd glued his hand to the handle.

'This place,' I gestured, sweeping my arm around the room, 'How long have you used it?'

No response. The tick-tock pulse in my neck continued throughout his attack of muteness, the thrum a reminder of my racing heartbeats. I wrung my clammy hands together into a ball in my lap. 'Charles?' I raised my eyebrows. 'I deserve an answer, don't I?'

'Yes,' he murmured. 'You do.'

The first time we'd met, he'd bounded into the house with energy, astounded by the passage of time. He'd slowly lost that vigour, and I remembered the transformation; deflating as he bore witness to the emptiness, showing sadness over Felicity's death. I was convinced he'd not faked those reactions. Which meant he'd been absent for five years. Where had he lived?

'You've been living rough here since I moved in, but not before. Why?'

He blinked, awaking from his stunned trance. 'I said before,' he said gruffly, forcing the words out through his lips, 'I'm itinerant. I sleep where I work.'

I tapped the surface of the table with a quivering finger; jitters stampeded across my body. 'This isn't a home. I know what makes a home and this isn't it. You have a bed, nothing else. How is this possible?' I scraped the base of the tin across the table. So many questions and I could barely think where to begin. 'Where did you find these letters?'

'In the cellar.'

'The cellar?' I guffawed. There was nothing of value in the cellar. 'Not Felicity's Chindi box?'

He finally let go of the door handle and ran his fingers through his hair, gathering the unruly strands in a bundle at the top of his head. He vigorously shook his head.

'Believe me, I've never taken her things. I recognised the box, but I'd not looked in it. I wouldn't—'

'Steal from her?' I pointed at the books on the shelf.

'She gave them to me.' He pressed his hands together as if to plead his case.

'You didn't know about the clearance – the locals in the pub knew the house had been emptied, but not you, unless you lied. Why didn't you help yourself to more of her things back then? And I don't get it, your absence. Five years,' I reminded him, 'How could you not know she'd died?'

'I've been away.'

I ignored his flippant reply. 'You've been sleeping here since I arrived. Less than a mile from the house. Have you been creeping around the house at night? Did you bank down the fire in the sitting room?' I rattled off my inquisition.

'Miriam, please…' The sentence hung incomplete. He'd a pained expression.

'You abandoned her, Charles. Took her things. What did you think was happening in the house? Are you like Maggie, a believer in ghosts, a seeker of evidence? Is that why you hang about Heachley, hoping to see something to tell the newspapers, the TV shows? Who do you think the ghost might be? Christopher Isaacks or Nuri Sully? Perhaps both? But not Felicity, no. She'd already worked it out.'

He shifted forward into the light and gaped, forming a wordless mouth while his pale face, now illuminated clearly, gave prominence to eyes as wide as opaque moons. His failure to give me a decent explanation for anything that had occurred over the past few months fuelled my disbelief, my frustration. Despair, too. He was supposed to be my friend. He was supposed to be…who the hell was this man and why had I foolishly fallen for him?

Strength returned to my legs and I rose. Instinctively, my hands clenched into fists, not to fight or protect myself, but because I feared I might reach out to touch him, to feel him. In that touch would I sense the reason for his lies? Would I fathom him through his clothes, know him any better just by forming a conduit? I doubted it. I'd been fooled from the beginning of our relationship. The theories to account for his behaviour, which I'd previously dismissed, the products of fragmented guesswork that I had used to paint him as a criminal and a social outcast, were brought back to life. I glared, buoyed by my reconstructed opinions – he was a liar. I pressed my lips together into a deep frown of misery.

Charles gasped, turned his back on me and ran out of the door into the woods.

I followed him, determined to harangue him into giving me proper answers. He stumbled a few times then picked up his pace. The mist flooded in from all directions. The miasma shot out from behind the trees, oozed up from the ground and hung from the bare branches. Within sight of me, the white haze enveloped Charles, and thickened around his legs and arms. He slowed as the veil descended, licking its wispy strands across his chest, darting up to his chin. He halted mid-stride.

Through the misty curtain, I barely discerned his features. Was he crying? His hunched shoulders juddered slightly and he buried his face in his hands.

'Charles?' A breathless exclamation and I ended my pursuit a few feet away from him.

He rotated, inch by inch, lifting his head as he pivoted. His eyes were dry not tear filled. From out of his translucent pupils, the hollow depths of his sockets shone a fiery glow.

I should have run away back to the sanctuary of the house, but it wasn't necessary. I wasn't afraid. The longer he remained captive in the fog, the more he seemed to merge into it, as if a mutual need had been met. I realised that as we stood face to face: Charles and the mist were a single living creature.

I tumbled into an abyss of tangled emotions fuelled by dark explanations for his behaviour, and I discarded each one until one remained: curiosity – naked, untainted curiosity. I had to know who he was. I reached out, slipped my hand through the protective blanket and touched his shoulder. The moment I made contact, his electrified tension shot into my fingertips and I felt a jolt of something inexplicable, almost calming.

Charles spoke with terrible clarity. 'I am Christopher Isaacks.'

With one deep, audible sigh, the mist vanished.

THIRTY

'What?' Stung into action by his bizarre announcement, I recoiled, whipping back my hand.

'I can't hide from you any longer.' The man I called Charles spoke in a strained voice, almost unrecognisable. He remained rooted to the spot. A waxy figure clothed in a timeless outfit. He might be at home in Madame Tussaud's such was his ability to freeze into a statue. His eyelids flickered, a brief reminder that as far as I was concerned, he was alive.

'Christopher is dead.' I stuck to the facts. Christopher had been a Victorian gentleman; what I saw was Charles, a handyman.

He looked at his feet, and as if to recall their purpose and moved one. The stained leather uppers creased into familiar ruts as he bent his toes, walking one step forward, then another. Colour, a minuscule hue of red, trickled into his cheeks and he nodded – in confirmation?

'Let me explain, will you?' He hurried towards the cabin, stumbling on a root in his haste. 'There is something I want to show you,' he called over his shoulder. Now it was my turn to force my jelly legs to respond.

A rush of blood pumped to my head, pounding against my temples. Anxious, afraid or excited? I had no idea how to tell the difference. I'd a puddle of adrenaline in my stomach and it controlled my emotions, bathing me in a confusing cocktail of sensations. I followed him more on automatic pilot than anything else.

He held the door open for me and offered me the bench. I sat and crushed my hands between my thighs. From out of the Carr tin, he extracted the letters, selected one and laid it on the table next to me. It was the last letter Kit had written to Beatrice: the letter of rejection.

He perched on the opposite bench and without touching the note, pointed a long, trembling finger at it. 'The man who wrote that letter was a selfish coward. He refused to stand up to his father or risk his inheritance to keep the woman he believed he loved. He threw her and the child she carried in her belly away – his baby. A young, foolish man who seduced a pretty girl with little care for her future. They talked of eloping in the heat of passionate love-making, but when his father found out, the heartless wretch demanded an end to their scandalous affair or else Heachley would not be his.'

I swallowed hard. 'She died in childbirth.'

He flinched, turning away for a moment before facing me with those sad eyes I'd come to see too often – were they really Christopher's?

'I...I'd already regretted mm...my decision by the time word reached me that day, the day of the fire.' He'd shifted his perspective, stuttering over the words. He forced the alien pronouns out. 'Regrettably, not due to my devotion to her, but because I believed somebody might tell her family.'

Her gypsy family. 'You feared them?'

'She was beautiful – dark eyes, jet black hair and the skin of a moor: rich and honeyed.' Charles hung his head and hid his eyes. 'She'd chosen Beatrice as her name because it hid her identity. Her father and uncle travelled afar to find work as thatchers. Her mother, long dead. They put her to work as a maid and my father employed her. It meant she had a roof over head and security. I ruined that sanctity.'

'Her honour, too, no doubt.' I touched the note. 'Christopher could have been a better person.'

'Yes,' he whispered, keeping his head bowed. 'It took me a long time to learn that.'

'He died in a fire.' I pushed the note across the table towards him. 'Which means, if you are him, you're a ghost. I don't believe in ghosts.' My voiced warbled. My faith in that belief was slipping away fast.

He continued, unperturbed by my lack of conviction, and he spoke as if from a great distance: a forgotten past lying dormant in his mind.

'She tried to reach me before she entered the workhouse, but I barricaded myself in the house, obeying my father's wishes. I was not to leave the house. In the village during the weeks of my confinement, rumours had spread, no doubt put about by the servant who betrayed us.' He leapt to his feet, unable to meet my eyes this time, his hands briefly clenching into fists. 'I hid in shame behind the curtains. My family and servants bravely went to church the morning she died – it was a Sunday – and I was left behind. My anguish grew with the realisation she might have lived if she'd remained at Heachley, if I'd insisted on keeping her by my side. The child, too.'

'Possibly,' I murmured, remembering the newspaper article about the treatment of pregnant women in the workhouse where Beatrice had died.

He swayed back and forth. His pasty skin was drawn tight over his cheekbones turning down his lips. An expression of agony or a grimace of disgust?

'I refused to answer the door. I heard a man's voice ranting, berating me. I heard, but didn't see.'

'Who?'

'Her father.' He'd lowered his voice and I struggled to hear him.

'He blamed you?'

'Worse.' He buried his face in his hands and released a low sob.

'Charles?' Not Christopher, not while I harboured doubts.

He sniffed and uncovered his face. 'He cursed me.'

'Cursed you?' I cast my mind back to when I'd first told Ruth about living in the house. She'd used the same words.

'I'm unable to leave Heachley until I find love again. I'm stuck here forever, never ageing. Unable to die. My body stuck in time while the world moves forward relentlessly.'

Goose bumps prickled up my spine. 'Christopher died in the fire. You,' I briefly shut my eyes, 'You died.' I reiterated.

He nodded, a strange acknowledgement of what he claimed to be the truth, one I fought to believe.

'I don't remember the fire. But these—' he rolled up his sleeves uncovering the white whorls on his skin, '– are scars. Something happened. When the fire started, I stayed and let it burn. I wanted to die, perhaps. That angry voice triggered a deep regret at my actions. In a rash moment, I cared not to live as Christopher any longer.'

'Or you fell asleep and a spark leapt out.' I drew the familiar picture of my own absentmindedness and saying it, I knew it didn't fit with what he described.

'Does it matter?' He pressed the heel of his palms into two harrowed eyes, 'Because the reality is I can't leave Heachley. I've not left this estate in over one hundred and fifty years.'

I shook my head in disbelief – why not simply walk out the gate? 'Then where were you after Felicity left? Why didn't you know she'd not come back from the hospital, that she'd died?' Flaws, there had to be flaws in his tale, something to end the illusion of Kit living in the cabin.

'I only exist in corporeal form when the house is occupied by females – women, girls. The moment a man or boy steps through the gate, I disappear.'

'To where?' I scoffed. Tony. Bert, too? Had they not seen him at all, not even working in the garden?

'I don't know, but not here. Whenever you leave, so do I. When you return I do too, and always in the closet or the cellar.'

'What?' I gaped as I mentally scribbled a list of unexplained events. All those strange noises echoing about the house. The ash-like dust that seeped through the floorboards and came out of the cellar and closet connected the house back to where the fire had raged. The handle on the inside of the closet door and the bolt missing off the cellar door – had he done those alterations? 'The closet door sticks.'

'I know,' he nodded. 'When you and Ruth came back from the village, I couldn't get out of the closet. My fear of being stuck there, not knowing how long I'd be there or having you find me trapped inside. I panicked. It's not like me. I've learnt to be patient and stay calm. So, while you made bonfires, I fitted a knob on the inside to help me open it. The bolt on the cellar door, I removed that too for the same reason. You saw, or heard me, I think. You called out to me as I hid in the dark cellar.'

I glanced up at the makeshift roof. What he said made sense. He offered substance to his story and the more the evidence fitted with what I'd seen, heard, almost sensed, the more his story convinced me.

'You disappear?' I rose and crossed the room. Reaching out I prodded him. Beneath my finger was hard muscle. Tentatively, I touched the back of his hand and although not warm, neither was it icy cold. I wrapped my fingers about his wrist, feeling for his pulse. There it was, plodding along at a steady pace, most unlike my racy one. He had all the attributes of a living person: breathing, pumping heart and warmth. 'You don't walk through walls or float about?'

Charles smiled. His expression was a welcome display of charm and pleasantness, the very thing that drew me to him each time we shared the same space. 'No. I'm quite un-ghostlike, am I not? But when the house is empty, that is what I become. I lose sense of time and emotion. I am lost; a spirit somewhere.'

'This curse keeps you here and you can never, ever leave?'

'I can be released,' he admitted.

'What? How?' I straddled the bench with my legs, determined to keep track of his convoluted tale. 'The man, Beatrice's father, cursed you never to leave until you find love again. That's what you said.'

The tension returned; he'd shrunken, hunched his shoulders down to avoid eye contact. 'That love would have to be reciprocated, given freely and consummated.' A whisper. The last word hurried out of his lips to the accompaniment of an embarrassed flush around his cheekbones.

'Consummated?' I raised my eyebrows.

'The passion of physical love; proof beyond the emotion.'

Sex. I wanted to laugh at his poetical expression, but his serious face, the tautness around his mouth, held it in check. 'And if you did?'

'Then, I assume, I'd be gone. Free. However, the curse extends to my lover; she would be left heartbroken and alone.'

Decades of celibacy. Not once had he – it was my turn to blush. 'And you've not sought this freedom?'

'To seek what I desire would be unfair; I've learnt that lesson the hard way.' Picking up the note, he placed it inside the tin and closed the lid.

'Over a hundred and fifty years and nobody tempted you?' I cringed at my own words. I didn't want to ask. My body, flooded with racks of adrenaline, could barely cope with the shock of what I was hearing never mind whether I should believe a word of it. I'd yearned for months to be something more to him than a friend. Now, my feelings for Charles were in turmoil.

He avoided making any eye contact with me and fidgeted with the tin's lid. 'Yes, I know the irony. But the reality is this house rarely had the occupancy of entirely women; men – the masters and servants – were always here, so I kept disappearing. I rarely had the chance to get to know women, nor they me, and if I did, well…it wasn't as I expected it to be.'

'Until Felicity.'

'Yes, Felicity,' he paused, clearing his throat. 'And you.' Finally, he glanced up and showed me two focused eyes; no tears or redness, nothing emotional. Yet, they weren't lifeless.

'When Felicity was here, you lived in this cabin and not the house?'

'How could I claim my place in the house I should have inherited? How to explain,' he said, fingering the tin that contained the last mementos of Christopher, the heir apparent. 'What would it do to have people know my predicament? To have me turned into a freak show?'

'The tenants who came and went, you've always been their handyman or gardener?'

He nodded. My interrogation seemed to relax him, help him open up. My questions were practical, not personal.

'Yes, what else could I do? I would appear on the doorstep and offer my services. Fortunately, the remoteness of the place and the changing occupants helped provide a cover story. I simply left no trace of my past in the house, so nobody suspected my time here had been more than a few years.'

'Like you did with me. Every time I went to bed, you returned here to this lowly shack, pretending you lived elsewhere. My God, your vagueness drove me nuts.'

A gentle grin spread over his face. 'I know. Sorry.'

The box. The beautiful decorations that hid the inquisitive mind of a lonely woman. I'd underestimated my great-aunt. 'Felicity worked this out, who you were. She started to collect things: the Chindi box contained newspaper cuttings about the fire and the death of Beatrice. But she lost interest, probably a long time ago.'

'Because once she confronted me a few months after she arrived here, she had the answers. I told her everything.'

I rose, uncomfortable with the realisation of exactly how long he'd been here with Felicity – not a few years, but decades: she'd arrived in the mid-1960s, while my grandmother lived here. The idea freaked me out.

'No,' I said empathetically, pacing the small space next to the table. 'This can't be true. You're imagining this all. You found stuff in the house and believed it.' I tried to ignore his increasingly tortured expression. 'You mentioned reincarnation, perhaps this is a fixation about that or maybe you're an amnesiac who has adopted these memories based on scraps of paper.' I lifted my hands in despair. I had to rationalise the excuses for his peculiar behaviour because the alternative – his version – was preposterous.

I stormed out of the hut.

'Miriam, please wait.' He ran after me and caught hold of my hand, gently tugging on it. 'Let me answer your doubts.'

'How?' I snapped and shook free my hand with an irritated jerk of my wrist.

'Walk with me to the gate. Please, trust me,' he implored, pressing his palms together as if in prayer.

'Okay,' I shrugged, striding off ahead of him until he caught up.

We walked side by side, weaving in and out of the trees, but staying close to the wall. For a while we covered the ground in silence, my thoughts jumbled up and incoherent. I replayed the last few months, dissecting our encounters, recalling the fragments of conversation.

'It can't be reincarnation,' he said abruptly. 'I remember only one childhood.'

It seemed Charles had the same idea. 'I see,' I murmured. 'Go on.'

'And I've no need to eat or drink. My hair doesn't grow beyond the length I had on the day of the fire. I don't shave either.'

Not once had I actually seen him drink the coffee I'd given him. I'd only seen the empty mugs in the sink. He'd declined all my offers of food and I'd assumed he stoically worked through the day with no need for it.

'The mist?' I asked, as we crossed the newly mowed front lawn. Tony had gone, leaving us alone. I would need to call by and thank him, but not yet.

'I think it protects me. I don't understand it. I'm not afraid of it, quite the contrary.'

We'd reached the gate and as we stepped closer, he slipped his hand into mine. Neither warm nor cold, it was a hand without callouses, unlike a workman's. Rather, I felt the smooth skin of a gentleman's palm.

'Don't be afraid,' he said. 'I don't feel any pain. You'll find me again.'

I held my breath and looked straight ahead. He squeezed my hand, his grip firm and present. I lifted my foot over the threshold, past the gateposts and in that instance, my fingers held nothing. Halting by the roadside, I tried to calm my breathing, aware of no sounds other than my rasping. I turned to where he'd been – next to me, right there, in my shadow.

Spinning around, I looked everywhere: down the lane, up the drive, and across the hewed grasses.

Charles had gone.

The gravel flew up beneath my feet. I ran, my heart pounding, and almost skidded on the slippery stones. Slowing up I jogged the last few yards to the back door. For a few breathless seconds I paused by the cellar door, listening for footsteps or any sounds of movement. Silence. I walked through the disused scullery, the cavernous kitchen with the Rayburn belching out a heat and into the hallway.

Charles was seated on the bottom step of the stairs with his hands loosely clasped together between his knees. He gazed towards the upper storey and sighed. 'Closet this time. There's no rhyme or reason to it, where I end up.'

Shocked, but not surprised at my discovery, I perched next to him. My stomach churned itself into knots of anxious bewilderment. He had disappeared from my side, there was no mistaking it – Charles was some kind of ghost or supernatural being. For months I'd been fooled by his ability to come and go, never noticing it as unnatural. Strange, but not implausible.

'The first time you came,' he said, as if to read my thoughts, 'I was upstairs. I darted between the rooms, trying not to bump into you. The suddenness of my reawakening gave me no chance to appreciate the empty house. The moment I had the opportunity to escape you, I ran outside into the woods and hid. Then, when you moved in properly, I stayed out of sight while you and Ruth cleaned up. I'd realised by then that Felicity had gone.' He wiped away an invisible tear from his wan cheek.

I'd missed the obvious clues, but they were there. 'You hummed the tune on my radio while I took a bath.'

He paused to recollect, then a swift nod of his head confirmed my suspicions. 'A little too boisterously, obviously. I would never have, you know, intruded while you bathed. The plumber left so I came out of the closet.'

'You banked the fire during the night?'

He'd a sheepish expression. 'Yes. I forgot to show you how to do it. I didn't think you'd notice.'

How often had he crept about the house at night, altering things? 'One night, I woke to hear noises in the attic, it seemed to be right outside my door.'

He paused to recollect. 'I knew you were keen to find that box of Felicity's. I foolishly thought I could intercept it by trying to contact the nursing home manager myself. Standing in her old bedroom, which I confess I did from time to time, I hatched this stupid plan. I tried to find the care home's telephone number and gave up. Truth be told,' he grinned for a second, 'I'm terrified of the telephone.'

'The box?' I had to know — was he trustworthy? Ghosts were one thing, but dishonesty about his relationship with Felicity was intolerable.

I didn't resist when he sandwiched my clammy hand between his larger ones — I needed that physical connection again. His hands shook; an uncharacteristic, perceivable quaking. I guessed he knew why I'd asked the question. He cocked his head and stared right into my eyes with an intensity that sent shivers sailing across my skin.

'Honestly, believe me, I've never looked inside it. I saw it in the library a few times, when she left it out, but I never intruded or rifled through her things. When Maggie brought the box back here, I panicked. I feared it might contain the truth about me — an unequivocal statement. I'd no idea of her plans for this place. Truly, I did not. She never discussed her will or legacy.'

I slipped my hand out and hugged my knees. Great-aunt Felicity had resilience, years of knowing who he was and never saying a word to anyone. 'Felicity stayed for *your* sake.' My remarkable aunt. I regretted calling her senile.

He sniffed and blinked several times. Was he capable of tears? 'I wanted…I asked her to go back to India, but she refused.'

'Why?'

He brushed the back of his hand against his nose. 'I think I became what she never had — a son. Also, to my shame, she saw her own parents' situation mirrored in my relationship with Beatrice. Two lovers thwarted by tradition and honour. We had that to bind us. She understood my regret.'

We sat so close to each other, I heard him breathing, softy, steadily. 'You do regret what you did?' I said slowly.

Whatever the nature of the functioning anatomy he possessed, he still had the ability to sigh, gasp and exclaim, which he did with a swift, 'Miriam, please.' He turned towards me and greeted me with another dazzling display of translucent discs. 'Absolutely. I was heartless. Bea died in a workhouse. Those places back then were appalling. She should have been a maid, safe and sheltered. She begged me,' his voice broke, 'I ignored her plea to be rescued. That last letter. Her father had every right to curse me. Although, in the end, he came too late to save her.'

'The fire, you don't remember it?'

'I was grieving that day. I do recall the guilt sinking in and consuming me. I loved her, I'm sure I did. My father said ending our relationship was the only option. My beloved but weak-minded mother offered no comfort and my brother hid in his bedroom. Then came Bea's father, crying out in anger at me.'

'I can't imagine what it was like for you. Years of haunting.'

'Not haunting. Existing.' He stood up. 'Could you wait for me? I want to fetch something from my cabin.'

I nodded. While he was gone, I made a much needed cup of coffee and forced down a slice of bread. I paced restlessly, trying to make sense of his life, his death and his curse.

If he loved another, he'd be free: the essence of his release from ghostly captivity, except as he pointed out, he wasn't a ghost. His heart beat, his breath warmed the air – he existed as a time-trapped being. However, he'd shied away from making eye contact with me when he spoke about love. I swallowed a mouthful of coffee and continued to patrol the hallway, hugging the mug to my chest. Was it possible for him to be in love with me? Did that explain why he'd told me the truth? He'd provided subtle, almost illusive signals, ones I had witnessed. Those little nuances he displayed whenever he came into my presence: the soft smiles, the warm greetings and when I danced with him. I sighed, recollecting his embrace.

Had I reciprocated? I groaned a slight sound of realisation, because I'd known the answer to that question for some time, perhaps since he'd clambered across the roof and I'd feared for his safety.

I stared out of the window of the sitting room. The ruts of Tony's tractor in the driveway showed his arrival and departure. No man, barring Charles, was on the property. Charles reappeared, carrying a book. Side by side we sat on the purple sofa, maintaining a discrete gap.

'This is my account of life at Heachley.' Charles handed me the journal, which was bound in leather.

'You want me to read it now?'

He nodded. 'Felicity suggested I write down what I remember, like a story, from the time I first became aware until, well I took heart, and I've added to it.' He paused and sneaked an appreciative glance in my direction. 'I plan to tell more about her life, but it isn't easy to write of her. Not yet. I'll have time to finish those missing years when I'm ready. Read it. I'm not gifted with the pen, but writing comes easier than speech for a man like me.'

I turned the page, noting the date – 1966 – the year after Felicity returned from India. The opening sentences were bleak, transporting me back in time to when he first reappeared and ran out into the woods to hide. Those trees had kept him company for over a hundred years. I read on.

·· ● ··

PART TWO

The Journal

"The best way to find yourself is to lose yourself in the service of others."

—Mahatma Gandhi

The Marsters Family (1873–1914)

July 13th, 1966

My father acquired Heachley Hall in 1850 and proudly aspired to be the most respected businessman in the area. By 1873 that dream was shattered by fire. My revival from its ashes threw me forward in time to a new century, to 1903, and the first of my many apparitions. The house, inhabited by strange women, brought me no comfort and only solitude; my home was no longer mine. The closet and cellar where I reappeared with increasing frequency became my prison, recalling me without warning, almost upon a whim. Both oppressive dark places. For the many times this happened, I struggled to understand where or who I was. It became easier and gradually I spent less time frozen to the spot, and more time attempting to understand my predicament.

I'd no notion of my ghostly behaviour. I learnt to escape my confines, whether to tiptoe downstairs or to guess the path across the dark cellar, and thence I headed out into the sanctuary of the woods. It was when I noticed my fingernails had stopped growing and I had no need to shave or trim my hair, that I deduced my body had frozen in time. Whatever power had put me in this position, I could not begin to fathom. My studies had not included the sciences and I turned my back on the religious teachings of schoolmasters and the clergy. I'd aspired to be a businessman, as my father had been.

I love to read and in my efforts to understand my dilemma, I borrowed books from the shelves in the library and filched the old newspapers left aside to burn. I discovered a journal belonging to Olivia Marsters in a bedroom drawer. From these pages, I elucidated what had transpired during my absence. I'm not proud of my spying, but I could not tolerate the vacuum created by my lack of knowledge.

I'd learnt much about the Marsters during those early awakenings. The master of Heachley Hall, Rupert Marsters, was an officer in the army. While Rupert furthered his military career, his brother, James, sustained the family business, travelling back and forth between England and India. James survived the ravages of tropical diseases, but on a visit to cold Norfolk, he succumbed to pneumonia, leaving his wife, Georgina, a widow. She resided, in part, at Heachley for the remainder of her short life, and left her son, Frederick, in India to run the company with his uncle. I never met Georgina. When in 1903 Rupert travelled abroad with his wife Olivia and his young daughters to fight the Boers in South Africa, Georgina spent those years seeking a new husband in London. Only the housekeeper and two maids remained behind to keep the house in order.

They'd covered most of the furniture in dustsheets, removed the paintings from the walls to protect them from the light and kept their chores to little more than cleaning. The housekeeper and one maid slept in the attic rooms overnight. I established the arrival of any man ended my visitation. Whenever a male caller crossed the threshold of the gates, whether to sell them goods, to deliver coal or to dally in the company of the pretty maid, whom I suspected had a lover, I lost my corporeal state. This I could only deduce by my singular inability to meet with a man or boy.

During my wanderings, having given up all hope of escaping the boundaries of the estate, I discovered the cabin in the corner of the woods. Sheltered by the outer wall and quite forgotten, I took up residence. The shack provided me somewhere to rest, read and contemplate, and allow me to be myself.

Sleep, you might ask, do I? Do I dream like a living person? No, I have no dreams and if I sleep, I am comforted by the fact I wake to find myself lying on the makeshift mattress and not had my body mysteriously propelled through space to the closet or the cellar.

My clothing, which always travels with me through time, was not appropriate to the period. Unfortunately, the fabric wears out in the way my body never does. I stole from the wardrobes the shirts and trousers of Rupert and what must have belonged to his brother, James, who'd died during my long absence. The change of attire inspired my adventurous nature, boosted my confidence and I decided to call at the house to determine if the occupants would welcome me.

I knocked at the back door, ensuring my status was that of a lowly servant and not a gentleman caller. I had no proof of my identity, no documents or portraits to compare my likeness. My name, Christopher Isaacks, I kept secret, instead I plucked one from a newspaper – Charles Donaldson. As I mumbled my introductions, Mrs Hyde, the housekeeper, treated me with caution, while I gaped in amazement that she had no fear of my presence; perhaps, I was not a ghost but a magician?

'Yes, what do you want?' she snapped.

I'd little forethought with regard to my plans. If I continued to exist in this bizarre in-between realm where I remained neither alive nor dead, then why not seek an occupation, a purpose? 'I'm here to offer my services as a gardener.' I blurted, surprising myself – I'd never spent any time in a garden other than to drink tea with my mother under the shade of a tree.

Naturally, my inability to reference a previous employer supported her suspicions that perhaps I'd fallen on hard times and had once been of a higher status. However, she made little suggestion of this at the time, although later, she confessed this to be her conclusion. In hindsight, I believe she simply took pity on me, treating me as a labourer made homeless by the lack of farm work.

Mrs Hyde turned out to be a blessed woman, whose stern exterior hid a gentler nature. She offered me employment and I begged, not for money, but items that I might put to use in my humble abode. I acquired, through my labours an oil lamp, bedding and more clothes. I believe because I worked hard she turned a blind eye to my circumstances. She might have guessed where I slept, knowing the estate well, but she never mentioned my squatting.

There I was, a gentleman who'd once expected to inherit Heachley Hall and his father's thriving business, forced through the nature of my peculiar situation to prune hedges, cut back the grass and lop the dead branches off trees.

For all my hard work, I develop no appetite, suffer no fatigue, the cold sweeps past me and my indifference to the heat repels the effects of the sun. Nothing, no habits of living are necessary for my existence. My skin never ages nor wrinkles, my teeth remain clean and my hearing sharp.

As for my scars, if I understood back then why they covered my arms, I had no memory of their origin. The events of that day were lost to me.

Then, one day, in the middle of tying back a splaying bush, the numbness, the unbearable sense of suffocation hit me. Plucked out of my fragile existence, it was sometime before I returned.

The Great War and beyond (1914–1934)

July 17th, 1966

Newly liberated from my spiritual captivity, I needed little time to adapt as I understood the reason for my re-emergence and the anticipated passage of time. I quickly established the house was yet again in a state of upheaval.

Rupert Marsters had gone first to London, then across the sea. A major war was being fought in France, driving the young men to don uniforms and join the army. Left behind at Heachley were Rupert's three daughters. They came and went in a manner of their choosing, each trying to ensure the house remained in good order. Frederick had a son, Hubert, but James's widow, Georgina, had passed away having never visited her son or grandson in India. The males of Heachley continued to be no more than portraits in frames, since I never met them, only hearing of their tales from the women folk.

Mrs Hyde had retired and in her place had been hired a new housekeeper.

My occupation as gardener was re-established with little difficulty. My excuse for avoiding conscription was explained by my scars – I claimed, falsely, that I had not the health to endure a war. Little did the occupants of the house know how often I escaped death. If I cut myself, no blood drips out and any pain seems momentary, as if a memory of it has been relived for a second, then mislaid. Any wounds will close swiftly without need of cleansing or bandages. If I fall from a height, which I once did while repairing the roof of the stables, I pick myself up, unharmed and continue.

Another oddity is the white dust, which forms during my absence and coats my clothing and hair. I often shake it loose during my dash up the cellar steps. This prevalent dusting caused the maids to complain and accuse each other of purposefully scattering the ashes from the fireplace. Then, as opposed to now, I knew not from whence it came, only that the dust seemed to dissipate whenever I walked about the house. The more frequently I appeared, the more the maids complained.

As an employee of the estate I took payment in cash, but managed to convince one of the maids to buy me clothes, proposing some preposterous idea that I could not venture into town for fear of being recognised by my debtors. She accepted my excuse because she'd taken quite a fancy to me. I had not encouraged her flirting, but my continuing youthfulness and affable nature aroused her attention.

I did not return her admiration, quite the contrary, I was incapable. She chose to express her feelings one day and in that instance, as she puckered her lips upwards and fluttered her long eyelashes, I remembered my lover, who'd also worked as a maid. I buckled over, as if an invisible hand had punched me in the stomach and ran out of the scullery – where she'd cornered me – and into the woods. The mist swooped in to collect me into its arms, but upon that occasion the embrace gave me no comfort, no sense of protection.

The words of Beatrice's grief-stricken father echoed in my ears.

'I curse you to drift, to exist betwixt life and death in neither one nor the other. If you choose to repent of your cold disposition, your meanness and lack of care, then you'll fear your affections will harm another and dare not show them. For if you love another woman and she loves you back with all her heart, with her whole body, giving herself to you with passion and desire, then the consummation of that love will cause you, the selfish man, to shrivel away and never come back. Consequently, you will fear to love, to consummate it, because to do so will bring despair and torture to your sweetheart. After your destruction she will be saddened to the point of despondency, and she will be unable to dispatch you from her memory. If instead you choose to spoil another's love, abandon her unwanted and rejected, just as you did with my beloved child and grandchild, you will harbour the regret and consequences for all eternity, while trapped in this meaningless existence.'

These words haunt me always, as I haunt Heachley.

Day after day, I deliberately neglected my duties and avoided the pretty maid with her plump lips. Eventually, she realised I'd scorned her, she gave up and refused to speak to me. It was a time when I came and went in short bursts, sometimes vanishing to my nothingness for weeks on end. This haphazardness was due to the house constantly changing in the nature of its occupancy. The daughters had husbands and sons, who stayed when on leave from the army. Other callers interrupted me mid-task, sending me spiralling into my abyss. Tradesmen called frequently including the vicar, who offered up prayers for one daughter's deceased husband. I saw nothing of these men, and only through careful eavesdropping did I establish the events that had transpired during my absences.

So the pattern of my bizarre existence continued. Rapid developments heralded the arrival of the motor vehicle, household electricity, the aeroplane, cinema with talking pictures, the wireless radio and the telephone. Each new invention necessitated a modicum of acquaintance with its advantages that I obtained mainly through careful discourse or books. Nevertheless, many of these new fangled devices I never experienced in person due to my inability to leave Heachley.

Rupert returned after the war and I slipped away. For many years I remained unaware and unseen until I stumbled out of the cellar, blinking in the bright light to find a house much changed. Music was blasting out, strange rhythmic pieces with combinations of trumpets, pianos and rasping vocals. Jazz – I later discovered when caught staring wide-eyed at the wireless.

paused in my reading, lowered the journal onto my lap and contemplated. I had so many questions to ask. Beside me Charles waited patiently. He'd closed his eyes and rested his head on the back of the sofa. He seemed relaxed, except his hands were tight fists, clasped together on his pointed knees.

I cleared my throat and he opened his eyes – beautiful eyes with their light irises. 'The letters – how did they end up in the cellar? Shouldn't they have gone with the Isaacks?' When I'd confronted him about stealing the letters, he claimed to have found them – how was that possible given the time lapse?

'There were many things down there which I recognised as belonging to my family. Postcards, the housekeepers' ledgers, maps of the estate, many trivial things. I can only guess they were left in the chaos that followed the fire. I don't think my father wanted to spend another minute in Heachley, what with the damage and my demise, so he abandoned many things and they ended up in boxes in the cellar. Gradually, subsequent occupants cleared them away, but I did retrieve the letters.'

'The letter from Beatrice to you, begging you to rescue her, surely that would have been in your possession and destroyed in the fire. It was your bedroom that burned down?'

'The letters from me which she had in her possession were returned after her death by the workhouse Master, but that particular letter had been intercepted by my father. I never saw it until I found it in the cellar. I supposed if they had been in his desk in the library, they would have survived the fire.'

'It must have been a shock to read it.'

'Yes,' he whispered. 'If I had seen it, I wonder if it might have been the spur I needed to rebel against Father. But, by then... read on. You'll see.'

I picked up the journal and turned the page.

The First Tenants (1934–1946)

July 20th, 1966

Upon Rupert's death the house passed to the ownership of Hubert Marsters, who lived in India with his children. Frederick never inherited Heachley. His wife, Alice, had died of the Spanish flu, which scourged India as much as Europe, leaving him bereft and apathetic – according to the domestic staff. He parted from his son, Hubert, and the spice trade, to return to England to reside with his uncle, Rupert. They died within a year of each other, widowers who haunted this house more effectively than I. In their final years, throughout the twenties, I existed in a void, their constant presence an encumbrance. With both men gone, an agent, who acted on behalf of Hubert, was established to manage the property and the start of 1934 began a long period of tenancy.

My first encounter with the Melrose family occurred not long after they arrived. Mr Melrose was a captain in the merchant navy and often departed on long journeys to distant shores. During his absence, while his boys attended boarding school, I reappeared.

Having snatched clothes from the washing line, desperate to lose my Edwardian appearance, I knocked on the door and pleaded my usual case for work. A long economic depression had descended on the world and the sight of a strange man begging for work about the house and grounds did not seem out of place to Mrs Melrose. She asked me to fix the broken shelves in the library. I'd never aspired to be a carpenter, but fortitude coupled with agile fingers enabled me to acquire the necessary skills to fashion things out of wood. She put me to good use: I chopped the felled trees for firewood, cut back the long grass in the garden with a scythe and pruned the apple trees.

The day her sons returned for the holidays I vaporised, the loppers falling out of my hands. I never heard them hit the ground. The pattern of infrequent appearances I'd experienced with the Marsters continued throughout the 1930s, then came a long spell of darkness, both for myself and the country.

Another war came, even greater than first and the house was used by the military. I had little awareness of this period until much later when I read about the workings of the Royal Observer Corp at Heachley. In secret, they spied upon the planes flying overhead, plotting positions of enemy aircraft. Only once did I come to be in the house during their occupation. I stirred from the closet and ventured out.

I gave the solitary woman quite a surprise as I shot downstairs.

'Who the hell are you?' She backed herself against a wall, her eyes wide with alarm. I suspected I looked somewhat pale, dishevelled and equally bewildered.

'Uh, window cleaner,' I declared. What year is it? How long had passed since my last manifestation?

'I don't remember the lieutenant mentioning a window cleaner.' She eased off the wall and from her pocket she dug out a cigarette and lit it. 'You didn't half give me a shock. The others have all gone to the pub to celebrate the news – the end of this bleedin' war. Left me in charge, only time ever.' She guffawed and sucked on her cigarette. 'Where's your bucket?'

I watched transfixed by the smoke spewing out of her mouth. She stood unladylike with legs apart, wearing a blue uniform with a skirt that came to just below her knees. I'd seen such garb on Mrs Melrose, but could not recall the skirt as short as the knee. The elderly Mrs Melrose wore hers to above the ankle.

The young woman had short hair, tucked about her face, rather than tied back in a bun. Her lips were painted bright red and her eyes blackened at the edges. When I failed to answer, she raised her eyebrows, which were neatly trimmed and her forehead creased with worried lines.

'I was checking access,' I explained. 'I'll go get my bucket.'

I hurried downstairs, grateful that my legs always sprang into action when I returned from my unearthly state. The kitchen had been changed, more cupboards with bare oak doors rather than the whitewashed ones. In the scullery, I caught a glimpse of a round bowl on legs: my first washing machine. I opened a cupboard, wondering where the bucket might be kept and slammed it shut.

What had I been thinking? I didn't know how to clean a window. Abandoning my preposterous idea, I dashed out of the house. There on the front drive were two motor vehicles, so different from the ones I'd seen before. These were less box like in the middle, rounded at the rear and larger, elegant almost. I reached out to touch one, when something else distracted me.

A whirring noise came thundering out of the skies. I stared up, seeing what looked like a rigid bird flying high above the trees. A bird with metal wings. I'd no comprehension of flying machines, how big they were, how loud they could be. The last pictures I'd seen of such things had shown wooden structures with cloth, bouncing along the ground. I ran, covering my ears, stumbling past nearly familiar trees, which were loftier than last time I'd seen them, but still upright. I sought out my meagre hut.

There it stood, unchanged and neglected, the interior overwhelmed by cobwebs and layers of dust. The old lantern remained on the table, as did the few personal objects I'd collected over the years, including a metal box in which I'd stored my tragic letters. Those papers had lain in boxes in the cellar and ignored by subsequent occupiers. During my erratic visits, and when chance permitted, I had retrieved any remembrance of the Isaack family and hid them in the cabin.

I shook out the bedding, brushed away the leaves and mouse droppings, before crashing on the mattress in despair. Too much time had passed for me to comprehend what I'd witnessed at Heachley Hall.

With a blink of my eyelids, I was gone again.

The Hinderton Affair (1947–1953)

August 2nd, 1966

For the next twenty years I continued my nomadic existence in time; sporadically jumping forward, sometimes in days or months, but rarely years. The next family to arrive at Heachley Hall was named Hinderton. Mr Hinderton was a wealthy businessman with interests in shoe manufacturing. His wife happily amassed a great store of footwear to try out on his behalf. Through her constant changing attire, and her need to appear attractive, I observed the shifting fashions.

They had no need of a gardener, they'd another who came intermittently to mow the lawn and weed the flowerbeds. I never saw this man, his arrival heralded one of my many departures. Instead, I offered myself as a handyman and Mrs Hinderton with her nylon stockings and swirling skirts always seemed to find something for me to do: painting, joinery and wallpapering, which I found most tedious. I listened to her on the telephone, a contraption I now accepted as not magical, but simply beyond my limited comprehension. Other machines appeared throughout their tenure: the refrigerator amazed me, as my experience of cold storage had been icehouses. The first occasion I witnessed the television switched on, I could not contain my excitement.

I crouched down before the cabinet, which housed the picture box, and gawped at the moving figures, cocking my ear to hear the crackling speech. I poked at the glass and peered behind the back of the wooden cabinet at the cables. Mrs Hinderton giggled at my fixation— 'had I not been to the cinema?' she'd asked. I lied and said, yes, but that the television, given my poor upbringing, was a fantastical object and one I could not afford. She agreed – the Hinderton family were privileged.

She paid me, but I had nowhere to spend my money. Consequently, I stole. Mr Hinderton was on the short side and his clothes fitted me poorly, necessitating the sewing of extensions on to the trousers. If Mrs Hinderton guessed at my ruse, she showed no inkling of the origins of those stolen clothes. I always picked the ones at the back of the wardrobe or bundled into bags to be given to charity.

She invited me to watch the coronation of the Queen Elizabeth. Another monarch to add to my tally. With the whole family in attendance and some of the village folk, I would not be in my corporeal form. I shrugged off her invitation, saying I had other matters to attend to that day: an excuse I used frequently.

Afterwards, I emerged from the cellar. The house had emptied of visitors along with her husband and son and I crept upstairs and out of the back door. As I walked towards the murky woods, Mrs Hinderton called after me. 'Charles,' she said softly, almost too quiet for my hearing. 'Do come in, won't you.'

I pivoted to find her stood on the doorstep, resting her back against the frame with her mouth slightly open and her tongue circling her pink lips. She ran the palm of her hand down her side, smoothing out the ruffles of her dress and it hovered by her hips, stroking up and down. She had a fine figure and elegant legs. In my era, men wooed women, not the other way around. Regardless of protocols, I'd no doubt what she sought from me.

Was I capable of consummating a frivolous affair without death arriving to whisk me to hell? It mattered little. I presumed an opportunistic sexual liaison would not meet the conditions required to release me from immortality. If I did not reciprocate with true love, the curse would remain unbroken. My natural ability to perform remained untainted by my state, something I am ashamed to admit to. Should I have allowed her to court my affection? The intrigue, and my curiosity, wiped away the guilt of interfering with a married woman. Mr Hinderton, from what I'd ascertained, merely came and went at meal times, often returning home late in the evening; hardly the behaviour of a doting husband.

However, if her husband returned, would I vanish before her eyes?

She might scream, denounce the house as haunted and uninhabitable. How would I fare if Heachley Hall was turned into a freak show that people visited expecting to see the ghost of Charles. Perhaps it did not matter as she would not say a word to anyone for fear of accusation of adultery. Law in my time had been harsh towards those who committed the sin; however, would the world of 1953 judge it as harshly?

Naturally, I was curious for other reasons. My curse restrained my desire to fall in love, and frankly, given my wayward appearances, I'd little opportunity to become enamoured with a woman. However, I was a flesh and blood human with urges that I'd crushed long ago. Now that they'd reawoken I stepped towards the door.

'Yes, Mrs Hinderton, is there something I can do for you?'

'Please, call me Vanessa.' She swung her hips as she walked and I followed her into the scullery.

'It's a pity you missed the coronation. So grand, quite glamorous and to see it on the television, most amazing. Some people managed to see it in colour, can you image that?' She lit a cigarette and wafted the burning match in front of her before tossing it into the sink.

'No.' I generally keep my answers short when I have little understanding of the purpose of the conversation. A habit that has saved me from ignorance on numerous occasions over the decades.

'Of course, you are of limited means.' She puffed out a smoke ring and it floated upwards before disintegrating. I hovered, debating whether to scarper, when she sauntered across the room and pounced, hooking her hand around my neck, she drew my head down to meet her lips. I smelt tobacco and perfume bundled into a strange concoction. Her lips were warm, suitably moist and inviting. I tasted them and, as she darted her tongue into my mouth, I found her methods pleasant. Then, I waited, wondering if some emotional eruption would take over me, but though I seemed capable of responding physically, I felt not one iota of warm feelings towards her.

'My husband and son have gone to the pub to celebrate. They'll be some time. Come.' She took my hand, leading me upstairs to her bedroom. I continued in the vein of curiosity, but also I wished company. It had been many lifetimes since I'd had intimate contact with a woman and although I'd given my heart to another once, I'd squandered that affection, resulting in my cursed existence.

'I…I have scars,' I declared as she began to unbutton my shirt.

'Many men left the war with scars.' She'd made an assumption and I let her believe it. My age always seemed to confuse those who met me. My style of hair I'd kept short in keeping with the current fashion. I discovered after trimming it, the hairs would grow back but no farther than when I first reappeared. My smooth skin, dark hair and firm muscles maintained my youthful appearance, whereas my manners and speech appealed to those who thought I was older. Vanessa Hinderton appeared not to mind what age I might be, since I clearly had a hold over her.

She complimented me on my performance afterwards, my attentiveness to her needs, although she hinted I had been swift in my approach. I had not the heart to warn her that the moment her husband reappeared I'd vanish before her eyes. Time was not on our side.

Throughout our brief coupling between the sheets of her bed, my emotions had failed to demonstrate anything more than carnal excitement. I'd lusted for her, as she had a glorious body and comely features, but nothing else materialised. She'd squawked in the moment of rapture, eager to show her pleasure and I found it somewhat excessive and unnecessary.

She'd insisted I used a rubber sheath, which she had retrieved from her bedside drawer. I'd accommodated her wishes. However, when I came to tidy up my person, I discovered that even though I'd experienced the delight of the spend, I had not produced one drop of liquid. I hid the evidence, believing my inadequacy was a symptom of my condition.

For a while, we lay side by side. She offered me a cigarette, which I politely declined having lost all interest in the taste since my ghostly term had begun. Did she realise that she'd made love to an apparition?

I find it hard to think of myself as a ghost, especially when I have no ability to pass through walls or hover up to the ceiling. I smiled, and she mistook that to mean I was content, whereas in reality, I merely felt relief that her husband had not returned, causing me to vanish mid-act.

Nor had I suffered the true parting of my soul from my earthly body, which would have released me from my undead existence. I doubted Vanessa loved me. Consequently, the curse remained in place.

She thanked me, quite sweetly. 'I do love Jeffery, but he's not the same man I married. I suspect he's fucking a woman in the village given the hours he keeps. As for that sod I call my son, he's no better.'

'I'm sorry that you are not happy.'

'Oh, I'm happy, in my own way.' She traced a finger along the reddish scar that ringed one of my nipples. 'How did you come by these?'

I shrugged. 'I don't really remember.' Which happened to be the truth, I didn't recall the details, although I knew they'd been caused by fire, and that conflagration had been here at Heachley Hall and resulted in my not so complete death.

'They look painful.'

'Once, they were, not now.' I'd never known them to cause me discomfort; nevertheless, they served as an indelible reminder of the life I'd once lived.

Our affair lasted a few weeks. Conveniently, she would harry her husband and son to leave the house on some business or other, so that she might invite me to her bed. I dutifully performed my role in a detached manner. I concluded that sex was not what she sought because afterwards she seemed to be quite talkative and spent more time incessantly nattering about her family and friends than she did in exploiting my manhood. I inattentively listened, my mind wandering as she sucked on her compulsory cigarette. What drew me back to her bed proved difficult to comprehend as I certainly did not love the woman; attractive as she might be, she had little in her nature that appealed to me. My need was more basic – companionship – and even if Vanessa lacked the intellectual capacity to thrill, she did at least welcome me into the house.

Towards the end of the coronation year Mr Hinderton's company went bankrupt. Vanessa tearfully announced their misfortune as I dismantled the bookshelves in the library.

'The useless rat has drunk it away, I'm sure.' She blew her nose ineffectively into her handkerchief. 'We can't afford the rent and we're moving to ghastly Peterborough to a measly townhouse.'

I commiserated. 'I'll miss you.'

'You've been a sport, Charles, keeping me company.' She ran her finger along the mantelpiece, staring right past me to a picture on the wall. The diamond ring she wore flashed brightly. I suspected she'd have to sell it. She sighed. 'I'll miss you, too.'

That was the last time I saw her. I piled the shelves into a corner and went to fetch a hammer from the shed. I never made it that far: I vanished somewhere between the hallway and the kitchen.

My inability to stay put often proves an encumbrance at the most inopportune moments. I frequently had to find excuses for my sudden absences, and also my lack of permanent abode, which meant as a consequence, I'd no apparent address. Due to the rise in popularity of the motorcar, my ability to appear at will without transport issues caused some degree of puzzlement from time to time.

I've learnt to think quickly on my feet, to cover up my ignorance of the ever-changing world beyond Heachley's wall, which I can neither see nor experience directly. Lying on my bed in my hut, as I will tonight, I dream of cities with their skyscrapers and terrifying traffic, and I draw mental images of picturesque mountains, lakes and the oceans. How I miss the rippling light on the sea and the crashing of white frosted waves.

Eventually, I was forced to emerge from my stupefaction by the arrival of a female at Heachley. She, unwittingly and unknowingly, transported me, without warning, back into the house.

The new arrival I shall write about brings me both joy and sadness.

Somewhat flabbergasted at Charles's affair with a married woman, I broke off reading and dispatched him a raised eyebrow. This time, his eyes were open and receptive.

'Vanessa?' I tapped the journal entry.

'I am a flesh and bone man,' he said sheepishly. 'The need was…organic.'

I chuckled softly. I wasn't upset by his adventurous spirit. I was hardly a virgin either. 'You don't need to apologise. I guess she was quite insistent?'

Charles's familiar crooked smile formed. 'Yes. And, I had to find out for sure. Sadly, nothing came of that experiment. If it had, I suppose I wouldn't have met you,' he added. 'Or…' he released a small sigh. 'I'm spoiling it. Please, continue.'

Keen to read on, I lifted the journal and turned the page.

·· ● ··

The Branston Family (1953–1965)

August 6th, 1966

I tripped on something lying on the cellar floor. Shuffling my feet forward, I scraped my fingernails along the outside wall until I found the candle and matches I'd left in a small recess. Lighting the wick, I used the light to guide me towards the far door.

Various discarded objects had accumulated on the ground, hindering my path. Their scattering indicated another passage of time. The chute remained in use, but the coal was no longer burnt in the boiler, it only served the fireplaces. During the Hinderton's stay, the absent landlord, John Marsters, had arranged for a new heating system to be installed and when structural weakness had been discovered, he also paid for the additional support columns in the basement. However, to my relief, his appearances had been rare and generally brief.

Opening the cellar door, daylight danced down the steps almost reaching the basement. I trudged up the stairwell. The fresh air reinvigorated my lungs, dispelling the weight of inertia from my limbs and the brisk draught scattered the usual accompaniment of dust from my clothing.

She screamed. A high pierce shriek, which only a small child can produce with little effort. The shrill cry almost shattered my eardrums and before I could calm her down, the young girl skedaddled out of the scullery, calling for her mother.

I used the opportunity to escape and ran for it, praying the familiar mist that typically greeted my arrival in the woods would come to my rescue.

That was my first encounter with Primrose Branston, daughter of Louise Branston. Unsure whether the girl had reported my trespassing, I hid behind the trees and waited, wondering if the new tenants would hunt me down. However, no search transpired nor had the police arrived, instead the end of day darkness replaced the mist. I retreated to the hut.

For a few days I watched the house – the husband absent for the duration of my spying. The weather improved and Louise, with her long, saffron hair that flowed and bounced against her cheeks, emerged outside. She wore a floral patterned dress with its narrow waist and broad skirt, which was common for the 1950s. With the summer heat baking the garden, she reclined on a deckchair under a sun parasol and read, while Primrose chased butterflies. Louise was a spellbinding beauty. For the first time in decades I awoke forgotten feelings and allowed them to evolve.

Unlike when I inhabited the hall, servants no longer lived at Heachley. Most tenants relied on domestic staff who came and went as needed. This situation yielded advantages for me and I approached her, clearing my throat in a less than subtle fashion.

'Hello, sorry to disturb.' I tugged my forelocks.

Louise rose and laid her book down on the chair. 'Yes?' She frowned, but the downturn in her lips barely impacted her beauty. If I were capable of a deep blush, then such a flush of redness would have been apparent on my face. She called for the child to stand close to her. I hesitated, waiting for the girl to recognise me, but she merely hid behind her mother's skirt.

I pointed across the lawn. 'I noticed your roses need pruning and the laurels in the corner have blocked the sunlight. I work as a gardener, a handyman, too. May I offer you my services?'

She asked my name and I gave it. 'Oh, yes. Mrs Hinderton mentioned you. We took over the tenancy. My husband is a lawyer and he is away in London, working at the courts there.'

My work was assigned, the pay negotiated, too. How fast money loses its value. What once would have been a monthly income in my day was now a daily fee.

'Mother.' The cry came from a bedroom window. An adolescent girl hung her head out, her dark hair swaying the breeze. 'Where's my green dress?'

Louise sighed, rolled her eyes with the seeming ease of practice, and called up to the sour faced child. 'In the ironing pile.'

'No,' she shrilled in reply. 'You promised me it would be ready for this evening.'

'I promised you it would be washed, not ironed.' Louise slowly shook her head; a gesture of despair. 'My daughter, Mary. I apologise, she is not in the best of moods. After living in London, she hates being here, but Terry and I wanted very much to live in the country, by the sea, for Primrose's sake.'

'It is near to the sea here,' I agreed. There had been a time I could smell the sea from Heachley Hall, now I have little sense of smell or taste.

She swept aside the blonde locks of hair from her daughter's face. 'Come, Primrose, say hello to Charles.'

I fell in love with Louise, but unlike Vanessa who seduced me into her bed, Louise was the loyal wife and devoted to her frequently absent husband. I could only admire from afar, as I planted clematis, buried tulip bulbs and picked apples from the yellowing trees. In my determination to avoid suspicious behaviour, I held fast to the pretence of indifference. The pain of unrequited love was great, and no matter how hard I tried to vanquish that cursed emotion, I failed. In a blink of the eye, Louise's dazzling smile or some other small gesture of friendship rekindled it.

During the dregs of the summer's day, I bit back my frustration and listened with quiet fortitude as Louise battled with Mary; the arguments between teenager and mother flew out the windows and into the garden. Women had acquired much freedom since my birth, but the changing way of life brought with it a lack of respect and the diminishing authority of parents. Following my father's demand, I had turned my back on everything of importance: my lover and my unborn child. The emancipation of women I admire. What next, a woman prime minister? I pushed the wheelbarrow to the rear of the garden by the outer wall. There I worked, whistling to myself.

In the distance I heard a car, the engine purring in the adjacent lane. I laid down my shears, closed my eyes and within moments I was gone from the garden.

Did anyone suspect that they had a ghost in their midst? Had my ability to evaporate into nothing been witnessed? My behaviour must have appeared extremely suspicious on many occasions. I'd once been caught coming downstairs from the closet by Mrs Melrose. I'd excused myself by telling her rather bashfully that I needed the bathroom and felt ashamed at relieving myself in the garden. She'd admonished me for not asking permission, but my excuse had been considered plausible, as she had not queried it. Sometimes, I'd concluded that other servants thought me mad or simple; the village idiot abandoned by an indifferent family and left to seek employment. I'd done nothing to dispel some of those rumours; they worked in my favour.

With each new occupant I had refrained from mentioning my long dead family. I'd manufactured fictional male companions. It tortured me to do so as I sorely missed the company of men. I'd kept my stories simple: trips to the horse races – using newspaper reports to describe the races I'd supposedly seen; the cinema – I resorted to regurgitating reviews, and so on. My imaginary life was packed with creative non-existent events and the recounting of each fabricated tale caused an ache in my lonely heart.

Dogs were especially bemused by my presence. The labrador, who lived with the Branstons, treated me, as do most creatures, with indifference. I'd expected barking or growling on my first encounter, something to arouse suspicion, but rather it appears I have no scent.

I'd grown accustomed to the nonchalant behaviour of the woodland animals, including the adventurous squirrels who bounce off my head and the sparrows who feed out of my hand. I am an object, not a being, and it re-enforces my incompleteness, my departure from normality.

Since my work was often solitary and enabled me to labour in isolated parts of the garden, I left my employees with the assumption I'd simply abandoned my tasks, which unfortunately, was not good practice, and on many occasions I had been reprimanded by the lady of the house about my sudden absences. I practised an apologetic expression and various plausible, but vague excuses. Mostly, I re-enforced the notion I was a mere labourer, unimportant and not worthy of their attention.

When working indoors I had to politely enquire when the man of the house might return, then excuse myself before his arrival. Unexpected callers proved to be most difficult and I prayed that in the eventuality of their arrival I would vanish without an audience. To help with the subterfuge and to afford the privacy I needed, I'd chosen one of the outbuildings as my workspace, and within those cold walls I maintained my activities. These various evasive techniques had proved sufficient until a small child occupied the house.

Primrose followed me wherever I went clutching a rosy cheeked china doll. At first, she said nothing, but as she overcame her shyness, she chattered, asking me endless questions. Factual ones, such as why petals were different colours, I endeavoured to answer to the best of my ability, but other personal questions proved trickier. Was I married, did I have children, where did I live, and so on. I made up a fantasy world, because it seemed the easiest solution and whether she believed in the magical land of Charles, it did not matter. Her mother found it amusing when Primrose informed her that I lived in an underwater palace by the sea.

Another ploy I used to protect myself was to play hide and seek in the garden. She loved to hide, and it kept her occupied, and if I hid, it gave me the opportunity to escape her. Sometimes she cried, frustrated by her fruitless search. In reply I gritted my teeth at the distress I'd caused, but the trickery was necessary to demonstrate my unreliability.

Sometimes, I truly vanished. Whether she cried or not on those occasions, I knew not.

A little before her seventh birthday her father came home from his offices in Norwich somewhat earlier than usual. Primrose had been digging holes to plant seeds – I took great pleasure in encouraging her interest in gardening – and she turned and began to smile. As the numbness struck, her eyes widened and her mouth gaped. I tried to speak, to offer words of comfort, but I disappeared too fast.

Had she told her mother? Ran indoors? Screamed? I could only guess at the nature of her shock. After the weekend, when Mr Branston returned to London, I lit my candle and tiptoed out of the cellar. Should I hide in the woods in the cabin or simply attend to my business as if nothing had happened? I chose the latter, on the basis I would laugh off Primrose's story as a childish fantasy.

The unhappy Mary was in the garden and when I calmly raked up the dead leaves she remained, unperturbed by my presence. Basing my reasoning on her reaction, I assumed my return had been expected.

'Hello, Charles.' She kicked at the pile of leaves.

'Miss Mary.' Ignoring her disruptive behaviour, I shovelled the scattered leaves into the wheelbarrow.

'Primrose thinks you're a wizard,' she announced.

'Does she?' With my head bowed, I presented Mary my rigid back, the spine locked in tension.

'She is a silly creature. She says you vanished into thin air, right before her eyes.' Mary laughed.

I put much effort into my chuckles, while continuing to rake the crisp leaves. 'She likes to play hide and seek with me, that's all.'

'Mother thinks the house is haunted.'

I tightened my hands about the rake. 'She does?' I swallowed hard. My heart should have pounded hard and the sweat should have formed on my brow, but my body never responds in tandem with my emotions. Feelings – those that exemplify raw, nervous energy – always remain locked in my mind and never manifest themselves in a physical response.

'She claims she hears strange noises – banging and the like – and she thinks the dust is weird, how it appears all the time. Personally, I think she watches too many scary films. She's hooked on this Quatermass Experiment television show. I'm not allowed to watch it. Too young.' Mary spat the last few words out.

'If it scares her then it can't be appropriate for a child.' I scrunched the leaves down to the bottom of the wheelbarrow.

'I'm not a child,' she declared and stamped her foot on the ground.

I stood straight and leaned on the rake. For nearly sixty years I'd shared my existence, such as it was, with females, mostly adults and throughout, I'd adapted my responses to their nature. I'd learnt to listen, not judge, to express sympathy and platitudes, rather than criticisms or what appeared to me to be obvious practical solutions. Women throughout those decades – even with their rising status in society that gave them the vote, the right to divorce, and to own property independently – reacted with little variety. Each generation take advantage of these social developments, but emotionally, women seem equipped the same.

Regardless of my experiences, an immature teenager was new territory. 'I gather you are a child until you're eighteen.'

'I'm eighteen next month,' she sneered.

Her age surprised me, I'd thought her sixteen, at most. 'Then, might I suggest you act that age.'

She glared, her lips trembling and her eyes turning into the dark moons of wide-eyed indignation. Tossing her head to one side, she stomped back into the house and I concentrated on the raking.

On another day, Louise requested I replace the light bulb in the library. Electricity unnerves me. It has taken many years to accept it isn't magic or dangerous if used wisely. I learnt that lesson when I fiddled with a plug socket with wet hands. Naturally, on that occasion, the electrocution did not kill me, as I am already quite dead.

I stood on a tall stool and twisted the bulb, unscrewing it slowly. Louise reached up and handed me the new one. 'You said something to Mary the other day, I'm not sure what, but she seems to be less obstructive than usual.'

'She is a challenging young lady.' I replied tactically, then secured the new bulb.

Louise chuckled. 'Oh, how true. The little minx has spent most her childhood determined to resist me as her mother. To Terry, she is all sweetness and courtesy. Me, she snarls and sulks, reminding us constantly that I am not hers.'

I looked down straight into her delicate blue eyes; they had a watery film glazed over their surface. 'Not hers?' I jumped off the stool.

Louise walked over to a bookcase and traced her forefinger along the spine of one of the books. 'Yes, not mine. Mary is my step-daughter.'

The revelation explained much about Mary and Louise's often fraught relationship. 'Mr Branston was married before?'

Her head hung lower and her trembling finger slipped off the edge of the book. 'No,' she whispered.

I waited, patiently, as she battled with her emotions. 'She was born just before the war. An unexpected outcome. Terry, in his youth, foolishly got carried away with a neighbour's daughter. Mary was the product. I do believe that he would have married her, but the war interfered. He joined the army, as many excited young men did in the beginning, and she remained in London with little Mary.'

I sat on the stool. Louise's recounting of Terry and his lover seemed to mirror my sad affair all too closely. 'Did she not wait for him?'

'Oh, I think she did. They wrote to one another. Terry still has the letters in his bureau.' She turned to face me and a lone tear trickled down her cheek. She brushed it away. 'Poor Mary. Her mother died in a bomb raid. They'd not made it to the shelter in time. Mary survived and remained in the care of her grandparents until Terry returned.'

'He honoured the memory of his lover by accepting Mary as his,' I said with a satisfactory nod.

Louise graced her face with one of her beautiful smiles. 'What a sweet way you have with words, quite quaint. The grandparents couldn't afford to keep her and left her at his door. By then, he was determined to finish his studies and practice law. She was an impediment. She desperately, so desperately, craves his attention. I think when he looks at Mary, he sees her mother and the image haunts him.'

I clenched my hands into tight fists and crushed a cry of despair. Would that have been my child's future, if she'd survived birth? Would I have been brave enough to fight Father's abhorrence and take my child under my wing, just as Terry had done? I will never know, will I? It is too late.

'I've made you sad. I'm sorry.' Louise rested her hand on my shoulder and I jerked. The one and only time she touched me and I repelled her. Such irony, because inside, I would have liked for her to have fostered more than a gentle offering of comfort.

I rose and stepped backwards. 'No, not at all. I'm sad for Mary. It explains her difficult behaviour.'

'Growing up illegitimate, even in these modern days, is still scorned upon. I have re-enforced over and over to her that I am her legitimate mother and will always care for her, but I'm not good enough.'

'Does she have any contact with her mother's family?'

'None. Her grandparents passed away.'

'A shame,' I redirected her attention to the bulb, gesturing upwards. 'Done. Is there anything else you need from me?' Oh, that question slipped out, unintentional in its delivery and today it still troubles me: the hope I had that she might express some kind of affinity toward me. But, naturally, she had no such thoughts.

She picked up a book from the desk and turned to face the shelves. 'Yes, actually, there is. We've run out of space. Could you make us another bookcase, to stand over there?' She pointed at the remaining bare wall on the other side of the room.

'It would be my pleasure. I love books.'

'You do?' She quickly smothered her mouth with her hand. 'I'm sorry, that's awfully rude of me. Why not, just because you work with your hands. What do you like to read?'

We passed the time talking about our favourite authors; how I loved the fantasy of Tolkien and the intrigue of Agatha Christie. All these books I'd borrowed from Heachley Hall's library, sometimes with permission, mostly without. I'd always returned them. I was surprised nobody declared a mysterious book borrower haunted the library.

Louise generously gave me free rein to read whatever I liked without asking first. 'As long as it's not one of Terry's precious law books.'

I assured her that such books did not interest me. Then the clock on the mantelpiece chimed and I realised it would not be long before Terry returned. 'I should be going.' I grabbed the stool and backed out of the door. 'I'll get to work on those shelves as soon as I can. I might have other jobs to do elsewhere for a while.'

It was two weeks later when Terry finally left the house, he'd lain ill with the influenza, preventing my return. When I materialised, I measured the wall in the library as if I'd been gone but a few hours, the delightful conversation with my fellow book lover still fresh in my mind.

Having completed the task and been paid with useless money, Louise announced the landlord, John Marsters, was due to visit to inspect his property. In a rush of anxiety, driven by the fear he might find fault with their tenancy, Louise tasked me with a few 'tidying up' jobs. No sooner had I finished them, I vanished again for a protracted period.

The closet welcomed me back. As was my custom, I stood still and listened, ignoring the oppressive darkness. I didn't have to listen hard; Mary was shouting. 'You hate me. You always had done.'

'Nonsense,' Louise replied. 'I love you as my own.'

'You say that to keep Dad happy.'

'Your father is most unhappy with all of us,' Louise snapped. 'You're being foolish.'

'I'm in love,' declared her step-daughter emphatically. 'How is that foolish?'

'With a man nearly twice your age?'

I heard the indignation and exasperation in her tone of voice as she continued to chastise Mary. 'Your father and I are in agreement. You will end this liaison immediately. You will write to John Marsters and insist he ends all contact with you.'

'I shall not!' A door slammed shut.

The argument continued unproductively for some time. There were more door slams, stamping of feet and poor Primrose sobbing in the background. I never made it out of the closet. Somebody else arrived, probably Mr Branston, and interrupted my eavesdropping.

I jumped from the closet to the cellar, which often happens when I fail to escape one portal: I mysteriously appear in the other location at a later time. On this occasion I crept out of the gloom, exited the back door and knocked on the front, keen to know what had happened in my absence.

Louise opened the door. She clutched a handkerchief. 'Charles, I'm sorry. I've nothing for you to do.' She dabbed at her nose and red-rimmed eyes.

The notion of walking away from a distressed Louise was impossible. 'Mrs Branston, I cannot possibly leave you in this state.'

She let me in, reluctantly, shuffling her feet to one side.

'What's wrong?' I asked. 'Is Primrose all right? Your husband, Mary—'

'Mary has gone. She eloped with John Marsters.' She spat out his name. 'She, barely twenty years old, with a man we know little about beyond being our absent landlord.'

I followed her into the kitchen. She filled the kettle and slammed it down onto the stove. 'What do I tell her friends? The gossip mongers in Little Knottisham? It's embarrassing. He came to visit, she fawned all over him – admittedly he's a handsome man – and he toyed with her, like a play thing. She stupidly fell for his ingratiating behaviour and I did nothing to stop it, according to Terry, who's livid and won't speak to me.'

'Surely Marsters didn't stay here?'

'No, he took up residence in the pub. An extended stay, unfortunately, and right under our noses. She swanned down there every evening, flirting with him. Terry can't control her, so what hope had I? How could that bastard snatch her away? She may no longer be a child, but she's certainly immature. But what could we do to stop her?'

Why hadn't they? Was there no threat to persuade her from leaving? I recalled my father demanding I gave up Beatrice. I'd fallen in love with a Gypsy, an outcast from society. Bea had betrayed her own kind and ended up in a workhouse without them knowing or seeking her out until too late.

I imagined Bea's despair at the thought of her family finding out and the dishonour of being shunned by their segregated community. Bea had held fast to her love, while I had abandoned it without standing up to Father. My mercenary attitude had been driven by my inheritance and reputation. In the absence of her itinerant parent, she'd tried in vain to contact me.

It came back to me then, and still does now, the memory of her last visit to Heachley Hall; the one before she entered the workhouse. I'd stood at the morning room window, hearing her distant screams as she'd attempted to open the locked gates. Over and over, she'd called out my name, beating her hands against the cold metal while Father stood guard over me and my unsupportive brother cowered in his room. I'd frozen rigid, fighting the desire to dash out and embrace her. Throughout her pleading, Father repeatedly threatened to disinherit me if I budged from the room. At twenty-nine years old, I was ambitious and selfish, and none of these traits would help save my lover. I'd closed the drapes and that had been the last time I saw Bea.

'Let her go,' I murmured to Louise. 'Yes, she might regret it, discover life is harder than she imagines, but it's her choice. Don't interfere.'

Louise lashed out. 'How can you know? You have no children.'

I bowed my head. 'I once abandoned my lover. I regret it. Maybe he will show her tenderness, treat her well. You cannot assume he is wrong for her just because they have little in common.'

Louise sighed. 'He's nearly twice her age, Charles. They've more than nothing in common.'

The kettle whistled, and she removed it from the stove. I declined her offer of tea.

'You never drink what I offer you.' She spooned the tea into the pot.

'I don't like tea or coffee.' I lied. I loved both and missed the flavours: the bergamot of an Earl Grey; the bitterness of the coffee bean. These were only memories. My taste buds remained inert, my belly empty and undemanding. Nothing I smelt or saw changed my inability to eat or drink.

'Let her go?' Louise repeated with a deepening sigh. 'That's what Terry says, and she is his daughter.'

'Are they married?'

'Yes, in Gretna. Now they're in Paris. We had a postcard. I'd been tearing my hair out with worry since I found her note on her pillow. So childish, she'd written such sentimental twaddle.'

'He married her. That's not the action of a frivolous admirer,' I remarked, sensing my optimism outshone hers.

'True.' She poured the tea through the strainer. 'We'll have to wait, shan't we? It has affected Terry more than I imagined. It has broken him, for all his bravado, and it's brought back his own sad memories.'

'You stand by him.'

'I love him, even if he…' the tea dripped slowly out of the strainer. 'He loves me in his own sweet way.' She stared into teacup, unsmiling.

'But not equally.' How I envied Terry and also wished he were a better husband. Two dichotomous feelings battled inside me.

'Is there such a thing? Are all lovers equal in sincerity or is it an imbalance of emotion, rarely, if ever perfect?'

I didn't answer. I sensed I had given her sufficient reassurances and I had to leave; I could do little, as I couldn't hold her, kiss away the tears or show my love. She was right. Love didn't always balance out: freely given, but not necessarily returned in an equivalent measure. I remained captive at Heachley with no chance of finding a lover of equal passion.

I had to wipe away the beginnings of teardrop from my eye before reading on.

Charles twisted to face me, caught my hand and squeezed it. 'What?' he said with obvious concern in his voice.

'You and Louise. So sad,' I rested my other hand on the page, covering up the words of a lover.

'How could I countenance acting on my feelings and ruining our friendship? It wasn't just the curse preventing me. She had children. A life bound to a man whom, for whatever reason, she loved.' He looked expectantly at me, as if yearning for approval.

I admired him so much in that moment and I offered in a reassuring smile in reply. He let go of my hand. At that point in his story he seemed so isolated, rather like I'd been when I first moved into Heachley. But there was hope for us. He'd admitted to feeling love again. I felt a welcome fluttering in my stomach. I had to keep reading and find out what became of Louise and her children, because I knew who Mary was now and it astounded me that Charles had actually met her, and several times.

Louise's sad affairs didn't end with Mary's elopement. Terry lost his job and he accepted a lesser position at a solicitor's in King's Lynn. Without Terry's prolonged absences in London, and due to his spells of ill-health, my appearances grew increasing erratic.

After what must have been a substantial amount of time, I knocked hard on the front door.

'Charles,' she exclaimed. 'Where have you been, it's been weeks, no, months surely? We had a tree come down in a storm. It nearly landed on the house. We needed you. I do wish you could afford a phone.'

The expense of a telephone had helped maintain my incognito whereabouts. However, little else could explain my haphazard appearances. For whatever reason, Louise never quizzed those absences. Maybe she saw me as unimportant and easy to forget, but that isn't how I wish to remember her. Her tired eyes and wrinkles, I ignored, because I met her each time with a renewed sensed of longing. Those months apart for her, which to me often felt like hours, turned swiftly into years. I strove to acclimatise to the constantly changing world to which I emerged. I grew my hair longer, in keeping with the pictures I saw in the discarded newspapers, and purloined Terry's discarded clothes, altering them to hide their origins.

Sometime early in 1965, I rematerialised again and much to my sorrow discovered packing chests and boxes lining the hallway. Having surreptitiously made my way to the front of the house, Louise welcome me indoors with a beaming, if fragile smile.

'We're moving out. Could you dismantle that beautiful bookcase you made? We want to take it with us.' She ran her fingers through her tangled hair. Deep shadows framed her bright eyes and the end of her nose seemed reddish, as if she'd been crying. Even with those impediments the beauty within her remained visible, burning like a fire. From upstairs came a childish giggle followed by a whoop. Primrose? It couldn't be, she would be a teenager by now. Louise followed the track of my eyes to the ceiling. 'Mary is here with my granddaughter – Anna.'

There was a pattering of footsteps coming downstairs and a young girl of five years or so dashed passed me. 'Catch me,' she shrieked. Stomping after the child, with her blonde hair tied back into a bun and wearing a ridiculously short skirt and knee-high boots, came Primrose – I gasped, she appeared fully grown.

'Charles.' A delightful smile erupted on her face before her next sentence wiped it off again. 'Mum's told you? About John?'

I shook my head.

'Keeled over. Heart popped and he's gone. Mary is beside herself and she's gone into deep, deep mourning. Refuses to leave her bedroom. I'm left looking after Anna, while Mum packs.'

'Your father?'

'In Peterborough, sorting out somewhere to live. Such a shame to leave, I love this house.'

'I don't understand why are you leaving Heachley? Surely, as his widow, the house belongs to Mary?'

Louise's face transformed into one of angry dismay, her eyes watering with unshed tears. It caused me anguish to see her upset. 'We found out John might have left his money, possessions and house in London to Mary, but Heachley Hall now belongs to John's sister, Felicity Marsters. Mary is relieved. Frankly I'm not surprised, she hated this place. She doesn't see it as our home or even the income it could generate if sold or leased. She gleefully informed us we'd have to vacate because Felicity, who lives in India, where John was born, is moving in next month.'

I hung my mouth open, gulping in her words as if they hung in the air. 'She's not contesting the will?'

Louise scowled. 'Terry has tried to persuade Mary. We don't know why John didn't include this place when he wrote this will. As far as Mary knows, John and his sister are estranged.'

'Clearly, he changed his mind.' I stared at the cardboard boxes stacked on the tiled floor.

'Rosie!' Anna piped up from the back of the house. 'Where are you?'

Primrose raised her eyebrows. 'Nice to see you again, Charles.' She went in search of her niece.

There was nothing I could do. While we chatted one last time, I helped Louise pack the books, dismantled the shelves of the bookcase and other odd hefty jobs she asked me to do. I never had the chance to say goodbye or to wish Louise and Primrose well. I faded, somewhere between the garage and the backdoor. In retrospect, it must have appeared terribly rude, disappearing without explanation, but perhaps it was for the best. Goodbyes are too painful.

'You met my mum?' I couldn't comprehend the time span that Charles's time at Heachley covered, nor could I believe that such an apparently young man had known my mother as a small child.

'Yes.' He'd replied with brevity, as if people's questions were something of an inconvenience, which I supposed they were to some extent given the restrictions he placed upon himself for answering anything personal. All those mannerisms of his, which I failed to understand over the last few months, now made sense.

'Please, I want to know more. You're the only person who can tell me.'

'Mary brought your mother here to visit from time to time, once she recovered from the shock of John's death. Mary rarely stayed long. Felicity put aside her feelings towards her half-brother for Mary and Anna's sake, partly because he'd left her the house, which initially she saw as a millstone around her neck, but she later came to love. As an adult, your mother came a few times with your father. Mary, her mind slipped away, and stopped visiting.' He spoke with that soft tone, the one I'd come to appreciate for its soothing ability.

My pulse started to race. He was speaking of my family as if they were so close in time to us. I quickly turned the page and gasped.

Felicity Marsters (1966)

December 2nd, 2015

I write this in the hope some day it will be read by those who understand the nature of solitude and despair. Sadly this account will not be read by Felicity, who has passed on. I wish it be known how she saved me, brought me back from the brink of madness and offered me companionship.

My aunt. He'd written about Felicity. I'd waited for this. He was the one person who could really explain her to me.

'You did this after I moved in?' I asked.

Charles leaned over my shoulder as if to verify what he'd written. 'She inspired me to start the journal, but when it came to Felicity herself, I couldn't shape a word of it until you came into my life.' The dejected tones were back on his face and in his voice. He'd written this for me, not her. I opened my mouth to ask a multitude of questions, but he spoke quickly, almost in a pleading whisper.

'Please read, because it's hard for me to describe those days. I hope I've answered some of your questions.'

The moment I stepped out the closet, I knew things were different. Even with my underactive nose, I smelt pungent spices and exotic fragrances. Immediately, upon regaining my vision I saw the first of many strange wall-hangings. Each was an elaborately woven collage depicting distant lands and people; their beauty and originality captivated me.

The library door was slightly ajar. I peeked through the gap and spied the new owner of Heachley Hall. She wore a rainbow dress as long as her ankles with glittering sequins embroidered onto the sleeves, her raven hair snaked down her back reaching her waistline, and her feet were clad in open sandals. She stood with her back to me placing books on the shelves – the original bookcase, which, since my early years, had remained fixed in the arched alcove. She hummed, and the melody was unlike anything I'd heard before. Transfixed by her strange garb, and dangerously close to exposure, I lingered, breathing softly. She paused in her reading, closed the book and snatched a glance over her shoulder. I ducked back and tiptoed away on the balls of my nimble feet. Had she seen me? Heard me?

The only facts I'd gathered about Felicity Marsters had come from Louise before her departure: she had lived all her life in India, she was unmarried and very independent. Beyond these things, I'd no idea what kind of woman she might be. Would she need a handyman or a gardener? What if she spurned my services – how would I live?

Unlike her predecessors, she lived alone with no gentleman callers, or boyfriends, as they'd become known. Such consistency of isolation and lack of male companionship meant I stayed in corporeal form not for hours, but days upon end. Then, if I vanished, it was for a short spell unless she ventured out on an extended trip. Her constant presence threw me – how to occupy my time, my empty mind?

Initially, I longed for Louise and consequently, I fell into a pit of depression. I banished myself to the lonely hut and lay on the bed for days, wishing myself gone forever. I confess my pining took me to such a black place in my soul that I tried new ways to escape the curse.

I hung myself by the neck from a tree branch. My legs swung beneath me and the rope creaked, cutting into the bark, and there I remained, neither dead nor alive, waiting for salvation and receiving none. The cellar rescued me as I suffered another breach in time. I landed on my feet, the rope gone, and the enveloping blackness hugged me. Feeling about my neck, there was nothing to show for my futile attempt at termination: no rope burn or scratches.

Eventually, I emerged from my macabre period of self-destruction and left the hut, weaving through the trees on the path to the house. The mist followed me, as it always did, until I reached the edge of the wood where my protective cocoon slipped away. I stepped forward and knocked on the front door. Tugging on the frayed hem of my shirt, I tucked it back in my trousers.

She would have been the first to admit she was no beauty, but that didn't mean she lacked presence; she certainly wasn't ugly or slighted in anyway. She maintained a grace about herself, always wearing long flowing skirts or strange dresses, quite unlike Louise, who'd followed the fashion of short skirts and tight fitting clothes. The colourful fabrics Felicity wrapped about herself – I later discovered she preferred to wear the sari – hid her figure and the shape of hips and waist.

Of middling years, perhaps forty or so in age when I first saw her, she possessed near black hair, so dark a brown it hid its true colour from the angles of light. She wore it in a plaited ponytail and the coarser, rogue hairs poked out of the braids seeking escape. When the loose strands flitted across her chocolate eyes, she brushed them aside. Her skin, for someone who lived an indoor life, had a golden shine to it, as if she had failed to hide from the sun and its blazing rays had chased her indoors, determined to colour her narrow face and stubby nose. India with its heat had left an indelible mark on her complexion and the more I gazed at her, the more I became convinced she had its blood running through her veins.

When I announced my services, she clapped her hands in delight. 'Thank God,' she declared, shooing me into the house. 'Charles, isn't it? Louise mentioned you. The blasted kitchen sink is blocked. I shouldn't have put the tea leaves down it.'

I followed her into the kitchen. The worktop was covered in bowls, spilt flour and my feet crunched on a scattering of sugar granules.

'I'm baking a cake. Lord knows why, but it seems the English thing to do, don't you think?'

I nodded in agreement whilst her head danced about on her neck. I detected a lilt to her accent, which I assumed betrayed her Indian origins. I examined the water in the sink. The tea leaves swirled about and pockets of air gurgled in the pipe beneath. I crouched down and inspected the u-tube underneath the sink.

'I'm sure I can clear this if I remove the pipe bend and clean it out. I'll try not to make a mess.'

Another brief round of applause. 'You're a star. Louise said you'd help from time to time. She also said you're a little erratic in your timekeeping, but very useful. I confess, I had servants in Bombay, but here, I can't afford the luxury. I'm learning to cook.'

'I'm sure you will make a fine cook.' I rose. 'I'll fetch some tools from the shed.'

'After that, you don't mind fixing the wretched toilet?'

The unblocking job began a long period of constant plumbing issues at Heachley. I told her many times that the pipes needed ripping out and replacing. However, she wouldn't budge and insisted she would make do. 'Tosh,' she would say with her hands on her hips. 'In India indoor plumbing is a rarity. There's plenty of life left in these old pipes.'

I disagreed, but her attitude to most things was grin and bear and avoid problems by ignoring them for as long as possible. Except for me. I, unknowingly, became something of a project for her while she kept me busy.

Weeks trickled by and I couldn't resist the books in the library. Boredom had set in – due to my inability to vanish – and it encouraged me to borrow books and take them to the hut in the evenings to read. Unlike Louise who preferred the Bronte's, Dickens and Jane Austen, titles that had been available in my time and of little interest to the enquiring mind, Felicity brought with her new authors. I devoured George Orwell and D.H. Lawrence with wide-eyed fascination. How the world had changed. I discovered Indian writers and poets with their epic tales of gods and heroes, and accompanying these books I poured over her collection of treatises on the history of Asia, Hinduism, with its reincarnation theology and many other distant cultures, such as Confucian and Buddhism.

For the first time in decades my intellect thrived on new knowledge. Instead of fearing change, I embraced the world beyond Heachley Hall. Although she cared little for the television, Felicity avidly listened to the Home Service on the radio and I enjoyed the debates, interviews, plays and comedies as much as she did. Of course, I hid my enthusiasm pretending to focus on my task, but conducting all my activities in a laborious, painfully slow fashion to ensure I didn't miss a favourite show

Although I couldn't taste or eat her cakes, nor try out her speciality teas, my existence didn't curtail emotional outbursts. I experienced loneliness, joy, tedium and despair. Still struggling with Louise's departure, Felicity, with her vivacious approach to all things kept me from descending into madness, something I've feared for years: my ghostly apparition roaming Heachley and scaring the inhabitants with my delusional mind.

Yes, I know fear, even if it doesn't quicken my heart nor cause sweat to form upon my brow. I'm quite capable of the emotion as I found out several months after her arrival.

Waiting in the closet I heard nothing: no creaks, footfalls or doors banging. I deduced she was occupied elsewhere in the house and I gave the door a shove and forced it open.

The shock was tremendous. Ironic, since is it not the responsibility of the ghost to incite terror in those who have the misfortune to encounter one? I froze to the spot. My legs were lead weights and my mouth gaped wide. She sat upon a small wooden chair with a blanket over her knees and clutching a set of knitting needles in her sun stained hands.

She seemed most unperturbed by my bursting out of the closet. Under the dim lighting I saw her eyes twinkle. She rested the needles on her lap and sighed. 'Finally, I'd begun to think I was mistaken. I wondered about the cellar, whether you came out of there, but then I decided it had to be this closet. It's that infernal ash, it collects right in front of the door.'

I blinked, looked down and saw the particles clinging to my trouser legs, waiting for me to shake them loose. My tongue cleaved to the roof of my mouth. Her appearance had stunned me into silence. How long had she sat there, facing the closet door, waiting for me to stir and step into her trap?

'It's quite all right.' Her face softened, and her lips curved upwards, shaping into a gentle smile. 'I know you are Christopher Isaacks.'

I slid down the closet door, which slammed shut behind me and I rested my back against it, drew up my knees, buried my face in my hands and sobbed. It was the first time I'd heard my name spoken in over ninety years. The tears didn't fall, they never did, but the emotion of relief, mixed with panic and uncertainty, was just as tangible as my tearless weeping.

She coughed gently, and I glanced up. She was bundling her knitting into a ball. She'd taken up knitting jumpers because of the cold, she'd told me. I'd spent hours chopping wood for the fires, but neither the heating system nor the fires managed to warm her constant coldness. I sympathised with her condition: the heat never touched me either, nor did the cold, but my indifference to temperature must have added to her suspicions – I don't wear coats, even on snow covered days. What else had she spotted?

'The books – you've been borrowing them,' she said, as if to read my mind. 'You didn't always put them back in the right place. You never change your dreadful clothes. Then there is the lack of interest in money, and avoiding my food, which I do take offence at – you might have tried. Then those darn mysterious noises. So hard to avoid given my solitary occupation. Your family – no mention of anyone, of your father, or even male friends or where you live.'

'Go on,' I urged, desperate to know how she came by my name.

'I wanted to know more about this place when I came over. I found out about the fire, did some more research at the county archives and discovered another name – Nuri Sully – a poor woman who died in a workhouse. Naturally, my curiosity rose as to why she had been abandoned. While you busied yourself in the frigid shed, I explored. I love exploring. Throughout my childhood my parents worried about my tendency to wander off. I went for a walk and found the little log cabin at the back of the woods. Had to fight my way through a pea-soup fog to find it. Not a problem; I'm use to battling the monsoon and I'm quite unstoppable when I put my mind to something.'

'I think you're the first to make it that far,' I said in a small voice.

'I saw the evidence of your habitation. I examined the contents of the tin box.' She halted, and I flinched as she bore down with her strikingly dark eyes.

'Please, don't speak of it,' I whispered. 'I don't open that box. The pain...' I hugged my legs and rocked forward. The letters inside are not for nostalgia or happy reminisces, rather they are a hateful reminder of my mistakes.

'I'm so sorry.' She rose and came over as I started to sob again, and she reached down to touch my juddering shoulder. 'You're a suffering soul trapped in this house, rather like me.'

I lifted my face. 'Like you?'

'Do you think the locals take to somebody like me? A half-caste spinster? A bastard? We're both outcasts.'

I calmed and took deep imaginary breaths. 'You're not afraid of ghosts then?' I tried a small smile and it shot across my face for a second, like a nervous twitch.

She lifted her hand off my shoulder. 'Louise, I think she suspected, but hadn't the imagination to think it through. We chatted a little on the telephone before she moved out. I'm different and I had a rather complicated upbringing that filled my head with romantic tales.'

'Louise?' I whispered.

'Yes. I'm so sorry to have taken her home. I hadn't expected to inherit this place from John. We haven't spoken in years. Then, I suppose, it's possible he saw me in a different light. After all, his wife was illegitimate before Louise adopted her. Maybe, I'm not quite the black sheep he considered me to be. I offered the house back to Mary, as John's widow, but she declined and seems determined not to come back here. Shame. I'd like to get to know my niece, Anna.'

'Louise couldn't persuade her?'

She shrugged. 'I don't know Mary that well. I've only met her a couple of times. When I flew into London she greeted me at the airport. She's a strong minded young woman. Wilful, my father would have said, but these days...' She picked up her knitting and blanket. 'I was furious when I found out what John had done – seducing her, marrying her at such a young age. But, having met her and seen her grief at his unexpected death, I do believe they loved each other very much and who am I to criticise? I myself am the product of a passionate affair, borne out of wedlock and despised by the people I live among.'

'What do you make of Christopher Isaacks, the man who left his over?'

'Come here and help me with this chair.'

I clambered to my feet and returned the chair to her bedroom.

She walked towards the top of the staircase. 'We shall be friends, Charles. We shall haunt this house together.' She led me downstairs into the library and bade me sit down in an armchair opposite her own. There, with the fire spitting in the background, I told her my sad story: the sweet woman I had spurned to my chagrin, my cursed existence and my years of haunting.

'I cannot be your lover,' Felicity said without embellishing and I wasn't surprised, because I simply knew in my heart I had not the capacity to love somebody who appeared older than me – she was more like my long dead mother: kindly and practical. 'I will be your friend and I will keep your secret as best as I can, so you may be free to dwell here on the estate.'

I thanked her profusely, which made her bronzed cheeks flush with redness and she offered to take my money, everything the Branston's had paid me and she would buy clothes, a fresh mattress and bedding, and other knick-knacks I might find useful. She also suggested I might use an attic room, which I declined.

'The woods protect me. I feel safe there. I haven't lived in a house for years and I need my space,' I explained.

'You must miss male companionship,' she remarked.

'I miss many things. However, I have met many wonderful people, too.'

'Write it all down for me, would you? So I understand.'

A simple request and here in this journal, I record my existence as a ghost – not quite what one might imagine it to be. Quite tedious, she had commented after I described the misery of my comings and goings. I laughed heartily, enjoying the sensation of uninhibited humour at my predicament. She joined in, then, left me to my penmanship, while she baked scones for tea.

PART THREE

The Grave

"We really have to understand the person we want to love. If our love is only a will to possess, it is not love. If we only think of ourselves, if we know only our own needs and ignore the needs of the other person, we cannot love. We must look deeply in order to see and understand the needs, aspirations, and suffering of the person we love. This is the ground of real love. You cannot resist loving another person when you really understand him or her."

—Thich Nhat Hanh
Peace Is Every Step: The Path of Mindfulness in Everyday Life
1992

THIRTY-ONE

I closed the book and due to my clammy palms I was unable to grip it; I rested it on my lap. I glanced at the man next to me, somebody whom I considered a good friend. The story made no difference: he remained Charles. He'd given himself a new identity and who he'd once been, Christopher Isaacks, didn't exist any longer. Kit might have died in a fire, but Charles had risen from his ashes, literally, it seemed.

Yes, many questions had been answered in his account, but not all. He'd lost his quiet repose and a vibrancy had returned to his crystal eyes. I steadied my trembling hands and flicked a few loose strands of hair out of my eyes; I had his attention.

'Those times when I visited Felicity as a child, you were here too, but we never met,' I said. 'Though to be honest, I don't remember much of my early childhood.' I wondered if Charles was a morsel of imagery hidden in my mind that was too small to recall.

'No, I never met you as a child. You always came with your parents or with your father.' He wove his fingers together, leaving one sticking out and pointing at me. 'Felicity was quite taken by you. She saw the talent in your drawings.'

I puffed out my cheeks. 'I don't remember doing drawings for her. I always drew for myself. A little selfish perhaps.'

'Perhaps your mother sent the pictures.'

Mum's family had never truly featured in my life compared to Dad's. It was too late to ask either of them. 'You actually spoke with Mum when she was younger, before Dad joined her?'

He gave me an apologetic frown. 'No. I kept out of the way. I watched from afar in the garden, always hiding.'

'Why?' I asked. Charles's ability to merge into the landscape didn't surprise me. How often had he lurked behind a bush or a tree, watching me move about the house and gardens, while he himself was unable to leave the grounds? A flurry of goose bumps sprung around my body. I'd never been alone once during my time at Heachley. Even when I slept, Charles had been half a mile away in the hut.

'You see,' he continued with a concentrated expression. 'Felicity, everyone, they all grow old, but I don't. It would have caused difficulties if your parents or grandmother saw me and noticed I never aged. Felicity kept her promise to keep me secret as best she could. I owe her a debt for her diligence and there is no way for me to pay it back. Because of her infirmity, I was exposed to Maggie more than anyone.'

'You never lived inside the house? Why not?'

'Eventually I did, but for many years we lived separately. Yes, we were friends, however, this was her home, not mine. I have no right to live here, and though she asked, I declined. Then, her needs changed. Maggie assisted with more than the cleaning. There was the cooking and other personal matters she helped do. Unfortunately, Felicity had grown frail. I stayed some nights in the attic in case she needed anything. Maggie never noticed that I kipped on the floor.'

His ease at deception didn't surprise me, because he'd been successful at it for years. He'd had to be. 'Maggie is still convinced this place is haunted, and I think, because she looked in the Chindi box, she knows it is Christopher. You.'

Charles laughed. 'She's right, it is haunted, but she doesn't suspect me, because I'm Charles. When she began to work for Felicity, a few years before she fell ill, I avoided Maggie as much as possible. You see, we didn't see eye to eye on Felicity. Maggie wanted her to move into a nursing home, whereas I respected Felicity's desire for independence. But, all the same, she fell and I wasn't on hand to help.' He pulled a glum face.

'Maggie called Tony.'

'Which explains why I quickly disappeared. I must have been in the garden when it happened. If Maggie was here that is where I stayed.'

'All those years, you and Felicity, together. Wow.' I held out his journal. Charles took it off me and clutched it to his chest. 'And she never lived with anyone else?'

'No.' He slowly shook his head. 'I don't think she cared for men.'

'Except you,' I pointed out, poking his arm.

He frowned, his posture slumping slightly. 'I'm half a man. A spirit stuck in time, not quite the same.'

'You're not half a man, not to me. I wonder if she…it doesn't matter.' I couldn't find the appropriate way to describe Felicity's solitary ways. Perhaps she was a lesbian or asexual, uninterested in sensual companionship. It didn't matter; she was dead. 'It must have been hard, coming back and finding her gone and me here instead.'

'Sadly I knew that day would come. I'd seen many occupants come and many are now dead, including your grandmother, but yes, I am upset by the loss of my friend.'

'Mary died some years ago.' Her departure had been the last family funeral I'd attended. A drab day spent in a cemetery in London with a handful of mourners, none of whom I recognised.

'Felicity grieved for both your mother and grandmother.' Putting the journal down next to him, he stroked the back of my hand with his fingertips and I swallowed hard, holding back the sudden arrival of tears in my eyes.

'You must have feared Felicity's death, what I might bring: new owner taking you back to the days of fleeting existence – the snapshots in time.'

'I selfishly wanted her to stay here, probably part of the reason I fought Maggie's idea of a nursing home. Nevertheless, Felicity, although increasingly infirm, had always been alert and aware of her surroundings. She witnessed my anxieties, what little I'd shown of them and she reassured me not to worry because she had in hand a solution.' He ceased stroking my hand and paused.

I digested the implication of his last statement.

'She said that?' I stared at Charles, my cheeks flushing with heat. 'Why, she planned this.' I sprung to my feet. 'She left me this house, wrote that stupid stipulation into the will to trap me here knowing I would likely uncover the truth within that time period of a year and a day, just like she had...' I ceased pacing and spun to face him.

Charles remained on the sofa. 'Yes, she worked it out within a year,' he murmured. 'Unlike the previous tenants, you and she live here alone. It makes it harder for me to explain my presence.'

'She wants me to free you. She couldn't love you, for whatever reason, but she believed I could and that if I did, do. Oh my.' I collapsed onto the sofa and sank into the sagging cushion. The constant flood of nervous energy over the last couple of hours was exhausting. 'She left this house to me for your sake, not mine – she never considered money as the motivation, she saw it as a temptation, but not the goal.'

'I'm truly in debt, aren't I?' He smiled weakly. 'Perhaps for both our sakes. A premonition maybe. Whatever, she gambled that I, we, you know, would—'

I didn't want to hear him say it. I wasn't ready to hear him admit to his feelings and for me to acknowledge them. I hunted for something else to say and interrupted his flow.

'Do you think the world is filled with ghosts like you? Amongst us, breathing, talking, interacting?' I bombarded.

He blinked and shot a look of bemusement in my direction. 'How can I tell, I'm a prisoner here.' He surveyed the room. 'So perhaps, there are others like me, walking about, looking alive, but only to those who can see them. Or maybe trapped and confined to small spaces.'

When Bert and I had entered the claustrophobic cellar, I'd struggled with the darkness, the oppressive gloom, yet Charles had been down there countless times without warning. 'That sounds horrible. That closet's like a grave, too. That's hell on earth.'

'So it could be I'm in hell, except—' he rested his hand on my knee and squeezed gently, '—I've had the fortune to meet decent, kind people.'

I tried to ignore the firm placement of his hand, but it triggered an odd tingling sensation in inappropriate places. Haste wasn't

ecessary was it? He, and I, weren't going anywhere in the near
ture. I cleared my dry throat and decided to keep to my tactic of
noring what needed to be said.

'Catholics believed in purgatory, an in-between place for the
ul.'

'That isn't my religion and I'm more than a displaced soul; I have
ving flesh and I feel emotions, sense the passage of time. I'm here,
n I not?' He spoke softly.

Another reminder he was not the ghost I'd imagined haunting
eachley Hall. No malicious spirit had pushed Felicity downstairs
: sought to harm either of us. Secretly, and without my knowledge,
harles had protected me, and Felicity had paved the way for him
 do it.

I swallowed; my mouth felt paper dry. 'So maybe there are
:hers. I always thought the undead were zombies.'

'Zombies?' He smirked. 'I don't recall that word in any book
ve read.'

'Flesh eating monsters who prey on the living. Stuff of horror
lms.'

'Ah. Films. I gather they like to scare for fun? Why I can't
nagine. So, I could be unique, then. The one ghost who lives and
:reathes, and never dies. The immortal man held captive by what?
'hat truly traps me here?' He rose and walked over to the window,
:eping his back to me.

'A curse?' I scoffed, still struggling to understand what bound
harles to the confines of the house. My constraints were easier to
:eak. 'We're both held hostage to the demands of another. Except,
 I choose, I can walk away from this place and wash my hands of
: sell and forgo the inheritance. You can't leave.'

Charles continued to view the freshly mowed grass, avoiding eye
ntact with me. 'I can leave. It's possible. But. I don't want to ask
r your help. It seems ungracious.'

'Ask me what?' My stomach twisted into knots, because I knew
:actly what he was alluding to and ungracious wasn't a word that
rung to mind. The awkwardness on both our parts was almost
nbearable. Such a polite discourse, and on any other occasion it

might have been humorous listening to us dance around the issue. I wasn't seeking a romantic cliché to justify what he needed from me, but he had to say something.

'To free me.' He turned to face me.

At last, a declaration, an acknowledgement of what I felt.

I glanced away from his searching gaze that called out for me to express what I'd nurtured for weeks, but left unsaid. A low sigh, quite unintentional, slipped out of my mouth before I spoke.

'She gambled we would fall in love, that is what you want to say. So you can die properly and be gone forever. Is that what you want?' I fought to hold back the tears.

For a second he closed his eyes, and I thought, maybe, that his lips trembled, then I realised that was my overactive imagination, my illusion. Nothing. Except his sad eyes, which once I'd considered translucent and empty, now I saw poured out his soul.

'What I want is to be with you and if I can't have that.' Another pause, another moment when he seemed on the brink of displaying his raw emotions. 'I'd rather not exist on any plane: physical or spiritual.'

I walked the few steps to stand in front of him and I placed my palms on his chest, knowing the heart beneath my fingertips still beat and always at the same unhurried pace. 'You said that because of the curse you would fear to love again.'

'I feared to have my love returned in kind,' he confirmed.

'It's too late. It's already happened.' I reached out and stroked my hand down his cool cheek. He didn't flinch, but briefly, he closed his eyes, allowing his long lashes to dip lower.

Covering my hand with his, he held my palm against his face. There was no hiding the warmth of my skin compared to his. 'You will leave here in a few months and I will remained trapped, with Liz possibly,' he said softly.

'Both of us heartbroken. In that case, what have we to lose by showing our love? I can release you, Charles.'

'You wouldn't see me ever again nor know what we could have been together. I mean if you wanted, you could stay, could you not, and live here, just as we've been doing'?' he suggested.

Like Felicity? I wasn't my great-aunt.

'I can't afford to pay the bills. The house would crumble about us: the wiring, plumbing,' I fretted, unfairly, because there was no need for me to live under the roof every day of the year. I would be free to choose when I came and went, but for how long?

'I'm sorry, I shouldn't have asked that of you. You're right, you should leave. Sell the house and live a full life. You'll meet a fine gentleman and marry.'

The tears swelled around the rim of my eyes. 'I've met a fine gentleman, haven't I? What the fuck are we to do?'

He chuckled. 'Such coarse language from so pretty a girl. Well, if you wish to be uncouth, we could f—'

I shook my head. 'No, I know what you're saying. Do it without passion and make a mockery of our feelings. No, I won't. Consummation is to share something special – our love.'

The smile slipped off his face. 'Then, if we truly make love, I shall cease to be Charles.'

The tears trickled down my cheeks. 'And you will be free, and I will be too. Free to move on and leave this place knowing you are resting in your grave and at peace.' A teardrop hung from my chin and he wiped it away with his thumb.

'Would you mourn me?' he asked, drawing me closer. His breath was surprisingly warm.

'Naturally, but don't pity me. Let's beat this curse, end it. One night with you is worth it. I'll cherish it.'

How much I wished we could find another solution, one that kept us both together. After Charles had been dispatched to his permanent rest, I would mope, commiserate myself in solitude, unable to mourn in public or explain my sadness. I would imagine those missed opportunities to grow together, the children we might have had. Love wasn't a transient emotion to be tossed aside and I realised, there in his arms, being in love was life changing and impossible to ignore. What of a broken heart? I didn't want to experience it.

I blinked, struggling with my blurred vision. 'I don't want to lose you.' I faltered.

He sighed. 'It is as I feared; I will leave you heartbroken.'

'But full of memories, which I'll cling on to and never forget,' I said fervently while wishing for something different.

For a while, we contemplated the impasse in silence. Such a dilemma we'd created for ourselves to solve. Great-aunt Felicity had conjured up this situation by tempting me into staying at Heachley. To ensure I discovered the truth about Charles, she'd dictated a timescale. Six months would have been too short, whereas even with her lack of foresight about the current state of the property, any longer than a year and I might not have taken up the proposition.

What had she envisaged would happen next given her understanding of Charles's captivity? If love had been the outcome, she would also understand how hard it would be to break that curse. What if I'd been indifferent to Charles's attentions and hadn't found him attractive or intriguing? If in those circumstances I'd learnt the truth of his situation would I choose to stay and give him an existence without interference from the world outside, as Felicity had done? She'd successfully borne the secret to her grave and then given me the opportunity to continue to help Charles. Could I be that selfless? The worse scenario would have been my failure to notice the unusual ghost in my house. Any lack of curiosity about the Chindi box might have left him undiscovered and struggling to cope.

I gently smirked: his clothes wouldn't have survived another winter. 'Charles.' I lifted my head from his shoulder and gazed straight into his pale eyes. 'What became of the money I gave you?'

He looked embarrassed, if that was possible for a supernatural man. 'It's under my bed.'

'Felicity never paid you with money, did she?'

'No,' he grinned. 'She gave me books, the radios, the wind up one especially is a blessing. Plus clothes and other necessities. I will return the money to you, it is of no use to me.'

I plucked a loose thread on his jumper. 'It would be if I used it to buy you clothes and a new pair of shoes.'

'Tomorrow—'

I pressed my finger to his lips, rose onto my tiptoes and supplanted the digit with my mouth. Our first kiss awoke more than I possibly imagined. I'd kissed other lips, felt the warmth of moist flesh and the flick of a tongue, but Charles had a delicate manner, quite unlike the hard pressure of other men's smothering mouths and I treasured its uniqueness.

'Miriam,' he murmured, breaking free. 'There will be no tomorrow for me if we do this.'

We could wait until nearer my final days at Heachley. Force him to linger in a tortured state fearing I might change my mind, but in doing so he'd be unable to demonstrate his love until the very end of my time here. My reason for keeping him at my side was unfair, because frankly, the house didn't need much else doing to it that would make a huge amount of difference to its price – only the garden required any effort to achieve a grandiose impression. But that would be the wrong reason to keep him at my side.

I gathered up both of Charles's hands and drew him away from the window and the light. 'I can't let you stay as you are. I couldn't bear to look at you, knowing I have the power to send you to your rest. There's always the chance that misfortune could strike one day and I might not be here to buy your clothes. I would rather have one night with you, cherish it, than have you exist in despair, uncertain of the future. I won't be broken hearted because I will have saved you. It's what you want, isn't it?'

He bowed his head. 'Yes, I wish to be free of this affliction, and if we delay this, I worry that your emotional attachment to me would grow and blossom. If you became dependent on me, my loss would be harder to bear. It would be too great a sacrifice. Nobody should be forced to grieve for their loved one. I know that now.'

The decision was sudden, or so it seemed, and that was necessary. Talk might persuade us to reconsider and neither of us could probably stand the agony of debating the right or wrong of it.

I led him out of the sitting room and up the stairs he had diligently renovated. With our backs to the nightmarish closet, we climbed higher into the attic and the bedroom. I closed the door behind us.

Whether he'd been in the room before or not seemed irrelevant. He paid no attention to the sprawl of discarded clothes or the unmade bed. I swallowed hard, aware of every nuance, every little signal of intent: was I eyeing his face too much, or too little; had I just licked my lips again; when had I last brushed my teeth? Charles stood rock still, not quite the startled rabbit in headlights, but he wasn't relaxed.

'Forget about the curse, Charles. Can you for me? Just pretend we are two ordinary people, in love.'

He broke into a broad smile and it melted all the doubt in my mind that I was doing the wrong thing: love isn't always about a lifetime, a commitment forever, because it is also just this – one moment in time to remember and enjoy.

Neither of us hurried in our preparations. I plucked at buttons and the clasp of my bra with quivering fingers. Issues over body image lost their relevance: Charles had vivid scars – my blemishes hardly matched up in comparison. I skirted around the outline of his body, tracking the contours of his ribs and waist, allowing myself a brief glance at his masculine feature, and I found it to be worthy and strangely reassuring. A ghost some might say, but not one that had lost his sexuality or attractiveness. Or realness, because I reminded myself, he wasn't a ghost.

I recalled his brief affair with Vanessa and how he'd modestly referred to his abilities. Neither of us were virgins, however, I guessed we weren't the kind of lovers who'd come to bed with vast experience. It helped, knowing we might fumble at it, and I suppressed a nervous guffaw. Charles frowned and cocked his head towards me. My cheeks must have flushed.

I shook my head. 'Nothing, just…I'm happy to be here.'

'Me, too,' he said and smiled.

I wriggled out my underwear, and immediately had to quash the temptation to mask his view. The subtle smile remained as he surveyed me. 'You're beautiful,' he whispered. 'Up to now, I daren't imagine this. Nights of listening to the owls, closing my eyes and wishing.'

How many nights? The awkwardness tied my tongue; it impeded him too. Instead of offering romantic overtures, I rearranged the bedding and created a welcoming nest.

We slipped under the cool sheets of the bed and I lay on my back with my hands tucked at my sides. Charles propped himself on an elbow and stroked my butterfly riddled belly. I shivered – a gentle tremble across my skin. I recognised the delightful sensation and it was desired; I understood it as a preamble to more intense ones.

'I think we should close our eyes,' he suggested, leaning over me. 'And savour these precious moments and make them last.'

I looked up at him, past his hollow eyes and mentally traced the gentle curls of his hair, the v-shape of his collarbone, the swirls of red and white scars which patterned his torso. I wanted to draw him again, keep all his attributes alive on paper so that I might remember him long past that day. The need in me triggered an emotional leap forward. 'I love you, Mr Charles Donaldson of Heachley Woods.' There, I'd said it. Made it real.

'Miss Miriam Marsters, Mistress of Heachley Hall,' he kissed my forehead, 'I love you, too.'

Naming him reminded me of the other man. 'Will you be Christopher again, when I wake?'

'I suppose,' he paused in his caresses. 'I don't know if I have a grave. You could lay flowers on it. If not, plant something in the garden.' He stumbled over his words, but the suggestion was good. I would lay flowers somewhere or perhaps plant a rose bush. He'd also reminded me of another grave; he should know of it.

'Nuri Sully. Beatrice,' I said. He tensed slightly, and I cupped my hands about his face to reassure him. 'She lies there in the churchyard. Your father paid for a headstone.'

'He did?' Charles's eyes widened. 'Then, please, lay some flowers on her grave, too. Tell her, I am sorry, that I—'

I nodded. 'I understand.'

He wriggled down under the covers. 'No more sadness. We are about to experience joy, aren't we?'

I giggled – a childish display of nervousness. 'Oh, I do hope so.'

Swiftly and with purpose, he drew me into a tight embrace, pressing himself against my body. So passionate, so ardent in nature. My heart pounded, bursting to be heard. Our breaths melded into one. I closed my eyes and curtailed my sight. Now we would rely on other senses to conclude what Felicity had envisioned years earlier.

THIRTY-TWO

I stirred from a deep slumber, pushed the duvet away from my nose and reached across the bed. There was a dint in the mattress where he'd lain, but the space had been vacated. Charles was gone.

I curled into a ball and stifled a cry, reminding myself I would not show grief at his belated death, but tears threatened to break me. I had to nip this melancholy in the bud. Charles was free. I'd released him from his curse, his fragile existence and somewhere his soul rested – hopefully in peace.

We'd achieved what he wished – what we both desired. It had been easy, uncomplicated and divine. It seemed a ridiculous tragedy that the best sex I'd ever had was with a ghost.

The magical moment had occurred late in the evening. We'd taken our time to properly warm to each other, to explore and enjoy what we each had to offer. As I suspected, Charles was not a novice. Although he'd had little opportunity to practise the art of lovemaking, he'd the wisdom of a man of many years trapped in the youthful, energetic form of a twenty-nine year old. It was all I desired in a bedfellow. I'd told him as much as he trailed kisses up and down my squirming body and he'd shushed me, which in turn induced another round of silly giggles.

What made it special had been the companion of love. Whatever I'd done in the past had lacked that necessary sentiment – the ability to whisper those sweet words as we made love without fear of regret or embarrassment in the morning. My regret took another form and it had been anticipated.

I sighed and sank into lethargy, allowing it to eclipse my sorrow.

My thoughts drifted to the future. I was determined to survive the last few months at Heachley Hall without him. The generous pile of wood would be burnt to a crisp: his last industrious legacy ironically consumed in fire. The weather would improve, the sunshine would warm the interior and the need for heating fuel would expire. If I needed help, I'd Bert and Tony to call upon, and Ruth too; she would visit, as she'd promised.

Did I tell her about my strange affair with Charles Donaldson? No. She'd probably think I'd gone bonkers with the loneliness and his absence could easily be explained: he'd gone to work elsewhere.

The house creaked and sighed a soft thud somewhere beneath me. Sounds of movement, except I'd never been as alone as I was that morning. I tensed forming a rigid pole. Footsteps. They grew louder, coming up the squeaky stairs towards the attic. I shot up in bed and hauled the duvet across my front to protect myself from the intruder. It seemed as if Charles's exit had triggered another supernatural force to awaken. Was Dickens's fantasy Christmas story coming to life with a string of apparitions to torment me or more likely; was I about to be the victim of the common burglar?

This was my fault. I'd left the back door unlocked too often. With Charles's departure, I was conscious of my vulnerability more than ever and the lack of security measures I'd put in place to protect my property. I was wrong; coping without him was going to be a challenge beyond heartbreak and isolation. I clenched my fists, ready to confront the intruder.

The door creaked, slightly ajar at first, then flung wider and from out the shadows of the corridor emerged a mop of unruly dark hair that failed to shadow bright eyes. I stared, disbelieving, as a vermillion blush flashed across his usually pale cheeks.

'Charles!' I screeched, leaping up onto my knees, allowing the bedding to fall away from my naked body.

He smiled – a broad toothy grin, quite unlike his usual suppressed one. He had a grip on the waistband of his baggy jeans; the top button was undone. 'I've just peed.'

'What?' My mouth remained open, stunned by his presence in the doorway.

'I woke up needing a pee. I haven't had that in a long, long time. And,' he came farther into the room, 'I'm hungry.'

'Charles.' I reached across the bed, desperate to touch him, to convince myself this man wasn't a dream or another apparition. 'Your skin.' I gestured at his bare chest, 'it's perfect.'

He glanced down and gasped. 'I'd not noticed.' He ran his hand up and down his smooth arms. 'My scars have gone.'

'I don't understand.' I wrapped the duvet around my cooling shoulders. 'You're not dead.'

'No,' He raised his hands above his head and stretched. 'I ache.' He cricked his neck from side to side. 'I'm cold, too.' He picked up his jumper and pulled it over his head.

I threw myself at him, ignoring my nudity and he captured me in his embrace. Tears cascaded down my face and I drummed my palms on his chest. 'You're alive, really alive.'

He laughed. 'Yes. And, ow, that hurts.'

I grabbed his wrist and hunted for his pulse. It raced, just like mine. 'What's happened? The curse?'

He shrugged. 'Gone, I assume – I feel quite mortal, vulnerable and hungry,' he repeated. 'Can we go and have some breakfast? I can't wait to eat.'

For a man who'd been born in the 1840s he had regressed into a boyish state. I hurriedly dressed and followed him down into the kitchen. 'What do you want?'

'Anything. Sausages? Do you have any? Oh, and coffee, please.' He smacked his lips together, then feverishly licking them with his tongue.

While I hastened to feed the ravenous Charles, he speculated. 'I think I have to be careful.'

'Careful?'

'That now, if I injure myself, like fall off the roof, I'd probably die, as in totally not come back from the dead.'

The Rayburn blasted out heat. I stabbed several sausages and tossed them into a frying pan. 'Quite possibly,' I concurred. 'I shouldn't put your theory to the test.'

'No, agreed.' He picked up a fork and waved it at me. 'I shall definitely need new clothes.'

I laughed. 'My goodness, you'll be stunned by men's fashion these days.' I poured hot water into the cafeteria. 'Seriously, why are you here? When I woke and found myself alone, I feared the worse.'

'I'm sorry, my love.' He kissed the top of my head. 'That was bad timing. I woke, and you were so sweetly curled up, I didn't want to disturb you. I thought for a minute I was not really there, in spirit, yes, but not in body, then my bladder told me otherwise. It was quite a shock. I'd forgotten how inconvenient the sensation can be. I had to go.'

I poked at sausages. The unfathomable mystery of Charles continued. 'You were convinced you wouldn't be here if we made love.'

He leaned against the worktop, and with an eager expression, watched me fry his breakfast. 'A curse should have a gruesome outcome. Isn't that the case?' He scratched his chin, which was already covered by a dark forest of morning bristles. 'I don't know. I can hear those words, over and over, warning me not to fall in love or be loved.'

'Maybe the Gypsy wanted you to live in fear of love, never daring to be with another,' I speculated – had that been the man's revenge? A cruel twist on words? The monstrous man, Christopher, had died, but Charles had been born out of the ashes, rather like the phoenix. A second chance?

'Then why release me and give me this happy conclusion?'

I removed the pan from the heat and walked over to him. 'Because you regretted what you did. You turned from a selfish young man into a considerate servant to everyone who lived here, including me. A selfless existence without material gain or comfort. I would like to think that deep down, the man who forced you into this supernatural state wanted to forgive you.'

'Perhaps,' he murmured. 'But still, it doesn't make sense. The anger he threw at me, that doesn't speak of a man who seeks to forgive me. I don't know. I grieved for Christopher, the man I once was. I hated him for a long while I think, but now he is truly at peace. We should go to the graveyard together, don't you think, and lay those flowers?'

I fetched two plates. 'Yes. After breakfast or maybe lunch.'

'Why later?'

'Because I want proof this isn't a dream. That we can repeat last night with our eyes open.'

'Oh, do you now.' He grinned. 'Sausages and coffee first. Then, after I've convinced you I'm real, I want to hold your hand, walk out into the lane and down to the village.'

..●..

THIRTY-THREE

We walked towards the gate, hand in hand, with me constantly squeezing his knuckles, checking that he was there. We both needed reassurances, but Charles especially. Having read his journal, I appreciated the terrible sense of dread he must feel in the moment before he would vanish – ceased to be, as he described it.

Two pairs of feet scrunched down the gravel driveway and I prayed the same footfalls would be heard on the other side of the gate. Why would they not, I'd told him earlier in the morning, as we lounged in bed. He'd drunk his coffee with relish, consumed a huge quantity of sausages and thankfully, it seemed his dormant digestive system functioned normally.

'No stopping,' I whispered, as the wrought iron gates drew closer. For the second time we crossed the invisible line that separated Heachley estate from the rest of the world, a world Charles had not experienced in over a century.

I held my breath and next to me Charles inhaled deeply as if we were about to dive into a pool of deep water. I grasped his hand as tight as I could, clinging onto him – *please, don't leave me.* Following one final stutter of uncertain feet, we passed the gateposts. I turned to look at him and smiled. His eyelashes were wet and he blinked, once, then again as he fought to contain his emotions. For a man accustomed to having his feelings locked inside, he seemed on the verge of letting them fly. Instead, he released my hand and continued to walk away from the gates.

Then I noticed where he'd gone. I dashed forward and tugged on his arm. 'Stop. You're in the middle of the road.' The last thing I wanted to witness was Charles mowed down by a passing vehicle.

I fizzed with both excitement and alarm, because the need to supervise him meant he was really alive.

He halted, glancing up and down the road, then he stamped his feet on the road. 'I've often wondered what this would feel like.'

I replaced my anxious expression with a solemn one. 'Being out here; I can understand.'

'No,' he smirked, 'Tarmac. Never stood on it before now. Cobbled streets, yes, but not asphalt.'

I thumped his arm and he laughed – a joyful sound – deep throated and hearty.

'Come on,' I urged, 'This way.' I maintained a firm hold of his swinging hand as we walked down the lane towards the village and the pub, where I'd promised him one of Glenda's steak and kidney pies.

'What's that?' He pointed to the distant electricity pylon.

So began a continuous stream of questions and answers. Our short stroll was more like taking a curious toddler out for a walk not a grown adult. Everything intrigued him: the white markings on the road at the junctions, the drain covers. Then as we approached the outskirts of Little Knottisham, he saw his first modern house. For twenty minutes, I experienced a vicarious innocence. I'd not seen houses as architecturally different or unusual, but Charles did. Garages attached to buildings – rather than separate stables – were a reminder he'd grown up with the horse and cart.

Wheelie bins left on the roadside for refuse collection were turned into a plaything. I dragged one along the pavement and tried to explain how it tipped up into the rear of a dustbin lorry. He'd seen the bins at the back of the Heachley Hall, but not witnessed the trucks at work on the lane.

A car drove past, and he jumped away from the kerbside even though the vehicle dawdled. He'd a familiarity with their design from picture books, but had never sat in one. He'd soon be my passenger.

We arrived at the Rose and Crown. The main entrance was wedged open and escaping from inside was the rhythmic beat of the latest chart topper. I halted in front of the door.

'Are you sure you're ready for this?' I asked.

Crossing the threshold would be a giant leap for Charles. After years of residing in the neighbourhood, he remained an elusive figure. If they started to interrogate him, he might expose his ignorance of the modern world. I doubted he would know how to use a hand dryer in the gents. Panic consumed me – there was so much to teach him, and we'd not tackled anything in preparation for this outing.

He squeezed my hand tighter. 'I'm not afraid to be out here.' Leaning forward, he brushed a kiss against my cheek. 'I have to start somewhere.' He understood his circumstances far better than me. I had to trust him, support him and without dampening his enthusiasm.

We entered the bar and immediately the noise and smells accosted us. Charles sniffed. I raised my eyebrows.

'Beer.' He licked his lips.

There was no sign of Glenda or Bert. The cheerful barmaid, whose scarlet blushed cheeks glowed under the bar lights, drew a pint of draught bitter for Charles. The pub basked in an unusual level of heat, adding to my discomfort as I baked in perspiration.

'Two steak and kidney pies with mash, is it, love?' She noted down our order. 'Which table?'

I pointed to my regular corner spot.

I'd feared the hustle and bustle of a busy bar, the swarms of people elbowing each other might intimidate Charles, who was a solitary man and accustomed to the open space of tranquil woods. However, he sat on the edge of his chair, eyes blazing and actively eavesdropping: he cocked his head to one side and soaked up the atmosphere and hubbub of voices and music. The radio had given him a familiarity with contemporary styles, but he preferred jazz and easy listening: the music of Felicity's era.

'Tell me,' I asked. 'Is it too much?'

He shook his head. 'No. How could it be?'

Over lunch, he developed a fascination with the flat screen television and the sports channel. Glancing in my direction, he spied my smile. 'What?'

'Blasted football. What is it with men and sports?' It was a half-hearted gripe. I didn't mind. He deserved a hobby, something other than carpentry and gardening.

He gestured at the television. 'I've had to picture this in my head. It's not easy to follow on the radio.'

This comment led to a surprise discussion about sports. Over the years, he'd listened to Wimbledon, rugby and cricket, the latter his favourite and he was knowledgeable, able to list the best teams, the trophies they'd won, not just recently, but over decades. His memory for details was terrifying – all that information locked away and unspoken for fear of revealing his true age. The thought of being the one to discover Charles was a thrilling adventure that awaited me.

'Miriam,' Glenda boomed.

I rolled my eyes upwards for a second. Glenda swept across the floor to stand by our table. She eyed Charles, taking in his rough clothes and tousled hair. He'd made little attempt at tidying himself up when he'd dressed.

'This is Charles,' I declared.

'Your handyman.' She wiped her hand on her apron and Charles shook it.

'Pleasure to make your acquaintance,' he said politely. I also had to work on Charles's quaint displays of etiquette – antiquated and tasteful, they stuck out as much as the string around his boots. Women might find it charming, but men would ridicule him. Perhaps introducing him to Mike and allowing a friendship to flourish would help educate him.

She chuckled. 'Dark horse you have here, Miriam. I can tell these things.' She gave me a wink. 'Handy man, my arse, you've found him handy, I bet.'

Charles's usual whitewashed face turned crimson.

'Glenda,' I shrilled softly, leaning toward her. 'You're embarrassing him.'

'Whatever,' she said and picked up the finished dinner plates. 'You two take care.' She bustled back to the bar, chortling loudly.

'Dear God,' Charles exclaimed, when she disappeared out of earshot, 'Did she just allude to—'

'You will have to learn to hide your embarrassment, those cheeks of yours are like alarm bells.' I giggled and pointed.

He touched his cheek and grinned. 'Can't be helped.'

'Come on.' I rose. 'Let's go find her grave.'

We walked past the fringe of the village green. I quickly plucked a few stray daffodils, and as we made our way to the church, I fashioned a rudimentary posy using sprigs of evergreen laurels from a nearby hedge.

Bright sunshine eked out the gaps between the trees and buildings and the wind nudged the branches with a gentle breeze. However, the odd gust still possessed a cold fringe, a reminder that winter wasn't entirely gone. I'd worn a jacket, but Charles only had his jumper; he'd never bothered with a coat, he'd told me before we left the house.

'Cold?' I asked.

'No, I'm fine.'

He lied – his hand was icy. The grass in the graveyard had been cut; spring smelt fresh and real in the abandoned cuttings.

'This way.' I directed him to the headstone in the shape of a cross.

Charles knelt on one knee by Nuri's grave. He traced her name with his forefinger. 'Poor, Bea,' he murmured.

'A daughter.' I pointed at the inscription.

'Yes.' He cleared his throat and placed the bouquet of daffodils by her gravestone. 'Rest in peace, sweet girls.'

I bit back a soft cry and wiped the tears from my eyes. This wasn't my grief. I hadn't known this woman, yet Charles's reaction to seeing her grave was touching. He stroked the granite, muttering: a prayer, perhaps, an apology? I couldn't hear. It wasn't my business to know.

He scrambled to his feet, perused the churchyard and scratched his chin. 'So, let's see if I'm here.'

I showed him my family plot, the familiar names, and he smiled, patting the grave of Rupert and Olivia. We split up and walked a circuit around the church; he one way, me in the opposite direction. We met on the other side of the church and shared a frown of failure.

'Try again,' I suggested.

We reconverged a few minutes later by the church porch, both our searches fruitless.

'Perhaps what little remains of me wasn't buried in consecrated ground. I committed suicide and dishonoured the family name.'

Nothing in the newspaper articles referred to suicide. 'That's unfair.' I crossed my arms. 'They gave Beatrice a plot.' I gestured to the crooked cross.

'Can I help you?' The deep voice came from a slightly stooped man in a dark suit wearing a white dog collar: the vicar. He walked up the path to join us.

Stood between graves with my foot resting on a low plinth, I cringed. Our intrusive search seemed to smack of sacrilege. Were we in trouble?

'Er, we're researching my friend's family history,' I said nervously.

The vicar introduced himself as Reverend Matlock and he shook our hands in turn. Charles hung onto the vicar's for longer, grasping it and shaking vigorously. The vicar's cheeks flushed pinker and I nudged Charles's elbow. The vicar might have been uncomfortable with Charles's fascination with touching a man, but I was secretly delighted – a poignant moment, rather than funny. It wouldn't be his intention to offend; he had missed the companionship of men and a handshake symbolised that relationship. Charles released his grip without comment.

'We can't find a grave.' I explained.

The reverend asked for the name.

'Christopher Isaacks.'

Charles's remained quiet, his hands stuffed in his trouser pockets.

'Ah. That name I do remember.' Reverend Matlock tucked a finger under his dog collar and scratched.

'Why?'

The vicar went on to explain he had recently taken over the parish and the neighbouring one. 'I like to familiarise myself with history of the parish, so I read the old records, the minutes of the parish councils, the diaries of previous priests. Riveting stuff. This place is blessed with a rich history, during the war—'

I fidgeted impatiently. Charles had adopted an impassive expression. He'd had much more practice at hiding his emotions than me.

'The grave?' I interrupted the vicar's narrative stream.

'Oh, yes. Some years back,' he started towards the porch, 'a heavy storm flooded the lower part of the churchyard. Quite unusual. Some of the older headstones toppled in the sodden ground. They were moved and placed over here.' He followed a path that veered across the graveyard, past the Marsters' plot. Beckoning to us, he ducked his head under a low branch of a yew tree.

Behind the curtain of ancient trees and propped against the brick wall were a dozen or so headstones.

'One of these.' He walked along the line. 'This one?' He'd stopped before a plain marker, which sat slightly lopsided and partly covered in bird excrement.

'Thank you.' I held up the daffodils. 'I suppose it's alright to leave these next to the headstone?'

'Naturally, please.' The vicar backed away. 'I'll leave you to your privacy.'

'Wait,' Charles said, abruptly. 'Why do you remember this particular grave?'

The vicar paused and fiddled with his dog collar again. 'In the records – the older ones – the vicar responsible for the burial of this man wrote about the funeral, about how well attended it had been by family and friends.'

Next to me, Charles flinched.

The vicar, unperturbed by or oblivious to the sight of colour draining from Charles's face, continued. 'The funeral was remarkable in that the family insisted on burying an empty coffin. You see, the fire that consumed the poor man left no trace of him. Usually, in these situations, a memorial plaque would be placed inside the church, but it seems the family wished to have a grave to visit, something of substance here in the graveyard. It's a great pity the stone toppled. However, the family are long gone and nobody is left to tend it.'

'So, they buried nothing during his funeral?'

'Quite bizarre. Hence the vicar's note in his diary and why his name stuck in my memory. I gather,' he paused, giving unnecessary dramatic impact to his revelation, 'they placed in his coffin a suit of clothes, as if he needed them in the afterlife.'

Charles stumbled, his legs buckling slightly, and I grabbed at his arm to steady him. The Reverend Matlock had the wherewithal to realise he wasn't needed any longer. He said goodbye, ducked his head under the yew trees and retreated.

Charles slipped down onto both knees before the gravestone. He leaned forward, rested his hands on his thighs and hunched his shoulders. I crouched down next to him to offer him the flowers, but the limp daffodils had lost any meaning – we weren't commemorating Christopher's passing. Something else had happened.

His face had the same pallor he'd worn during his haunting days and his eyes appeared hollow once again having lost their brightness. I shrank back, almost expecting him to vanish before my eyes as he reverted to his former self – the shadow of a man.

'Charles?' I said gently, my voice wavering with tension.

His stoop shoulders shuddered, as if burdened with some immeasurable weight. My own palms had gone sweaty and in an instance, my mouth turned parched. Barely a few hours had passed since we'd passionately made love, and now, when he suffered, I struggled to touch him. I thought I'd healed him. I was wrong. My optimism was premature and lacked a deeper understanding of his mind.

'Talk to me,' I insisted.

'It's me.' He blurted.

'Your stone, yes.' He'd gone crazy, lost his mind after decades of clinging on to sanity.

His face portrayed so many emotions as if he'd rediscovered them all – shock, anger and despair – in one instance. The graveyard hadn't brought him closure. It had snapped him open. Charles was fracturing before my eyes. He shook his head. 'No, not this. It was always me.'

'I don't understand.'

'Nobody came that morning.'

'What morning?'

With his fingertip, he touched the death date on the headstone – Christopher's last day. 'Everyone left for church, just like usual, but I couldn't go. I hid behind the walls of the house. I was filled with shame at my disgrace, and worse, remorse. I also expected anger at her tragic death, but there was none. Nobody came.'

'You said Beatrice's father—'

'*Nobody*, Miriam,' he rasped. 'She died alone. Her family didn't care, that was obvious, because her father abandoned her at Heachley. He never planned to come back for her. A daughter had no value to him.'

'I thought Gypsy honour—'

'Honour,' he guffawed, frowning deeply. 'There was no honour or loyalty shown by her family.'

'But the curse, if he – her father – didn't say those words…' I floundered.

Charles's glassy eyes locked onto mine. His lips trembled as he spoke. 'I said them. I cursed myself.'

I rocked backwards, almost losing my balance. 'You?'

'Seeing this grave – my grave – hearing the vicar tell of my mourners, who came out of obligation to my family. They came anyway. It has shamed me. I've buried those memories. Abandoned them like Bea.'

'Your father—'

'Cared about his reputation. That day, that awful day, I raged alone in the house, because nobody came. Not one representative of Beatrice's family. I deserved to be punished for neglecting her, shunning her when she needed me most. But not one vengeful relative came.'

Vengeance is mine. The biblical quote sprang into my mind. Charles, even without a religious belief, wanted penance. He'd burdened his own shoulders with the guilt. It wasn't fair; Beatrice's family had left her in a workhouse.

'That wasn't your fault.'

He stared at the gravestone. 'I couldn't forgive myself because she sent me a letter. It was the last one.'

'What letter?' The only letter I'd seen from her was the one pleading for him to rescue her from the workhouse.

'She wrote a scrawled note, barely legible, covered in tears and blood. The baby, our child, had died in her arms, a few minutes after it had been born. It came too early. Bea knew she was dying and that nobody was coming. In her last moments, she wrote to forgive me.' He released a gut-retching cry of anguish, which the breeze collected and echoed about the yard.

I pressed the back of my hand to my mouth, halting my own exclamation. 'How did you get this letter if she wrote it the night she died?' I asked. Charles wasn't making sense, yet he spoke with utter clarity. His voice, although strained, was steady.

'The workhouse sent it on. A messenger boy ran across the fields at dawn. She'd confessed my name on her deathbed, wishing to be absolved of her sins, and with the aid of my love letters, which had been found amongst her things, the workhouse master knew where to find me. The boy arrived after the others had left for church. This very church.' He crushed his hands into a ball. 'I burnt the letter.'

I guessed the answer to my unspoken question – now I knew how the fire started.

'I struck a match in my bedroom and let it burn, but not in the safety of the fireplace. I put the lit note against a thread of the rug and I nursed the flames. Let them breed and spread. I blew on them.' He spoke with such bitterness and self-loathing. He screwed up his face, fighting back the tears.

Charles described more than an attempt at suicide: he'd committed a wanton act of destruction of his home, and for years afterward it remained his prison. 'Did you try to escape the fire?'

'No. People came running from the village. I watched from the window. The heat rose behind me and I turned and lifted up my arms to cover my face. Then, I ceased to be.'

His first vanishing, one of hundreds, may be thousands, that had happened since then.

Still crouched next to him, I ignored the cramp in my legs. 'You cursed yourself, but in order for it to work you had to die.' Had I met a mad man, or maybe, I was delusional and imagined he'd left my side when we first passed through the gate. Somehow, I had to rationalise the bizarre story into something believable.

'You,' he murmured, 'brought me back.' He reached over and captured my clenched hand between his shivering ones. 'By allowing love back into my life and having it returned, I forgave myself. If Beatrice could forgive me at such a terrible moment, then I must accept what I did. She died alone, but here in her grave, she found the peace I've sought for years.'

A mellowness descended over him. I watched him shift from the rigidity of shock to sombre reflection. No longer was he hiding abandoned memories. He was embracing them. I had to look to our future. The past had folded back on itself, releasing Charles in its wake.

'You had the ability to curse yourself into becoming a kind of ghost. Would you do that again?'

He laughed, softly under his breath. 'I'm not a magician. I know what you fear. Is it important – knowing how it happened? I can't explain it. But I know I feel it in my heart: I will live out my life and die. I don't doubt that end. Do you have faith in me?' He snared me with those translucent, frankly enchanting eyes of his and held my gaze. I didn't flinch.

'I do have faith in you.' Such a simple statement, but it settled my nerves.

We scrambled to our feet and he enveloped me in a swift embrace, the kind of hug that nearly crushed me. Then it abruptly weakened. 'I will keep you safe,' he murmured, and he patted my back gently. 'And you can show me the world – if you'll take me?'

Charles had offered an arrangement no previous boyfriend could ever have given me. I liked it.

I eased myself off his shoulder. He looked exhausted. Fatigue had drained his body of energy. With fingers interlocked, I led him out of the churchyard. We said little as we returned to Heachley Hall. He'd recalled a huge hole in his life and filled with it with raw emotion. What magic he had conjured up on the day of the fire, I couldn't fathom. Perhaps the house lay at the heart of it. After all, the place had held him captive, almost protecting him with its mist and walls for decades. However, he was right, it didn't matter. We had each other.

The instance he collapsed onto the sofa, he fell asleep. I fetched a blanket and draped it over him. Fearing he might think I'd abandoned him, I left a note on the armrest explaining my plan. The hard part was going back to the log cabin. I really didn't want to see that place again and imagine the multitude of fragmented instances he'd spent there. I rummaged underneath the slight trundle cot and retrieved the paper bag. Inside it were countless bank notes.

I laid them on the bed, spreading them about. Amongst the current tender were a few older currencies showing the heads of bygone monarchs. I extracted the recent ones, the notes I'd paid him and counted close nearly a thousand pounds. I pocketed the whole amount and abandoned the old currency.

Leaving behind the sleeping Charles, I drove to the largest supermarket in Hunstanton. There was a sufficient range of clothes and shoes to make a selection on his behalf. I had noted his shoe size before I'd left the house. I spent nearly half the amount, which included other things he might need, and not required in the past: toiletries, a razor and a wallet to keep his own money.

Returning home, I drove fast; he shouldn't be left alone for too long. As soon as the car wheels skidded on the gravel Charles hurried out of the front door and shouting, 'Miriam. Miriam.' His hair was ruffled, cheeks flushed, but the shadows under his eyes had gone.

I retrieved the shopping bags from the car boot. 'I left you a note.'

'Yes, I saw it.' Together we carried the bags into the house. 'I wondered if I'd scared you off and the note was a flimsy excuse.'

'Really?' I huffed indignantly. 'Have more faith in me.'

'I know, I'm sorry. It's just this is the first time I've been left alone at Heachley in over a hundred and fifty years.'

I halted. The bags knocked around my ankles. Had he never been alone? I'd not thought about it that way. I'd assumed his entire existence had been a lonely affair.

'You lived in that cabin in the woods.'

'It's like I'm a reclusive neighbour. Sometimes I'd come up to the house at night and look at the lights, the smoke pluming out of the chimney. It comforted me to know that you were in there.'

The two of us living alone without ever knowing we could have kept each other company day and night. What if under different circumstances a boyfriend or even a husband had visited – Felicity's will had been drawn up some years ago when I was barely an adult – would I ever have uncovered the truth? Possibly, but it would have required greater suspicion on my part and Charles would probably have spent more time adrift and invisible. A horrible thought. And, worse still, I wouldn't have been free to love him, perhaps only able to help him survive as a trapped man just as my great-aunt had done. Felicity had gambled with my future and it had paid off. I had been there for him.

'But, darling,' I balanced on tiptoes and gave his lips a tender peck. 'While I was gone shopping, you didn't disappear on me.'

He smiled softly at first, then as the realisation dawned on him, it gradually transformed into a broad grin. 'True.'

He liked the new clothes and tried each of them on. 'Such soft fabric, and the shoes stretch about my feet. What is it about the soles? They're springy.'

I shrugged. 'It's just the materials used.'

'Thank you. You're very kind and thoughtful.'

Something about his endlessly polite manner touched me deeply. I never wanted to lose that part of Charles to the modern world out there. Which made me think – where next?

'What do you want to do?' I asked.

He straightened up and stuffed his hands in the pockets of his new trousers. 'I'd like to see the sunset over the sea again.'

I knew exactly where to take him.

THIRTY-FOUR

'You can let go of the car seat now.' I patted the back of his hand. For the entire journey, he'd clawed at the car seat turning his knuckles white whilst his face had developed a green tinge.

It was like taking somebody on their first rollercoaster ride. Aware of his increasing anxiety, I'd kept my acceleration gentle, my braking gradual, but to Charles, who'd only ridden a horse, the speed was too much. I'd driven slowly and in doing so, I'd collected a small queue of cars behind me. Every time I'd picked up speed, Charles winced as if struck and clutched the edges of the seat. I'd nearly laughed at his petrified reaction to his first trip in a car, but didn't. It must be a strange experience: the speed, the constant change of scenery flashing by the window, and even the confusing traffic systems that forced me to halt without warning – at least from his perspective.

I came around to his side of the car and opened the door. He staggered and uncoiled his long legs. Before we'd left, Charles had bathed and washed his hair using the toiletries I'd bought, and when I pointed out they weren't particularly fashionable, he'd shaved off his sideburns. He'd eyed the modern razor nervously, peered at his reflection in the warped mirror and slowly scraped off the stubble. I'd observed, mesmerised, appreciating the significance of such a small daily routine.

'Amazing,' he muttered, stepping away from the car. 'Is it normal to feel sick?'

I offered him my best sympathetic smile. 'Not at thirty miles an hour.' I glanced at my watch, conscious of the time and approaching sunset.

We weaved through the dunes of Old Hunstanton beach. Charles's new shoes sank into the sand, his hand in mine as it had been for much of our waking day. The cloudless sky remained blue and with the approaching dusk it had deepened into a richer azure. The air was pungent with seaweed and salt. We emerged from the rolling dunes just as the sun touched the horizon. Charles halted. He inhaled deeply. I watched him and not the sea. I was fascinated by his animated expression of delight.

Finding a comfortable spot, we settled on our bottoms. Nearby the shallow waves rippled and caught the last rays of bright sunshine, reflecting it in all directions. Dazzled by the orange sun, I shaded my eyes with my hand. Charles tucked his knees up and rested his chin on the kneecaps, hugging his legs with his left arm, his right wrapped around my shoulders. We'd not let go of each other as if we both feared he might vanish once more.

During my dash out to buy him clothes, I'd time in the car to re-visit what he'd told me in the graveyard. All those jaw-dropping spikes of adrenaline-induced emotions had flattened out, allowing me to think clearly.

I nudged my shoulder against his. 'Charles?'

'Mmm,' he stirred.

'Why do you think you believed that Beatrice's father had cursed you?' I waited; he didn't rush to answer.

'It took thirty years for me to emerge from where that fire took me. It was immensely confusing, overwhelming, trying to find me, who I am, where I was. That awful rage had gone, the anger at myself and what I'd done. If I imagined that day, I couldn't picture the details, especially how the fire began. I conjured up Bea's father, a man I'd never met, but I knew through her sad stories to be a neglectful, cruel father. I wanted him, for her sake, to be a loving one. My father was loyal and caring – at least within the confines of the traditions he rigidly followed. He'd had my future planned out and it was filled with opportunities, but no lover, and certainly not a Gypsy girl. She should have had the support of her family.'

'So, you wiped out your penance and gave the responsibility for the curse to another in the form of an entirely imagined scenario.'

'I suppose. Guilt, shame, such negative emotions for me to hold, so I gave the anger to another and he became its vessel, reminding me of my punishment, my curse.' He briefly shuddered.

I leaned against him and spoke softly, fighting to be heard over the crash of waves. 'But, you know, after punishment comes the guilt and remorse, then forgiveness and redemption; you've travelled a long journey to reach here, Charles.'

'Yes,' he agreed. A gentle, subtle acknowledgement. He blinked several times, visibly fighting the tangle of emotions.

There was one other mystery I wanted to solve before he went completely quiet on the subject. 'You call her Beatrice; why not Nuri?'

'It was the name she chose when she arrived at Heachley. She wanted to hide her background and her given name had unfortunate connotations, the kind which would have made life difficult for her. However, all the servants knew she was a Gypsy and behind her back they spoke cruelly about her. To me, she was beautiful and intriguing. I wanted her, as an eager young man does. In secret, away from prying eyes, I seduced her with ease, and we quickly arranged our trysts. She wasn't educated beyond rudimentary schooling and I lent her books to read. It led her to trust me.' His voice had grown quieter, almost inaudible over the crash of the waves.

We'd spoken enough of the past.

The sun had almost disappeared and only the fringe of it poked above the shimmering water.

'So, where now? For us?' he asked, breaking the awkward silence.

'Heachley. I still have six months to live there before I can inherit the place and sell. But you don't want to be there, so...' I stared out to sea, chewing on my lip.

'I don't, I admit.' He squeezed my shoulder. 'However, I've realised during the terrifying drive over here that I'm not suited to life beyond Heachley.'

I twisted around to see his face. The smooth skin had lost its paleness. His eyes dazzled once again, reflecting the low beams of the sunlight. 'I don't understand. You don't want to leave Heachley?'

'The world beyond the walls is so very different to my imagination. I've been a prisoner for a hundred and fifty years and to expect me to simply walk away from Heachley and live as you do, without some kind of preparation, it's not possible. I'm sure I would go crazy. It's a scary world you live in.'

I chuckled. 'Sometimes it is for me, too.'

'Cities, cars, all these electrical things you take for granted: the television, the cinema and aeroplanes – just seeing them fly overhead makes my knees go weak.'

I needed to inject some optimism into his bleak vision. I believed in Charles's abilities, his intelligence and versatility, just as Felicity had done. She'd quietly educated him, giving him books to read and the radio to listen to, not only to feed his knowledge, it unconsciously taught him another thing: he'd lost his Victorian style of speech – for the most part, now and again, something antiquated slipped out of him mouth – otherwise, he looked and sounded like he belonged in the 21st century.

'You'll adapt. You're very adaptable.'

He blushed, and the colouration enriched his face. 'I need time to complete my transformation from ghost to what I am now.'

'We have that time: six months of it.' I settled myself between his knees and held his hands in mine. 'You would cope with Heachley?'

The pink tinge in his cheeks remained. Hands, rock steady, ready to saw and chop once again. 'Yes, because I can walk out the gates. I can learn to ride a bicycle. But please don't ask me to drive a car.'

'One day you'll want to do it – most people do.' My laughter brought out his. 'You need little doses of modern life. A gradual emergence and then, when I inherit, we can move on?' Heachley needed to be free as much as Charles. The house would fall quiet, no creaking or rattling, and no more ash. The mist would shrink back to the seashore and the skies would lighten again. The little cabin in the woods would fall apart and the ivy would swallow it up.

'Yes. Sell it. For six months I can paint and mend, re-hang the doors, pull up weeds. I don't know, whatever needs doing to the place to make it attractive to sell. We're a team.'

'Felicity always intended me to sell it. She knew you were my real prize, not the house or money. I simply don't have the income to maintain it if I stayed. When I'm finished here, my year and a day, we can move out.' I thought about my poky flat and the view out of the window, which lacked greenery. The constant noise of traffic. 'You won't like Chelmsford.'

He chewed his lip. 'I do prefer the country, but of course…if you…' Urban life must terrify him. It didn't me, but I'd changed my perspective from simply visual to something more encompassing of other senses. I felt places now.

'Me too, the country, as long as it has broadband,' I said, remembering the practicalities of working, but not too hard. Dad had got that part wrong.

He sighed. 'Once again you speak of things I know nothing about, but I'm sure there will be somewhere for us both.'

'By the sea.' A vast space was a tonic to a life spent trapped in the woods and it showed in the sparkle of eyes and the way his tense body uncoiled. 'Yes, the open sea. We'll find a smallish property and I can draw and you can—'

'Make things. I've learnt to use my hands and I can fashion wood. Is there much need for a carpenter?'

'A good one, yes, one who makes bespoke furniture. I'm sure you can make a living from what you've done over the years.'

I'd arrived at Heachley expecting to be alone for a year. Instead, I'd met a kind soul and I was about to join him on a journey that began over one hundred and fifty years ago. We still had a lifetime ahead of us. I gave him an encouraging nod.

'Maybe I'll try gardening. I like being outdoors.'

'You'll have a trade, like me.' I wanted him near me, not too far away, as we'd always been since we'd met.

He pursed his lips and nodded. 'A thoroughly modern couple.'

We fell into a comfortable silence.

With the sun gone, I suggested we walk a little to keep us warm. The tide had uncovered a stretch of rippled sand and isolated rock pools. We skirted around the banks of seaweed and I picked up a few shells, putting them in my coat pocket. Charles kept sniffing, inhaling deeply through his nose and licking his lips. At one point he stuck out his tongue to taste the air. I laughed, but not at him. I understood the awakening of memories was a sensory experience.

If we decided to stay in Norfolk, which I was coming to see as something I would find more than agreeable, I'd have to sell my flat in Chelmsford. Two places to sell would be headache. I groaned as I imagined how that might go.

'What's the matter?' he asked.

'God, I'd hate for Liz to buy Heachley.'

'Me, too. She showed determination in wanting it. Pestering poor Felicity, threatening her behind Tony's back.'

'I came to Norfolk convinced Felicity had been a senile old woman. I had to know why she wanted me to live in the house.' I turned away from the attentive Charles and looked behind us. In the soft, wet sand, we'd left two lines of footprints. A revelation bolt shot through me and a forgotten image sprang forward, and not of two tracks, but rather three: two side by side, and the third alone and some distance behind.

'Something wrong?' He placed his hands on my shoulders and I leaned back against him.

'I'd been convinced I only remembered Felicity from when I was small, before Mum died, but now, I have this vivid memory of coming to visit her after Mum died. I think we'd come to tell her about Mum's passing. Dad trailed behind Felicity and me – he was so sad, couldn't speak, so we talked.' I paused, recollecting the dark shadows under Dad's red-rimmed eyes.

'Go on,' Charles murmured.

'It was a miserable day, but Felicity had been determined to take us out. Dad wasn't keen. I would have been ten. We talked about my love of art, especially drawing pictures. She suggested I shouldn't shy away from drawing sad things.' I swivelled to face Charles and he cupped his hands around my cheeks. The cold wind, which had picked up since the sun had sunk below the horizon, had cooled his palms, but I didn't mind. I loved him touching me, knowing he was real.

'How does one draw sadness?'

'With tear filled eyes and an emptiness.'

'So you did? I wonder why she suggested such a melancholy activity to a child.'

'Oh, she was wise, in her strange way, don't you think? Creativity is sparked by all kinds of emotions. Those pictures, inspired me to draw others, happier ones, not straightaway, but it was good therapy. She understood grief, loneliness, rejection – all those tough emotions – and she saw past them to better times. I remember it clearly now. That day me and Dad went to Heachley to tell her Mum was dead.' Walking up the drive...the lavender, the birds singing.

'A challenging day.'

'I didn't want to go. But he wanted me to. I played in the garden while they spoke. And then we went for a walk on the beach. She told me don't rush, be comfortable with yourself before finding...love, although I don't think she used that word. I was ten. If she made me captive at Heachley for a year and a day, it was because she wanted the rest of my life to be even happier. And you, I do think she had your interests at heart always. She did love you, like a son perhaps.'

Now wasn't the time, but one day when Charles felt secure in his future, I would tell him the reasons for Felicity's decision to stay at Heachley and that I believed it was her faith in karma. She'd not gone back to India or pursued her dream of travelling elsewhere, instead she'd become a recluse, and believed, I was sure of it, that her self-sacrifice would lead her to a higher plane of tranquillity in death. She would see her fulfilment in another life, just as Charles would from this day on. I might not believe in ghosts but I was warming to the idea of reincarnation. As for myself? What had I achieved? I'd given Charles a second chance at love and life. Yet, I liked to think that wasn't Felicity's only intention. Her foresight was more remarkable than rescuing Charles.

I'd last seen her when I was a fragile child, an introvert shielding my memories behind doors, grieving for one parent and in the process of losing the other. By returning me to Heachley,

Felicity had dismantled those barriers and given me the confidence to love, to thrive in companionship. Grief comes in many forms, for Charles it was anger then despair and retribution, for me isolation. Time healed us; memories brought us together.

'You're a kind soul, Miriam. Brave, too. I wonder how many other people would live in a haunted house.'

'I can think of a few who did.'

We chuckled over our secret.

The drop in temperature ended our sunset stroll and heralded the arrival of dusk's thin red horizon, glowing clouds and darkening skies. The tide would turn soon and wash away our footprints. But that was okay, I told Charles as we walked back to the car. We'd make plenty more in the years to come.

EPILOGUE

Lynn News

Heachley Hall, an elegant Victorian house built on the outskirts of Old Hunstanton in 1843, has been sold at auction. The house and grounds, which include an extensive ancient woodland, had been the home of the Marsters family since 1875. The death of its previous owner, Miss Felicity Marsters, brought to an end the long lineage. Or did it? The surprise outcome of the auction, which involved a feverish amount of bidding by two parties – taking the offer substantially above its guide price of 1 million pounds and selling at 1.2 million – had led to speculation the house had been bought by a boutique hotel chain. The new owner, who outbid a local farmer, declared she'd purchased the house with the intention of renovating it and bequeathing it to her grandson.

Lady Primrose Fitzgerald, who is married to the successful entrepreneur and former Ambassador to Malaysia, Sir Hugh Fitzgerald, is a relative of the Marsters family through the marriage of her sister to John Marsters, the late Felicity Marsters's brother. She lived in the house as a child and fondly recalls playing hide and seek in the gardens.

MEET THE AUTHOR

Many sparks ignited this project and bringing them together has been a labour of love for several years. My earliest memories of walking along Old Hunstanton beach with my grandmother helped craft Miriam's relationship with her great-aunt. All those fragments of memories I retain, but can't quite piece together into a coherent picture of one particular day, are the relics of my childhood, as well as Miriam's. The house is a composite of many I've visited and the woods are those I battled through as a Wellington clad child armed with a stick.

The story of Heachley Hall really belongs to the Charles. By telling his life through the women he met, I wanted to protect him from ghost hunters and create a different approach to solving the haunted house mystery. He was never simply going to die.

This book was made possible by the invaluable help of many. To my beta readers and editor, Kate, thank you for your input and advice. Thank you to my support network of family and friends who encouraged me to keep going when I lost my words. Also, many thanks to those I met at the Festival of Writing; the authors and writers, agents and publishers, all of whom has helped contribute to this publishing adventure.

For most of my working life, I've been a scientist and my love of creative writing has never ceased even when surrounded by technical reports and impenetrable patents. Among moments of mummy taxi, delving into museum archives, drawing pictures and flute playing, I shall continue to pen my stories.

If you enjoyed exploring Heachley Hall and you would like to leave a review, you can find me on Amazon and Goodreads. But please remember Heachley's secret and don't spoil it for others!

Find out more about my forthcoming books at rachelwalkley.com

Beyond the Yew Tree

Rachel Walkley

'Beyond the Yew Tree' stands out as a mystery simply because of the seamless way the author brings together three seemingly different elements of the story. ~ Trail of Tales

Whispers in the courtroom.
Only one juror hears them.
Can Laura expose the truth before the trial ends?

In an old courtroom, a hissing voice distracts reluctant juror, Laura, and at night recurring nightmares transport her to a Victorian gaol and the company of a wretched woman. Although burdened by her own secret guilt, and struggling to form meaningful relationships, Laura isn't one to give up easily when faced with an extraordinary situation.

The child-like whispers lead Laura to an old prison graveyard, where she teams up with enthusiastic museum curator, Sean. He believes a missing manuscript is the key to understanding her haunting dreams. But nobody knows if it actually exists.

Laura is confronted with the fate of two people – the man in the dock accused of defrauding a charity for the blind, and the restless spirit of a woman hanged over a century ago for murder.

If Sean is the companion she needs in her life, will he believe her when she realises that the two mysteries are converging around a long-forgotten child who only Laura can hear?

The Last Thing She Said

Rachel Walkley

It was a gripping story of family dealing with loss and love with an added sprinkle of magic for good luck! ~ Amazon Reviewer

**A sister and her lover bring turmoil to a family.
Was her grandmother's prophetic warning heeded?**

"Beware of a man named Frederick and his offer of marriage."

Rose's granddaughters, Rebecca, Leia and Naomi, have never taken her prophecies seriously. But now that Rose is dead, and Naomi has a new man in her life, should they take heed of this mysterious warning?

Naomi needs to master the art of performing. Rebecca rarely ventures out of her house. She's afraid of what she might see. As for Rebecca's twin, everyone admires Leia's giant brain, but now the genius is on the verge of a breakdown.

Rebecca suspects Naomi's new boyfriend is hiding something. She begs Leia, now living in the US, to investigate.

Leia's search takes her to a remote farm in Ohio on the trail of the truth behind a tragic death.

Just who is Ethan? And what isn't he telling Naomi?

In a story full of drama and mystery, the sisters discover there is more that connects them than they realise, and that only together can they discover exactly what's behind Rose's prophecy.

Three sisters. Three gifts. One prophecy.

Printed in Great Britain
by Amazon

84567286R00202